Crescent Summer
All rights reserved. Copyright © 2021- Kellie Bellamy Tayer

ISBN: 978-1-942728-40-5

Spider Books Publishing
Fort Myers, FL USA

Cover design, and formatting services provided by
https://www.SpiderBooksPublishing.com
Illustrated by Jennifer FitzGerald

Dedication:

To anyone who loves a love triangle…this one's for you.

Acknowledgements:

Special thanks to E, C and J for not giving up on this story and for staying on my mind long after I wrote the magic words…*to be continued*…

Prologue: Part One

Charlie

"Slow down, Sarah! You're gonna freakin' kill us both!" I jammed my right foot down hard into the floorboard as though doing so would somehow miraculously slow us down. "Slow the fuck down!" I'd been trying—politely—for the last ten miles to get her to slow the damned car but she wasn't listening.

"Shut up, Charlie!" Sarah screamed, her voice choked with tears. "I'll pull over…just don't yell at me!" She took one hand from the wheel and swiped it across her blotchy face. The car swerved dangerously close to the shoulder of the road and I had to stop myself from grabbing the wheel which would have undoubtedly resulted in a collision with the logging truck that came around the blind corner toward us at that same second.

We were flying at a speed of seventy-five miles an hour in Sarah's Toyota Camry—an invitation for an early death on these curving roads—racing along the highway, nothing but towering evergreens on either side of us, blind curve after blind curve as far as the eye couldn't see. My heart jack-hammered in my chest--if Sarah didn't kill me, a massive coronary surely would.

We entered the parking lot of Indian Point State Park and I began to feel a sense of relief that our deaths weren't imminent. The park was deserted and it was almost sunset, just starting to get dark. Through a break in the trees, I caught a glimpse of the Pacific Ocean and the setting sun as it cast an orange glow over the horizon. Rain clouds hung low over the trees. Sarah pulled fast into a parking spot, came to an abrupt stop and put the car in park. She adjusted the AC, removed her seatbelt and then slumped over the wheel. She sobbed quietly, her shoulders shaking.

"Sarah…we can figure this out. It isn't the end of the world." It was all I could think to say but I knew it wasn't enough. I wasn't a girl—

how the hell could I begin to understand what she was going through?

She shoved herself up off the wheel and laid her head back against the headrest, pushing her auburn hair out of her face. She turned toward me and looked at me with empty eyes. "Yes…Charlie…it is the end of the world—my world."

I reached over and touched her arm, giving it a gentle squeeze. "Sarah…I promise it's gonna be OK. You have options. This isn't the fucking 1950s. You're not the first girl this has happened to and you won't be the last."

"Oh, my god. You sound just like my mother." She opened the glove box and pulled out a wad of napkins and wiped her nose.

I sucked in a breath. "Your mom knows?" I had assumed Sarah hadn't told anyone about her pregnancy yet.

She didn't respond right away. She just stared straight ahead through the windshield, unblinking. Then she turned toward me. She looked frightened…and lost. Tears fell down her cheeks as she answered.

"I'm dead, Charlie. I can't go back to Westbrook. I can't show my face in that town again. I can't tell my mother. I can't tell…"

"Wait. I thought your mother knew. You just said she did."

"No, I didn't." She let out a shuddering, lung-cleansing sigh. "What you just said about my not being the first girl this has ever happened to? That's what she said…the last time."

I didn't answer right away. I was too dumbstruck. And I knew I would sound judgmental if I wasn't careful with my words. Finally I shrugged and still managed to say the wrong thing. "OK…so…this isn't…the first time…you've been…"

"No!" she said harshly. "It's not. I'm a whore. Go ahead and say it. I know that's what's going through your head. That's what my mother said the last time. So go ahead and say it, Charlie, cuz I know you're sure as hell thinking it."

I ran a hand through my hair and shook my head. "I'm not thinking anything. Whose was it…last time? You and Johnny haven't even been together that long."

"Of course it wasn't Johnny's. And before you ask…it wasn't yours either. It happened at summer camp last year, way before you and I hooked up this February and before Johnny and I started going out in the spring. I got rid of it just before school started." She began to sob again. "And now school is about to start again—junior year—and it's fucking happening all over again. I can't get another abortion, Charlie. I can't put myself through that nightmare a second time."

I closed my eyes and put my hands on top of my head. I felt like I was getting a headache. "Are you saying you're gonna have it?"

"I don't know what I'm saying. But I'm scared to tell Johnny.

He'll freak. He thought I was on the pill. I mean…I am on the pill…but I forgot to take it once or twice." She slumped over the wheel again, her shoulders shaking.

I sighed. I also felt a wave of relief knowing I hadn't been the cause of her last pregnancy. But Johnny…fuck. "You have to tell him."

"I can't tell Johnny. I have this bad feeling he's gonna break up with me. This," she passed her hand over her stomach, "will put him over the edge. You're his best friend. You know he won't handle it well. And my mother will throw me out. She told me if this ever happened again she would send me to South Carolina to live with my dad. My dad's a fucking lunatic. I can't go to South fucking Carolina." She hit the steering wheel with the palm of her hand and winced at the pain.

I wracked my brain for something intelligent—or at least something comforting—to say to her, but my mind was in a twist. Johnny was my best friend and not what one would call daddy material. He would most definitely freak. "Does Johnny know about the other time?"

"No. It didn't seem relevant to our relationship. And I don't want him to know so please keep it between me and you. He doesn't even know you and I hooked up after the Valentine's dance last year. That was before he asked me out so it shouldn't matter anyway…but still… he doesn't need to know." She turned to me and tilted her head sideways, her gray eyes glistening. "What am I going to do, Charlie?" Her question came out as a shaky whisper in the gathering darkness.

Before I could answer, her cell phone rang. She pulled it out of the cup-holder between the seats and glanced down at it, grimacing. "Damn it. It's my mom. I can't talk to her right now." She put the phone down on the dashboard and turned her head to stare out the window.

We were quiet for a couple of minutes. I stared out my own window toward the ocean. It was twilight now…the moonlight shone on the water and I could see the waves gently rolling toward the beach. The sound of my cell phone pinging with an incoming text message disturbed the silence. I pulled it out of my pants pocket and saw Johnny's name on the screen. I glanced at Sarah but remained quiet as I opened the text and read:

where you at dude? we need to talk. ive made a decision about sarah. im ending it with her. im just not feeling it anymore. shes too much drama all the time and i want my last couple of years of high school to be fun and stress free. i don't want to be tied down. shes smothering the fuck out of me. text or call me when you get this. or better yet, come over. ive got a six pack chillin in my mini fridge and three of the bottles have your name on em.

I shoved the phone back in my pocket and swallowed a lump of anxiety. I stole a glance at Sarah. She seemed to have calmed down a bit. But I felt anything but calm inside. I didn't know who I felt sorrier for—Sarah, Johnny or myself for being in the middle of it.

Sarah's phone rang again. She grabbed it off the dash and glanced at it but slammed it back down again. "Dammit! My fucking mother again. Who was your text from? It wasn't Johnny, was it? Looking for me?"

I blinked...and lied. "No. It was my dad, wondering where I am. Maybe you should call your mom. She's called twice now. It could be important."

"I don't really care but I'll see if she left a message." She picked up the phone and pressed the voicemail button. A few seconds later, we heard her mother's recorded—and angry—voice:

"Sarah. Imagine my surprise when I gathered up the trash and found a used pregnancy test in your bathroom trashcan. You think burying it at the bottom is gonna hide it from me? I saw the plus sign. You're pregnant again? How could you? Don't even bother coming home. I warned you what would happen if you did this again. Stay the hell away from this house. You're nothing but a slut and a whore. I'm done with you."

I looked over at Sarah and saw her face contort in agony. "Oh, my god...Charlie. I'm so fucked. My life is over." She began to cry hysterically and yanked at her hair as if to pull it out by the roots.

I felt panic-stricken. I didn't know how to comfort her. I reached toward her, intending to take her hand and offer her some sort of support but she suddenly sat up straight, threw the car into gear and pulled out of the parking spot. She drove fast out of the park and onto the main highway heading away from Westbrook and home.

"Sarah? What are you doing? You need to slow down. Pull over and let me drive." I tried to keep the panic out of my voice. I grabbed the door handle and felt my foot automatically smash into the floorboard again, trying to slow us with my invisible brake. "Slow down this goddamned car!"

"I have to get out of here, Charlie. I need to think." She drove faster in the darkness. I watched in horror as the needle on the speedometer inched upward...thirty...forty...fifty.

"Sarah! Pull over...now!" My words rang inside the car. Up ahead I could see a vehicle approaching, its headlights the only visible entity in the gathering darkness.

Sarah zipped past the car, hugging the center line. I heard the honking of the other driver's horn as we passed. Sarah looked like a zombie—her face pale and streaked with mascara. I went into full-on panic mode. I was acutely aware that in less than a mile we would hit the sharp curve that led into the neighboring town of Kenilworth. We would never make the turn at this speed.

"Sarah! You have to slow down!" I yelled. I had to do something before she killed us both. Instinctively, I reached over and grabbed her leg, pulling it up off the gas pedal. I felt the car slow the tiniest bit.

"Charlie! What the fuck?!" Sarah glanced down at her leg and knocked my hand away. The sound of a horn blaring caused us both to look up. We were crossing the center line in the sharp curve, heading toward an oncoming car.

"No!" Sarah screamed and jerked the wheel back to the right—too hard. I yelled as she smashed her foot onto the brake. The car jerked hard and I felt my seatbelt tighten across my chest as I fell forward toward the dash. We went airborne, flipping sideways down an embankment and crashed into a grove of trees. The horn sounded—one long, never-ending noise—engaged by Sarah's arm jammed over the steering wheel, her airbag billowing all around her body which lay at an unnatural angle on the mangled driver's side. My airbag had also deployed but it hadn't prevented me from feeling like I'd been hit by a sledgehammer. I pushed myself up, my head turned in Sarah's direction. I saw her still body and I felt shock setting in. Then I felt pain inside my body followed by a strong desire to go to sleep. My right leg and arm felt like they were on fire, making it hard to move, but I managed to turn my head away from Sarah and noticed that my window was still mostly intact, except for a thin, straight-line crack running down the middle of it. I was amazed by that. I heard the sound of a soft rain beginning to fall. I forced my head back toward Sarah and saw the rain washing over her auburn hair which was exposed to the night sky. I tried to call out to her but my voice didn't work. I wanted to touch her…to make her speak… but I went numb and slumped further into the airbag. As I slipped into unconsciousness, I instinctively knew that Sarah's nightmare was over and I was keenly aware that mine had just begun.

Prologue: Part Two

Johnny

Nothing made sense. I heard the words coming out of my father's mouth but my brain wasn't grasping it: Sarah was dead. And Charlie was seriously injured. He'd been airlifted to a hospital in Seattle with multiple broken bones and internal injuries. There had to be some mistake.

"I'm so sorry, son," said my dad. "This is so unbelievable." He grasped my shoulder hard. I was fairly certain he was thinking how easily it could have been me in that car. I was usually with Sarah every day, but today...we'd had a fight on the phone—a fight about her clinginess. I'd felt like she was smothering me and I wanted out. I was going to tell her it was over but before I got the words out, she'd hung up on me. And somewhere along the way, my best friend, Charlie, had ended up in her car with her. And now she was dead and Charlie was half dead. It just didn't make sense.

I paced around my room while my dad stood in the doorway and watched me. He looked as distraught as I felt. I needed to do something. I had to see Charlie. "I've gotta get up to Seattle. I need to see Charlie." I grabbed my car keys off my dresser and made to push past my dad.

"Johnny...I don't think that's a good idea. We don't even know what hospital he's in yet. We should talk to his parents first. His dad didn't leave any details on the answering machine other than he or his wife would be in touch as soon as Charlie was out of surgery."

"I'll call his brother. Will should know what's happening." I grabbed my cell phone and called Charlie's older brother. He picked up on the third ring. We talked for a few minutes and after answering my questions as best he could, we hung up. I noticed that my mom had joined my dad in the doorway. She looked stricken—white as a ghost.

"He's in Seattle General. His right leg apparently got jammed under the dash and it's messed up bad. He has internal bleeding and I think Will said his arm was broken, too. Now I can't remember everything he said. He said not to bother coming for a day or two because Charlie won't even know I'm there. Not that I care about that." My room was starting to feel too small, like the walls were closing in. I needed air. "I've gotta get out of here." I tried to push between them but my mom grabbed my arm.

"Don't you think you should go see Sarah's mother?" she asked the question softly, probably fearing my reaction. Sarah's mother had never been my biggest fan. Come to think of it, my mother wasn't all that crazy about Sarah either.

I shook my head. "I don't want to go over there. Her mother hates me. She'll probably find a way to blame me for this."

"That's crazy," said my dad. "This had nothing to do with you. But your mother's right. You need to go over there and offer her mother some solace. Your mom and I can come with you if you want us to."

"No! I'll go over there when I'm goddamned good and ready!" I tried to push between them again but my dad grabbed me in a bear hug too tight to break.

"Johnny…listen, son. You're hurting right now. I understand. But Sarah is gone. And her mother needs all the support she can get. Please go over there and see her. She needs you."

I felt his arms relax enough for me to pull myself out of his embrace. I backed into my room and grasped my head in my hands. I felt so much pressure in my head that I thought I was stroking out or something. And though I fought to stop them, I felt tears burning behind my eyes like fireballs. I didn't want to cry. It wasn't my style. Oh, my god. Sarah's dead. I didn't love her, but I never wanted anything to happen to her. Was this somehow my fault? Did I kill Sarah?

"Alright, I'll go."

My parents walked with me out to my car and watched as I drove away to Sarah's house. There were several cars in the driveway including a police car. I parked on the street and walked up to the front door, my stomach churning with every step. A friend of Sarah's from school—Tania—came to the door. She stepped out onto the front porch to talk to me, closing the door behind her.

"Hey, Johnny," she said, her voice low. I could see that she'd been crying.

"Hey," I said, glancing down and all around—anywhere but directly at her. "How's Sarah's mom holding up?"

"Uh…not good. And, Johnny…" Her voice dropped even lower. "She saw you drive up and she called you some pretty nasty names. She said not to let you in."

"Why? Does she think this is somehow my fault?" I felt my anger rising and my stomach felt like a hurricane was tearing through it.

"I don't know what set her off but you are persona non grata here so you should go."

"What the fuck, Tania? I cared about Sarah. She was my fucking girlfriend."

"Yeah, I know. And I also know you guys hadn't exactly been getting along lately."

"So…what…that makes me guilty of something then?" I started to slowly back away. I needed to go. Sarah's mother was proving herself to be the bitch I already knew she was.

"I'm sorry, Johnny. I'll let you know about the funeral arrangements as soon as I know them. I need to get back in there." She turned and went back inside the house and I got back in my car and drove off.

I drove around town for a while trying to settle my nerves. I couldn't believe this was happening. I decided to drive toward Kenilworth to see the accident site. When I'd talked to Will he'd told me where the accident had happened. I drove the twisty roads…imagining Sarah speeding in and out of these curves. Why was Charlie with her? What had been going through her mind? Would I ever know? Did I even want to know? About a quarter-mile from Kenilworth's city limits I saw police tape stretched alongside the road, tied to trees. Though it was dark, my headlights lit up the area well enough for me to get a good look. I could see where trees had been smashed by the car falling down the ravine into them. The car had already been towed out. I pulled over to the side of the road and sat, staring at the fallen trees. I felt numb inside like I was standing beside myself staring at the place where Sarah had died and my best friend had been nearly killed. This was crazy…pure crazy, fucking bullshit. I drove home in a trance, refusing to believe it.

Sarah's funeral was held the day before school started. I went to the funeral home with my parents and brother. We got as far as the guest sign-in registry when an employee from the funeral home asked our names and then, upon learning we were the Beaumont family, asked us kindly to leave. I saw Sarah's mother standing in the doorway that led to where Sarah's body lay. She gave me a death stare and turned her back on me. I wanted to barge in there— I started to—but my father grabbed my arm and pulled me outside.

"What the fuck?" I exclaimed as we went back to our car.

"Watch your language, John," my mother said, her voice shaky from trying to suppress tears.

"Let it go, son," said my dad. "We don't have to understand Sarah's mother's reasoning but we have to abide by her wishes. For whatever reason, she doesn't want us here."

"She doesn't want me here. It's not you guys. I don't even know what the fuck I did," I spoke through clenched teeth.

We drove home and I went to my room. I sat on my bed trying

to make sense out of senselessness. Eventually I went out to the fridge in the garage where my dad kept his beer and I brought four bottles of Heineken to my room where I proceeded to pound them back one after the other in rapid succession. When I had a good buzz on, I lay back on my bed and tried not to think about Sarah. I wouldn't get to pay my respects to her or tell her how sorry I was for hurting her—for being on the brink of breaking her heart. I wouldn't get to see her body so I could know this was real and not some fucking nightmare I couldn't wake up from. And what about Charlie? Poor fucking Charlie. I didn't know why he'd been in Sarah's car but knowing Charlie, he was probably trying to help her. She'd probably turned to him for advice on how to deal with me and what did it get him? A brush with fucking death. I felt the effects of the beer taking over…I got sleepy…and finally I nodded off, thinking this was a fucking hell of a way to start my junior year.

Prologue: Part Three

Emma

The house wasn't as big as the one in Portland but it was nice. I was pleased with the soft lavender color of my bedroom's walls. My dad had clearly gone to a lot of trouble to make me feel at home. I wondered if he'd spend every waking moment trying to be Super Dad—trying to make up for leaving Mom and marrying Nanette. I doubted it though. If he stayed true to form, he'd get over the novelty of having me around pretty fast. My mother was bitter and unhappy and she'd been more than OK shipping me up to Westbrook—out of her hair. Never mind the fact that if she hadn't cheated on my dad in the first place, they might still be married and we'd still be living in our Portland house. And my dad probably wouldn't have turned to Nanette, his masseuse, for comfort. But now everything was different. My brother, Eric, had joined the Air Force right out of high school and now it was just me and my new stepmom in this house in Westbrook, Washington. At least I was closer to the ocean here than in Portland. And in a few days I would start my junior year at Westbrook High.

"Emma?" Nanette tapped on the door. "I've got something for you." She tentatively pushed open the door and stuck her head inside. She had a shopping back in her hand from J. Crew. "It's just a little something for your first day at your new school. I hope you like it." She extended her hand to me offering her gift.

I walked over and took the bag. "You didn't have to get me anything. My mom already took me back-to-school shopping before I left Portland. I don't need anything else."

"I know. But I wanted you to have it. It looked like something you might wear. There's a gift receipt in the bag so if you don't like it, you can take it back and get something else." Nanette sounded nervous—and very eager to please.

I opened the bag and pulled out a pale blue oxford-style shirt. It was cute and did indeed look like something I would wear. "Thanks. It's nice." My face reddened at my stepmother's act of kindness. Nanette was actually a nice woman—nicer than my own mother sometimes, but I would never let on to anyone that I felt that way. She was also young—

obscenely so—as in only ten years older than me.

Nanette smiled and I saw a look of relief wash over her face. "I'll just let you get back to whatever you were doing." She started back down the hall but stopped at the top of the stairs. "Oh, and your dad had to go back to work. Apparently there was some car accident between here and Kenilworth that he has to cover—a couple of Westbrook teen-agers were involved. I guess one of them died. They're going to try to get the story in tomorrow's paper if he can make the deadline in time."

"OK. Thanks for letting me know." Nanette went downstairs and I hung my new blouse on a hanger in my closet. I lay down on my bed and tried to talk myself out of being nervous about starting my junior year in a new school where I didn't know a single soul. But I had always been pretty good at making friends and never really considered myself all that shy, so maybe it wouldn't be so bad. I grabbed my book from the nightstand and settled in to read myself to sleep.

OK, so Westbrook High School was nothing like Portland Central High. It was considerably smaller and everyone seemed so morose. But when I heard the principal's announcement over the intercom in homeroom, I understood why everyone was so depressed and unfriend-ly. They were in mourning. Principal Anderson informed the student body that grief counselors were available in the guidance department for anyone needing to talk out their feelings in regard to the death of fellow student, Sarah Lennox. The student body was also informed that cards and well wishes could be sent to Charlie Channing who was hos-pitalized in Seattle and would probably be there indefinitely. I didn't know these people but I certainly felt the sadness of my fellow students. It was palpable and hard to ignore.

At lunch I sat alone at a table near the windows watching the dreary rain fall and tried not to feel awkward about being the new kid. It was hard enough not knowing anyone, let alone when the whole student body was wrapped up in grief over losing one of their own. I glanced around the cafeteria as I sipped from a carton of grape juice and watched students come and go. I listened to the low hum of voices in conversation all around me and forced myself not to feel out of place and lonely. I would make friends in time. Suddenly a hush fell over the cafeteria. The sudden silence was almost louder than the noise that had preceded it. I noticed all eyes turned toward the doors. A tall, blond boy had just walked in and had stopped just inside the entrance. I watched as he looked around at the faces that stared back at him and I wondered what the hell was happening. This kid's appearance in the lunchroom was certainly causing a reaction. The boy looked around the room and then headed over to purchase food. I watched as he paid for his lunch of pizza and bottled water and then stood beside the cashier, surveying the room. He was handsome but his face was impassive…emotionless. I thought he looked empty. I wondered what his deal was. I glanced around at the other students who were watching the boy. He made his way over to my table and sat down at the opposite end, but on the other side from where I sat. I watched as he picked at his pizza, sipped from his water bottle and stared off into space.

A couple of big guys who looked like football players walked past him and squeezed his shoulder. I heard them tell the boy they were sorry for his loss. He mumbled something incoherent and continued to stare at his pizza. He took another sip of water and then glanced up in my direction. I looked at him for a moment and then turned my eyes away. I couldn't be sure, but if I were to guess, I'd say he was somehow connected to the girl who'd died in the accident. Whoever he was mourning, my heart went out to him.

Later that afternoon in math class, I sat in the back row and waited for the teacher to call the class to order. I hated math but somehow I would endure. At least it was Algebra and not godforsaken Geometry. The seats filled up quickly except for the one next to me. I guess no one wants to sit next to the new kid, I thought. Someone dropped a notebook down on the one unclaimed desk next to mine. I glanced up and saw that it was the boy from the lunchroom—the one whose very presence had silenced the entire cafeteria. He settled into his seat and looked at me.

"Hi," he said. "I don't know you. Are you new?"

I nodded. "Yeah." I felt my face redden just a little bit. "I'm Emma Davis."

He forced a smile that didn't come close to reaching his eyes. "Nice to meet you. Welcome to good old Westbrook High. I'm Johnny Beaumont."

Chapter One

Johnny

Nine and a half months later, end of junior year, 2015

Charlie's coming home today. My best friend was finally coming back to Westbrook and I should have been happier about it. But I was ashamed. At first, just after the accident, I'd gone to visit him at least two or three times a week up in Seattle, but I got busy with football and school work and my visits tapered off. When he was discharged from Seattle General he'd moved into an apartment with his mother near his rehab center where he did his physical therapy. His parents had decided to lease an apartment up there so Charlie wouldn't have to spend too much time in the car travelling back and forth between Westbrook in the western portion of the Olympic Peninsula and Seattle. It wasn't that long of a drive, but the traffic could be heavy and so it just made sense to live up there, I guess. Then winter hit with a vengeance and driving in the snow up to see him seemed crazy, so we talked sometimes on the phone or texted. But then I got sidetracked in the spring by baseball and Emma, and I felt Charlie pulling away from me—or maybe I was pulling away from him. So I was a little nervous to see him today—not sure how I would be received. In all the time he'd been away, we'd never really talked about Sarah. About why he had been in the car with her that night. About why she'd been driving so fast…and why Charlie shut down every time I had tried to talk about her. For Christ's sake… she was my girlfriend. If it was gonna be hard for anyone to talk about her, it should have been me. But I'd decided to push aside my shame for not being a better friend and make a fresh start. And I couldn't wait for him to meet Emma. Emma was like a breath of fresh air. She brightened every room she walked into. She'd been a good friend to me in the weeks after the accident and she'd let me cry on her shoulder about Sarah and Charlie—not in the literal sense because I wasn't a crier but more like my own personal sounding board. She was smart and funny and a little bit of a clutz and I loved that about her. She was all soft edges and velvet where Sarah had been hard edges and tough as nails. I'd wanted to ask her out almost as soon as I'd met her, but I was still in shock over Sarah and I knew people wouldn't understand if I jumped too soon into a new relationship. No one knew I had been about to break up with Sarah—except for Emma…and Charlie. I'd waited till February to ask Emma out and our first official date was the Valentine's dance. We'd been going out for almost four months now but I felt like I'd known her forever. I mourned for Sarah and I missed Charlie, but Emma filled the big void their absence made in my life and then some. I loved this girl—she didn't even know how much. I hadn't yet said the words but I was planning to—soon. Funny…I was gonna break up with Sarah because I wasn't feeling anything for her anymore…not that I ever really had…and I hadn't wanted to be tied down. But then along came Emma…beautiful, sweet, amazing Emma—the brightest star in the darkest sky…that was my Emma. I was excited for her to meet my best friend. Charlie's gonna love her.

"We're free! No more junior year. Don't you think it went by fast?" Emma asked me over pizza and Cokes at Alfredi's Pizzeria. She had mozzarella cheese hanging from her chin and if we'd been alone I would have used my tongue to get it off of her. God, she was beautiful. Her black hair looked almost purple in the weird lighting of the restaurant. Purple—her favorite color. And those eyes—as green as emeralds. Every time I looked at her I wondered how I'd survived seventeen years on the planet without her.

"Not really," I answered. I leaned across the table and wiped her chin with a napkin. "But I'm glad it's over. I only wish I didn't have to work for my dad all damned summer."

"Ah…it'll be good for you. All that manual labor—mowing, planting, weeding, landscaping—you'll be all tanned and buff and ready for football in the fall." She smiled at me and proceeded to spill pizza sauce down the front of her t-shirt.

I shook my head at her. "I can't take you anywhere, can I?" I laughed.

"Seriously…I'm batting a thousand today. I should come with a warning label—trips, falls, spills and faints in the presence of needles, blood and loose teeth," she said grinning. She pushed her plate aside and reached across the table, taking hold of my hands. "Hey…you haven't said much, but I know you're seeing your friend today. You must be excited, huh?"

I looked down at the table for a second, considering her question. Emma didn't know Charlie. She'd started at Westbrook right after the accident. She'd only been here for one school year but it was like she'd been here forever. I literally couldn't remember a time before her. "Yeah...but I wonder if it'll be weird. I haven't seen him in like a month. I feel badly about not visiting him more often. He might not be happy to see me."

Emma rubbed her thumbs over my palms. Her fingers were soft and gentle. They felt like rose petals. I was quite intimately involved with roses since they were my mother's favorite flower and we had tons of them around our house. And I'd certainly planted enough of them—and would plant more this summer when I went to work for my dad at his landscaping company.

"You guys are best friends, right? He'll be happy to see you. And I can't wait to meet him. But I think you should go alone to see him first. I can meet him another time."

"Maybe you're right. The last time I talked to his brother, Will said he looked normal—like himself, but who knows how he's really feeling inside. I'll feel him out and see if he wants to hang out or something. According to Will, Charlie can do everything he used to...mentally and physically, I mean. It's just emotionally that he's still kinda messed up... but that makes sense, right?"

Emma squeezed my hands. "Of course. I imagine it takes a very long time to get over something like what happened to him. You two catch up and call me later tonight."

I paid for our meal and we walked out to my car. It was raining again but even through the misty rain I could still feel the warmth of the early June sun. We drove to Emma's house and parked in her drive. Charlie lived exactly two blocks away from her and I found myself wishing it were farther. I couldn't believe I was nervous about seeing my best friend. Charlie and I had been buddies since second grade. We'd been in Scouts together and camped together many summers at Lake Crescent and hiked all over the Olympic Mountains. I only hoped he'd be happy to see me. In any case, I planned to make my absence up to him. If I had my way, we'd be back to normal in no time.

"When I leave Charlie's later, I could come back here. You want me to?" As I asked, I leaned across the middle console and unfastened her seatbelt so I could pull her closer to me.

"Call me first. Nanette is having people over tonight for her book club and she wants me to help out with food and stuff."

"Hmm...OK." I cupped her cheek and pulled her in for a kiss. I breathed her in—green apples and cinnamon. "How do you smell like apple pie when you just ate pizza? I should be smelling—and tasting—tomatoes and garlic."

She grinned at me. "Lip gloss." She pressed her lips to mine and I melted into her. I wound my fingers into her hair and held her as close as the damned console would allow.

"You're like a drug…Emma Davis…a green apple, cinnamon, pizza drug and I'm an addict." I kissed her long and hard and I absolutely did not want to stop—ever.

She giggled against my mouth and pushed herself away from me. "I think you've been away from Charlie long enough. You'd better go." She opened the door and stepped out, then leaned back inside again. "Hey, Johnny…?"

"Yes, beautiful?"

"Does Charlie know about me? Have you ever mentioned me?"

"I've mentioned you, yes. But tonight I intend to tell him all about you. You're my favorite topic of conversation."

She laughed and rolled her eyes. "Oh, my god. You'll bore the poor guy. I'll talk to you later." She waved and disappeared inside her house. I sat still for a minute, watching her through her living room window. I shook my head in wonder and headed over to Charlie's.

"Hey, Johnny. It's so good to see you." Charlie's mom, Grace Channing, threw her arms around me and gave me a tight hug. "He's in his room." She pointed up the staircase. "Go on up. He's expecting you."

I felt my face redden. I was surprised at how nervous I was. It was strange and foreign to feel this way. I realized I hadn't been inside Charlie's house since last summer—so weird…and unnatural. I'd practically grown up here. "Uh…OK. Is he…uh…doing alright?" I sounded like an idiot.

Grace smiled. "He's good, Johnny. I'm glad you're here. You'll be good for him. Go on up." She went into the kitchen and I headed upstairs. I stopped in front of Charlie's door and took a second to calm myself. If I wasn't an atheist I would have crossed myself or something. Instead, I tapped on the door.

"Come in."

I opened the door and stepped inside.

Chapter Two

Charlie

I looked up at Johnny and noticed instantly that he was different. Not physically so much, but different in the way he moved…the way he seemed. He looked the way I used to feel—happy.

"Hey, Charlie. You look good, man." Johnny sounded nervous—like he didn't know me—like we were meeting for the first time—ever.

"Thanks." I pointed to the loveseat in the corner. "Have a seat… take a load off." I heard him sigh as he sat down, as if he'd been holding his breath for a very long time.

"So…how're you feeling? Back to normal?" He was nervous and it made me want to laugh. It was absurd.

"Normal as I'll ever be, I guess. So school's done, huh?"

Johnny picked up a guitar pick from the bookshelf next to him and turned it around in his fingers, clicking it against his thumbnail. "Yeah. We finished this morning. Glad as fuck the school year's over. We're gonna be seniors next year, man…about damned time, huh?" As soon as he said the words, he dropped the pick and looked at me funny. "You're gonna be a senior, right?"

I nodded. "Yep. I had a tutor. It's a hell of lot easier to get good grades when you're the only student in the class. I had to take some state-mandated tests to prove I was worthy though. But, yeah, I'll be back at Westbrook this fall." I'd been sitting on the edge of my bed but now I scooted back against the wall and leaned my head back. Johnny watched me move and I knew he was wondering if I hurt when I moved. I didn't—not any more. At least…not much.

"So, what're you gonna do this summer? Working? Going any-where? Going up to your folks' cabin at Lake Crescent?" He reached for the pick and started playing with it again. It was getting on my nerves and I was tempted to snatch it out of his hands.

I didn't answer him. I'd stopped planning for the future nine months ago when I almost lost mine. I looked out the window and stayed silent until the awkwardness in the room got the best of Johnny.

He cleared his throat. "Listen…Charlie…we need to talk about it, man. About…you know…that night. I have questions that only you can answer."

I looked at him…considered his comment and the way I should—would—answer. "I don't like talking about it. It's over now. Time to move on." Even as I said the words I knew I was fooling myself. You didn't just 'move on' from watching someone die and nearly dying yourself.

"Fuck, Charlie. She was my girlfriend. I deserve to know what happened—why you were with her that night—why she was speeding—why her mother wouldn't let me come to the funeral. What did I fucking do to her?" As soon as he said those words his face paled. "Damn it. That text I sent you. Did you let her see it? Did you read it to her? Did she know I was gonna end it?"

I glared at him as the pit in my stomach filled with anger. "No. I didn't tell her. I didn't read the text to her or show it to her. She died thinking you loved her. And I was with her because she…was giving me a ride." I wasn't ready to tell him the truth. Not just yet.

"Why was she speeding? Why didn't you stop her from driving like a maniac?" Johnny got up and moved over to the window, his back turned to me.

"She was angry. Anger makes people drive stupid. And I did try to stop her—to make her slow down. You think I wanted to die that night?" I ran my hands through my hair and then over the scruff on my chin. I felt the tiny scar behind my left jaw where it had been cut by flying glass—my little souvenir…one of the many.

Johnny turned and faced me. "Why was she angry? And why does her bitch of a mother hate me? I went to the funeral home and her mother threw me out—with no explanation…no reason. She acted like I'd killed Sarah, for Christ's sake."

I noticed that his hands were shaking. He paced in front of the window, finally stopping and coming back to sink into the loveseat. He leaned forward, resting his elbows on his thighs, holding his head in his hands. It was now or never. I guessed I should just put it out there and get it over with. "She was pregnant."

Johnny jumped as if someone had come up behind him and scared him. I heard his intake of breath. After a few moments, he lifted his head and looked at me, wild-eyed. His face was red. "What the fuck, Charlie…that's impossible. We were always careful. And she was on the pill."

"Not careful enough, Johnny—neither one of you were. She was afraid to tell you. She was scared. She wanted me to help her. Like I would even know how to deal with something like that. And her mother knew and was threatening to send her to South Carolina to live with her dad."

He turned suddenly and punched the back of the loveseat. I watched dust particles rain down on his arm. "Fuck. This is fucking shit."

"Yeah? Well, it's the truth. So now you know." I wanted him to hurt—as much as I did. He'd sailed through this nightmare with no ramifications—no consequences, while I was scarred for life—physically and emotionally. I wasn't worried about the physical pain or scars—they were almost non-existent now, but the other pain…I couldn't get away from it.

I watched as he got himself under control and put his frustration in check. "Well, things make sense now, I guess. Thanks for telling me… and for being there…for her." He sighed and it sounded very much like a sigh of relief. He was pissing me off and he didn't even know it.

"Yeah, whatever, Johnny." I got up and walked across the room… further away from him. "So Will tells me you have a new girlfriend— some new girl from Portland. Didn't take you long to move on, did it? Must be nice to be able to bounce back that fast."

Johnny jumped to his feet and stepped toward me but checked himself, stopping half-way. He was breathing hard and his face was red with something—anger…annoyance…embarrassment? "What the fuck is that supposed to mean, Charlie?"

"It means what it means. You've moved on…from Sarah…from me. Why'd you stop coming to visit me? Too far to drive? Not enough time in your busy schedule? Too much fucking around with your new girl?" I knew I was being unreasonable but I was past the point of caring.

"Are you fucking kidding, Charlie? What do you want from me? You want me to cry? You want me to apologize for knocking her up? You want me to stop living just because you almost did?"

"You say that like it was my choice.…my choice to almost die… to have broken bones and have my internal organs moved around like a tornado cut threw my gut."

"I'm not saying that and you know it. I've been walking around for nine months not knowing what happened that night. Wondering about her state of mind. We'd had a fight earlier that day and I was afraid maybe I'd somehow caused her to become irrational…not careful behind the wheel…or something."

"Well, that about sums it up. I guess that makes me collateral damage then."

"Damn it, Charlie. Why are you acting like this? We shouldn't be arguing, man. Can't you just tell me what happened that night? Why'd she talk to you about the…pr...problem…instead of me?"

I studied his face and for a moment I thought I saw a hint of anguish. Just a hint but not much more—not enough. "She couldn't talk to you. She knew how you'd react. She saw me at the track and called me over to her car. She was crying and almost hysterical. She asked me to ride with her...that she had a problem to do with you and since I was your best friend she figured maybe I could help. So I got into the car and we drove around awhile. And the more she talked, the more upset she got and the faster she drove. And don't think I wasn't yelling at her to slow down because I was."

Johnny didn't say anything for a minute. He seemed to be taking it in. Finally he asked, "Did she tell you we'd had a fight that afternoon? I can't even remember what it was about...you know us—me and Sarah—we used to fight about the most ridiculous small shit."

"She told me she had a bad feeling that you were gonna dump her. And in light of the text you sent me when I was sitting right next to her, she was right on the money."

We stayed silent for the next five minutes. I went back over to my bed and sat on the edge of it. Johnny stared out the window. Finally he turned around. He looked scared now. "Did she... suffer?"

I looked up at him and shrugged. What a loaded question. "I'd like to think she didn't. That's what I choose to think. For what it's worth she didn't make any sounds or move after it happened. She'd taken her seatbelt off earlier so the only thing that kept her from going out the window was the thick foliage that blocked the windows. It just seemed like she went to sleep. And her arm got tangled in the steering wheel over the horn. I remember the sound of it before I passed out."

Johnny blew out a long breath and stared off into space. We were silent again.

I'd had enough of remembering. I decided to give him a break and change the subject. And what a reaction I got. "So, who's this new girl that Will says you're all into—the Portland chick?"

And just like that, Johnny transformed...right before my eyes. It was like watching every light coming on at once inside of a dark house.

"Emma." He said her name like just that one word explained it all. "Her name's Emma Davis and she's new this year—moved up from Portland. Her dad got a job here at the Westbrook Daily News. And, Charlie? She's seriously fucking amazing—beautiful, smart, funny. You should hear her sing—she has this amazing voice. I mean she could be famous if she wanted to. I've never met anyone like her." His voice cracked on the end of his sentence, causing me to lean forward a little to really look at him. His eyes were glassy like wet marbles and the smile on his face was massive.

"She's all that, huh?" I was astonished. He was choking up over the girl who was alive, but hadn't shed a single tear for the girl—his girl—who'd died. Wow. It was very hard for me not to call him out on that. "She sounds like she might be too good to be true."

Johnny shook his head. "She is too good to be true—too good for me anyway, but I'm not letting her go. She's fuckin' perfect and you know what the best part about Emma is? She's mine. I can't wait for you to meet her. I was gonna bring her over here but she thought maybe you and I should talk first before I introduced her. She's so intuitive. It's almost like she has special powers or something. You're gonna totally love her, Charlie, I just know it. By the way, she's friends with Claire McShane. Remember she had a crush on you in ninth grade? Maybe we could double date or something."

"Or something." I closed my eyes for a second so he wouldn't see me roll them in exasperation. I had zero interest in Claire McShane. I hadn't given a thought to dating anyone seriously since last summer when I'd briefly dated Donna the Ditzy Cheerleader. It's kind of hard to date when you're in traction and physical therapy—not exactly a priority. I thought back to a question Johnny'd asked me earlier about my summer plans. "You asked me about my plans earlier and I never answered—my summer plans. I'm gonna work part-time at the music store in town—same as last summer. Mr. Jameson wants me to teach guitar lessons again. And I'm sure I'll spend some time at Lake Crescent at the cabin."

"Cool. We always said it isn't summer if we don't get up to the cabin at least once." He stood then and walked over to the door. "I'm gonna head out. It was good seeing you. And I'm sorry I didn't visit more often. I should have. But you're back now and that's what counts."

I stood up, too, and walked with him down the stairs to the front porch. He walked down the steps and turned back to me. "Charlie? Are we cool? Cuz if we're not, I won't give up until we are."

I felt a tightness in my chest and a strange, burning sensation behind my eyes. "We're cool. Life's too short not to be. See ya later." I stepped back inside the house and closed the door. My mother came around the corner and stopped. She was holding a plate of apple pie in one hand and a fork in the other. I watched her study my face—checking to see if I was stressed.

"I made your favorite dessert," she said, smiling. She handed me the pie and the fork and I forced a smile.

"Thanks, Mom." I could tell she wanted to talk to me about Johnny but thankfully she held her tongue and let me walk away without an interrogation. I went back to my room and ate the pie. It was good. I walked over and grabbed the pick Johnny had been holding and sat down on the loveseat. I put it between my teeth and reached for my guitar in the corner. I put it across my lap and took the pick and began to strum. I played chords and finally started picking out a tune. I liked the way it sounded and I didn't want to forget it so I got out a notebook and started writing it down. I did this for two hours. When I was finished I stared at the configuration of notes and rests and I liked the way it looked on the page. I didn't know where this tune had come from or what it meant, but I liked the way it made me feel. I had no lyrics yet. I didn't even know what the song was about but I knew it would be beautiful. I decided to give it a name—just as a placeholder—until I knew what the song was about. I stared off into space, thinking, humming, imagining. And finally, a title popped into my head. I still had no lyrics but at least it had a name: "She's Mine."

Chapter Three

Emma

"So how'd it go with Charlie? Was he happy to see you?" I lay back on my bed, my phone to my ear. I had just finished helping Nanette clean up the kitchen when Johnny called.

"Not the way I thought it would. He looks like the same old Charlie...but he's different. I guess that's to be expected. And, truthfully...he didn't seem all that happy to see me."

I heard sadness and disappointment in his voice. My heart went out to him. "Give him time. He's been gone away awhile so he just needs time to readjust to his old life."

Johnny sighed. "I wish you'd met him before the accident, Em. That Charlie was funny as hell...very sarcastic...and, I swear, he never got down or upset about anything. He was like Mr. Happy-Go-Lucky. Now he's just...like a shell."

I looked up at the ceiling...watched the fan turning in slow circles. "Are you going to get together with him again soon?"

"I hope so. That reminds me. I was thinking about maybe setting him up with someone. Did Claire ever tell you she had the hots for Charlie back in ninth grade? Maybe we could set them up and all go out together...to a movie or dinner or something. Think she'd go for that?"

I thought a minute. It sounded like a good idea in theory but... "The bigger question is...would Charlie go for it?"

"I kinda mentioned it to him and he didn't seem all that enthusiastic, but I caught him off guard. Maybe if we actually put some thought into...made a plan...it could work. Cuz you know what, Emma Davis? I want my best friend back. I've missed that guy."

I smiled to myself. "Hey, Johnny? True story...everything's going to work out. I can feel it. Now, I've gotta go. I have a 7:30 a.m. dentist appointment and I'm sleepy. I'll talk to you later."

"Hey, Emma? True story...I frickin' love...everything about you. Good night."

I turned off my phone and stared at the ceiling fan again. I felt my heart beating faster. It sounded like he'd been about to say the other thing...those three words that frightened me just a little bit. I went into the bathroom and brushed my teeth, then changed into my pajama pants and a t-shirt. As I crawled under my blanket and turned out the light, I whispered into the darkness, "Hey, Johnny? True story…If you do say it, I'm not sure I can say it back."

After my dentist appointment I drove to the public library. It opened at nine o'clock and it was ten till now so I sat and played Words with Friends on my iPhone with my friend Liane back in Portland. She played Words with Friends constantly so I knew she'd be up and at it. At nine on the dot I saw a librarian unlocking the door so I messaged Liane that I had to go and shut off my phone and went inside. I stopped at the information desk.

"Good morning. I was wondering if the library keeps copies of high school yearbooks on hand?"

The librarian smiled and stood up. "Yes, I'll be happy to show you."

I followed her to the section where books on genealogy were kept. "I'm guessing you're looking for a particular year?" she asked me.

"Yes. Westbrook High School—the yearbook from the last school year. Not the one that just ended…I mean the one from the year before."

The librarian found the yearbook and handed it to me. I thanked her and went over and settled into a lumpy chair. The yearbook looked brand new. I had the sense that I was the first person breaking its spine. I opened it and began to peruse the pages. I found Johnny's sophomore picture. Ah, gorgeous, I thought. I smiled at the sight of his handsome face. The photos were in alphabetical order and a few faces over I found the picture I was looking for: Charlie Channing. I checked the names running along the side of the page to make sure I was matching the right name with the right face. He looked like a Charlie—also handsome, with perfect teeth and dark brown hair. I studied his face for a few minutes, not sure why I felt compelled to do so. I continued to turn the pages and found more pictures of Johnny and Charlie in various group montages: Johnny with the football team…Charlie and Johnny with the band—they were holding drumsticks…Johnny in the cafeteria sitting in the midst of a bunch of girls…Charlie playing a guitar up on stage in the auditorium. Near the back of the book I saw a picture of Johnny and Charlie together with other students out on the ball field. They were both wearing baseball uniforms. I knew Johnny was a first baseman. I wondered what position Charlie played. I found a picture of Sarah Lennox. I stared at her face and was surprised to feel a knot form in my stomach. She had been Johnny's girl and she was pretty in a sort of hardened way.

I knew that Johnny had been on the verge of breaking up with her but still…he'd cared enough to date her. And Charlie had seen her die. I couldn't imagine going through something like that. I thought back to the beginning of the school year when I didn't know anyone. I'd heard all sorts of rumors about Sarah…and Charlie…and Johnny. Everyone had assumed Sarah was cheating on Johnny with Charlie, but after I got to know Johnny he'd told me he'd never believed that. He'd said Charlie was his best friend and that they'd had a code of honor—they'd never take the other's girl…or the other's spot on the team…or anything that the other wanted first. They had each other's backs. Johnny loved Charlie like a brother. I closed the book and put it back on the shelf. I left the library, thanking the librarian again on the way out. As I drove home I couldn't seem to shake the melancholy that enveloped me.

When I got home I called Claire. "Hey…what're you up to?" I was home alone so I put her on speaker while I fixed myself some peanut butter and Nutella toast.

"Nothing. I just painted my toenails fuschia. It looks cool. What's up?" she responded.

"I was thinking about going to the mall later this morning and I thought I'd see if you wanted to come?" I poured myself a glass of iced tea and took my breakfast to the kitchen table. I glanced out the window, thrilled to see that the dark clouds that had threatened rain earlier this morning had lifted. The sun was shining now and it looked gorgeous outside.

"Sure. I need a new swimsuit. Can you pick me up? My mom took the car to go golfing."

"I'll pick you up at noon." We said good-bye and hung up. Just as I put my phone down on the table it rang. I glanced down at the caller ID. It was Johnny.

"Hey, baby. I'm about to drive by your house. Can I stop over?" he sounded excited about something.

"I'll open the door for you." I put the phone down and went to the front door. Johnny was already in the driveway. I smiled at him as he walked up to the porch. "Did you call me from the driveway?"

He laughed. "Maybe." He skipped over three stairs and bounded to the top of the porch, grabbing me. He pulled me into his arms and kissed me—a very passionate and eager kiss. "Yum. Peanut butter and Nutella…my favorite. I like having my breakfast this way." He leaned down and kissed me again. Then he brushed his thumb across my bottom lip. "Oops…I missed a spot of Nutella."

I shook my head at him and smiled. I noticed he was dressed for work. "No rain means work for you."

He frowned. "Yep. I was sure it would rain...I'd bet on it. I owe my brother five bucks now. I always lose bets to Scott. You'd think I'd learn."

"I think you should watch the Weather Channel before you bet on the weather. Although, this being the Pacific Northwest, the odds were in your favor."

He took my hand and pulled me over to the wicker loveseat. We sat down and he pulled me into his arms. "Hey, Em...I was thinking... maybe we should throw a party for Charlie...you know...to welcome him back...and so everybody can see him again." He ran his hand through the length of my hair, then leaned into me and buried his nose in it, breathing deeply. "Your hair smells like peanut butter and strawberries."

I grabbed his hand and pulled it out of my hair, down onto my lap. "I know you're excited to have Charlie back. But you're talking about fixing him up and throwing him a party. Maybe he's not ready for all that. I personally think you should talk to him about this stuff. You said yourself that Charlie's not quite the same. He might not appreciate being the center of attention. You should check with him first and make sure he wants a party. It's not like he's just back from Afghanistan or college or a summer abroad. He's just returned from a hell we can't really understand, so go easy on him."

Johnny sat up straighter and cupped my face in his palms. "Have you always been this mature? And thoughtful?" He kissed the tip of my nose and grinned at me.

"Mature? No. But I'm a thoughtful kinda gal. Speaking of being thoughtful...I'm going to the mall with Claire later and I could try to feel her out about Charlie. But we're not springing any surprise dates on him. He has to want to go out."

"Look at you...you've never even met him and you're already looking out for him. You're so damned amazing...and sweet...and beautiful...and..." He kissed me again...a tender kiss that left me feeling strangely wistful. "I've gotta go. Dad'll kill me if I'm late on the first day. You have fun with Claire and let me know what she thinks about Charlie. I'll call you later."

We walked together down to his car. I waved good-bye and watched him drive away then headed back into the house. I tidied the kitchen and went upstairs to my room and sat down by the window. We lived on a leafy street and the sunshine was bringing out the neighbors. I heard a lawn mower start up. I saw the neighbor kids out playing in their front yard. While I watched the activity outside, I tried to ignore the strange feeling—something I couldn't identify—that was settling into my bones. It was like the premonition I'd had about my mom last year. I'd had a feeling that something was wrong but I couldn't figure it out. And then she told me she and Dad were splitting up. I'd known then just as I knew now that something weird was in the air. I shook my head and grabbed my purse. I needed a new swimsuit, too. As I jumped into my silver Honda Civic, I figured a little retail therapy would make me feel better.

Claire and I scored in the bathing suit department. She found a pink bikini that didn't leave much to the imagination and I found a slightly more modest two-piece sporting a palm tree and coconut motif.

"Johnny's gonna love your lovely bunch of coconuts," Claire joked as she sat down across from me in the food court with her plate of bourbon chicken and fried rice from Asian Chao. I rolled my eyes as I bit into my sandwich from Chick-Fil-A. A glob of barbecue sauce fell out, narrowly missing the front of my white t-shirt. I wiped the mess off the table and decided to begin the 'feeling out' process.

"Hey, Claire. You know Charlie's home, right? He's Johnny's best friend and I haven't even met him yet. What's he like?" I took a drink from my Coke and tried to act like I was just making casual conversation. She leaned back in her chair and stared somewhere off behind me.

"Charlie Channing was…is…" She stopped and looked at me. "He's pretty amazing, Emma. I wish you'd met him before this happened. I heard he isn't the same as before—I mean emotionally. But the Charlie I know is smart and very funny. Always smiling. And man, can he play the guitar. And he can sing, too. When he sings he sounds like Adam Levine mixed with that guy from Muse. Oh, and he's hot—dark brown hair, blue eyes. I had a major crush on him a few years ago. It's weird you go to Westbrook but you don't know him. He's like one of the most popular guys in school. Everybody loves Charlie."

I took another sip of my Coke and thought about what she'd said. Charlie sounded too good to be true. "So you had a thing for him, huh?"

Claire laughed. "Oh, yeah, but then every girl in school had it bad for Charlie…and Johnny. Nobody could figure out the whole Sarah thing. She was kind of a loner and not always the friendliest person to be around. But she was crazy about Johnny." She stopped and sucked in a breath. "I'm sorry. I probably shouldn't have told you that."

"It's OK. I'm glad you did. No worries." I ate my last fry and asked another question. "Did Charlie have a girlfriend?"

Claire shook her head. "I think he might have dated some dumb blonde cheerleader for about five minutes. Charlie really never did the girlfriend thing. He pretty much had any and every girl at his beck and call. I always assumed he didn't want to tie himself down and limit his options. Why be with one girl when every girl in school was throwing herself at you, right? I heard he even hooked up with Sarah last year." She clapped her hand over her mouth. "Shit, Emma. I definitely shouldn't have said that. I heard it was long before she and Johnny got together. Please don't tell him I said that." Her face was red and she looked like she'd just been caught cheating on a test.

"I won't. But I was wondering…would you ever go out with Charlie?"

Claire laughed. "Oh, my god. There was a time when I would have given my left nipple to go out with Charlie Channing…but not now. He would never ask me anyway. I'm afraid he might be damaged goods now and I'm not the fixer-upper type. And I don't mean that in a disrespectful way toward Charlie—don't take that the wrong way. Besides…I've got my eye on Jason Flanagan."

I raised my eyebrows and forced a smile. We gathered up our trash and headed out to the parking lot. I dropped Claire at her house and just as I pulled into my driveway, my phone beeped with a text message from Johnny. I opened it and read: hey, babe…i talked to charlie a few minutes ago. he's gonna meet us at denny's tonight. you're finally gonna get to meet him. pick you up at 6:30?

I sucked in a breath and felt that strange feeling again—racing pulse and breathlessness. I blinked and typed my answer: See you then.

Chapter Four

Johnny

I was surprised that Charlie had called me. I'd assumed, based on our visit, that I'd have to take the initiative in our getting together. He'd called just as I was about to clean out a bunch of dead stuff from the mayor's flower beds. He'd suggested meeting for dinner at Denny's and said I could bring Emma if I wanted. I was thrilled. I couldn't wait for my two favorite people to meet. His call had given me an adrenaline rush and I was able to get through the afternoon without losing my patience over the condition of some of the lawns I'd had to service. And now I was showered and ready to head over to Emma's. I was excited and for some strange reason, a little nervous.

Emma's father greeted me at the door. I didn't know him very well because he worked a lot and was hardly ever here when I came over, but I'd read stories he'd written in the paper. I still had his articles on the accident tucked away in my nightstand.

"Hey, Mr. Davis. How're things at the paper?" I glanced around the foyer, hoping Emma would hurry so I wouldn't have to spend too long in the purgatory of parental small talk.

"Not bad. Busy. There's always something going on to write about in Westbrook. No rest for the weary here." He smiled and stepped aside so I could enter. I always felt a little awkward around him—he was so serious all the time—always seemed to be in another world. Even now he looked like he was thinking about a million other things. I wondered where his hot wife was. I had a sneaking feeling if Emma knew I found her stepmother attractive, she'd not be pleased. Nanette was a SMILF of the highest order.

"Hey," said Emma from the upstairs hallway. I watched her float down the stairs. That's what it seemed like she was doing. She looked amazing—as usual—the only thing missing were her angel's wings. She was wearing a sun-dress. It was green with some kind of tiny, white unidentifiable pattern on it. Her long, sleek black hair hung down her back and her toenails were painted some dark pink color. The closer she got to me, the wider my eyes opened. I stole a glance at her father and noted that he seemed unfazed by the beauty of his daughter. Probably just as well, I thought. Holy fuck but I wanted to run my fingers through that hair. My stomach clenched at the thought of kissing her plump, juicy pink lips. And my hands and stomach weren't the only body parts reacting to the sight of Emma Davis. I slipped my hands into my pockets and stepped a little closer to the door, turning my suddenly bulging crotch away from her father's line of sight. If he knew what I wanted to do to his daughter I'd probably be tomorrow's front page headline—and not in a good way.

"Hi, Em. You look nice," I said, showing great restraint with my compliment. She smiled at me and gave her dad a quick hug which seemed to snap him out of his trance-like state for a second.

"I thought you said you were going to Denny's?" he said, eyeballing her dress and sandals.

"We are. Why?" Emma slipped her arm through mine and slowly propelled me toward the front door.

"Never mind. Have fun." He nodded at me and disappeared into the living room.

Emma rolled her eyes and pushed me out the front door. Out on the porch she burst into a fit of laughter. "My dad is so weird…but he means well."

"Well, he does always seem a little preoccupied. Does he ever do anything besides work?" I opened Emma's door and stared at her beautiful legs as she settled into the front seat of my Ford Escape. I needed to get her away from her house…down the street…so I could pull the car over and kiss her. She was making me crazy. I backed out of the driveway and sucked in a deep breath of her essence as I shifted into gear.

"Believe it or not, he does have a hobby. He's into wars—big time."

I looked over at her to see if she was being serious. "You mean like video games and war movies?"

"Not video games though he does love war movies. But, no, I mean he reads about them and he's into Civil War reenacting and visiting scenes of battles and stuff like that. He has a collection of war memorabilia but Nanette won't let him display it so it's boxed up in the attic for now. When he left the Portland paper he was offered a job in Virginia which he would have loved since it's so close to a lot of old battlefields but my mom guilt tripped him into staying out here and not moving so far away from his children. And then as soon as he and Nanette bought the house and he settled into his new job, she packed me off to live up here with him. My brother had joined the military and once she got rid of me she had the house all to herself so she could be free."

I pulled the car over at the end of the street and turned to her. "Well, your mother's loss is my gain. True story, Emma Davis: The day you moved to Westbrook was the day I came to life. Funny how the

CRESCENT SUMMER | 39

world works—two people I've never heard of get a divorce down in Portland and next thing you know, Johnny Beaumont is the happiest damned guy in the world." I unbuckled my seatbelt then and leaned toward her. The moment I tasted her cinnamon and green apple lips I felt light-headed—my whole body was on fire for her. I slipped my tongue into her mouth and tasted her sweetness. Her hair fell across my cheek and I swear it felt like silk. I nuzzled my nose against her delicate jawbone. "Hmm, Emma…maybe we should blow Charlie off and go to my house. My parents aren't home…we could watch war movies…or something," I whispered against her lips.

She pushed me back a little and smiled. "We are not blowing off your best friend for a make-out session no matter how tempting that may sound. I'm looking forward to meeting him. I even dressed up a little so I could make a good impression."

I kissed her again and forced myself to drive. "You're gonna make one hell of an impression in that dress. I'm starting to think maybe I shouldn't introduce you two. He'll take one look at you and try to steal you away. If the situation were reversed I know I sure as hell would—our childhood code of honor be damned." I looked over at her and grabbed her hand. "When I told you earlier that you looked nice, what I actually meant—but obviously couldn't say in front of your father—was that you look amazingly hot…sexy as hell. If your dad's hobby was mind-reading I'd be up proverbial shit creek right now."

"Ah, Johnny…you're sweet…thanks. Sometimes I think you put me on too high of a pedestal. I'm not as perfect as you think I am."

I squeezed her hand. "I know, Emma. You're right." I glanced sideways at her, waiting to see if my agreement about her state of perfection would get a reaction. It did.

"You didn't have to agree with that so fast," she said, giggling. I loved hearing that giggle—it was like fucking musical notes were floating out of her mouth into the air when she laughed.

"No…you really are right, because, Emma…I have another true story for you: Perfect doesn't begin to describe you—you're beyond perfect."

She looked down and then out her window. I saw a hint of pink shading her cheek. I'd embarrassed her. I pulled into the lot at Denny's, parked and turned off the car. "So, you ready to meet Charlie Channing?" I grabbed her hand again and brought it up to my mouth. I kissed her knuckles and the tender spot on her wrist. I was so fucking horny right now. I didn't want to go inside and eat or talk to Charlie. I just wanted to get her alone—not that that would have necessarily led to sex. Emma and I had fooled around on more than one occasion but we'd never consummated our relationship. Every other girl I'd ever dated had been as eager as I'd been about getting it on, but Emma was more reserved and I respected her in ways I'd never respected other girls. She was fiery and passionate and kissed like a house on fire, but she said she wasn't ready for sex and I was willing to wait until the end of time for her to be ready. I'd promised I'd be patient and never push her. But lately, that promise was getting harder and harder to keep.

"Yes, let's go meet Charlie," she said, her voice quiet.

Once inside the restaurant I glanced around the interior but didn't see Charlie. We were seated and the waitress brought us glasses of iced tea. I was sitting next to Emma in the booth with a good view of the door so I could see when Charlie got here. I noticed Emma fidgeting in her seat. She seemed rattled. I draped my arm over the back of the seat and pulled her close into my chest. "You OK?"

She fiddled with her straw wrapper, folding it into some sort of origami configuration. "Yep, but I have to admit, I'm a little nervous about meeting him. What if he doesn't like me?"

"Are you kidding me? That's like asking, 'what if I buy a lottery ticket and accidentally win a million dollars?' Charlie will love you almost as much as I do…you don't have to worry about that." I'd never known Emma to feel insecure about anything—she generally oozed confidence but, for some reason, meeting Charlie certainly seemed to have her feeling unsettled. She began to fold her straw into another origami shape. It slipped from her hand and fell to the floor under the table. She picked up her glass of iced tea and brought it to her lips. As she sipped the drink the ice shifted and iced tea erupted from the glass raining down on the front of her pretty green dress. I smothered a laugh and grabbed a handful of napkins.

"Damn it!" she shrieked, tea dripping down her chin into her neck. She looked down at her dress front and cursed again—almost. "Son of a…" She began to blot her face and swipe at her dress. "Why does this always happen to me?"

"It's OK. You still look hot." I grabbed more napkins and pushed them against her breasts to blot the tea before a stain could set in. She grabbed my hand and pushed it away.

"I'd better go to the bathroom and try to wash this out before it stains. Let me up."

I slid out of the booth and watched her walk away to the back of the restaurant. I cleaned up the table and shoved the wad of napkins off to the side out of the way. The waitress walked by and I asked her for new napkins and another straw. I was keenly aware that Emma's mood had changed. She rarely got rattled by anything, but now she seemed the tiniest bit off. Probably just nervous, I figured.

"You haven't even ordered food yet and you've already made a mess?" said Charlie, sliding into the booth across from me. I hadn't even seen him walk in.

"Hey, man." I laughed. "Yeah…a little tea spillage. Emma's in the bathroom trying to save her dress—the ice shifted."

"I hate when that happens," said Charlie. He leaned back against the banquette. He looked thin and I wondered why I hadn't noticed before when I was at his house. Of course, he'd been wearing baggy sweats and a t-shirt then and now he was dressed in jeans and a button-down black shirt. It was easier to see the physical changes in him now.

"How're you doing?" I asked. I felt a slight awkwardness between us and it bothered me—like I couldn't relax completely in front of my best friend who I'd known forever. We'd shared every experience two best friends could have together—we'd played baseball together every summer in Little League—I played first base to his pitcher. We'd gotten drunk together for the first time when we were fifteen. We'd told each other about our first sexual experiences, again when we were fifteen. For him it was Amy Sanders and for me it had been Amy's identical twin sister Anna. And later we'd been shocked to learn that I'd actually fucked Amy and he'd done it with Anna. We'd mixed them up. We'd smoked pot together up at Lake Crescent at his family's cabin after we'd accidentally sunk his dad's boat and nearly drowned trying to save it. We even got our driver's licenses together on our sixteenth birthdays, which happened to be the same day: January 23. And now he felt like a stranger…someone I had to get to know all over again. Just like for Emma, Charlie was new to me, too.

"I'm OK. I gave a lesson to the Munson kid today—you know, Keith's little brother. That kid is tone deaf and doesn't know a guitar from a shovel. I've got my work cut out for me."

He sounded like Charlie just then—it made me breathe a little easier. "Keith never learned to play the fucking drums right. They should stick to football and leave music to the experts."

The waitress came over and took Charlie's drink order. She asked if we were ready to order and I asked for a few more minutes. I observed Charlie's body language. He seemed a little tense and yet, almost the old Charlie—like he was warring inside himself to be old Charlie or some new, more reserved version. He reminded me of someone who was observing life as opposed to actively participating in it and I was suddenly filled with a strong desire to bring my friend back to life. And I would start with Emma. She could bring anybody to life.

"I'm psyched for you to meet Emma. She's without a doubt the coolest girl I've ever known."

"Cooler than Sarah?" He said it quietly but with some kind of unspoken intent. I felt a rush of heat creep up my chest, into my neck.

"Why'd you say that? I don't want her name mentioned tonight—not in front of Emma." I fought to control my temper.

"Oh, right. Cuz Sarah doesn't exist anymore...I almost forgot." Charlie stared at me, his head cocked to the side, his eyes dark with some unrecognizable emotion.

I slammed my fist down on the table...hard...and caused my iced tea glass to jump. "What the fuck, Charlie? I thought we were cool. What's your problem?"

He leaned forward, his palms against the edge of the table. "What is my problem? Good question. Let me think. Maybe it has something to do with the fact that Sarah's death doesn't seem to mean anything to you. She was more like a problem that solved itself by dying. And now you want me to meet your new precious Emma who walks on fucking water." He jammed his elbows backward into the green vinyl-covered banquette. "Well, guess what, Beaumont, I can't move on as fast as you. Sarah may have been your girlfriend but I was the one who watched her die. You treated her like fucking shit, Johnny. You use girls. You're probably using this Emma chick, too."

I was boiling. I wanted to reach across the table and wring his fucking neck. "You don't know what I went through, Channing, after she died. I mourned for her, but you wouldn't know that because you weren't here to see it."

"That's because I was up in fucking Seattle trying to live. Oh, but you forgot that part, didn't you? Considering how many times you came up to see me. You know what, Johnny? You're a selfish prick. Tell your precious Emma I said hi." He slid out of the booth and was gone.

I sat there stunned...frozen in place. I felt sick. I wasn't sure what the hell had just happened or how things had gotten so out of control. I saw Emma approaching and I could see on her face that she could tell something was wrong. She came to a stop beside the table and touched my shoulder.

"Johnny? What's wrong? What happened?" I looked up at her and felt a fucking tear escape my eye. I dashed it away, hoping she wouldn't see. I am not a crier. I simply don't cry—ever, not even when I'm physically hurt. But now I wanted to cry and rage and tear up fucking Denny's. I slid out of the booth, pulled a ten dollar bill from my wallet and slammed it down onto the table for our drinks.

"I've got to get out of here." I walked fast to the door, with Emma close on my heels. I made it to my car but before I could get in, she grabbed my arm and turned me around. Her eyes were wet and she looked scared.

"Johnny?" She said my name quietly, on a whisper, and I heard something in her voice—a tenderness that calmed me. I took a deep breath and leaned back against the car…passed my hands over my face and tried to focus. My stomach hurt and my heart felt like it wanted to crack open. But Emma was here. I had Emma. She'd make everything OK.

"Did something happen while I was away from the table? Did Charlie come?"

I nodded but couldn't speak. I unlocked the doors and opened hers. She climbed in and I walked over to my side. I got in and leaned back against the seat for a moment, trying to process what had happened… trying to remember what Charlie and I had said to each other… tried to figure out what had gone wrong but nothing made sense.

"He came, sat down, and within sixty seconds we…we…exchanged…words. I don't even know what happened. He seemed like himself…like the Charlie I've known my whole life but then he…turned on me. I don't fucking get it." I turned toward Emma and I knew I couldn't hide the damned tears that threatened to spill from my eyes. I fought to stifle a sob.

"Oh, Johnny. I'm so sorry." She leaned over the console and placed her hands on my cheeks. She used her thumbs to wipe away my tears. "It's gonna take time…he's been through hell. You've just got to be patient."

I pushed her hands away and pounded the steering wheel. "Godammit, Emma! Why are you defending him? You don't even fucking know him! I didn't do anything wrong in there. I fucking care about Charlie, Em, but I don't think he cares one shit about me or our friendship. Your allegiance should be with me."

"It is. You know that. But I think you're expecting too much from Charlie and from yourself. You want Charlie to be the same as before and he will never be that Charlie. And whether you want to believe it nor not, Johnny, the accident changed you, too. You might not have been there when it happened but you're still a part of it. Don't be hard on Charlie and more than that, don't be hard on yourself."

I didn't say anything. I knew she was right but I couldn't think straight. I started the car and drove through Westbrook, back toward Emma's neighborhood. Maybe I should have offered to take her somewhere to eat, but I wasn't hungry. I felt sick and, more than anything, I wanted to go home, sit in my room and drink some beer. I needed to take the edge off and try to get a handle on this situation. I didn't want to lose my best friend. I'd die before that happened.

Chapter Five

Charlie

"What's the big hurry, son?"

I looked up at the officer and shook my head. "Sorry. I wasn't paying attention." I handed him my license and registration and stared straight ahead at the endless line of trees on both sides of the highway.

"Not paying attention—and speeding—can get you killed. You stay put. I'll be right back."

I watched him walk back to his cruiser in my rearview mirror. I hoped like hell he wouldn't recognize my name. I knew all too well what driving too fast and not paying attention could get a person.

I couldn't get my mind off of Johnny. I wondered if I was being too hard on him. He was right about the fact that I had no idea what he'd been through in the days and weeks after Sarah died. The times he had come up to Seattle to visit me in the hospital and later at the apartment my parents had rented, we hadn't talked about Sarah. I hadn't wanted to and he hadn't asked many questions. He'd wanted to ask about that night—to get details…I could tell—but I figured he was afraid of upsetting me. So we talked about sports or shit on TV or school. Then his visits lessened and finally stopped altogether. I guessed his visits stopped right about the time he started seeing the perfect Emma. He certainly seemed different now…like she had some kind of hold over him.

"Son, I'm giving you a break today. You've got a clean record and I'm feeling generous. But don't speed in my town again. And keep your mind on your driving. If I pull you over again, you're gettin' a tickct, OK?" Hc handed me back my license and registration. I looked up at him and forced a smile. I knew that I, of all people, didn't deserve this break.

"Thank you, officer. I appreciate it. I'll be careful." He gave me a nod and walked away. I pulled back onto the road and continued toward home. On the way through town I drove through the Wendy's drive-up and got a burger and fries. After nine months of not caring much about food, I was finally getting my appetite back and nothing satisfied me like a Wendy's double cheeseburger.

I parked my Dodge Durango in the garage and went up to my

room. When I finished my food I picked up my guitar and started play-ing the song I'd been writing. I'd been working on it a lot lately, making changes to it and perfecting it. Lyrics had been forming in my brain and I checked my notebook to see what I'd written last. I jotted down more notes and played for the next hour. I sang my song but didn't like the way it sounded. Suddenly the lyrics seemed dumb—inauthentic. I was getting frustrated with it and decided to stop altogether before I lost pa-tience and hurt my guitar. I stretched out on my bed and brooded for a while. And I knew I had to admit to myself what was happening—what was wrong with me. I was scared to think the word, but I knew if I acknowledged it, I could maybe—just maybe—fix it. I was depressed. Charlie Channing, known around Westbrook High for being the happi-est man on campus with not a care in the world was suffering from de-pression. I didn't like feeling this way. I felt worse now than I did after my surgeries to fix my broken leg and messed up insides. I wanted to be myself again, but I had no idea how to make that happen. I pressed my head deeper into my pillow, closed my eyes and tried to trick my mind into thinking about things that made me happy. Things like baseball and music and cars and being at the cabin at Lake Crescent. That's where I needed to go. Depression didn't exist at Lake Crescent. It was impos-sible to be anything but content there. As I felt myself drifting to sleep, I decided I'd tell my parents I wanted to go up for a long weekend by myself. They wouldn't mind. They didn't usually start going up till the Fourth of July holiday weekend. I loved the idea of going up there alone or maybe with my brother Will if he could tear himself away from his high maintenance ball and chain, Amanda. Of course, I could always invite Johnny up—without his precious Emma—so we could maybe… just maybe…make peace and get back to the way things used to be be-tween us. His friendship meant too much to me to let Sarah's death and the accident hurt the lifelong bond we had. I'd figure this out one way or another because more than I missed Johnny, I missed myself. I wanted to be happy Charlie Channing again—the kid everyone expected me to be.

I was standing at my bedroom window watching the neighbor kids play basketball in their driveway when I saw her walking up the street. Even though I'd never met her, I knew it was Emma. I'd just gotten out of the shower and was in the process of towel-drying my hair. I dropped the towel to the floor and quickly rubbed on some deodorant under my t-shirt. On the way downstairs I caught a glimpse of myself in the hall mirror. Man, I need some sunlight, I thought, as I ran a hand through my damp hair. For some inexplicable reason I felt a knot forming in my gut as I opened the door and stepped outside onto the front steps. I watched her turn up the drive and walk toward me. She had some amazing hair—long and black. She didn't look all that tall—maybe 5'4" or so and kinda skinny but with big boobs. At first glance I had to admit I could see the appeal for Johnny—physically anyway. But if she was anything like his former girlfriends, Sarah included, I was fairly certain that when she opened her mouth and started speaking she'd be just as ditzy as the rest of them. Johnny had a type and though this Emma chick didn't look like his type, I was willing to bet she acted like it.

She stopped at the bottom step and looked up at me with the greenest eyes I'd ever seen. Definitely not Johnny's usual type—for sure. I waited for her to speak first.

"Hello," she said in a voice that sounded musical. "Are you Charlie?"

"I am." I felt like a giant looming over her. "I'm guessing you're Emma?"

"Yes." She let out a breath—a nervous breath it sounded like—and said, "I was wondering if you and I could talk…maybe get to know each other. I'm worried about Johnny."

"Did he send you here?" Because nothing would surprise me more.

She blushed and her pink cheeks stood out like tiny balloons against her pale skin and black hair. "No, he has no idea I'm here and I'm pretty sure if he knew, he'd be mad at me. I do plan to tell him though, but you know what they say—it's easier to ask for forgiveness than permission."

"Yeah, I've heard that before." I stepped over to the front door and opened it, beckoning her inside. "We can talk on the back patio."

She walked up the steps and when she passed me to go into the house, I noticed that the top of her head only came up to my armpits. She was certainly a tiny little thing. I directed her down the hall, through the kitchen and out onto the back patio. She sat down in one of the patio chairs and it seemed to swallow her up.

"Would you like a drink? Coke or water or something?"

"Coke is fine but only if you're having some, too."

I shrugged and went into the kitchen for two glasses of ice and Cokes. I glanced at her through the open door and studied her a moment. The knot I'd felt in my gut earlier now seemed like it had grown considerably in the two minutes since I'd first seen her. I was suddenly nervous and I didn't like the feeling. I took the drinks and joined her on the deck. She took the glass and sipped from it, then set it down on the small, wooden table between our chairs.

"So what do you want to talk about? What's up with Johnny?" I leaned back in the chair, stretched out my legs and tried to pretend that I didn't have a care in the world.

She cleared her throat and looked around the backyard for a second, then turned toward me. "Johnny talks about you all the time. And he misses your friendship. He was one of the first people to befriend me when I moved here from Portland just before school started in the fall. And on the first day of school I heard about…you know…"

"The accident."

"Yes. Johnny told me about you and Sarah—that she'd been his girlfriend. And he told me how close you two were…are. It's hurting him that you guys aren't as close as you used to be and I was hoping that maybe I could help bridge the gap or something."

I raised my eyebrows at her. "And just how do you plan to 'bridge the gap?' You don't even know me."

She smiled and leaned forward in her chair. "You're right…I don't know you…but I'd like to…get to know you."

"What…any friend of Johnny's is a friend of yours?" I knew there was an edge to my voice—a slightly antagonistic edge—and I knew it wasn't fair. I needed to tone it down and get over myself.

"Well, truthfully, Johnny has a few friends that are most definitely not friends of mine so, no, that blanket statement doesn't apply."

I couldn't help but chuckle at that comment. This girl had some spunk in her. "I bet you're talking about at least half of the football team."

She giggled. "Maybe slightly more than half." She reached for her Coke without looking and bumped it, knocking it over, spilling its contents down the leg of the table and onto the deck floor. "Oh, darn it! I'm so sorry." She picked up the glass and began scooping ice cubes back into it. "I do this kind of thing all the time."

"It's OK. I'll get some paper towels." I went inside the kitchen and grabbed the roll of Bounty from the counter. I pulled a handful off the roll and bent down to clean up her mess.

"I can do it. I made the mess." She reached for the paper towels, her hand grabbing the towels along with a couple of my fingers. She snatched back her hand fast. "Ooh, sorry."

"I've got this," I said, glancing up to look at her. For a split second I was three inches from her face. It's amazing what a person can discover in three seconds—long black lashes…a tiny mole just under the right jaw…a nose that turned up just the slightest bit at the tip. I looked away from her and cleaned up the Coke, then took the paper towels and her glass into the kitchen. I got her a new glass of Coke with fresh ice and brought it out to her. "Sorry, I don't have any sippy cups…with lids." I smiled when I said it so she'd know I was kidding.

"Ha, ha. Very funny," she grinned. "The sad thing is…I could make a mess even with a sippy cup. It's a gift."

I took a long drink from my Coke just for something to do with my hands and then asked her a question. "Johnny mentioned you're from Portland. How'd you end up in Westbrook?"

"My dad got a job here at the local paper. He's a reporter. I live with him and my stepmom right here in this neighborhood." She pointed over her head in the direction of the street. "I just live two blocks from you on Spruce Street."

I asked her more questions about herself so I could, hopefully, avoid talking about me. She told me she had a brother named Eric in the Air Force and that her stepmother was very young—that the age difference had creeped her out at first, but she'd eventually grown fond of her. She told me she'd had a cat named Martino that she'd wanted to bring with her to Westbrook, but Martino had run off the week before she'd moved here and never came back. She said she was passionate about music and had played clarinet in the band at her old school but hadn't joined Westbrook High's band. And then she told me something that nearly made me fall out of my chair. She played guitar.

"I play, too. It's kind of my passion. While I was recovering I played a lot when I was finally strong enough to sit for long periods and hold my guitar. I think I drove my mom crazy in our little apartment up in Seattle. But she's a patient woman and never complained. I think she was just so happy to see me doing something fun that she would have even endured drums if I'd had my drum set with me."

"Your mom sounds great." She crossed her legs and I noticed they were muscular as if she ran track or played tennis or something. I cleared my throat and studied my Coke glass.

"Yeah, my mom's awesome actually. The accident really disrupted her life. She quit her job so we could stay up in Seattle for my physical therapy and surgeries. Seattle's not that far but she hates to drive and she didn't want me sitting in cars for long periods of time so it was easier to stay up there until I was finished with therapy."

"What's she do?" Her voice was soft…quiet…interested.

"She's a first grade teacher. She doesn't seem to miss teaching though. Lately she's been helping out at her friend's bakery in town—more for fun than for the money. She's totally into making pies all of a sudden. She made a cherry pie this morning if you'd like some."

Emma laughed hard at that. I wasn't sure what was so funny about cherry pie. I raised my eyebrow in question.

She grabbed the bottom of her shirt and pulled it away from her stomach an inch. "Look at this. I'm wearing a white blouse. Bright red cherry pie is an invitation for disaster. No matter how careful I would be, I would still end up wearing half of it. Even if someone fed it to me I'd still make a mess. I bet it's good though."

I had an instant vision of feeding her a bite of cherry pie and that knot I'd felt earlier in my stomach suddenly unraveled, making me weak. I was glad I was sitting down.

She finished her Coke and set the empty glass down. "I came here to get to know you and I feel like I've done all the talking. That wasn't my intention. And we really haven't talked about Johnny much."

I leaned back in my seat and stretched out my legs. I had the sense that one of my legs equaled both of hers stacked toes to thigh. She had pink toenails and a gold chain holding a gold coin around her neck. And that hair. Damn...it was beautiful. Every so often a breeze would blow, leaving the scent of strawberries in the air.

"Charlie?"

I snapped out of the trance I didn't know I was in. "Oh, sorry. Yeah...Johnny. Listen, Emma. He's still my best friend...probably always will be. These past few months I haven't been myself but I'm coming around. And I hope things will get back to normal. I want that. I just need to ease into things around here. We'll work everything out. It's what I want, too."

"Now that makes me very happy. Johnny's glad to have you back. Shoot...I don't even know you but I'm glad to have you back, too." She smiled another killer smile and stood up then, picking up the empty glass which immediately slipped out of her hands and landed, by some miracle, in my lap. "Oh, damn! I am so sorry. I'm gonna go now before I break your house."

I shook my head in wonder at this clutzy, gorgeous girl and followed her through the house out to the front steps. We stood for a moment eye to chest and she suddenly and very impulsively threw her arms around me and hugged me. "The next time we meet, you're gonna talk and I'm gonna listen." She dropped her arms and stepped back, smiling up at me. "I'm going to tell Johnny I was here. He might get mad or he might not. He's never really been mad at me before so we'll see."

"If he gets mad at you, I'll set him straight. Don't worry."

She walked a few steps down the drive and turned back again. "Oh, Charlie. I should mention something. Johnny wants to throw you a party and fix you up with someone. He thinks it'll help with your... readjustment. For the record I told him it wasn't a good idea. Was I right to think that?"

I felt my face redden. "Dead right. You tell Johnny I said no parties and no fix-ups. I don't want people coming around gawking at me and I don't want him picking out girls for me. I'll take care of that myself in due time. I mean it—no parties, no fix-ups. If he wants our friendship to get back to normal, that is not the way to go about it."

"I'll be sure to pass that along. It was really nice to meet you, Charlie. You're just as great as Johnny said you are. See ya." She waved and walked away.

I stepped back inside the front door and watched her through the screen until she turned the corner out of sight. I purposely kept my mind blank as I headed back to my room. I walked over to my guitar and touched it—I almost picked it up to play it but I knew I wouldn't be able to manipulate the strings right now. My hands were a little shaky. I felt like I'd been hit by some sort of natural phenomenon. I lay back on my bed and relived the entire conversation I'd just had with Emma from hello to good-bye. My head was spinning. Johnny was right about her. She was beautiful, smart, funny, sexy. She really was too good to be true and so against his usual type. I felt that knot forming again. Holy shit. Emma was something special. She was a natural phenomenon. And I knew from this moment on, I would have to continually remind myself that Emma was Johnny's. She wasn't mine. Never was…never would be.

Chapter Six

Emma

I couldn't stop thinking about Charlie. In a way, he was exactly as I'd imagined him to be and in other ways, he was not what I'd expected at all. I had thought he'd be smaller—and angrier. But he seemed like a peaceful guy…slow to anger and not the type to carry a grudge. And I was surprised at how tall and big he was. I wondered if he played football, too. He was so different from Johnny who had a bit of a temper although he'd never really directed it at me—good thing, too, because I'd never tolerate that. Charlie was soft spoken where Johnny could be a little loud on occasion. I sensed he was patient and that was definitely not one of Johnny's traits. Sometimes Johnny acted like an over-grown kid with his sports and video games—an overgrown kid who liked to drink beer. They looked different, too. Johnny was blond with brown eyes and he was a couple of inches shorter than Charlie, who was probably six feet or more in height and had dark hair and dark blue eyes. I'd had to be careful when I was sitting next to him so that he couldn't tell I was staring. I'd never seen eyes that dark blue before. Charlie's hair was thick and curled the tiniest bit around the ends. Johnny had thick hair, too, but he kept it short—almost military style—and Johnny was clean-shaven but I had seen a hint of a shadow on Charlie's jaw and I'd noticed the hair of his moustache above his lips—nice, full lips.

Damn it. I snapped out of my daydream, not happy with where my thoughts were going, and looked closer at Nanette's note on the kitchen table. She and my dad had gone out to dinner and a movie tonight and she was letting me know they'd be home late and that there was salad and homemade macaroni and cheese in the fridge for my dinner. Yum—that sounded good. I picked up my phone and scrolled through it. I had several texts from friends back home in Portland and one from Claire. There was also a text from Kerry, a friend from school who I'd hung around with occasionally. I was surprised to hear from her so I read her text first. She was just saying hi and wondering if I wanted to hang out, go to the mall, see a movie. That was a pleasant surprise. I made a mental note to text her back and tell her it sounded like a plan but I didn't feel like texting her now. My phone beeped with a new text and made me jump. It was Johnny: hey, sexy. i just finished work and as soon as i shower i'm coming over. whatta you wanna do tonight?

I smiled and replied: my dad and nanette are out for the evening. wanna have mac and cheese and salad with me?

His reply was instant: hell, yeah. see you in 20.

I smiled to myself as I took the pan of mac and cheese from the fridge and slid it into the oven, turning it on to 375 degrees. I set the table with plates and silverware and bowls for salad and found croutons and slivered almonds in the pantry. I got out two glasses and napkins and in a sudden burst of creativity, I folded the napkins into funny-shaped birds. Johnny would get a kick out of that. Then I went upstairs to change and freshen up. I moved about my room, rearranging things—the books on my bookshelf...the toiletries on my dresser...the clothes in my closet. I touched up my make-up while I hummed my favorite song by Chris Brown, "Forever."

"It's like I waited my whole life for this one night...it's gonna be me you and the dance floor... cuz we've only got one night...double your pleasure double your fun and dance forever ever ever..."

I felt like I was having an out-of-body experience...I felt buoyant...excited...like I'd suddenly made some momentous discovery—of a new planet or a cure for cancer or the lost city of Atlantis. I'd finally met Charlie and I was going to tell Johnny as soon as he got here. He might get mad at me for going behind his back but it was worth the risk. And as long as things went back to normal for them, that was the main thing anyway. The doorbell rang and I ran down the stairs and opened the door.

"Hey, gorgeous," said Johnny. His right hand was behind his back and he had a sweet smile on his face. He brought his hand around and presented me with a bouquet of wildflowers.

"Wow...they're beautiful...thanks." I took the flowers and stepped into the circle of his arms. He hugged me tight and leaned down, kissing me long and slow and tenderly.

"I missed you today." He kissed my nose and followed me into the house. We went straight to the kitchen where I found a vase under the sink and filled it with water.

"Did you work hard today?" I asked as I trimmed the ends of the flowers so they'd fit better inside the vase. I set the vase on the table and it looked nice with my bird napkins.

Johnny stuck out his arms and flexed his biceps. "I lifted mulch and fertilizer all day and I feel like Tarzan," he said, chuckling. "Where is everybody?" he asked as he sat down at the table.

I went to the fridge and got out the lemonade and poured two glasses. I set the bowl of salad on the table with a couple of bottles of salad dressing. The timer on the over dinged and I took out the macaroni and cheese. "Dad and Nanette went out for dinner and to a movie."

A huge smile spread across his face. "So we're alone?"

"We are."

"Uh, oh," he said, wiggling his eyebrows.

"Uh, oh, what?" I said, putting on my best innocence act.

"Uh, oh, I might not be able to keep my hands off of you, that's what." He helped himself to a large serving of mac and cheese while I filled our bowls with salad.

I smiled at him but let his sweet comment go. I needed to tell him about Charlie and see how he'd take it. I was just about to tell him when he asked about my day.

"So, what did you do today? Anything special?"

I looked down at my plate and pushed around a clump of macaroni. Here we go, I thought. "Actually, I did do something special today."

Johnny poured French dressing on his salad and asked, "Oh? What was that?"

"I went to see Charlie." I waited for the ax to fall. Johnny continued dressing his salad, sprinkling slivered almonds over it and adding some croutons. He set the bag of croutons down and leaned back in his chair and regarded me.

"Yeah. Charlie really likes you…I knew he would." His voice was even—he didn't sound angry…or pleased.

"He told you?" I didn't know what to think about that. I felt my stomach clench a little, not knowing what Johnny would say next. I couldn't tell by the way he was acting if I'd made a mistake or not.

"Yeah. He called me. He was worried that I'd be mad at you and he wanted to make sure that didn't happen."

I took a sip of lemonade, hoping it would calm my suddenly nervous stomach. "And were you…mad at me?"

He looked at some spot over my shoulder and remained quiet for a minute. Then he sighed and answered. "I was disappointed. I wanted to be there when you met Charlie for the first time. It was kinda important to me but, no, I'm not mad. I know you were trying to help and it's OK."

I let out a sigh of relief. "I'm sorry. I probably should have waited but I hated seeing you so sad. I wanted to help."

"No worries, Em. You're an angel and it's really OK." He winked at me and went back to his food. "So what'd you think of Charlie? Nice guy, huh?"

"Very. Not really what I expected. I guess I thought he would be just like you—all Alpha male…bad ass…in charge…Mr. Tough Guy. But he seems like a gentle, quiet guy…the silent, artistic type or something. I was surprised."

Johnny laughed. "Don't be fooled, Em. Before the accident Charlie was all those things you just said about me. And quick to laugh or tell a dirty joke and even though it kills me to admit it, if Charlie and I were to get into a fight, he could have kicked my ass to Canada and back. I'm not sure about now. Did he tell you about his injuries from the accident?"

"No, he didn't go into any detail. We really didn't talk about the accident."

"His leg was messed up pretty bad. He's got long legs and his right one got busted up. And he had internal bleeding. He also had a messed up right arm and cuts from flying glass on the left side of his face. He had great doctors though. You can't even tell from looking at him that he was ever in an accident. But I know he hurts sometimes…still…his leg aches and I'm not sure he'll be able to pitch for the team next year. He's ambidextrous though so he might be able to pitch left-handed with some practice if he decides to play again. I hope he does."

I felt my heart crack the tiniest bit—for Charlie and the pain he suffered. Life could be so unfair. And then I thought of Sarah and felt even worse—for this girl Johnny had cared for. And Charlie must have cared for her, too, since he'd been with her that night, and had watched her die even as he clung to life himself. "So, did Charlie have anything to say about me? I hope I made a good impression."

"He thinks you're great. He made a comment about your hair… said it looked like night or something like that. He's such a poetry man."

"That's sweet…I think." I laughed. "He told me he plays guitar. That's cool. Maybe he and I can jam sometime. You can play percussion. We could start a band." I rolled my eyes when I said it so he'd know I was pulling his leg.

"If he heard you sing, he'd be all over that. Charlie has an amazing voice, too. Maybe you guys should try out for the school musical this fall. Every year the music and theater departments alternate between a play and a musical and since we had that fucking Shakespeare thing last year, it'll be a musical this year."

"Fucking Shakespeare thing, huh? You're not a fan of the bard then?"

"Pardon my Freudian slip, but, no, I never cared for the dude and all that taketh and killeth and loveth and believeth shit. Why couldn't he just talk in plain English and make things simple?" He finished his dinner and carried his plate and bowl to the sink.

"I hate to break it to you, Johnny, but that's the way they talked five hundred years ago." I took my own dishes to the sink and rinsed them out and loaded the dishwasher. Johnny put the salad fixings away and wiped off the table, then tossed the dishrag over my head into the sink. I picked it up and rinsed it out, hanging it over the spigot to dry. He came up behind me and slipped his arms around my waist. I turned in his arms to face him and he leaned down and kissed me.

"I'm very proud of you, Em. You didn't spill a single drop on that pretty, blue blouse." He nuzzled his nose into my neck and I felt his lips snaking along my collar bone. My heart hammered in my chest and my dinner felt funny in my stomach. "Let's go up to your room and get comfortable." He took my hand and pulled me gently toward the stairs. I followed him up and with every stair my nervousness intensified. I knew what Johnny wanted—what he'd probably gotten from every girl he'd ever dated—but I wasn't ready to go down that road. I'd dreamed of it many times…wondered what it would feel like to give myself to Johnny that way…to feel his naked body pressed against mine. Johnny had no idea how close I'd come to giving in on several occasions. But something always held me back…some little voice in my head that said 'hold on, Emma,' 'not just yet, Emma, 'wait a little longer, Emma.' I trusted that voice and I listened to it even though it wasn't always easy to resist.

Johnny closed the door and pulled me close. He buried his nose in my hair and breathed in. "Strawberries…and cheese…yum," he said softly against my cheek. "Can I have you for dessert?"

"I'm awfully high in calories," I said, pressing myself into his chest. I could hear his heart beating fast against my cheek…felt the rhythm of his lungs as his breath quickened…as his desire grew.

"I know a great way to work off calories," he whispered. He kissed me, his tongue finding mine, tangling with it. I could feel myself wanting to melt into him but I also felt myself needing to resist. But my reluctance was different somehow, like there was a new reason to wait… to be sure…to know in my heart that Johnny was the one I wanted to give my virginity to. I was confused…unsure…nervous. He moved over to the bed and lay back against the pillows, pulling me down beside him. He pushed himself up on his elbow and leaned over me…began to sift the long strands of my hair through his fingers. "You do have hair dark as night…Charlie's right. And it always smells so edible." He leaned down and began to kiss me, his tongue stroking inside my mouth. I heard a low groan in the back of his throat…felt him press his lower body against my hip. He brought his hand up to my waist and slid it slowly upward under my blouse.

I was torn…by the desire I felt inside my body and by the voice in my head that said to be careful. He'd said Charlie's name and now I could see Charlie's face in my head. I closed my eyes…tried to shut out the image. I hadn't expected to see Charlie in my mind. What was he doing there? I barely even know Charlie. This is crazy, I thought.

"Em?" Johnny spoke against my lips and looked into my eyes. His pupils were huge.

"Yes?" I was afraid of what he was going to say next.

"Do you have any idea how badly I want you right now? I'm dying for you." He kissed my lips, sucking on the lower one. The sensation felt like a lightning bolt running through me.

I put my hand on his chest and gave a gentle push. "That sounded a little Shakespearian."

He chuckled. "I should have said, 'I dyeth for you.'" His hand moved further up my stomach and came to rest just beneath my bra. I reached down and slid my hand under my shirt and placed it over Johnny's, but I didn't pull his hand away. He'd touched my breasts before and I'd touched him before…this was nothing new…but today it seemed new…different. I felt different and I didn't know why…or wasn't ready to acknowledge why.

"Johnny…" I murmured his name against his mouth as he kissed me with a growing passion. He slipped his fingertips under my bra and gently moved them across my breast. He groaned in the back of his throat and cupped my breast, applying a little pressure, and my back arched automatically.

"God, Emma. You're so beautiful and I know this isn't the time to be saying this but I can't hold it back any longer…I love you. I seriously freaking love you. I have never felt this way about any girl before…like I might die if I'm not with you. And I want you so, so, so much that it hurts. Let me make love to you."

I sucked in a breath. A strange sensation pricked behind my eyes. Twenty-four hours ago I would have said yes…I would have given in… given him my body…but now…I couldn't…it didn't feel right. He pulled his hand out and started to unbutton my shirt. I knew I had to stop this even as my body begged for him. But my mind…and my heart… said no. My body was outnumbered two to one. I had no choice.

"Johnny…stop…" I grabbed his hand, squeezed it gently. "I'm not ready."

He looked hurt but thankfully not angry. "Why, Em? What are you afraid of? I promise I won't hurt you. I'll be gentle and take care of you. Don't be afraid to let yourself go. I can feel the way your body responds to me…I feel it when you kiss me. Tell me what to do so I can make you feel safe. I want so much to make love to you. And it wouldn't be just sex or fucking, Em. I'm talking about love here…the real thing… the forever kind of love. I love you."

A sob escaped from my throat. I put my hand up to my chest and fastened my buttons as I pushed him off me and sat up. I had never felt so confused about anything before in my life. "I'm sorry. I don't know what's wrong with me." I dashed away tears before they could fall.

Johnny stood up and walked over to the window. His back was to me but I could see in the way his shoulders slumped and the way his head hung down that he was hurt and I felt like a monster for being the one hurting him this way. Finally he turned around and came back over to me. He knelt down before me and pulled me close, pressing his cheek against my chest. "I'm sorry, too. I know I promised not to push you. But sometimes it's hard to be close to you when all I want to do is..." He didn't finish his statement...but he didn't have to.

"I know," I whispered against the top of his head. I felt like I owed him an explanation even though I truly didn't understand it myself. But my guilt forced me into trying to soothe him somehow. I tucked my hand under his cheek and lifted his face so I could look into his eyes. "I want you to know, Johnny, that I'm crazy about you. And I'm not holding onto my virginity because of some old-fashioned notion either. I just have this sense that the when the time is right, I'll know it instinctively and nothing will stop me. And I hope when the time comes, you're the guy on the receiving end."

Johnny stiffened. He pushed back on his heels and stood up, the expression on his face one of hurt and confusion. "Dammit, Emma... you say that like there's the possibility I might not be the one on the receiving end. Are you trying to fucking tell me something?" He walked away to the other side of the room and again looked out the window. I jumped up and ran over to him, putting my arms around his waist and resting my head against his back. I'd said it all wrong and I'd hurt him—again.

"I didn't mean it like that. I'm sorry. I'm sure you'll be the one." But even as I said the words I doubted their validity. I wasn't sure any more that Johnny would be the one. I wasn't sure of anything anymore.

He turned around and held me against him. "You're making me crazy, Emma. But no matter what, I'm not gonna lose you. You're mine, OK? Only mine."

I pressed closer to him and sighed, fighting the threatening tears. "Yours, Johnny."

Chapter Seven

Johnny

"That sounds awesome, man. I'm sure I can talk my dad into letting me get off work early on Friday. Once we get up to Lake Crescent it'll really feel like summer." It was my lunch break and I was on the phone with Charlie. He'd called to ask me if I wanted to spend the weekend at his folks' cabin. We'd made peace over the incident at Denny's—he'd apologized—and I'd silently thanked Emma. I was sure it was her visit with him that had smoothed things over. And now we were talking about Lake Crescent. I loved it up there. His parents owned a nice place in Crescent Springs, nestled in the woods. It had four bedrooms, two bathrooms and a deck that overlooked the lake. The kitchen was huge and had two refrigerators and two dishwashers. His parents could certainly afford it. His dad was an eye doctor and owned a large practice in Westbrook and his mom had been a teacher until she'd quit to take care of Charlie after the accident. They'd remodeled the place last year and had the second dishwasher and fridge installed to accommodate all the family and friends that stayed there throughout the summer. We even went up in the winter sometimes and that was a whole different experience. But I couldn't go without Emma. If Charlie or her dad said no, I'd have to stay home. Lately I'd been consumed with thoughts of Emma—more so than usual. It had been easier during school because we'd had classes together and I saw her every day. But working for my dad kept us apart during the day. I only saw her in the evenings and on weekends and it wasn't enough. She'd invaded every part of my being and I'd become dependent on her…addicted to her. Sometimes when I looked at her, I had to literally turn away and close my eyes because the sight of her green eyes, pink lips and black hair overwhelmed me. I wondered if it was normal to feel this way about another person. If I was being totally honest with myself, I had the sense that what I was feeling might not be completely normal…or healthy. I'd had a dream recently that had awakened me from a sound sleep. My heart had been pounding so hard I'd thought I was having a heart attack. I hadn't been able to breathe and I was disoriented. Within five seconds of waking, I'd known what had caused the night terror: I'd seen Emma's broken body inside that car, in that embankment, dying next to Charlie and for a moment I'd thought it had been her who had died instead of Sarah. I knew in that moment that if anything ever happened to Emma…if she was ever taken away from me…my life would be over. And if it was a person who took her away from me, his life would be over, too.

I could hear Charlie's voice in my ear trying to get my attention. "Sorry, dude. I got distracted for a second." I hesitated. "Hey, Charlie… what would you think about Emma coming up for the weekend, too? Maybe she could ask a friend to come along and we could make it a foursome…someone like Claire McShane or even that hot chick Kerry Westfall."

"Kerry Westfall? Are you kidding? Didn't you have a thing going with her for about five minutes freshman year? Forget it. Yes to Emma. No to anyone else. I know you want to fix me up so I can be all in love and happy like you, but it's not gonna happen. Not for a long time anyway. So, if Emma's OK with being at the cabin with just the two of us then she's more than welcome."

I laughed. "OK, OK. I hear ya. I'll ask her…but Charlie…if she can't come, I'm not sure I can either—at least not for overnights. I hate being away from her. And don't give me any shit about that either… cuz you just wait…your turn's coming and when you fall for some girl, you'll know why I'm a little crazy where Emma's concerned."

"Whatever. By the way, you sound like an idiot, but it's cool. If she can come, tell her to bring her guitar. I want to see if that girl can play."

"Trust me, Chuck…she can play."

We hung up and I called Emma immediately. "Hey, baby. What's up?"

"Hi. I was just about to head to the mall. I was thinking about filling out some job applications at a couple of the stores there. And I'm meeting Kerry at the food court."

"Job applications? If you get a job at the mall that means you'd be working some nights and weekends, right?"

"I'm sure I would. Why?"

"It would take you away from me. I'm not OK with that. I miss you every day as it is." I was more than not OK with her getting a job. I'd have to make sure it didn't happen. Hell…if it was money she needed, I'd give her my whole damned paycheck.

"Johnny…you sound like some pre-historic, Neanderthal cave man. Are you covered in body hair and wielding a giant club?" She giggled and the sound of her laughter caused my body to react in ways inappropriate for the workplace.

"Sorry. I get carried away where you're concerned. But, hey, I've got a question for you…how would you feel about going up to Charlie's cabin for the weekend? I was just on the phone with him and he's going up Friday around one o'clock and coming back Sunday afternoon. It would be fun. And I already checked with him about you. He said you're more than welcome and he wants you to bring your guitar. He's not convinced you can play. Boy is he in for a surprise."

I heard her sharp intake of breath. "He said that? That…brat! I'll show him my guitar skills. We'll have a guitar-off or something. Is that even a word?"

God, but I love this girl, I thought. "It is if you say it is. So, that means you'll come?"

"I'll check with my dad. He probably won't care. He's not even likely to notice I'm gone."

We talked a few more minutes and I reluctantly said good-bye. I was excited about going away with her for the weekend. So what if we weren't going to be alone. Having Charlie there would make it great. I'd bring my drum and we'd jam. We'd cook out and go boating…maybe even go skinny-dipping. On second thought, maybe not. Charlie might be my best friend but I didn't want him seeing Emma's naked body. I shook my head at the direction my thoughts had taken and went back to work.

I threw some steaks into the cart and moved on to the frozen foods aisle. I'd told Charlie I'd bring food even though he'd told me not to worry about it. I grabbed some frozen pizzas and a couple of cartons of ice cream—mint chocolate chip for Emma and cookies and cream for Charlie—and threw them in, too. I added cereal and bananas and two packages of Oreos and finally some Coke and root beers. I wanted beer beer but I'd have to sneak that from my dad's stash from our extra fridge out in the garage. I remembered Emma's love for peanut butter and Nutella so I got jars of those and a loaf of bread and a gallon of milk and figured I had enough to feed three people for three days. If we needed anything else we could always go to the general store in Crescent Springs.

When I got home I grabbed two six-packs from the fridge. I wanted to take more, but my dad would miss them if I took too much. I was pushing it with two as it was. I also grabbed four blackberry wine coolers knowing how much Emma hated beer. Those were my mom's but she wasn't likely to notice that some were missing. I was pretty sure my parents knew Scott and I helped ourselves from time to time. They'd never said anything directly but we often were treated to off-hand comments in passing about the dangers of drinking and driving.

I was so ready to hit the road with Emma beside me in my Escape. Charlie had left at noon and was probably already there. I'd gotten off work at 12:30 and while I was getting the groceries and then later sneaking beers, Emma had been helping her stepmother with some home improvement project. Just as I pulled out of my driveway heading over to pick her up, she texted me: OMG, JOHNNY. I'M GONNA DIE.

I opened my eyes wider and felt the car swerve a little. I looked up and caught a glare from my neighbor whose mailbox I'd gotten a little too close to. I didn't think Emma was literally going to die, but she wasn't usually so melodramatic so her text kinda freaked me out a little. I wanted to text her back but decided that speeding to her house was safer than texting a response asking her to explain.

Five minutes later I pulled into her driveway. She was sitting on the front porch, her overnight bag and guitar at her feet. I jumped out and hurried up the steps to her. She'd been crying and she looked pale. I pulled her to her feet and wrapped my arms around her and held her tightly. "What's the matter, baby?"

"I'll tell you in the car. Let's get out of here." I grabbed her bag and guitar and put everything in the back with the groceries and climbed in beside her. Once we were out on the street and heading away from her house I reached over and took her hand in mine and gave it a squeeze.

"Tell me."

She looked at me with those emerald eyes swimming in tears and let out a puff of air. "My stepmother is pregnant."

"Whoa." I raised my eyebrows and shook my head. "No kidding."

"I wish it was a joke. Johnny…this is embarrassing. Nanette told me while we were cleaning out the spare bedroom. She had me carrying all these heavy boxes up to the attic and on about the fourth box the light bulb came on in my head and I figured it out. And then she confessed."

"Confessed? You make it sound like she committed a crime or something."

"It is criminal. I will be eighteen in February and I will be a sister to a screaming infant. My brother Eric is gonna flip when he finds out. This is not good. The only thing that would be worse is if my mother suddenly calls and says she's pregnant, too. That's all I need to hear."

I laughed. I wasn't quite sure why this was such a big deal but clearly it had touched a nerve. "Explain to me why this is so bad…?"

"My dad barely paid attention to me and my brother when we were growing up and now he'll have a new baby to ignore. Don't get me wrong. I love my dad and he is a good man—very kind and very patient. But…I mean…he didn't even bat an eye when I asked to go away with you this weekend. Shouldn't most dads be a little concerned if their teenage daughter is going away for three days to a cabin in the woods with two boys?" She crossed her arms over her chest and sighed deeply.

"Hell, Em, I'm glad your dad didn't question it. If he'd thought too long about it, he might have said no. So when's the little one due?"

"January.

"Don't dwell on it. There's nothing you can do about it anyway. And I bet, when the time comes, the little critter will win you over." As soon as I said those words, I felt a negative impulse hit my chest. I looked away from Emma and concentrated on the road. I felt the memory of what Charlie had told me about Sarah wash over me and I felt guilty. Sarah had been pregnant with my baby and it had freaked her out so badly that she'd driven too fast, wrecked the car and died, nearly taking out my best friend in the process. Emma didn't know about the baby and I'd told Charlie she was never to be told. Until now, I had not spent even a single second thinking about Sarah being pregnant. But I thought about it now as I drove, letting the sounds of Band of Horses play from the CD player. If Sarah had lived, my life would be vastly different right now, depending on the choice she would have made re-garding the baby. And I knew in my heart it was wrong to feel the sense of relief that was washing away that guilt.

Emma started singing along to the CD and I listened to her voice. She had a magical voice—perfect pitch—just like Charlie. They'd sound good together. As we drove north along Highway 101 she pointed out sights—a herd of elk standing in a field…a field of wildflowers in bloom…the turn-off to the Hoh Indian Reservation. I loved listening to her talk. Every so often I would glance her way and I started imagining a life with her after high school and college. I imagined marrying her and having a family. I thought of babies again and I had to push Sarah out of my head. Sure I wanted to have kids one day…in ten or twelve years. I looked down at Emma's flat stomach…at her perfect breasts… and I imagined her body filled with my baby. Holy fuck. What the fuck. I must be having some kind of mental fucking breakdown. As soon as we got to the cabin I was going to drink some beer…a lot of beer.

When we got to Forks we stopped at a gas station so Emma could use the bathroom and get us some candy bars and drinks. I filled up my gas tank and watched one of those crazy Twilight Tour vans drive by filled with tourists who were probably inside taking sides—Team Edward vs. Team Jacob. I'd seen every one of those damned movies with a different girl—the first couple of times it had been with a bunch of friends because I'd been too young to date--and it had always been the same: every girl was Team Edward. Except Emma. She'd been Team Jacob. Oh, my god, idiot, you're thinking about Twilight now. What the fuck was wrong with me? I wondered if Charlie's brother had left any weed hidden around the cabin, because at this point, it was going to take more than beer to help me get my head on straight. I was turning into a fucking girl.

Emma came back with a bulging bag of junk food and pop. "I got chips, microwave popcorn and...check this out...all the candy bars were buy one get two free. Of course they only had three types to choose from. Hope Charlie likes Butterfingers and Hershey bars cuz I've got dibs on the Reese's peanut butter cups."

I grinned at her and we hopped back in the car and drove on. Soon the road began to curve—sharply at times. I drove slowly around the blind bends hoping the damned tourists were paying attention to their driving. The closer we got to Lake Crescent, the darker the skies got. It was probably going to rain on our parade. But the sun came out just as the lake finally came into view for the first time. Emma sat straight up and gasped.

"Holy cow, Johnny! Look at that! Is that it? Is that Lake Crescent?"

"Yep, that's it. Gorgeous, isn't it?"

"Unfreakingbelievable. It's huge. It looks almost fake. The water's not even moving...and it's turquoise!"

Emma was beyond excited. She began to bounce in her seat like a little kid. She pulled out her phone and snapped a few photos as we drove. When we came to a run-off spot along the side of the road I stopped the car so she could get better photos. She hopped out of the car and crossed the road. I stayed in the car, and while she took pictures I sent Charlie a quick text to tell him we were almost there. He responded quickly: ok. see you shortly. drive safely.

I slipped the phone back into my pocket and thought about those last two words. Charlie'd never told me to drive safely before. It was nice—it gave me a damned warm fuzzy. I glanced up at the mountains around the lake. They were beautiful and Emma looked so damned tiny in contrast. She finished taking pictures and slipped her phone back into her pocket. I smiled as she started across the road. She was half-way across when a car suddenly zoomed around the curve too fast coming right toward her.

"Emma!" I screamed and dove out of my door, nearly stumbling as I rushed to get to her. I heard her scream, saw her hesitate in the middle of the road, frozen on the center line. The driver hit his horn as he swerved past, just missing her. I saw her hair fly up in the wind tunnel from the car's wake. I reached her and grabbed her up in my arms and ran back to the car, getting her as far off the road as the terrain would allow. She was sobbing and shaking and I was dying inside.

"Oh, my god, Emma...oh, my god." I sank down into the side of the wall of rock and vegetation and cradled her in my arms. I rocked her back and forth, blinded by the tears pricking my eyes.

"Johnny…I'm sorry. I didn't see it. I'm sorry. I looked both ways. I didn't see it." She sobbed into my chest and I held her as close as I could without crushing her.

"I know, baby. That motherfucker was speeding. It wasn't your fault. You're safe now. I love you." I continued to hold her until she finally calmed down enough to stand. Suddenly I just wanted to get her to the cabin…off the fucking road…and safe.

We got back in the car and I buckled her up, then I drove the last few miles into Crescent Springs. I took the turn-off to the cabin and pulled up next to Charlie's Durango. I turned off the car and looked over at Emma. She was pale and still shaking and more than likely in shock. "Don't move, Em. I'm coming to get you." I got out and ran around to her side and reached in, unbuckling her seatbelt. I picked her up and headed up the walkway to the door. She felt lighter than air in my arms. Charlie opened the door. He saw instantly that something was wrong.

"What happened?" he asked, his voice sounding as hollow as I felt inside.

"Some motherfucking asshole nearly hit Emma when she was crossing the road. We'd stopped at one of the run-offs so she could take some pictures. The fucker was speeding and he almost…" My voice cracked. I walked over to the couch and put her down, then sat next to her, my arms around her. "Emma, baby…are you OK?" I looked into her eyes. "You're safe now."

She pushed her hair out of her face and sniffed. "I'm OK. I can't believe I didn't get hit." She looked up at me, her eyes bright. "Johnny…I should be…I was almost…"

I crushed her lips with mine to silence her. I couldn't let her say what I was trying not to think—that she should've been killed—that she should be dead right now. Only a miracle had a saved her…or a guardian angel. I kissed her hard and then tucked her into my shoulder. I looked up at Charlie who was still standing by the front door, watching us. And I could swear I saw tears in his eyes.

Chapter Eight

Charlie

At first I'd wanted to come up to the cabin alone...or with my brother if he was available, which he wasn't. But my mom wouldn't let me. She didn't want me to be alone so far from home even though I'd tried to reassure her that I'd be fine and was perfectly capable of taking care of myself. My doctors had given me a clean bill of health—for the most part. But that clean bill had come with rules: no extreme sports, no heavy lifting unless it was strength training for my arm, and I had to continue with physical therapy for my leg at the Westbrook hospital throughout the summer. I was also supposed to see a counselor, but, so far, I'd managed to blow off that rule. So I'd called Johnny and apologized for acting like an asshole at Denny's and invited him to the cabin. I'd known he wouldn't come without Emma and that was why I hadn't wanted him to come. I'd tried to convince myself that having her here wouldn't be a big deal, but I had a feeling I'd end up being wrong about that.

Emma was sitting out on the back deck while Johnny was unloading the car. I'd offered to help but he'd asked me to sit with her—he didn't want her to be alone. So I went out and sat down on a deck chair next to her and hoped I could say something that wouldn't upset her. They were both still shaken up about the incident. Even though I hadn't been a witness to it, I felt off-balance, too.

"You OK? Can I get you a drink or something?"

She looked over at me and shook her head. "I'm OK. I'm gonna try not to dwell on it. And I'll get something to drink in a bit—thanks, though." She turned her gaze out onto the lake. The sun was moving in and out of gray clouds that signaled rain before nightfall.

"Did you bring your guitar?" I asked her.

She slowly turned to me, smiling. "I did...and about that...I understand you don't think I can play it. Is it because I'm a girl? Cuz if that's the reason, then Charlie, boy...don't close your eyes tonight." She emitted some sort of musical giggle sound that cracked me up...not to mention her threat was pretty funny, too.

"Oh, I love a challenge." I grinned at her. "But for the record...I believe you can play it. I'm looking forward to hearing you." I heard Johnny in the kitchen popping tops off bottles. He joined us with two beers and a wine cooler. He passed me a beer and pulled a chair close to Emma and pressed the wine cooler into her hand.

"Thanks," she said. "I don't usually drink alcoholic beverages but what the heck."

Johnny raised his eyebrows. "I brought you four. One for tonight, two for tomorrow and one for Sunday. I'm rationing you."

"And the same goes for you two with the beer?" she asked. She put the bottle to her lips and took the tiniest sip.

"Uh…no. For us it's more like two or three tonight and double that tomorrow. We'll try to be strong on Sunday."

Emma rolled her eyes. "I don't think you brought enough."

"Trust me, there's plenty. I'm sure Charlie brought some, too. We can always get more if we run out."

I watched the two of them together over the top of my beer bottle. It was my first time seeing them together as a couple and their dynamic fascinated me. Johnny had always gone for blondes or redheads. They were usually either bimbos or hard-ass chicks. I'd never known him to go for someone…soft…feminine…breakable. That's what Emma seemed like to me although I sensed that underneath her delicate exterior lay a steely strength of character. I mentally checked myself—I was going off on some philosophical tangent in my head and it wasn't likely to lead anywhere good. I drank my beer and tried to relax. My leg was aching from the long drive up and I knew I'd need to exercise it before I went to sleep tonight.

"That lake is taking my breath away," said Emma. She set her wine cooler down under the edge of her chair and walked over to the end of the deck to stare at the lake. I saw Johnny slide her bottle further under the chair out of feet range. I smiled to myself remembering the spilled Coke on my deck back home. "It's so still, like it's made of glass…and that color is surreal," she said.

Johnny finished his beer and went over to her, putting his arms around her waist, staring out at the water over her head. When he bent down to kiss her neck I turned away…looked toward the kitchen and thought about food…and my guitar…and the funny sound I'd heard in the engine of my Durango on the drive up here. I'd have to get it checked out when I got home. The sound of kissing caused an instant annoyance to take hold in my gut. I stood up and shook out my leg, flexed it a couple of times and grabbed our empty beer bottles. I cleared my throat and Johnny turned around.

"You guys hungry? For food I mean? I'm gonna make a sandwich. My mom packed a lot of lunchmeat and cheese." I slid open the screen door and went inside the kitchen. They joined me inside and I began to set out sandwich fixings.

Emma walked through to the living room and returned with her overnight bag. "Where will I be sleeping?" she asked.

I pointed down the hall. "You and Johnny can have the last bedroom down the hall on the right. Johnny'll show you. I'll have to get you a set of clean sheets. I doubt the beds are made." They disappeared down the hall. I went to the laundry room where the linen closet was located and found a set of queen-sized sheets. I walked back to the bedroom and placed the sheets on the end of the bed.

Emma stepped across the hall into the other bedroom and dropped her bag to the floor. "I'll take this room. Could I have a blanket, too? I tend to get cold even in the summer."

I raised an eyebrow at Johnny. He shrugged and started putting the sheets on his bed. I stepped back into the hall. "Uh, sure. I'll be right back."

OK, so for whatever reason, they weren't sleeping together. That didn't sound like Johnny, but, whatever. I grabbed more sheets and the heaviest blanket I could find and took it to Emma's room.

"Thanks. I'm gonna make my bed and change into something warmer. I had a feeling it would be cooler here by the lake. So, if you guys will excuse me...?" She smiled and closed the door. Johnny came out of his room and followed me down the hall. We set about making sandwiches. Johnny was uncharacteristically quiet so I addressed the elephant in the room.

"And here I thought you two would be going at it like rabbits so I took the bedroom on the other side of the house to give you privacy," I said as I peeled the plastic wrap off a piece of Velveeta.

Johnny stopped slathering a ton of mayonnaise on his bread and looked at me sideways. "It's not like that with Em. This relationship is different...she's different."

"OK. You don't have to explain." I squirted mustard on my bread and piled on thin slices of turkey.

"You may find this hard to believe, Charlie, but I can actually have a relationship with a girl that isn't all about fucking." I heard a slight edge to his voice as if he felt some weird need to explain his sex life—or lack thereof—with Emma.

This was so not the Johnny I knew that I had to ask for clarification. "So if this isn't about sex, then what is it about?"

He stared off into space for a few seconds then picked up the knife and resumed his slathering. "It's about the fact that Emma is the one, man. I mean the one. She's like some goddamned amazing treasure and I don't want to fuck it up." He lowered his voice. "And she's a virgin and I respect that she's not ready to give that up and so I'm gonna wait for however long it takes for the moment when she is…ready." His voice hitched and I sensed it hadn't been easy to say that.

I decided I needed another beer and he probably did, too. I grabbed two more from the fridge, popped the tops and pushed one over to him. "Damn, Johnny. You've changed."

He picked up his beer and took a long pull on it. He gave me a half-grin and said, "It's her…she's changed me. I can't fucking explain it but there it is…you heard it here first: Johnny fucking Beaumont's in love."

I grinned and held up my bottle, clinking it against the side of his in a toast. "Here's to being in love."

"What're you guys toasting?" Emma walked into the kitchen and climbed up on the bar stool at the end of the counter. She was wearing a Portland hoodie that seemed to swallow her up. Her dark hair fell around her shoulders and her green eyes seemed to pop out against the pink color of her hoodie.

I could smell her perfume—berries and roses blending together. I grabbed my sandwich and moved a little further away from her. Oh, fuck. She was gorgeous and I didn't want to think about how her presence was affecting me. For someone so tiny, she cast a huge metaphorical shadow in the room. I sneaked a look at Johnny. He was watching me, his face expressionless.

"We were toasting summertime at Lake Crescent. I'll get your drink." I went out to the deck and got her wine cooler…brought it back and set it down in front of her. She picked it up and raised it in the air.

"I want in on this toast." We clinked bottles and I slid away from her again, trying to get out of range of her perfume which was doing strange things to me. Ten minutes ago I'd been starving and craving this turkey sandwich, but now, it felt and tasted like cardboard going down my throat.

Emma began to make herself a sandwich. I watched in total amazement as she pretty much trashed her end of the counter. She made one hell of a mess while she made that damned sandwich. When she grabbed the mustard bottle and held it up to shake it, Johnny grabbed her wrist and stopped her. He took the bottle and squirted the mustard neatly onto her sandwich and handed it to her. And when she put it to her mouth to take a bite, I was pretty much done for.

"Be right back." I went into the bathroom and leaned against the sink, pressing my palms into the sides of it. My body felt tightly coiled and I was breathless. Even my head was spinning. I glanced down at my crotch and shook my head. Fuck. This wasn't going to work. I'd never make it through an entire weekend with Emma in the house. What the fuck was wrong with me? I pretended to use the bathroom, washed my hands and stared at my reflection in the mirror. Get your shit together, Channing. She's off limits and always will be.

I returned to the kitchen and forced myself to finish the sandwich. It started to rain as dark clouds passed over the lake. Emma slid off her stool and walked over to the sliding door to look out.

"I feel like I'm in one of those horror movies and any minute Jason's gonna rise out of the dark depths of Lake Crescent and come for us. I swear the whole lake, surrounded by all those tall trees, which are surrounded by those huge mountains, is some sort of movie trick." She turned back to us. "I know I keep commenting on it and, yes, I have seen mountains and trees and water before…but never like this."

The girl was positively beaming. But I knew what she was talking about. I'd been coming up here for years and the sight of the lake never got old. And I never took it for granted.

"I was gonna suggest going for a hike, but that's out of the question until the rain stops," said Johnny. "So how about you guys get out your guitars and I'll get my drum from the car and we can have a little jam session?" He looked over at Emma. "I seem to recall someone saying something about a guitar-off in the car on the way up here." He winked at her and she blushed, her cheeks turning the same color as her hoodie. She looked over at me and raised an eyebrow.

"You up for playing, Charlie?" Emma asked. "I'll show you mine if you show me yours."

Johnny cleared his throat loudly. "You better be talking about guitars, girl."

She let out that little giggle-sound again. "Of course…what else would I mean? But I want us to play together. This isn't going to be a contest to see who's the best. Let's just play for fun."

"I'll get my guitar." I went into my room and took my Martin Dreadnought out of its case. I slipped a pick in my pocket but I didn't think I'd need it. I wanted to use my fingers and feel the strings while I played. I tried to ignore my nerves—nerves not caused by any doubt in my ability to play but rather, if I was being honest, nerves caused by the thought of watching Emma handle her instrument…of watching her fingers moving over the strings and hearing her voice. I seriously hoped I wouldn't lose my shit in front of her and Johnny.

We gathered in the living room. Johnny brought a kitchen chair to sit on, his drum on the floor between his knees. Emma and I sat across from each other on the sofas. I noticed she had an Epiphone Hummingbird model. I strummed a few chords to warm up and she did the same.

"How about you start playing something and if I know it, I'll join in," Emma said, letting her fingers come to rest over the guitar's bridge.

"OK." I strummed over the strings for a second thinking about what I wanted to play. I'd have to steer clear of original music for now and stick with something she might have heard of. Finally I began to play…a song by one of my favorite bands. And I knew Johnny would recognize it: "Endlessly" by Muse—my own bare, stripped down version. A few measures in, Johnny began to drum softly, keeping time with me. This song had a heavy drumbeat but he played it conservatively so as not to overpower me. Every so often I glanced up at Emma. She was listening with her eyes closed, her fingers moving over the strings but not actually touching them yet. When I went into the second verse and she'd figured out my version of the tune, she joined in and matched me stroke for stroke. When we neared the end of the song, she said, "Play it again, with vocals this time." I nodded and began again.

I started to sing and she joined in, her voice an octave higher, singing melody. And then on the chorus she switched to harmony. And she was freaking amazing. I glanced at Johnny and he was smiling. I was beyond impressed that Emma knew the lyrics. If she liked Muse then she was a goddess in my eyes. When we finished the song, which had an abrupt ending, the cabin rang loudly in its silence.

"Fucking amazing." Johnny banged his drum hard once and grinned, shaking his head. "Pure fucking amazing."

"I've got one now. You guys join in if you know it," said Emma. She played a few chords, finding the key, as we waited to see what she'd chosen. Finally she began. I heard the familiar opening notes and I knew exactly what she was about to play. And it felt like a knife cutting through my gut. I joined her in harmony on the chorus of "Fix You" by Coldplay. Johnny joined in, too, and when we finished, and the room was silent again, nobody said a word.

Chapter Nine

Emma

I loved Lake Crescent and this cabin. In spite of the fact that I'd been nearly mowed down on the road, I still felt at home here. It was warm and cozy and even though we'd only been here a few hours I knew I'd hate to leave on Sunday. Plus being here was making it easier to deal with the fact that my stepmother was pregnant. The idea of it made my stomach churn. I pushed thoughts of Nanette away and relived our afternoon concert. After we'd played music together for a couple of hours, I'd told the guys I needed another snack/drink break. I really didn't, but the music was starting to get to me. It seemed that every song Charlie and I chose had some kind of hidden message in it. I almost felt like the two of us were speaking some kind of secret language in front of Johnny. I doubted Charlie was aware of the undercurrent flowing in the room because I'd pretty much convinced myself it was all in my head and only one-sided anyway. I was sure Johnny was unaware of it, too. Even though I'd only known Charlie a few days, I sensed he was more intuitive than Johnny or at least intuitive in a different way.

The rain continued to pour down and it got dark really early. While the guys talked in the kitchen, I'd toured the cabin, checking out the rooms. It was really nice and modern and tastefully decorated. The living room where we'd played had taupe walls and big, over-stuffed couches perfect for curling up on to read or watch movies. There was a large-screen TV and a well-stocked DVD cabinet and another wall of shelves filled with books and board games. The kitchen was painted a soft olive green and there seemed to be two of everything in it: two refrigerators, two dishwashers, two sinks and even two ovens. I had a sudden urge to bake and if I'd had the ingredients I would have made a cake or a batch of chocolate chip cookies.

I came back into the kitchen and when Johnny saw me he beckoned me over. When I got close to him, he grabbed the sleeve of my hoodie and pulled me into his arms.

"Where've you been, babe?" He kissed my forehead and held me tight. Charlie watched us from his spot on the stool at the end of the counter. When Johnny leaned down and kissed my lips, I saw Charlie turn his head to look away. I was afraid that if Johnny didn't stop, Charlie would leave the room and I didn't want that, so I broke off the kiss and pressed my hand to Johnny's cheek for a moment to lessen any sting he might feel at my separation from his lips.

"I was checking out the books and DVD's in the living room. There's a nice selection. Maybe we should watch a movie tonight since this rain is seriously hampering any possibility of outdoor activities."

"As long as it's not a chick flick, I'm down for a movie." Johnny said, tightening his hold on me. For a split second I felt like I was being smothered.

"Anybody hungry?" Charlie asked. He got up and went to the fridge.

"I could eat," said Johnny. "It'd be nice to cook steaks on the grill, but that will have to wait till tomorrow. We could have pizza, Oreos and ice cream."

"Sounds good," I said. "You guys put the pizza in and I'll go pick out a movie."

I went back to the living room and perused the shelves again. I decided I'd pick three movies and give the guys a choice. I picked a James Bond flick, a Jason Bourne movie and the third Mission Impossible. I'd be happy with any of these. I took them back to the kitchen and spread them out on the counter next to Charlie. He looked down and smiled.

"I vote for Jason Bourne," he said. I was secretly thrilled. I had a thing for Matt Damon.

"I second that," said Johnny. He slid the pizza in the oven and set the timer. Then he pulled out a drawer hidden in the center island and exclaimed excitedly at what he saw inside. "Let's get fancy with our Italian dinner. How about a bottle of…" He reached down and pulled out a bottle of red wine…, "a Cabernet Sauvignon 2010 vintage."

"Since when do you drink wine?" Charlie asked, grinning.

"Hey, I have a sophisticated palate. Besides…you know me, Chuck…I'll drink damned near anything." He opened several drawers until he found a corkscrew. "We need to let this baby breathe."

I shook my head. "Wow…aren't you full of surprises? Am I allowed to have some? I'm being rationed, remember?"

Charlie brought out three wineglasses and Johnny divided the entire bottle among the three of them. "Yes…I'll lift your restriction just for tonight." He winked at me and brought me the glass. "You going to be able to drink this without spilling it?"

"Ha, ha. I can manage." I made a point of being careful as I sipped the wine. It tasted a little bitter but it was tolerable. I took a few more sips trying to get used to the acidic taste.

Charlie brought out a radio and tuned it to a rock station. The sounds of The Cure singing Lovesong floated about the kitchen. I loved this song. I raised my glass of wine to my lips, took a big gulp and began to dance around the kitchen. As I was just about to sashay past Charlie, Johnny called out in an alarmed voice, "Holy shit, Charlie, take that glass out of her hand before she spills wine all over herself and the floor."

As I twirled past Charlie he caught me gently around the waist and removed the glass from my hand. A little bit of wine spilled over the edge of the glass onto our hands and I laughed. He dropped his other hand from my waist and turned around abruptly for napkins. He was smiling but his face was red. He pressed a napkin into my hand and wiped his fingers and wrist then cleaned the drips from my glass.

"And that's me…sober!" I continued my dance around the island toward Johnny and he caught me in his arms. He suddenly picked me up and set me on the counter and pushed himself between my legs, pulling me into his chest.

"If this is you sober, I'm quite curious what drunk Emma would look like." He leaned down and kissed me, running his tongue inside my mouth, moaning. "This wine tastes so much better second-hand," he said softly against my lips.

The oven timer went off, coinciding with the crash of a glass hitting the floor. Johnny jumped and turned toward Charlie. I slipped down from the counter and made a beeline for the paper towels.

"Yay! I'm not the only one!" I screeched. "Welcome to my world, Charlie!"

"I didn't want you to be alone so I sacrificed a glass for you," he joked as he took the paper towels from my hand and began to wipe up the mess. "Johnny, will you grab the broom and dustpan? They're in the laundry room."

Johnny left and I helped Charlie clean up the mess. He picked up the larger pieces of glass and put them in a paper towel. We both reached down to swipe up a puddle at the same time and our hands met, just like before, when I'd accidentally grasped his fingers through the towels on his back deck. We were squatting on the floor, side by side, three inches apart. I looked into his blue eyes and felt myself blushing.

"This is becoming a habit," he said quietly. I stared at his lips as he spoke and for one second I wondered what they would feel like against mine.

"Yeah, but this time, you spilled…not me," I said softly.

"Then we're even," he replied.

"Here we go." Johnny returned with the broom and dustpan and helped Charlie sweep up the remainder of the broken glass. I slipped out of the kitchen and dashed into my room. As soon as I was alone I let out a long, quiet breath. I felt hot and sweaty under my hoodie. I pulled it over my head and threw it on the bed. I was purposely not thinking. Not thinking about Charlie and what his full lips would taste like or the way his fingers felt touching mine. I didn't think about his blue eyes and how they were only slightly darker than Lake Crescent. Or about his brown hair and what it might look like entangled with mine on a white pillow case. A shudder coursed through my body and goose bumps broke out over my arms. I shrugged back into my hoodie, smoothed out my mussed hair and went back to the kitchen, putting on a calm face to mask the sudden turmoil swirling inside me.

It was almost midnight and Johnny was a little drunk. He'd had a few more beers and the majority of another bottle of wine. He'd fallen asleep halfway through The Bourne Identity and Charlie and I had finished the movie together over a bowl of popcorn into which we'd crumbled Oreo cookies, then poured melted butter over the top of it. It was freakishly delicious. During the closing credits Johnny roused himself from sleep long enough to use the bathroom before falling into his bed. He wasn't even aware that I'd tucked him in and kissed his cheek good night. I came back out to clean up the kitchen but Charlie had already beaten me to it.

"So, did you get the baby put to bed OK?" he asked, grinning.

"Out like a light," I said. I walked over to the sliding doors and noticed that it had stopped raining. An almost full moon shone over the lake and if I thought the lake was beautiful by day, it didn't compare to the way it looked now. "Charlie…come look at the moon. It's freaky gorgeous."

He left the light on over the stove but flipped off the overhead, casting the kitchen in shadows. He hung the kitchen towel over the handle of the oven and joined me at the door.

I slid the door open and we stepped out onto the deck. I breathed in the night air. The lake rippled the slightest bit from a soft breeze and the moonlight cast a narrow swath of muted gold from one end to the other, fading into the dark water where the lake curved in a northward path and disappeared into the trees and mountains beyond. Nightsounds played all around us—crickets, a hooting owl, rustling grasses and leaves brushing against one another in the breeze. The wet trees and grass sparkled in the moonlight. It was chilly and I shivered. I'd spilled pizza sauce on my hoodie earlier and I'd had to wash it out in the bathroom sink. I was in a t-shirt now and the air was cold on my arms.

Charlie saw me shiver and unzipped his sweatshirt. "Here, put this on," he said, holding it open for me. I slid my arms inside and he pulled it around me, adjusting the collar around my neck, his fingers brushing against my skin. I pulled it close around me, wrapping myself in it. It was huge and I almost disappeared inside of it.

"Thanks," I whispered, turning my gaze from his face back to the lake. "This night is so beautiful that I might actually start crying. You won't laugh at me, will you?"

He leaned against the railing on his elbows and smiled. Out of the corner of my eye, I saw his teeth flash white in the darkness. I peeked over at him and saw his eyes sparkling, just like the lake was doing now under the moon's glow. My god, he's beautiful, too, I thought.

"Nah...you can cry if you want to," he said, his voice low and husky. "This place'll do that to you."

"I'm not really a fan of winter but I bet it's just as magical here in a snowstorm. Do you come here in the wintertime?"

"Yeah, sometimes. We cross-country ski and rent snowmobiles. It's pretty cool, but I think summer's better."

"Hmm," I murmured. "Maybe you'll invite me up here some winter weekend so I can compare and see if you're right."

"Sure, any time." He turned around then and leaned against the railing, his back to the lake. I felt him looking at me so I turned to him, waiting for him to speak. When he didn't say anything I did.

"I enjoyed playing with you today. I think you are the better guitar player."

He chuckled. "You held your own...I'd say it was a tie. But you beat me in the singing department. You sound like you could sing opera if you wanted to."

"I can. I took voice lessons for years down in Portland with an emphasis on opera. I still love it and I love pop and rock and country, too. But I really love indie rock the most."

"You know Muse. That won you a ton of points with me. Most girls are all about Taylor Swift and the Justins, as in Timberlake and Bieber." He shuddered and I giggled.

"Hey, now...don't knock the Beebs. For about five minutes I had a case of Bieber fever."

"Oh, my god...please, no," he exclaimed, his shoulders shaking with quiet laughter. "Anything but that."

"Ah, he's not all that bad," I replied. "I can't believe I'm defending Justin Bieber. I must be crazy."

"I'll forgive you if you promise never to let it happen again."

He turned around to face the lake again, his body brushing up closer to mine. My heartbeat sped up and my breathing slowed, threatening to stop altogether. Standing this close to Charlie made me feel things I shouldn't be feeling…made me think things I shouldn't be thinking and worst of all…it made me want things I could never have. I suddenly couldn't swallow or talk and I knew I needed to go to bed… to put some distance between us. I was under no illusion that he was experiencing any of the things I was feeling right now and I allowed myself to take comfort in that even though it hurt a little to think it. But Johnny was sleeping a few feet away and I knew he'd be hurt if he could read my mind right now. Whatever this was happening inside my head, I'd ignore it…push it away…concentrate on Johnny…my Johnny who loved me.

"I'm gonna head into bed," I said quietly. Right then I should have given him back his sweatshirt but I pretended like I'd forgotten I was wearing it.

"OK…and thanks again for the jam session today. I really enjoyed it."

And I know I shouldn't have, but I just couldn't help myself. I put my arms around him and gave him a hug. "Good night, Charlie."

He put his arms around me, too, and gave me a squeeze then dropped them quickly down to his sides. "Night, Emma."

I walked silently down the hall and stopped in the bathroom to brush my teeth. Once in my room, I snuggled down under the blanket and pulled Charlie's sweatshirt up to my face and buried my nose in it. It smelled like him. I held it tightly to my breasts and closed my eyes. I tried not to think about him. I tried really hard, but it was a battle I had no chance of winning.

Chapter Ten

Johnny

There were a dozen tiny hammers tapping inside my head. I rolled over and picked up my phone. It was 11:30. I sat up and considered going back to sleep but then thought of Emma. I missed her. I noticed I was still in the clothes I'd been wearing yesterday. And then I realized I desperately needed to take a piss. On my way to the bathroom I made a mental note to stick to beer. I did not like the aftereffects of wine. When I finished in the bathroom I shuffled down the hall to the kitchen where Charlie sat at the table drinking orange juice. There was an empty cereal bowl next to him and an open box of Honey Nut Cheerios.

"Hey, man…where's Emma?" I went to the cupboard for a mug—there had to be some instant coffee in this place. I put water in the kettle and turned on the burner. I grabbed a carton of milk from the fridge and fixed myself a bowl of Frosted Flakes.

"She walked down to the lake. She went down there with a notebook and a pen to write. She didn't say what she was writing…a story…poetry…a book…a song…all of the above?" Charlie turned the Cheerios box around and stared at the back of it.

"Probably her journal. She says journaling keeps her sane. I'd love to know what she says about me in that thing," I remarked, joining Charlie at the table.

"I don't suppose you'll ever know," said Charlie. "On another note, the weather looks great. You oughta take Emma up to Lover's Leap. She could take some nice pictures up there. I'd go with you but I don't trust going that far with my leg. It's been a little achy the last few days. Anyway, I don't want to be a third wheel."

"We didn't come here to abandon you…although…I wouldn't mind being alone with her. Isn't she amazing?" I wanted Charlie to love her as much as I did—well, not quite as much but close.

He pushed his chair back and took his glass and bowl to the sink. "Yeah, she's great." His answer sounded flat and unconvincing. I couldn't imagine anyone not loving Emma.

"She's more than great. She's fucking awesome." The kettle whistled and I got up to get my coffee. Charlie moved away from me to stand at the sliding door, his back to me. I had the feeling he was avoiding me. "Everything OK, Chuck?"

He turned his head a fraction in my direction. "What? Oh, yeah, fine. Just my leg's bugging me today. I'm going to my room to do some exercises. Here comes Emma." He moved away from the door and disappeared down the hall.

I watched Emma bounce up the dirt path like a beautiful female version of Tigger. Her boobs bobbed up and down and I felt it right in my crotch. I needed to talk to her about sex again. This waiting was almost too much for me to take. She'd jokingly referred to me recently as a caveman but, truth was, where she was concerned, I was a Neanderthal and I had a strong need to make love to her so I could somehow officially mark her as mine. I slid open the door and grabbed her as she bounded up onto the deck.

"Good morning, Tigger," I said, as I pressed her against me and kissed her. She tasted so damned good. "You're full of energy this morning."

"Hi. How're you feeling? Hung over?" We walked into the kitchen and she went to the fridge, pulling out the orange juice.

"Are you kidding…Johnny Beaumont doesn't do hangovers," I gave her a sly grin as I finished my coffee.

"Riiiight," she said, clearly not buying it. "Where's Charlie?"

"He said his leg was bothering him so he's in his room exercising it. What time did you get up this morning? I feel kinda bad I slept so late and wasted the morning."

"Around 9:30. I went for a walk along the lake…took some pictures…collected some interesting rocks. And I was writing in my journal. I'm finding Lake Crescent to be very inspirational." She grabbed a handful of Cheerios from the box, put them in her mouth and didn't even bat an eye when half the handful showered down the front of her t-shirt. I shook my head in wonder and began to pick them off of her chest. When I touched her breast I let my hand linger there, unable to resist.

"Hey, no getting fresh at the breakfast table—Charlie might see," she said, pushing my hand away and giving me a frown. She had her hair in a pony tail and all I wanted at that moment was to pull out that damned rubber band and let her hair rain down all over me. Fuck all but I needed to snap out it.

I pulled my hand back and sighed. I'm going to behave…I'm going to behave…I'm going to behave, I repeated silently. "Charlie suggested we go for a hike up to Lover's Leap. What do you think about that? It's maybe about a mile from here to the base and then another half mile or so to the top. We can get there along a path that winds around the lake."

She hesitated, glancing down the hall toward Charlie's room. "Maybe we shouldn't leave Charlie alone, if he's not feeling well. We could do something around here."

"It's just his leg. But he's fine with our going out for a while, and anyway, we won't be gone all day—just a few hours. And maybe when we get back we can take the boat out. Charlie's dad keeps a small one here with an outboard motor. It's not very big but we can squeeze three people into it, especially considering you take up about as much space as a peanut."

She laughed—that musical sound I loved. "OK. Let me change clothes and check on Charlie. We should make sure he's not just being polite about our going off and leaving him." She dashed off down the hall. I put my dirty dishes in the dishwasher and considered her concern for Charlie's well-being. She was such a caring girl—it was one of the million things I loved about her.

I went into my room and put on some tennis shoes and grabbed a sweatshirt. I heard Emma talking to Charlie in his room. She joined me in the kitchen and we left out the back door and headed for the path edging the lake. I couldn't help but notice Emma's mood seemed less buoyant than it had been ten minutes earlier, but I let it slide. I had a feeling she felt a little sorry for Charlie and his bum leg.

"You're not gonna get us lost out here in the woods, are you?" she asked as we made our way down the trail. The sun was shining but it was still a little cool for June. The water level was high because of all the rain and it made me wonder about taking the boat out later. Usually the lake was quite calm and placid but now it had a good ripple going.

"Don't worry. I know my way around here just fine. For your information, Lover's Leap is where Charlie and I smoked pot for the first time. Ah…such fond memories." I glanced back to see her expression and as I expected, she had a frown on her gorgeous face.

"Pot, huh? That stuff's bad for you. It kills your brain cells."

"Hey, don't knock it till you've tried it," I said. "It's a naturally growing substance so it's perfectly safe to smoke it."

"Poison ivy is a naturally growing substance, too, and you know what happens when you get too close that," she said, making a valid point.

"OK, I'll give you that." I slowed down my pace and waited for her to catch up. We were at the part of the path now where it began to veer away from the lake, turning inward further into the woods. "Speaking of poison ivy…beware of that patch on your right."

We walked on and Emma began to hum some song that sounded vaguely familiar. I listened to her hum as we walked and after a few minutes I could feel the pull in my thighs from the subtle yet steep incline of the hill. Overhead, the foliage thickened enough to block out the sunlight but it was still warm as we climbed. I eventually had to take off my sweatshirt. I looked back at Emma and saw that she had removed hers, too. The sight of her breasts in the tiny white tank top nearly caused me to lose my footing. I'd decided that as soon as we got to the top of Lover's Leap I was going to bring up the sex topic and see if I could get to the bottom of her hang-up. It if was fear of getting pregnant or some other psychological or emotional issue holding her back, I could fix it. I'd put up a convincing argument. Thinking the word pregnant made me think of Sarah and I immediately forced my thoughts onto something else. I didn't want to deal with guilt anymore.

Eventually we emerged from the woods onto the flat summit of the hill. It was covered in a field of tall grasses and wildflowers in their early stages of growth. The sun shone down on us and it was hotter here than in the woods. The clouds were thick and low and the sky was a killer shade of blue. I looked over at Emma to see her reaction. She'd come to a stop in the center of the field and was slowly turning in a circle and staring all around at the view.

"Geez, Johnny. Look at that lake. This view is to die for." She took out her phone and began to snap photos. "I'm putting these on Facebook right now. My friends back in Portland will be so jealous."

"I've been to Portland a few times. The views are pretty nice there, too," I said. I walked over to her and spread my sweatshirt on the ground for us to sit on.

"Yes, but not like this. Lake Crescent is different. It's almost like it's alive." She fiddled with her phone and muttered something under her breath about the lack of service then shut it off, joining me on my sweatshirt. As she moved to sit down I grabbed her and pulled her onto my lap.

"I have the best view of all," I said, kissing the back of her neck… tasting the saltiness of the sweat there and groaning. "Damn, girl…even when you're all hot and sweaty you still taste good."

"Ick…I somehow doubt that, but I think you're biased." She turned sideways giving me better access to her lips. I leaned down and kissed her, a little harder than I meant to. I wanted to taste every inch of her luscious lips and tantalizing tongue. Sometimes I feared losing control with her—she was so fucking desirable. I had a feeling she was completely oblivious to the effect she had on me. She returned my kiss but finally pushed away to catch her breath.

"That was…passionate," she breathed, panting a little. The panting did it. I had to bring up the 's' word now.

"Hey, Em…," I decided not to over-think it. I'd just dive right in.

"Can we talk about something kinda serious?"

A look of apprehension passed over her face before she said, a little hesitantly, "O…K…?"

I swallowed and lifted her so that she straddled me. We were now face to face. I wanted to watch her reaction to the subject matter—to see if I could read her. I sensed she might be a little cagey with her answers. "I want to talk to you about sex."

She let out a nervous giggle. "Is this the talk about where babies come from? Because if it is, maybe you should've clued my stepmother in a few months ago."

"Ha, ha. No, it's not about the birds and bees. It's about us—me and you." I waited for a reaction but she remained still…expressionless…waiting.

"Emma…true story…I love you…like I've never loved another girl…ever. And I swear on a stack of friggin' Bibles I'm not saying that just to get in your pants. I really mean it like I've never meant anything before. And I want to have every part of you—inside and out. I want you. So, I'm asking you…what can I do to reassure you that you're safe with me and that I would never hurt you and that, more than anything, I want to make love to you? What can I do?"

I studied her face. Her eyebrows rose and she sucked in her lower lip, biting down on it in a way that wasn't helping to stem the need I felt building up inside of me right now. I could see in her eyes that she was thinking about how to respond to my deep question.

"Johnny…wow…I don't know how to explain this," she said, her voice quiet. "I know I'm safe with you and I know you would never hurt me. It's nothing to do with that."

"Then tell me what it is, Em. I promise I won't get mad or upset. I just want to understand where you're coming from." I made sure to control the emotion in my voice even though a part of me wanted to beg her.

She looked away, her hands in her lap, resting dangerously close to my crotch, which was in the process of giving away just how badly I wanted her. I finally grasped her chin gently and turned her to face me. Her emerald eyes were glassy with unshed tears.

"What is it, babe? Tell me," I urged quietly. I dashed away her ears with my thumbs as they fell.

"I'm worried about feeling guilty for one thing…and, I do fear pregnancy…I won't lie. I'm not on the pill." She spoke quietly and I heard shyness in her voice.

I smiled and kissed the tip of her nose. "First of all, we'd use condoms…problem solved. Second of all, as far as guilt is concerned, there wouldn't be anything to feel guilty about. It's me, Em. I'll treat you like the gift you are. I'll make it special…damned unforgettable…you'll be so impressed you'll be begging for more." I chuckled, hoping my joking would ease her fears.

She leaned into me and pressed into my chest, wrapping her arms around me. I held her securely…rubbed her back…breathed in her hair. And I waited.

Finally she pushed back from me and looked into my eyes. She bit her lip again and I shook my head, trying not to let it affect me. "Let me think this over for a few days and in the mean time maybe I should see a doctor about getting on birth control. But even then, I have to think about how I'd handle my conscience. Can you bear with me?"

I had to rein myself in from jumping into the air with happiness. Her response sounded promising, but if she sensed my eagerness, I could scare her off. So I calmly responded, "Of course. That's a great idea. Being on the pill will probably make you feel a lot better—take some of those fears away." I wanted to crush her to me like the fucking caveman I was, but instead, I pulled her to me gently and kissed her as tenderly as possible. She responded and I convinced myself that it was only a matter of time.

Eventually we stood and wandered around the hilltop a while so Emma could take more photos and then we headed back down the hill, through the woods to the lake. The water level was still high enough that I decided taking out the boat wouldn't be a good idea. We walked along the shoreline, hand in hand, and just before we headed up the path to the cabin, I grabbed Emma in a hug and kissed her again—hard enough and long enough to leave her a little breathless.

"Johnny Beaumont…has anyone ever told you that you're incorrigible?"

"Incorrigible? Ooh, I like being incorrigible." I laughed as we walked up the path onto the deck. Charlie was sitting on a lounger drinking a Coke.

"Hey, Chuck. How's the leg?" I asked as I joined him. Emma glanced at him and smiled then went inside to the fridge, returning with two Cokes.

"Better, thanks. I checked on the boat but the engine's acting up. It needs a tune up or something," he said.

"No worries. The water's too high anyway. One rogue wave and Emma'd bounce right out of the thing." I grinned at Emma who'd taken the seat next to Charlie. I tried not to let it bother me that she'd not taken the one beside me.

"I also noticed that we're out of propane for the tank and there's not even any charcoal in the shed. I could go into town and get some," said Charlie.

"I'll go. We need more beer and I have a much better chance of buying it than you, Mr. Baby Face. I think I still have a fake ID in my glove box, if my brother didn't take it."

Emma stuck her fingers in her ears and began to hum loudly, her eyes closed. After a few seconds of this, she cut her eyes at me, shooting me a look of chastisement. "I'm trying not to hear your plans for breaking the law. You guys are so bad," she said, grinning.

"Hey, I'm not the one with the fake ID," said Charlie. He finished his Coke and stood up. "While you're getting the propane—and the beverages—I'll start marinating the steaks." He went inside—straight to the radio first—before setting out his marinade supplies. Soon we could hear an old song by Depeche Mode playing softly.

"I'll make a salad," said Emma. She got up and I followed her to the kitchen. I wasn't sure if it was my imagination, but I was picking up on a vibe—a sort of negative vibe—and I wasn't sure if it was because our talk was on her mind or if maybe Charlie was causing it. I was certain she liked Charlie, but, unless I was imagining things, she seemed to get a little sad around him. I decided that if I continued to notice it, I'd bring it up with her. More than anything, Charlie would not want her pity. Charlie was fine now—almost completely healthy again. There was no reason for her to worry about him. But she did have that nurturing side to her. I shrugged off those thoughts as I went to my room to grab my wallet and car keys.

"Do we need anything else?" I asked as I headed for the front door.

"If we think of something, we'll text it," said Emma. I waved goodbye and went out to my car. As I pulled out of the drive and headed to the general store in tiny Crescent Springs, I felt that weird vibe again... like something wasn't quite right. But I couldn't figure it out, so I let it go as I drove with the music cranked. It was probably my imagination anyway—where Emma was concerned, my imagination was often out of control. I chuckled to myself as I drove on into Crescent Springs.

Chapter Eleven

Charlie

"Do you like spicy foods?" I asked Emma. I was about to dust the steaks with some red pepper flakes but caught myself in time. She was standing next to me, drying her hands on a dish towel.

"Love it—the hotter the better," she said, smiling. She pulled out bags of spinach and romaine lettuce from the fridge and poured them into a bowl. I watched as she began to peel a cucumber and chop it into tiny pieces. I noticed how small her hands were—and delicate—and I was amazed again at how proficiently she'd handled her guitar with such small hands.

"Good. I'm gonna lay the heat on these steaks then. Johnny likes hot stuff, too." I almost laughed at the double meaning behind those words but stopped myself in time. I peppered both sides of three steaks and then poured some barbecue sauce over them to soak. I put them back in the fridge, then sat down at the end of the center island and watched Emma peel carrots. "So when did you and Johnny start going out? I think he told me before, when he came up to see me in Seattle, but I can't remember."

"Well, we met the first day of school and just started talking and then eventually hanging out from time to time. We didn't really start dating until February. He asked me to the Valentine's dance. After that, we just kinda started going out." She threw the peels away and started chopping the carrots into pieces. Every so often a tiny piece would shoot off the knife blade and go flying down the counter or onto the floor. I watched her in fascination as I picked up the pieces that landed near me and popped them into my mouth.

"It seems kind of serious between you two," I said. I was testing the waters—curious about what she would reveal—and what she'd withhold.

"I guess so," she said, her voice dropping. She put the knife in the sink and began to clean up her mess. When she didn't continue, I pressed a little further. I just couldn't help myself.

"You don't sound so sure," I said quietly.

When she didn't respond immediately, I felt bad. I'd gone too far and made her uncomfortable. I was just about to apologize when she spoke.

"Johnny's kind of intense...sometimes. He can come on rather strong. Sometimes he pushes me a little to change the relationship in ways that I'm not ready for." She looked up at me then, a troubled expression on her face, and I swear my heart did something strange in my chest...something unnatural. It seemed to leap. I did a mental head-shake and tried not to let my expression show anything unusual.

"Yeah, that sounds like Johnny. When he's crazy about something, he loves the bejesus out of it." I remembered Johnny telling me that Emma was still a virgin. It didn't surprise me that he wanted to change that.

She moved a little closer to me--a worried look in her eyes. "You're not gonna say anything to Johnny, are you? About what I just said?"

"No. Anything you say to me is between you and me—no worries." I noticed a tiny piece of carrot was caught in her hair. I could have just told her—pointed it out to her—but I decided to punish myself instead. I wanted to touch that beautiful, black hair. I reached into her hair, pulling the piece of carrot out of it and, just as I figured, the strands felt like silk. I held up the carrot and grinned. "You're sort of a loose cannon in a kitchen, aren't you?"

She laughed. "You have no idea." She sat down next to me on a stool. She was close enough that I could feel her leg brushing up against mine. "What about you, Charlie? You don't have a girlfriend?"

I shook my head. "Nope. I was kinda dating a girl last year before the accident but it didn't work out. Just as well, too, cuz when you're laid up for as long as I was and somewhat too far away for regular visits, dating doesn't exactly work well."

"Well, her loss," said Emma, giving me a sweet smile. She moved back down the counter and pulled out salad tongs, then began to toss the salad. When she was satisfied that it was mixed enough, she put it in the fridge and held up the carton of lemonade. "Wanna join me in a cocktail?" she grinned.

My eyebrow shot up at that remark. "You're kidding, right?"

"Yeah. I like my lemonade straight up and on the rocks." She got two glasses and poured some for both of us, then joined me at the end of the counter again.

"What's with Johnny rationing your alcohol intake?" I asked.

She laughed again—that infectious laugh. "It's just a joke. Johnny calls me a lightweight—which I totally am. And anyway, I really don't like the taste of alcohol, although those blackberry wine coolers aren't too bad."

We were quiet for a time, drinking our lemonade as I tried to control my thoughts. I was way too aware of her presence next to me—for someone so small, she really did fill up a room. And then a song came on the radio that caught her attention. "Ooh, I love this song," she said. "This is an awesome radio station." She began to sing along to "Ho Hey" by the Lumineers. Suddenly she jumped off the stool and began to dance around the island. She danced around to me and grabbed my arm, pulling me off my seat. "Dance with me, Charlie."

I didn't have a chance to say no—not that I would have. She moved her body in time to the music as she held my arms, twirling us around. She pressed herself closer to me, her head not even reaching the level of my shoulders. I knew this song well—it was up-tempo and I let Emma lead us around the island again, finally veering us off into the dining room. I noticed my leg actually felt good and it occurred to me that I should scrap physical therapy altogether and just dance with Emma. I took her hand and twirled her around a couple of times. She smiled and fell into me—my arms automatically coming around her. The song ended and I should have let her go…but I didn't. She could have let me go, too, but she held on, her fingers caressing my back. I could feel her in my gut. My mouth watered as if someone had just placed my favorite food in front of me. I wanted to taste it…to taste her. I sucked in a breath as she looked up at me, those green eyes sparkling. She licked her lips and I knew I had to do something…now…before I screwed up everything I was trying to fix. The sound of Johnny's car door slamming saved us both. I dropped my hands and stepped away, going back into the kitchen. I drained the last of my lemonade and tried to collect myself. It wasn't easy.

"OK, guys…we're covered both ways—charcoal or the fast way," said Johnny. He came in with a twelve-pack of Corona and a bag of charcoal. He set the beer on the counter and carried the bag of briquettes out to the deck. I slipped my hands into my pockets and walked around the island, trying to act normal. Emma had disappeared down the hall. Johnny went back out front and returned a second later with the propane tank. He went out and affixed it to the grill. "What's your preference, Chuck?"

"Charcoal," I said. "So they fell for the fake ID, huh?"

"Nah…I didn't even have to show it. The chick at the counter took one look at my baby browns and didn't even question it. Gotta face it, man, I have a gift." Johnny laughed. He went back inside and found a pack of matches in a drawer then returned to light the grill. "Where's Emma?"

I could hear the shower running at the end of the hall. "Sounds like she's taking a shower," I responded. I suddenly had a vision of

Emma…naked…and wet…under the shower spray. Oh, Jesus.

"We should have another jam session after we eat if Em's up for it. What do you think?" Johnny asked. I watched as he filled the grill with charcoal. "Got any newspaper?"

I went inside to the living room and found some old newspaper and brought it back for Johnny to tear up. In a few minutes he had the grill up and running. While I watched him poke around in the charcoal, a thought passed through my brain and tried to take root. I tried to block it but it wouldn't go away: Johnny didn't deserve Emma. He was my best friend…but…he wasn't right for her. She was out of his league. I wondered if he was aware of that…aware of the precarious hold he had on her. I had no real reason to think this way other than gut instinct. What would Johnny do if Emma broke up with him? Would he freak out like Sarah and get himself killed? Somehow I sensed that if it ever happened, someone would get hurt.

When the grill was finally hot enough, I laid the steaks out on it and sat back with a beer on the deck, breathing in the scent of hot coals and roasting meat. Johnny disappeared down the hall and within seconds of his departure I heard Emma let out a screech. Johnny had probably invaded her privacy. I closed my eyes and immediately my mind conjured up a vision of Emma, stepping out of the shower, dripping water on the floor, wrapped in a white towel...the towel slipping down her body…exposing her perfect, round…

"Earth to Charlie," said Emma. I jumped at the sound of her voice and opened my eyes, straightening up in my chair. She knocked gently on my head with her fist. "Anybody home in there?"

Emma was standing in front of me in tiny white shorts and a tight black tank top. Her long hair was wet and shining in the late afternoon sun. She smelled like citrus and berries and some other unidentifiable scent that was uniquely Emma. I tried to keep my eyes moving so they wouldn't linger on any particular body part. If I didn't know better, I'd swear she was…somehow…taunting me.

"Uh...sorry…I zoned out for a minute. Oh, hey…how do you like your steak cooked?" I got up and checked the steaks, turning them over with a meat fork.

"Well done, please." I kept my back to her as I made my way to the kitchen to get a plate to put the steaks on. I heard the shower going again—and Johnny singing an old Radiohead song. I had to give him props—he could carry a tune, too. I returned with a platter and attended to the steaks. I heard her settle herself into the lounger next to mine.

I could feel Emma's eyes on me as I moved. I knew it was not my imagination that there was a strange vibe in the air between us. I didn't know what it was, but it was palpable. Finally I stole a look at her. Her face was unreadable and I would have given anything to know what she was thinking right now. I had the feeling she was studying me…dissecting me like a fetal pig in biology class. I set the platter of steaks on the patio table and settled back into my lounge chair next to her. Finally she spoke.

"Have you thought about what you want to do after graduation? If you want to go to college and if so, where?" she asked. As she spoke she ran her hands through her hair, fluffing out the damp strands.

"Yeah…there's this music and theater school in New York City I'm interested in. I've actually already filled out the application. Geez…I didn't even tell Johnny about it." I gazed out at the lake as I drained the last of my beer.

She sat up straighter in her chair. "Wait…it isn't by any chance the Jenkins School of Music and Theatrical Arts, is it?"

I glanced at her sideways. "Yeah, that's it. How did you know?"

A slow grin spread across her face. "I'm applying there, too. Wow. What a coincidence." She leaned closer to me. "And I haven't mentioned it to Johnny yet either. He says he's applying to the University of Washington and he wants me to apply there, too. I haven't gotten up the nerve to tell him I don't want to go there."

"Wait…back up…you're applying to Jenkins?" This news astounded me. Whatever weird vibe I thought I was feeling earlier…it just grew exponentially. My stomach actually tightened.

"Yeah. As a matter of fact, I'm going to put in for my audition sometime in the next couple of weeks. Have you put in for yours yet?" She sounded excited and I noticed she was still speaking in a hushed voice.

"Not yet. But I will. Don't they hold auditions in the winter?"

"Yes, but the slots fill up fast and you have to request one early. A friend of mine from Portland just finished her freshman year there. She loved it. She says it's hard but she's already been invited to play on Broadway and in the Met's symphony for some special concerts. Her name's Maggie Cho—she's Chinese—and she plays violin like nobody's business."

"Wow…cool. Thanks for letting me know about the auditions. I knew I'd have to, but I didn't realize the slots filled up that fast. I'll get right on it when we get home."

"This is amazing, Charlie. It would be so awesome if we both got in. It would be nice to have a friend there…in the big, bad city." She giggled and then, hearing Johnny coming, she quieted and put a finger to her lips. I nodded and winked so she'd know our secret was safe.

"What are you two talking about? You both look guilty as hell," Johnny came out and leaned against the deck railing.

"We were talking about you. About how crazy you are," said Emma. She smiled up at him and I watched him melt under her magical powers. I shook my head and got up. I debated getting another beer and decided to keep a clear head. Emma was already messing with my psyche enough as it was—I didn't need to get wasted, too.

"You guys ready to eat?" I called out from the kitchen.

Emma came in and grabbed plates and silverware while I set out the salad and dressing. I watched Johnny open a can of corn and pour it into a bowl and microwave it. Emma brought a bag of knot rolls and three Cokes to the table. We all sat down and dug in. I was surprised at how hungry I was. I watched as Emma cut her steak into tiny pieces and was impressed that none of it ended up on the floor. I'd half expected Johnny to cut it for her. I looked on in amazement as she proceeded to drown her steak with half a bottle of ketchup. I glanced at Johnny and he just grinned and rolled his eyes in her direction.

After dinner, Emma and I got our guitars and strummed chords, warming up. Johnny started a jungle rhythm with his drum and soon we were in music heaven. I listened to Emma sing an amazing acoustic rendition of Karmin's "Hello" and she blew me away. I never would have guessed she could rap, too. I had no doubt she'd be a shoe-in for Jenkins. I didn't feel as confident about my own chances of getting in but I knew if I continued to play with Emma, I could have as good a chance as anybody. Without even knowing it, she was pushing me to be a better guitar player…a better singer…and even a better songwriter. She had no idea how she was influencing me with her talent. I heard new songs writing themselves in my head, including "She's Mine." She'd inadvertently given me a new set of lyrics for the song. I only hoped I wouldn't forget the words running through my brain before I had a chance to write them down. We continued to play and drink—beers for me and Johnny and one wine cooler and a lot of lemonade, straight up and on the rocks for Emma. I couldn't remember when I'd had a better time…with music… with my best friend…and his girl…sexy, sweet, amazing Emma…with whom I was falling in love…deeper with every passing second.

Chapter Twelve

Emma

It was long past midnight and I couldn't get to sleep—couldn't shut my brain off. We'd sung and played music all evening long until my voice had gotten hoarse. And Johnny had drunk way too many beers again but at least he hadn't passed out like he had the night before. Now I was thinking about Charlie—again. It was becoming a habit and that fact scared me a little. Thinking about Charlie would only cause problems for everyone. And though I couldn't be sure, I was starting to get the feeling that Charlie was thinking about me, too. There was something about the way our voices blended when we sang…about the way we were so in tune with each other musically—literally and figuratively—and the look in his eyes the few times I'd caught him staring at me, that made me think my feelings weren't one-sided. I'd convinced myself that he was feeling something for me. I'd just about decided I'd turn on the bedside lamp and write in my diary—just pour my heart out onto the pages—when I heard a sound in the kitchen. One of the guys must have gotten up for a late-night snack or a drink. I got up, tiptoed to my bedroom door and pulled it open a fraction. I could hear Johnny's rhythmic snoring across the hall. I knew the smart thing to do would have been to go right back to bed, but I didn't do the smart thing. I did the crazy thing and walked silently down the hall toward the kitchen. Light from over the stove was casting a soft glow on the far side of the room. I stopped in the doorway a moment and observed Charlie, sitting at the end of the counter, his eyes downcast, shoulders drooping, his hands loosely grasping a glass of chocolate milk in front of him. I must have made a sound because he turned his head and looked at me over his left shoulder.

"Hey, Em," he said softly. My heart fluttered at the sound of my nickname rolling off his tongue with such familiarity.

"Hey…you couldn't sleep either, huh?" I said as I walked past him to the fridge. I poured myself a glass of chocolate milk, too, and joined him at the counter.

"Nope. I thought sleep would come easy to me here at the cabin. I'd figured I'd sleep for forty-eight hours straight and actually end up exhausted from too much sleep…but that didn't happen. What about you? What's keeping you awake tonight?" He sipped his milk and turned his gaze toward me. His hair was mussed from his attempt to sleep and his eyes looked tired. I noticed his facial hair—a goatee was forming around his beautiful mouth and I had an urge to trace it with my fingertips. I swallowed the temptation along with a mouthful of chocolate milk and answered him.

"I couldn't shut my brain off. I kept thinking about our jam session tonight—and last night's too—and how much I enjoyed it. We seem to blend well together. Did you think so?" I sensed we'd blend well in other ways, too, but I remained silent about that.

"Uh…yeah…we do sound pretty amazing together. You're actually the first girl I've known who is talented and not stuck up about it. Westbrook High is full of girls who are either good at something but shallow, or bad at everything and uninteresting." Charlie cast a sidelong glance at me then turned back to his drink.

"Thanks…that's a sweet thing to say," I replied, my cheeks reddening at the unexpected compliment.

"You're welcome." Charlie got up and put his glass in the dishwasher and moved over to the sliding doors to look out on the lake. I finished my drink and joined him there. I stared out at the mysterious moon hovering over the lake—not quite full anymore with dark clouds passing over it, preventing much light to shine over the water.

"You know what kind of moon that is?" Charlie asked me. "That nearly full moon missing a tiny piece in the upper right corner?"

"As a matter of fact I do," I said. "It's a waning gibbous."

He looked down at me and grinned. "Ah…talented and smart, too." He gently bumped my shoulder with his elbow.

I chuckled quietly. "I'm just full of surprises, aren't I?" I bumped him back, wanting so much to leave my arm pressed up against his.

"You certainly are." His voice sounded funny and it made me look up at him. I heard something in those three words—a weightiness that made my pulse race. I suddenly had a runaway train feeling…like something significant was about to happen…something dangerous…if I didn't stop it. He met my gaze and his eyes were dark—so dark they looked black instead of deep ocean blue. I'd never wanted to kiss someone or be kissed by someone so much as I did in that moment. My breath hitched in my throat as I forced myself to take a tiny step back— my eyes still locked on his.

"Well…I'm…uh…gonna get to bed," I stammered out the words as if I were trying out speech for the first time. "Night, Charlie."

He turned away and looked up at the waning gibbous moon and said, "See you in the morning."

I went back to bed and tucked myself in, once again alone with thoughts of Charlie. As much as I was having fun and sorry our weekend at Lake Crescent was coming to an end, another part of me was relieved. If I spent too much more time this close to Charlie I was seriously fearful I might do something stupid or say something ridiculous. My ability to use rational thought around him was starting to malfunction the way a computer's proximity to a magnet could wipe out all of its data. Once I got back home I'd be fine. I'd put some applications in at the mall and request an audition with the Jenkins School. Maybe I could even muster some enthusiasm at the prospect of becoming a big sister. I highly doubted it but I could give it a try. I turned over on my stomach and burrowed down under the blanket and counted sheep. I didn't remember getting past twenty-nine.

The next morning we cleaned the cabin and packed up the perishable food items we wanted to keep. I made my bed and Johnny's, too, while he packed the car. Charlie walked through the cabin, making sure all doors and windows were locked. He covered the grill with a tarp and swept off the back deck. He and Johnny gathered the trash, making sure not to leave any empty beer or wine bottles around for an adult to find. I climbed into Johnny's Escape and glanced over at Charlie getting into his Durango. As we waved good-bye and left for home, I fought back the negative impulses coursing through me…tried to ignore my yearning to be inside that Durango, next to Charlie, listening to Muse or Arcade Fire or Iron and Wine. I sighed as we drove away and when Johnny reached over and took my hand, I gave his a squeeze and remembered how much he loved me. No way would I ever hurt Johnny.

We pulled into my driveway and Johnny hopped out, pulling my bag from the back. He carried it up to the front porch where I took it from him.

"It was a fun weekend, wasn't it?" he asked, pulling me into his arms.

"Yes…I loved it. I love that lake. I hope we get to go back again."

"Oh, no worries, Em. We'll be back there for the Fourth of July for sure. We won't be alone though. Charlie's folks will be there and his brother. Sometimes my brother goes, too. And occasionally random weird-ass Channing cousins show up. I hope that doesn't happen this time." He leaned down and planted a kiss on my lips…a kiss that deepened into something I wouldn't want my dad to see if he happened by the front windows. I kissed him back and then stepped back, grinning up at him.

"I'm going to do my laundry and then take a nap. I'll see you later, OK?"

"You know it. Maybe we should see a movie tonight or something. Call me when you wake up." He leaned down to whisper in my ear. "And Em… don't forget to call tomorrow and make yourself an appointment to see the doctor. Remember what we talked about?" He spoke earnestly like he was telling me to get a lump checked. My stomach flip-flopped at the thought of making that appointment. But I nodded.

"OK…thanks for reminding me," I said, forcing a smile.

"Like I could forget." He kissed me again and bounded down the steps to his car. "Later, baby." He waved and drove off. I let myself into the house, trying not to think about birth control pills and the implication of them.

My stepmother was in the kitchen chopping vegetables. She was wearing a maternity shirt and I was somewhat astonished by the sight of it. It seemed a little premature. I said hi as I walked down the hall to the laundry room where I emptied out my overnight bag into the washing machine and started the load. Back in the kitchen, Nanette was assembling the vegetables into a baking dish.

"What are you making?" I asked.

"An Italian-style chicken and veggie casserole. Will you be home for dinner?" she asked, pouring some kind of sauce over the mixture, then dropping in pieces of pre-cooked, chopped chicken and giving the whole thing a stir.

"Yep," I said, glancing at the casserole. "That smells good."

"It's Martha Stewart," Nanette said, as if that was the only explanation needed—the end all, be all, of casseroles. "How was your weekend at the lake?"

"Very nice. It's gorgeous up there. I could live there forever." I realized I was gushing and figured I should tone it down before she mistook my enthusiasm for something it wasn't meant to represent. "Is Dad home?"

"He's out back, doing a phone interview for some story he's working on."

I yawned, grabbed a Coke from the fridge and headed down the hall. Over my shoulder I called back, "let me know if you need help with anything." I went to my room and dropped onto my bed with my phone. I'd gotten several texts from friends while we'd been gone, many of which I had responded to and several new ones that needed my attention. One of them was from Kerry. She'd texted me about getting together to hang out. I sent her a text telling her I'd love to. I figured I could skip a nap for some girl talk. I asked her about coming over and would she mind if I included Claire, too. I knew they were friendly with each other—I'd seen them talking at school though I didn't think they'd ever hung out together. They both responded that they'd be over soon. I tidied my room and went back out to put my load of laundry in the dryer. I could smell the casserole baking in the oven. It smelled divine. I couldn't remember my mother ever making casseroles. It wasn't that she couldn't cook—when she did it was always good—but she never got the pleasure out of it that Nanette did.

Thirty minutes later Kerry and Claire pulled up into the drive within seconds of each other. I met them at the door and we went back to my room. While they made themselves comfortable on my loveseat, I went to the kitchen for some snacks. I returned with cheese and crackers, Doritos and three Cokes. I shoved my door shut with my foot and dumped our goodies onto my desk.

"Help yourselves," I said, grabbing a handful of Doritos for myself.

We launched into typical girl talk: celebrity gossip, make-up, clothes and boys. They asked me how things were with Johnny and I asked them if they had their sights set on anyone in particular. I remembered Claire telling me she liked someone but I couldn't remember who.

"This reminds me of Charlie Channing," said Claire. "Remember you mentioned setting him up with me but I've got this thing starting with Jason Flanagan. But Kerry…," she glanced at Kerry with a sly grin. "What do you think about Charlie Channing?"

Kerry's answer registered on her pretty face in various shades of red. It made her blonde hair seem brighter and her blue eyes sparkly. "Ooh…Charlie Channing. I've had a crush on him since freshman year. Please don't tell anyone I told you that." She stared off into space, absent-mindedly chewing on a piece of cheese, a blissful expression on her face.

I felt my stomach nosedive at her confession. A new emotion gripped me—one I'd never considered an issue for me before—jealousy. I didn't want to fix Charlie up with anyone. Besides, Charlie had made his feelings known quite clearly on this subject—he wasn't interested in being fixed up. I decided a change in topic was warranted.

"I think I'm going to try to get a job at the mall. What do you guys do for money?" I asked the question brightly as if their answers might hold the secret to eliminating the national debt.

"Babysit," they both said at the same time and laughed. And then Claire went right back to Charlie talk.

"Seriously, though, Emma. You're Johnny's girlfriend and he's Charlie's best friend. Maybe you could fix them up. I mean they know each other so it wouldn't be like a blind date or anything. And Johnny and Charlie know Jason from sports. We could go on a triple date or something. Wouldn't that be cool?" She certainly seemed excited about her idea. She turned to Kerry. "What do you think, Kerry? Would you go out with Charlie if he asked?"

Kerry didn't hesitate. "Absolutely. I'd give anything for a date with him, but…he might not be interested."

"Are you kidding? A gorgeous blonde like you? He'll want to." Claire turned to me. "OK, Emma. You have an assignment. Get Johnny to ask Charlie to ask Kerry out. What do you say?" She sounded down-right giddy at the prospect.

I plastered a fake smile on my face and answered. "OK. I'll see what I can do." I felt bad at the sight of Kerry's excited face but I just didn't think Charlie would go for it. Kerry wasn't the right girl for Charlie—it was so obvious. And I certainly wouldn't say anything to Johnny. He'd love the idea. My stomach was hurting and the smell of the Doritos was making me queasy. I tried again to change the subject, mentioning senior year and college after graduation.

A couple of hours later, the girls had to go. I walked them out and said good-bye on the porch, promising we'd all go to the mall later this week. Back inside the kitchen, I found the casserole on the stove, covered in foil. Nanette and Dad had obviously eaten already. My stomach was still goofy so I decided I would eat later. I remembered my laundry and grabbed it from the dryer. As I was folding t-shirts and pajama pants, my cell phone rang. I pulled it from my pocket and looked at the screen—Johnny.

"Hey," I said, tucking the phone between my ear and shoulder as I gathered up my laundry and headed down the hall to my room.

"Emma," Johnny said, his voice cracking the slightest bit. I heard something bad in the tone—something was wrong.

"What is it? Is everything OK?" I asked, feeling my pulse quicken.

"No. It's my grandpa. He died today. He wasn't even that fucking old, Em." His voice cracked again and I thought I heard him break off a sob.

"Oh, my god, Johnny. I'm so sorry. What happened?" I'd met Johnny's grandparents twice—once at Easter and again when they'd come for his brother Scott's graduation a few weeks ago. They were a sweet and very youthful couple. I couldn't imagine something happening to his grandfather.

"He had a stroke while he was out working in his garden. My grandma found him but the doctors think he'd probably laid there in the garden for a couple of hours before she got to him. She'd been at a friend's playing cards. She found his cell phone in his hand but he wasn't able to call for help, I guess. I cannot fucking believe this."

"I'm coming over. I'll be there in ten minutes, OK?" My heart was breaking for him. I knew how much he loved his grandfather.

"OK, thanks, babe." He hung up. I held the phone in my hand, thinking about him and how much this must hurt. I didn't have grandparents—well, not exactly. My dad's parents had died in a car accident when he was young and my mother's parents were alive but I'd never met them. They lived in Florida and had never come to visit nor had my mother ever taken me to visit them. I wasn't even sure I could remember their names. I'd tried a few times some years ago to talk to my mother about them but she'd always stopped the conversation immediately and asked me to please never mention them again. So I'd asked my dad and he didn't have anything to share about them either—or so he'd said. So I just accepted that they'd always be a mystery and left it at that.

I changed into a pair of jeans and a pink blouse and pulled my hair into a low pony tail. I stopped in the living room where Nanette and my dad were cuddled together on the couch watching TV. It occurred to me that I had never seen him cuddle my mother like that.

"I'm going to Johnny's. He just called. His grandfather died today."

"Oh, that's so sad," said Nanette. "Please give his family our condolences."

"Yes," said my dad. "If there's anything they need, tell Johnny to let us know."

"OK, I will." I waved and walked out to my car, wondering what my dad would do if Johnny or his family actually needed something. He wouldn't know how to respond. My dad wasn't the get involved type. He preferred to stand back quietly and observe. If it didn't involve world wars or military action, Dad wouldn't have a clue.

I drove to Johnny's and pulled into the driveway, parking right behind Charlie's Durango. The brake lights were still on and I saw his head above the headrest. I waited for him to exit his car so we could walk in together.

"Hi," I said as I followed him up to the porch. "Johnny called you, too?"

"Yeah. It's so sad. Grandpa Beaumont was one cool guy," said Charlie. He knocked on the door. A minute or so passed before someone answered. Johnny's mother, Andrea Beaumont, opened the door.

"Charlie...Emma...thanks for coming. Charlie, you look great. It's so good to have you back home. Johnny's in the family room. You two go on in. He's taking this so hard."

"We're sorry for your loss," said Charlie. He gave her a hug as I tried not to dwell on the plural pronoun he'd used and its significance. It was probably a slip of the tongue. I hugged her, too, reiterating Charlie's words, and then Charlie and I went to find Johnny.

Chapter Thirteen

Johnny

It felt good to have Emma and Charlie here. I held her in my arms and regarded Charlie over the top of her head. He was sitting in the brown leather recliner across from us. I noticed he looked pale like a frickin' vampire and I considered telling him so, but changed my mind.

"How's your grandmother holding up?" Emma asked against my chest. She was rubbing her hand up and down my arm and I liked the feel of her hand there.

"She's trying to keep it together. She's blaming herself. I don't know if she'll ever get over this. My dad and brother are already on the way there. My grandparents live in Kalispell, Montana. Mom and I are flying out tomorrow." I squeezed Emma closer...kissed the top of her head. "Charlie...do you think you could take us to the airport in the morning...to Seatac? It's OK if you can't. We could just leave the car in the long-term lot."

He didn't hesitate. "Of course. What time's the flight?" I watched him stretch his leg out, flexing it a couple of times and I immediately felt bad for asking. He didn't need another lengthy car drive after the long drive home from Lake Crescent.

"You know what...don't worry about it. We can leave our car there." I was looking at his leg when I said this, hoping he wouldn't think I was pitying him.

"Don't be ridiculous. What time's the flight?" Charlie repeated, giving me a look.

"Our flight's at eleven o'clock, but my mom will want to leave way earlier than necessary because of her paranoia about missing flights." Emma shifted in my arms and sat up straighter.

"Want me to come, too?" she asked. For a minute I thought she meant all the way to Kalispell and I got excited at the thought. But then I realized she meant to the airport. I nodded.

"Of course," I said. "We can take my Escape."

"No...we'll take my car...it's roomier," said Charlie.

My mom came in then and asked if we needed anything—food or drink or some other unnamed thing she wanted to offer to keep herself occupied. My mom didn't handle crises well so I was impressed that she hadn't fallen apart yet. I decided to give her something to do. "Sure…is there any more lemonade?"

"Three glasses, coming right up," said my mom, looking relieved.

"Oh, no thanks, Mrs. B., I'm…," Charlie started, but Mom had already turned tail and run off to the kitchen.

"She needs something to do to keep her mind occupied or she'll start crying. Just humor her," I said, shaking my head in resignation at Charlie. He grinned and nodded in understanding.

Emma pushed back from me and stood up. "I'll help her carry," she said and disappeared into the kitchen.

I noticed that Charlie looked pensive. I couldn't tell if he was experiencing physical discomfort or something deeper…something other than physical. "Everything OK, Chuck?" I asked.

"What? Oh, yeah. I was just thinking about the time your grandpa smoked weed with us up at the lake. Remember that summer your whole family came up to Lake Crescent with us?"

"Oh, yeah. That was fun. That was our first time smoking pot and he caught us—up on Lover's Leap. We thought we were totally busted and grounded for life but what does Grandpa do? Pulls out his own stash and smokes right along with us. Awesome dude, my gramps."

Charlie laughed and leaned forward in the recliner. "And then later we went back to the cabin and ate the kitchen."

"Good times," I said, shaking my head at the memory of my Grandpa Beaumont, higher than a kite and pissing in the trees…trying to make designs with his pee on tree trunks. I wondered if Charlie remembered that, too. I could hear Emma and my mom talking quietly in the kitchen. I could also hear the clinking of silverware and plates. Mom was really making herself useful, whether we liked it or not. They returned to the living room bearing plates of cake and glasses of lemonade.

"You guys have this cake or it'll go to waste while we're in Montana. Eat up," she said, passing plates of butter pecan cake to me and Charlie. Emma gave us lemonade and sat down next to me on the couch. Mom said she was going to pack for the trip and left us alone. We ate in silence for a few minutes.

"I don't know how long we'll be in Montana…probably through the end of the week or maybe a little less. But while I'm gone I want you two to do me a favor." I turned to Charlie. "Chuck…you take care of Emma and don't let anybody steal her away from me while I'm gone." I grabbed Emma's hand and gave it squeeze. "And you, babe… don't let Charlie sit in his room brooding, writing music all day. Dude needs some sunlight before somebody mistakes him for Edward fucking Cullen and stabs a stake through his heart."

Emma threw back her head and laughed…so hard her cake toppled from the plate and landed in her lap. "Oops," she said, her face reddening. She began to pick up the cake pieces and put them back on her plate.

"Why does this not surprise me?" I said, handing her my napkin then moving her lemonade further back on the coffee table out of her danger zone.

We finished our cake and talked some more about my grandpa. Just having Charlie and Emma here made me feel better. And knowing my Grandpa Beaumont like I did, I knew he wouldn't want me sitting around going all maudlin all over the place. I was half-tempted to smoke a joint in my room tonight in his honor but my mom would get wind of it—literally—and flip out. Finally Charlie said he had to go. We all stood up and walked to the front door.

"How about I get here around seven o'clock tomorrow morning?" he asked. To Emma he said, "I can pick you up on the way since you're just around the corner."

"OK. I'll be ready," she responded.

We walked out to their cars and Charlie reached to shake my hand but I pulled him into a bear hug. "You'll keep an eye on Em, right, Chuck?" I whispered near his ear. He patted my back three times and nodded. A three-thump back pat—code for 'OK, enough with the hugging.' I had to suppress a grin at that. He waved and went to his car. I walked Emma to hers.

"I love you, Em…you know that, right?" I whispered the words in her ear as I pulled her close to me, pressing her body into mine. I smelled strawberries in her hair and when I kissed her, I tasted butter pecan cake and frosting. She was a regular walking bakery and I'd never get my fill of her. She looked up at me…her eyes watery.

"I know…I…love you, too," she said. "I'm so sorry about your grandpa." I squeezed her tighter and felt my stomach react to her words. Finally she'd said it back. It felt like a victory. I completely ignored the tiny hint of reluctance I thought I'd heard in her voice at the unexpected declaration. I noticed Charlie watching us from his rearview mirror, waiting for Emma to move her car. I opened her car door and she climbed in, started the car and rolled the window down. I leaned in and kissed her again. "You'll make sure to keep Charlie busy, right? Otherwise, he will literally sit in his room, playing guitar, writing music and getting depressed."

"I will," she said. "Don't worry." I kissed her once more and stepped back, watching her and Charlie drive away. Later, as I was packing my suitcase, I thought about how lucky I was to have Emma for a girlfriend and Charlie for a best friend—and thankful they had each other. I thought of Grandpa Beaumont then and smiled. Wherever he was at this moment…he'd be alright.

Chapter Fourteen

Charlie

I had no right to be excited at the thought of being alone with Emma in my car on the way home from Seatac Airport. But that was exactly how I felt as we said good-bye to Johnny and his mother outside of the departures terminal the next morning. I'd picked Emma up a little before seven. She'd been sitting on her front porch with a mug of coffee and I was secretly relieved when she stood up from the chair, drained the last of her coffee and shoved the cup under the seat. I'd had no doubt that the coffee would've been all over her and my seat before we ever got out of Westbrook's city limits—even with a lid. And now I looked away as Johnny kissed Emma good-bye while Mrs. Beaumont handled their curb-side check-in. We waved as they hoisted their carry-on bags over their shoulders and entered the terminal. I was standing beside the front passenger door and I opened it for Emma to climb in. For a moment I thought I'd have to give her a boost. My Durango was a little higher off the ground than Johnny's Escape.

"I feel so sad for them," said Emma, her voice soft and low, as I pulled the car out into the flow of traffic and headed for the exit. "I remember thinking when I saw Johnny's grandfather at Scott's graduation party that he seemed like the youngest grandfather I'd ever met—not in terms of his actual age but his youthful countenance and zest for life."

I chuckled at her choice of words. "Youthful countenance and zest for life, huh? That's very poetic. I think the word countenance is bigger than you."

"Ha ha… very funny. I get so much grief for being…tiny." She said the word like it tasted bad on her tongue.

"Well, I'm 6'2" and I've heard more than my fair share of Jolly Green Giant jokes," I said in commiseration. I pushed the radio buttons on the dash until I found a station that wasn't playing bad music. I finally found a station playing a Coldplay song and figured Emma would like it.

Emma began to hum to the music as we drove along, leaving the congestion of the city behind. I felt my stomach grumble and wondered if Emma was hungry, too. "You wanna stop for breakfast when we get around Olympia?" I asked.

She shifted in her seat, tucking her left leg under her body and faced me. "Yes. I'm starving. I'm craving waffles and bacon...and maybe eggs, too."

"Sounds good. I seem to remember a diner just after we get onto 101. We can stop there." I kept my eyes on the road, both hands on the wheel. I played the alphabet game in my head with the passing road signs in an attempt to ignore my awareness of Emma's proximity. I made it to 'F' before she broke the silence.

"I had a good time this weekend. Lake Crescent had quite an effect on me," she said somewhat quietly. Or maybe it was wistfulness that I heard in her tone.

I looked over at her. "Oh? How so?"

She glanced out her window as she answered. "I used to write poetry and short stories and songs just for fun, but I haven't felt compelled to write anything since I moved to Westbrook—well, except for writing in my journal. I try to be faithful with that. But I actually wrote a song this weekend. I have the lyrics and most of the tune worked out. It just suddenly came to me when I was sitting by the lake. And I was thinking if it's any good when I get it finished that I might sing it in my audition for Jenkins...well, if I'm lucky enough to get an audition, that is."

"I bet it's great. If you need any help with it or just need to try it out on someone, I'd love to hear it. As a matter of fact, I've recently written a new song, too, so maybe you could return the favor."

"I'd love to hear your song. You know...I heard that the decision-makers at Jenkins tend to favor people who perform original music." Her voice sounded peppier now, the melancholic tone fading. A new song came on the radio just then and she began a rhythmic bounce in her seat in time to the opening measure. It was some song from a British boy band whose name I couldn't remember at the moment. I listened to her sing along, watching the bouncing out of the corner of my eye. She was certainly into the tune. And I was thankful for the invention of seatbelts, holding certain body parts in place.

I saw the sign for the diner I'd eaten at with my mom once and took the exit. It was another half-mile to the diner, which was nestled in the trees—Dunston's Diner. I pulled in and parked in the half-full lot. I didn't turn the car off until the song finished. I didn't want to end Emma's bouncing concert prematurely. I watched her dance in her seat, an amused grin on my face. It occurred to me that even when she wasn't moving—when she was just sitting quietly—her body still seemed to hum with excitement...with an energy that I was coming to realize was just uniquely Emma.

We entered the diner and the hostess seated us in a corner booth with menus and asked for our drink orders. We both ordered orange juice. I pretended to study the menu but in actuality I studied Emma. I watched as she carefully removed the paper from her straw, being careful not to tear it, and folded it into some strange shape. When she was satisfied with her creation, she dropped the paper onto the table and cupped her orange juice glass in her hands. I wondered how safe it was from disaster. I had to resist the urge to lay a blanket of napkins across the surface of the table just in case.

"Did I tell you my stepmother is pregnant?" she said, not sounding pleased with the information.

I raised my eyebrows and leaned back in my seat. "No, you didn't. Wow. You don't sound thrilled."

She grimaced. "I'm not. It's humiliating. I'm almost eighteen—too old to have a little sister or brother. I find the whole concept kind of gross."

I really didn't know how to reply to that so I didn't. The waitress returned and took our orders—waffles, eggs and bacon for Emma and sausage, eggs, toast and hash browns for me. I could feel my appetite kicking in and I wanted to indulge it. I heard my cell phone buzz in my pocket. "Excuse me a sec," I said, pulling it out. It was the music store where I taught guitar lessons calling. I took the call and, after a short conversation, I hung up.

"Everything OK?" Emma asked. She was now making some sort of creature out of a napkin. I suddenly wondered if she had ADHD. She definitely seemed to be in constant motion, even when she wasn't moving at all.

"Yeah. It was the music store where I work. Apparently a bunch of new people want to take guitar lessons and my boss was wondering how many new students I wanted to take on. It sounds like he has more people wanting to learn than teachers to teach them."

Emma cleared her throat. She was about to say something but was stopped by the arrival of our breakfast. When the waitress left, Emma said, "Um…I was thinking about getting a job at the mall, but maybe you could use my help at the store. I've taught guitar before…back in Portland…I mean…if you needed me. I'd rather do that than sell purses or underwear at the mall." She emitted a nervous giggle and shoved a large bite of waffle into her mouth.

I swallowed a bite of hash browns before I answered. Emma working at the store…with me. Wow. Not that I'd actually see her during a lesson…but…just knowing she was there…wow. I liked the idea of it. Too much. I wiped my face with a napkin and answered.

"Yeah…that sounds great. When I get into the store later today

I'll mention you to the manager. His name's Luke Jameson. He's a nice guy. If he's interested he'll probably want to 'audition' you." I used my fingers to make quote marks around 'audition.'

"Sure. I have no problem with that. Let me know." She dug into her scrambled eggs which were drowning in ketchup, just like the steak I'd watched her eat at the lake house.

While we ate away at the edges of our appetites, I pretended not to watch her eat. Every time she put the bacon in her mouth I felt a stirring sensation in places that shouldn't be stirring in a diner off Highway 101. When she licked maple syrup off her bottom lip I almost choked on a piece of sausage. I grabbed my orange juice and drained it, then signaled for the waitress to bring me a refill. I was well aware that I needed to keep my shit together. My brain—both of them—was venturing off into dangerous waters and I knew I had to redirect it elsewhere.

We finished breakfast and I signaled for the check. Emma opened her purse and pulled out her wallet. "It's my treat," she said, giving me a smile.

"No way. Put your wallet away." I took a twenty from my pocket and put it on the table. Emma plopped a few ones on the table beside my twenty.

"I'll get the tip then," she said. "And I've gotta go to the ladies' room. Back in a sec." She slid out of the booth and headed to the back of the restaurant in the direction of a restroom sign hanging crookedly from the ceiling by a back hallway. I watched her walk away, bumping into two chairs on the way. My eyes drifted to her hips. She had a heart-shaped ass covered in skin-tight dark jeans. I closed my eyes and turned my head away toward the tiny packs of jelly on the table, stacked neatly in their condiment caddy with salt, pepper, artificial sweetener and hot sauce, wondering what I was going to do about Emma. No…not Emma. Me. What was I going to do about me? I felt something negative flowing through my veins. That feeling you get when your subconscious wants something unattainable before you allow yourself to acknowledge it consciously…the want…the need…the desire for something off-limits. I already knew I was falling for Emma. But after sharing breakfast with her…alone…I was beginning to understand that I would never be able to ignore that feeling. I had the sense that, as sure as I was sitting here, that there would never be a time when I did not want her.

Emma came out of the bathroom and we left the diner. Just as we stepped out into the parking lot, a tiny white kitten appeared out of nowhere and darted across the parking lot into the path of a car backing out of a parking space. Emma and I both saw it at the same time. She screamed and ran after it, waving her hand wildly to get the driver's attention. The kitten meowed softly and froze in place, as the car's tire came dangerously close to it. Emma ran to the car and smacked the back end of it with her open palm. The driver came to an abrupt stop and immediately put the window down.

"What the hell are you doing?" shouted the female driver. She looked like Honey Boo Boo's mother crossed with Rosie O'Donnell.

Emma scooped the kitten up into her arms. "You almost hit this kitten," she said, stepping away from the car. I walked closer to Emma in case Honey Boo Boo Senior O'Donnell decided to get nasty.

"Well, too bad I didn't. I'da done the world a favor if I'da run it over." She rolled her window up and backed the rest of the way out and drove off.

I looked at Emma. She looked like she wanted to do more than smack the woman's car. She held the meowing kitten up to her face as it squirmed in her hands.

"That woman was a bitch. I hope she gets four flat tires," she said, nuzzling the kitten. "I'm going inside and see if anyone knows who owns this kitten."

"I doubt anybody in there will know," I said. But she was determined so we walked back inside the diner. She spoke to the hostess who told her that a cat that hung around the diner had recently given birth to a litter and this was probably one of the babies. She told Emma to take it out and put it down and it would eventually find its way back to its mother.

"If it doesn't get run over first," said Emma, sounding agitated. She turned away from the hostess and we went back outside. "I have to keep him…or her…I can't just let someone run it over." She nuzzled it again and it meowed…that high-pitched yet soft mewling sound that kittens are famous for. The kind no one could resist. "Can I bring him in your car?"

"Of course." It wasn't like I could deny Emma anything. Johnny must feel like this all the time, I thought.

We got into the Durango and Emma fastened her seatbelt and held the kitten in her lap. I was just about to pull out of the spot when she asked me, "Do you know how to tell if it's a boy or a girl? Can you check?" She held out the kitten to me and I looked down at it like it was an alien life form. I'd always been more of a dog person…not that I had anything against cats per se. I took the kitten and turned it over in my hand. I moved aside the little critter's fur and took a look. When I found what was I looking for—or didn't find it as was the case—I grinned and handed the kitten back to Emma.

"Congratulations, Miss Davis. It's a girl."

Emma let out a squeal of delight and hugged the kitten to her chest. As I watched her pet the kitten and talk sweetly to it, I really wished I could be that kitten right now. I sat still watching her with the kitten for a moment before I shook away the illicit thoughts taking hold in my head and pulled out of the diner parking lot.

"I hope my dad and Nanette don't freak out about this," said Emma. The kitten continued to squirm in her hands and meow in a steady stream of noise that would probably last all the way to Westbrook.

"What are you gonna name her?" I asked. I couldn't wait to hear what name Emma would come up with.

"Hmm…I'm thinking…" Emma studied the kitten, her eyebrows furrowed. "Any ideas?"

I reached over and stroked the top of the kitten's head. "You know what she looks like to me?" I said, casting a sideways glance at Emma.

"What?"

"She looks like a little freshly popped kernel of popcorn." I smiled at Emma and resisted the urge to stroke her hair, too, like I'd just stroked the kitten's soft fur.

"Popcorn…popcorn." Emma tried out the word. She brought the kitten up to her face again and stared into its blue eyes. "Hey little kernel of popcorn. Should we call you Popcorn?" She began to bounce in her seat again, causing the kitten to meow louder. "Ooh, Charlie. It's perfect. She is officially Popcorn. I love it."

I laughed and turned my attention back to my driving. "Let's hope your stepmother isn't allergic to Popcorn."

She giggled and turned up the radio. An Adele song came on and Emma sang along. Popcorn sang, too, for a while, before finally settling down into Emma's lap and falling asleep. When the song finished…and before the next song began…I heard a faint purring sound. I wondered who it was coming from…Emma…Popcorn…or me.

Chapter Fifteen

Emma

Yes! Charlie'd gotten me an interview with his boss about teaching guitar lessons. When he'd dropped me off at home, we'd exchanged phone numbers, with him promising to call or text if he had any luck. He'd texted me the next day to tell me that his boss wanted to see me. And now I would meet with Luke Jameson tomorrow morning. I was to bring my guitar and a lesson plan. I was psyched. Charlie'd told me I'd make a lot more money teaching guitar lessons than working at a mall store anyway so I was excited. I needed to save money for a possible trip to New York this winter if I was granted an audition at Jenkins.

I'd just hung up from scheduling my interview with Luke when Johnny called. He and his mother had spent the last couple of nights reminiscing with relatives about Grandpa Beaumont and he said everyone was doing fine and in good spirits in spite of the circumstances. He'd been texting me regularly to check in and he told me that his father and brother had discovered that Grandpa Beaumont had been growing marijuana in his garden and Grandma Beaumont was under the mistaken impression that it was some kind of wild herb. Johnny's dad had found a bunch of it trimmed and washed inside of a plastic bag in the refrigerator. When he'd asked Grandma Beaumont what it was doing in the fridge, she'd said, innocently, that it was for lasagna.

"Dad told her it wasn't an edible herb and convinced her to throw it away. Of course, when no one was looking I retrieved it. I couldn't stand by and let Grandma's new wave basil go to waste."

"Oh, my god, Johnny, you're crazy," I laughed. "You guys should get that stuff out of the garden before the wrong people find it and your poor grandmother gets arrested."

"Oh, don't worry. My brother already took care of it. Technically it's legal now but I think you have to have a license to grow or something to be legit, but not to worry, Grandma's in the clear."

"I'll bet," I laughed. I had told him about finding Popcorn outside of the diner on the way home from the airport. Popcorn was currently biting at my ankles and pawing at my feet—Johnny could hear her soft meows. He told me about the funeral plans and I made a note of the funeral home so I could send flowers from my family. We talked a few more minutes and finally hung up, but not before he reminded me once again about making a doctor's appointment. I'd had to fight to keep the irritation out of my voice at his bringing it up again. I dropped my phone on my bed in exasperation. I didn't know the first thing about getting birth control. Should I go to Planned Parenthood? Or find a gynecologist? I supposed I could ask Nanette who she used but the thought of using her doctor made me nauseous. I decided I would ask Claire. I called her and got her voicemail so I left a message to call me when she had time.

I went downstairs to the kitchen for a snack and found Nanette at the table making a list of baby names. I saw that her boy's list was considerably longer than the girl's list.

"What do you think of Trapper for a boy?" she asked. "Or Fisher?"

"Don't forget Hunter," I said, making a joke. "May as well cover all the outdoor activity bases." When she didn't laugh, I turned back to her to make sure I hadn't hurt her feelings. But she was staring at the list, biting on the end of a pen. I saw her cross some names off the list and write something new down on the paper.

"What about Kevin or Steve or Vance?" she asked.

"Now you have a 'V' thing going," I said, hating all three of those names. I thought a minute. "How about Thomas or Samuel? Those are good, strong, manly names."

"Those are good. Of course, we could just name him Anthony after your dad," she said, writing more names on the list.

"My brother's name is Eric Anthony Davis. He already has that name," I said, a hard edge to my voice that I hadn't intended to inflict. "Maybe it'll be a girl anyway."

"I have three girl's names picked out. Tell me which one you like best: Lily, Daisy or Tulip?"

I stared at Nanette, dumbfounded. She was bound and determined to attach a name to this baby that pertained to nature one way or another. I fought to control my irritation as I answered, "Daisy seems to be the cutest of the three. Of course, there's also Rose and Dahlia and Hyacinth."

Nanette looked up then. "Emma…are you teasing me?"

I gave her smile that didn't reach my eyes. "Yeah…sorry. I do like Daisy. That's cute." My cell phone rang then, saving me from more baby name talk. I glanced at the dial, saw Claire's name and waved at Nanette as I went back upstairs to my room.

"Hey, Claire. Thanks for calling me back."

"Sure. What's up?"

I hesitated before launching into the dreaded topic. I knew I was about to open a can of worms but I asked anyway. "I was wondering about something kinda personal."

Claire laughed in my ear. "Are you gonna ask me if I'm a virgin? Cuz the answer is no."

I grimaced. "No...not that. But I was wondering about birth control. Are you on it? And who's your doctor?"

She breathed out a long sigh. I felt my stomach lurch. "Birth control, huh? You've never been on it?"

"No. I've never really needed it before." I felt my face redden in spite of the fact that Claire wasn't there to see my embarrassment.

"Ah...but you do now?" she asked. "You mean you and Johnny have never..." She stopped and I felt my gut twist again.

"No...and that's not even why I'm asking. My periods have been a little irregular lately and I heard the pill can help with that."

"Riiight," said Claire, obviously not buying it. "OK, then...whatever you say. I use Dr. Karen Abernathy at the Westbrook Medical Center downtown. She'd great. I have the number. Gotta pen and paper?"

"Hang on." I grabbed a pen and notebook from my nightstand drawer and wrote down the number. "Thanks."

"You're welcome. Let's me and you and Kerry go to the mall this week. I need new sandals."

"OK. Let me know when. I need some shorts anyway." We talked a minute more and hung up. I stared at the paper in my hand with the doctor's name and number and felt ill. I hated going to the doctor. I decided to call right this minute before I chickened out. My fingers shook as I dialed the number. Five minutes later I had an appointment for tomorrow afternoon. It was just my luck that the doctor had had a cancellation moments before I called for an appointment. I wrote down my appointment time and shoved the paper into my purse so Nanette wouldn't find it. I didn't think she came into my room when I wasn't home, but I didn't want to take any chances. It occurred to me that I hadn't talked to my mother in a while so I dialed her number. She didn't pick up so I left a message. I put my phone down and turned my attention to Popcorn. I would need to find a vet now, too. I thought about the interview tomorrow and hoped I would get the job. It seemed like I was going to need money for a lot of things now.

I saw Charlie's Durango in the parking lot of Westbrook Music Center but I didn't see him inside the store. I figured he must be in a back room giving a lesson. A youngish man with a name tag that read Luke Jameson, Manager, approached me. I introduced myself and he led me to an office where we talked and I played my guitar and gave him a demo of my teaching method. He pretended to be the student and I pretended to teach him a few chords and guitar etiquette. Within thirty minutes he'd offered me a job, a schedule and some paperwork to take home to fill out. I was thrilled. I would get to choose my available times on the schedule and all classes would be conducted at the store in one of the music rooms at the back. He took me on a tour of the store and showed me where I could find sheet music for the classes. I was so excited that I had to rein myself in to keep from bouncing right out the door. This was going to be so much better than working at Westbrook Mall.

I lingered out in the parking lot hoping Charlie would come out, but when fifteen minutes had passed and he still hadn't shown, I drove to Arby's for lunch. It was almost time for the stupid doctor appointment and I just wanted to get it over with. I could see the Westbrook Medical Center just across the street. The sight of it was almost enough to put me off my roast beef with cheddar and curly fries. I finally decided to suck it up and get over there so I could get this bit of unpleasantness out of the way.

An hour later I left the clinic with a prescription for birth control pills and a bruise on my dignity. That was one of the most humiliating experiences of my life. I drove to the pharmacy and dropped off the prescription and while I waited for it to be filled, I picked up some kitty treats and toys for Popcorn. I bought some new lip gloss and a packet of hair ties and collected my pills and headed home.

Nanette was gone when I got home. I could hear Popcorn meowing plaintively in my room and I hurried up the stairs to comfort her. Nanette had surprised me regarding Popcorn. She'd told me she loved cats but was concerned about breathing in kitty litter due to her pregnancy and about Popcorn clawing at the furniture so I had to keep her in my room. I wasn't crazy about having the litter box in there, but I could deal with it for a while. I sat at my desk scrolling through the yellow pages on my phone looking for a vet clinic when my phone beeped with an incoming text. It was from Charlie: congrats on the job. luke told me. my last lesson of the day ends at 6. wanna celebrate with dinner?

My heart skipped and began to pound a new rhythm in my chest. Dinner with Charlie. My fingers fumbled over the keys as I typed my response: sounds great. should I meet you somewhere? what are you hungry for?

Less than a minute later he answered: you like mexican?

I giggled as I answered: *si...es mi comida favorita.* I wondered if Charlie had taken Spanish in school. In a few seconds I had my answer:

Yo, tambien. te recogeré a las 6:30.

Holy crap! Charlie knew Spanish! I didn't know why this thrilled me so much but in any case he was picking me up at 6:30. I texted back a quick, see you then and went to take a shower. I was still feeling violated from the doctor's visit. I needed to wash that nightmare away. And I wanted to make myself beautiful…for Charlie.

Chapter Sixteen

Johnny

We were in the church for Grandpa Beaumont's funeral. Grandma hadn't wanted to wait. Apparently Grandpa had told her that if he happened to die before her he wanted to be buried within forty-eight to seventy-two hours of his demise so his good parts could fertilize the earth before they lost their potency. We'd chuckled at the absurdity of this request, but followed her wishes on Grandpa's behalf. My dad's sister, Kathy, and her three kids didn't live far, just on the other side of Kalispell, so it was fairly easy to get the family together quickly for the funeral. I was amazed at how many people came on such short notice. Grandpa apparently had a lot of friends. I sat at the end of the front row while my dad spoke to the priest who would be performing the service. I wasn't feeling great—mentally. My mind kept playing tricks on me… trying to make me think there was someone else in the casket even though my grandfather was right there in front of me. I'd close my eyes and see Charlie dead. Or Emma. It made my stomach churn, causing a sweet taste to develop at the back of my tongue. And then I thought I saw Sarah in the casket. I hadn't thought about Sarah much since Emma had come into my life but I couldn't stop thinking about her now. I had not been allowed to attend her funeral and now as I sat in the pew of the church about to hear the eulogy for my grandpa, I wondered what words had been spoken for her. Who had eulogized her? Had her friends gotten up, one by one, and said nice things about her? Had her father come up from South Carolina to see her dead body? Sarah had hated her father and had told me that he had walked out on her mother before Sarah had taken her first breath. And he'd missed her last breath, too. I wondered if he cared about missing such milestones in his daughter's life. Is a last breath considered a milestone? It must be—the final one in a human life—the only milestone we didn't get to see the reward of or the fallout from.

In the weeks after the accident with Sarah dead and Charlie gone, people had left me alone for the most part. When someone had spoken to me about her, they'd been mostly considerate and non-judgmental. I was fairly certain people had seen us argue and fight in public…a lot. Everyone knew our relationship was of the volatile variety. I had been a shitty boyfriend to Sarah and I knew it. Other people probably knew it, too. I'd used her. I had taken advantage of her love for me and used it for selfish reasons—mostly of the sexual kind. I would always wonder if I could have saved her if I hadn't been such an asshole. If I'd been a good boyfriend she wouldn't have been in the car that night. If I'd been careful with birth control and made sure she was careful, too, she wouldn't have been freaked over being pregnant because she wouldn't have been pregnant...with my kid. And Charlie...Charlie Fucking Collateral Damage Channing...wouldn't have had to pay the price for my bad behavior. My stomach began to tense up at the thought that I had broken Charlie's leg and his arm and scrambled his insides like a dozen fucking eggs. I felt a tightness in my throat...it was hard to swallow and not all that easy to breathe either. It had been almost ten months since that goddamned accident and only now, in St. Michael's Catholic Church in Kalispell, Montana, was I feeling something real. Why now? I looked up at the casket and stared at my grandpa's face, eyes closed, hands folded across his chest...asleep forever. That had been Sarah ten months ago. I hadn't seen her in her casket but I could just imagine how pretty she must have looked. Sleep had always made her features look softer. But now I needed to get out of this church and away from death even though I knew I couldn't do that to my dad. It was his father in that fucking casket and for him I would sit here in this wooden pew and suffer in silence. I deserved to feel this way. I suddenly remembered something my grandpa had said when he'd caught me and Charlie smoking pot up at Lake Crescent. The profundity of his words had been lost on me then—I'd been well on the way to getting high as a kite at the time—but I remembered those words now...clear as a bell. The pot had made him quite philosophical. He'd said, "Johnny... Charlie...you boys are young pups...you've got your whole lives ahead of you. It's OK to smoke a little weed once in a while and drink a little beer or whiskey on occasion...but let me tell you boys what's not OK. There are two things in life that can eat away at a man's soul faster than cancer: Guilt and regret. Don't let 'em get ya. If you treat people right and aren't afraid to take chances with no guarantee of the outcome, then you'll have a lifetime of immunity from guilt and regret."

As I approached my grandfather's casket along with my brother and father and several of Grandpa's friends as pallbearers, I acknowledged to myself that my emotional immune system was down. Guilt and regret had found their way in and I was feeling the effects of it now. As we slid the casket into the hearse, I stepped back and thought of Emma. I wished she was here with me right now. She was the antidote I needed to rebuild my immune system. I missed her...Emma...my cure.

Chapter Seventeen

Charlie

This morning my mother had asked me again about seeing a therapist. Every once in a while the subject would come up and I always deflected off topic by steering the subject to anything other than me. Right after the accident I'd spent months dealing with the pain of my body as it tried to fix itself with the help of surgeries, medications, physical therapy and sheer force of will. Friends from school would call or drop by on occasion or send cards, notes and emails which usually buoyed my spirits. But the times I'd actually felt depressed mostly coincided with visits from Johnny, so even though his eventual absence had hurt my feelings, I'd also felt less depressed. It had angered me, but that was different. It was a double-edged sword. And now that I was home, I had the sense that I was on some sort of emotional roller coaster—up and feeling almost like myself again one minute, then down at rock bottom the next, wallowing in self-pity but without a valid reason for my self-inflicted pity party. It had been ten months since the accident and I couldn't let that be my excuse anymore. And since meeting Emma, I was losing interest in my occasional pity party. As clichéd as it sounded, just being around her made me feel like a better version of Charlie Channing and I couldn't wait to have dinner with her.

I'd finished my last lesson and hurried home to take a quick shower and change clothes. I splashed on some Armani aftershave and even put on a black, button-down dress shirt instead of a t-shirt. And the whole time I was getting ready I heard a voice in the back of my mind asking me what the hell I thought I was doing. I dismissed the voice and headed out to my car. I was on the upward trajectory of my metaphorical roller coaster ride and I wanted to stay there for the next couple of hours. The descent would come soon enough.

I arrived on time at Emma's house and she met me at the door. She looked other-worldly in a purple sun-dress and a white sweater. I noticed she was wearing sandals with heels and she still barely hit my shoulders. And she smelled crazy awesome…like berries and orchids and grapefruit all rolled into one. I breathed her in slowly then held my breath to contain the scent for as long as possible.

"Hola," she said. "You take Spanish, huh?" Her eyes sparkled and her lips were shiny with gloss. Her hair was a curtain of darkness under a bright moon. She was like a magazine advertisement—whatever she was selling I was buying.

"I do, but I must confess, I Googled that response. I couldn't remember how to say 'pick you up.'"

She smacked her forehead with the palm of her hand. "Darn…you just shattered my illusion."

I laughed and followed her to my car. I opened the door for her and when she climbed in, I caught a glimpse of her thigh. I wanted to touch it…to touch her. I blinked and shut her door, closing my eyes for a second as I moved around to my side of the car. But her thigh was still there…on the backside of my eyelids. I sighed and climbed into the Durango.

"So, where are we going?" she asked as she fastened her seatbelt.

"There's a place in Kenilworth called Tio Taco's. They have great chimichangas. Have you ever been there?" I asked as I exited the neighborhood and turned onto the main highway. Driving the route to Kenilworth was like being in a dark green tunnel…a twisty highway lined on either side by tall western hemlocks, Scotch pine, spruce and fir trees.

"No. I don't really go to Kenilworth often." She turned sideways in her seat. "Before I forget…thanks for the job. I owe it to you. The manager seems nice."

"Mr. Jameson…Luke…yeah, he's a really nice guy. He's also a phenomenal keyboardist. He used to be in a band called The Gunrunners. I'm not sure what happened to his band but sometimes he plays his own music over the store's sound system. It's pretty amazing. You'll hear it one of these days."

"Cool. I'm going to fill out the paperwork and take it and my schedule to him tomorrow. I'm anxious to get started teaching. It'll be fun."

I glanced at her and shook my head. "It'll be fun for about five minutes and then you'll realize that most of the students are tone deaf and you're gonna want to shoot something. Give me a heads up so I can take cover."

She laughed and fiddled with the radio buttons. I loved that she wasn't afraid to make adjustments to the dials—that she felt comfortable enough to do it on her own without asking. I noticed we were about to approach the curve in the road where the accident had happened. It would be my first time seeing it since that night. I wondered if I should point it out to Emma but I didn't want to alter the mood so I stayed silent as we rounded the bend. I glanced over at her and saw her study the trees where Sarah's car had crashed and then she looked over at me. She had a knowing expression on her face, but she remained silent. I gripped the steering wheel tighter…looked down the embankment, too, and showed no reaction as we drove on, leaving the scene behind us. Neither of us mentioned it as I entered Kenilworth and drove in to the parking lot of Tio Taco's.

Once inside we were shown to a booth, given our complimentary chips and salsa, and placed our drink orders. The restaurant was fairly busy and mariachi music played over the sound system. I watched Emma adjust herself in the booth, tucking her legs under herself, her hands immediately in search of something to fiddle with. She settled on the miniature bottles of sauces in varying degrees of heat. I hoped all the lids were on tightly.

"Johnny's coming home tomorrow night. It's a fast trip for a funeral," Emma said.

I nodded. "Yeah, he texted me this morning and said they'd be home early," I replied.

"Are you picking them up?" she asked. She took a tortilla chip, dragged it through the salsa and put it up to her lips. I held my breath waiting for the pile of onions, peppers and red sauce to fall, but, miraculously, it didn't.

"No. His dad left their other car at the airport so they'll all ride back together. Oh, hey…how's Popcorn?"

Emma grinned. "She's good, but she kept me awake all night between meowing and trying to nip at my feet. I've gotta find a vet so she can get a check-up and shots and I'll have to see about having her fixed. One baby in the house is all I'll be able to deal with…when Trapper or Daffodil is born."

I raised an eyebrow. "Do I even want to know?"

"Nanette and her crazy baby names," Emma said.

The waiter arrived then and took our orders—a beef chimichanga for me and a taco salad for Emma. When he left, Emma pushed the bottles of sauce aside and leaned slightly over the table. Her face had clouded over. "Can I ask you a question?"

"Oh, boy…this sounds serious…but…sure…go ahead." I shoved a salsa-covered tortilla chip in my mouth, dripping salsa onto the table. I wiped it up and looked at Emma, grinning at my own messiness.

"It's about Johnny…and Sarah. I was wondering about their relationship…what it was like." Her voice was quiet and traces of red began to splotch across her throat. It looked like she was breaking out in hives.

I leaned back in my seat and sighed. This was a loaded question that I'd just as soon avoid answering. "Johnny never talked about her?"

She blinked, her green eyes seeming darker than normal in the light of the lamp that hung low over the table. I watched the splotches on her neck grow larger and begin to connect themselves across her throat.

"No. Well, he talked about her in the abstract, but not as someone he dated. I mean he talked about her more as if she were just a fellow student that something tragic had happened to, more than someone he was…involved with…or cared about. I thought it was weird and when I pushed for more details he always turned the subject to you. He talked way more about you than Sarah. He was sad for a time and I was new here and didn't know anybody so we were just a couple of lost souls at the beginning of the school year. I could tell he didn't want to talk about her so I really don't know much about their relationship. Was it very serious?"

I glanced down at a scratch mark in the table top and began to pick at it with my finger. I really wished Johnny were the one at the receiving end of this question, but then she wouldn't get a fair answer. I decided to be honest without harming Johnny's character too much.

"I think it was more serious on Sarah's part than Johnny's. But I don't think anyone should hold that against him. Sarah knew what she was getting into with Johnny. He was kind of a playboy and most girls were aware of his reputation. Every girl he dated thought she could 'tame' him. And to tell you the truth, Emma, until you came along, I doubted that any girl ever could. But he certainly is different with you."

She sighed and tilted her head into her shoulder, her body tensing up into a half-shrug. "He told me he loves me, but it did occur to me that maybe he said that to all the girls he's dated just so that he could… well…you know…." Her face reddened and she looked away. I noticed her hives were slowly fading now. I wondered if she was reacting to the salsa or the conversation.

I could feel my own face heating up. Talking about Johnny and his modus operandi with girls made for unpleasant table talk. And if any other girl were sitting across from me right now, I would have agreed with her…but this was Emma, and I really did believe that Johnny loved her.

"Uh…well…that does sound like something Johnny would do. He is a smooth talker, I'll give him that."

Emma sipped her drink, her gaze wandering around the restaurant, but not focusing on any one thing. Whatever she was thinking, she kept it to herself. And then she turned the tables on me. "What about you, Charlie? Are you a smooth talker, too?"

I breathed in a bit sharply at the unexpected question. "As much as I'd like to think so…no…I'm not. I probably lean more toward subtlety when trying to get something I want badly."

She dipped another chip into the salsa and this time it did drip when she put it up to her lips—onto her chin and down onto the table-top, narrowly missing her sundress. She giggled and grabbed a napkin, bumping her glass in the process. I saved the glass while she shook her head at her clumsiness and proceeded to wipe her chin and the table. I kept her drink closer to me and waited to see where she would take the conversation. She started to speak just as our meals arrived. As soon as the waiter left us alone, she continued—her voice low and damned sexy.

"So…is there something you want badly?" she asked, as she poked her fork into her salad and began to mix it up to her satisfaction.

I opted to take a bite of rice before answering. It was damned hot and I had to fight not to react to the fire I'd set inside my mouth. I sipped my Coke, brushed my tongue against the roof of my mouth and confirmed that, indeed, a layer of skin was now missing from my tongue—and probably my palate, too. I looked down at my chimichan-ga, studying it…looking for an answer. "I want a lot of things."

"Like what?"

Like you. My brain threatened to go as mushy as the refried beans on my plate. I refocused and gave Emma a proper answer. "I want my body to feel normal again. I want to be able to pitch left-handed for the baseball team next spring. I want to get into Jenkins. I want the Munson kid to be able to play at least one song on the guitar before school starts this fall…just to name a few."

"Maybe I could help you with some of those," she said.

I glanced at her then. Her hand rested on the table beside her plate—an open invitation for me to take it in mine, though I really didn't think that was her intent. Our eyes locked and I could no longer hear sounds in the restaurant. My peripheral vision stopped working, too. All I could see was Emma's beautiful face…glistening emerald eyes… shiny black hair. I wondered which of the four things I'd mentioned I wanted she could help me with. I knew which one I preferred. I forced myself to snap out of it. I took a bite of my chimichanga…chewed… swallowed…answered.

"You really think you could teach a Munson kid not to kill a minor chord?"

She laughed…leaned back in her seat. "Well, I don't know the Munson kid but, yeah…maybe that…and maybe the Jenkins thing. Not sure about the baseball issue though."

She didn't comment on the other thing I wanted—probably just as well. But I knew she most definitely could help me with that. We stopped talking for a while and finished our meals. The waiter brought the check and asked about dessert. We both declined. She tried to pay and I wouldn't let her. But I let her leave the tip. We walked out to my car and once we were headed back to Westbrook, she brought up music...specifically my song.

"When do I get to hear that song you've been working on?" she asked, turning to face me.

"Any time. It's pretty much finished but I'm still working on the tune."

"Can I hear it tonight?"

I hadn't expected that. I hadn't actually performed it in front of anyone yet. I was unsure how it would sound to someone else's ears. But I wanted to play it for her. And so I said, "Sure."

"I can't wait."

We didn't talk much on the rest of the ride back into town. Emma found an alternative rock station and turned it up. We sang along to an old Strokes song and when we rounded the bend where the accident had happened, I almost didn't notice it—almost.

Chapter Eighteen

Emma

When we got to Charlie's house, it was dark except for the porch light. He parked in the driveway and left the engine on while we finished listening to a song on the radio. I could barely see his face in the darkness with only a half-moon overhead, sitting directly over the sun roof of the Durango. But the porch light coupled with the interior dash lights cast one side of his face in a shiny glow leaving the other side of his face hidden in the shadows. For a moment he reminded me of the Phantom in The Phantom of the Opera. I had to bite my tongue to keep from belting out "Think of Me" or "The Music of the Night."

"My parents are at some barbecue tonight and it doesn't look like my brother's home either. You wanna come inside? Or we could go out on the back deck if you want," Charlie said, sounding a little nervous.

"Inside is fine. I want to see your room. Is that where you write and play music?" I asked.

"Yep…mostly." We walked up to the front door and he unlocked it, then let me enter first as he reached his hand inside to turn on the foyer light. "Can I get you a drink or anything?" he asked.

"No, thanks…I'm good." I followed him up the stairs, down a long hallway with a floor plan just like my house. Our rooms were even the same—the last one on the right. He went in first and flipped on the light. I entered and took in his room—the walls covered in posters of music groups he liked—and I liked, too. I saw sports trophies arranged on several wooden shelves intermixed with the posters. The walls were painted blue and the curtains had musical notes on them. Against one wall were a dresser and a desk and chair. Dominating the room was a queen-sized bed with a navy blue comforter over it. And in the middle of the bed was…a teddy bear? I went straight to it and picked it up.

"Cute," I said, flashing him a grin. "What's this little guy's name?" I brought the chocolate brown bear to my chest in a hug.

Charlie grimaced and came toward me, reaching for the teddy bear but I put it behind my back out of his reach. "Uh…that was a gift and I just never got around to getting rid of it."

"Oh…a gift, huh? From a girl?" I brought the teddy bear back around in front of me but when Charlie grabbed for it again, I turned my back to him. He reached around me, trying to get it from my hands but I turned again, part-way, into his arms. I was mere inches from his chest. I could smell his cologne and the scent of a dryer sheet on his black shirt. I slowly raised my head to look into his eyes. His cheeks were pinking and I was certain mine were, too. I was acutely aware of his arm still around me. My breath hitched in my throat and my mouth watered. I looked at his mouth…those perfect lips and I…swooned… literally…and fell back onto the bed. "Oops," I said, emitting a nervous laugh. Charlie dropped his arm from mine and stepped back.

"It was from some girl I was seeing before the accident. She came to visit me and brought me that," he said, pointing to the stuffed animal. "You should take it for Popcorn to teethe on…or something." His voice sounded funny…higher-pitched…like he was talking through nerves.

I could feel my heart pounding wildly in my chest and I resisted the urge to press my hand against it, as if that could calm it. I watched as Charlie went over to his guitar in the corner and took it out of its case. I was still seated on the end of his bed. He sat across from me on a loveseat and began to tune his guitar.

"So, what's the name of this song?" I asked. I made a conscious effort to control my breathing and appear calm. But being this close to Charlie was messing with my head…and my body, which was suddenly tingling all over.

"It's called 'She's Mine.' It's still a little raw so bear with me."

I nodded and watched his fingers work the strings. I saw the way he held the instrument like it was precious to him and…in that moment…I so badly wanted to be that guitar…to be held by Charlie and played so gently just like he was playing it now, as the opening notes of his song unfolded on the strings. And then he began to sing.

> I didn't plan it,
> That's not my style,
> She came just to talk,
> I said stay for awhile.
>
> In the blink of an eye,
> In the rush of the wind,
> It happened so fast,
> Now she's under my skin
>
> When she's mine it's for good,
> When she's mine it's for real,
> I hope this goes easy,

I don't wanna steal,
But I will,
I will.

An exchange of hellos,
A whispered good-bye,
I know that it's only
a matter of time.

It's a lightning fast moment,
It's a thief in the night,
It's a promise unbroken,
It's a turn on a dime.

When she's mine it's for good,
When she's mine it's for real,
I hope this goes easy,
I don't wanna steal,
But I will,
I will.

There's no giving up,
There's no letting go,
There's no backing down,
There's no saying no.

I'm sorry it hurts,
Not much of a friend,
Just gotta believe,
It's alright in the end.

When she's mine it's for good,
When she's mine it's for real,
I hope this goes easy.
I don't wanna steal.
But I will.
I will.

I will, I will,
Cuz she's mine,
I will, I will.

Charlie never looked at me as he sang. He looked either at his hands on the guitar or at the floor...but never at me. Until he was finished. When the room grew silent and the last note had faded away, he glanced up at me. My eyes were burning...stinging...pricking with hot tears. I felt breathless and strange. I sat on the end of his bed, stiff... nervous...my stomach jumping...my lungs faltering. I'd listened to the lyrics. I'd heard every word. And now I was swimming in a sea of confusion...wondering if I'd truly heard what I thought I'd heard. One damned tear fell and as I dashed it away, Charlie placed his guitar down on the loveseat and came over to sit beside me on the end of the bed.

"Is this a sign that you liked my song?" he said quietly. He pressed a thumb to my cheek and wiped away a tear. His touch was electrifying and when he removed his thumb my skin burned from the memory of it.

"It's...beautiful," I said on a whisper. "The melody is haunting... and Charlie...the words...what do they mean?" I turned to look up at him and as I turned to him, I pressed my hand into his. He looked down at my hand in his and I half-expected him to push it away. But he didn't. He clasped it in his and his hand seemed to swallow mine. His was warm and mine was cold but within seconds our temperatures matched. We looked at each other, our thighs resting against each other's...our arms touching.

"I think you know what it means," he said softly. My fingers touched the pulse point on his wrist. It was beating fast like a runaway train. I was sure mine was beating just as fast if not faster. I tried to speak but a lump prevented me from getting any words out. I swallowed, licked my lips and Charlie sucked in a soft breath. He leaned down toward me as I shifted my body into his. His arm snaked around my back and he pulled me close and I let out a small puff of trapped air as his lips met mine.

His kiss was everything I imagined it would be and more. His lips were soft and warm and sure. There was nothing tentative about the kiss...no fear...no doubt. His tongue touched my lips and I heard myself moan as I opened my mouth welcoming him inside. Every part of my body burned with desire for him. It burned hotter than it ever had for Johnny...Johnny...oh, my god, Johnny. This was wrong...so wrong. But how could something that felt like this be anything but right? Charlie pulled me into both of his arms then, deepening the kiss and I kissed him back with everything I had. I heard him groan in the back of his throat. I reveled in the feel of his hands rubbing up and down my back as I pressed closer, trying to erase any distance between us. And as we kissed I knew now why I had been so reluctant to give my body to Johnny. Because he didn't make me feel like this...like a furnace being lit for the first time...an inferno that threatened to burn out of control...

an all-consuming beautiful fire that I never wanted doused. And then Charlie's cell phone rang.

He stopped the kiss, but didn't pull away. He pressed his forehead against mine as he sighed and reached into his pocket for the phone. He glanced down at it. "It's Johnny. I can't answer it right now," he whispered against my lips. After a few seconds, the ringing stopped...and then my phone started buzzing. I recognized the special ring tone I'd set just for Johnny's calls.

"Should I answer?" I asked. I knew I should but I was afraid to hear Johnny's voice right now. I was afraid my own voice would betray me.

"If you want," said Charlie. He held my hands on his lap and leaned back from me a little bit.

"I'll let it go to voicemail and call him when I get home." I looked up at Charlie...into his dark blue eyes and I wanted to live there...to stay forever right there in his eyes. "I'm not sure what happened just now, Charlie. I don't know what's happening. Do you?"

He gave me a half-smile and let go of my hands. He put his arms around me and folded me into this chest and I rested my head there against him...where I could smell him...so good...so intoxicating. I felt dizzy and drunk on Charlie Channing.

"All I know for sure, Emma, is that I'm falling for you. And I know it's not right and that you're really not mine, the lyrics to my song notwithstanding, but I knew the moment you spilled your drink on my back deck that you were important...almost like your presence that day was a gift from the universe."

"Oh, Charlie..." I sighed into his chest. My brain was sparking with confused thoughts, feelings, desires. "What does this mean? What happens now?"

He leaned back and cupped my face in his hands and kissed me tenderly...one short, chaste kiss on my lips. Then he dropped his hands and stood up. And the words that came out of his mouth next were not the words I expected to hear.

"Here's the thing, Em. Johnny is my best friend. And in spite of the very shitty...pardon my French...year I've just had, and the conundrum I now find myself in, I cannot take something I want...from him... something that's his. No matter how much I want it...you. I can't do that to him. And even if you break up with Johnny tomorrow and come straight back to my arms, I'm not sure I can wrap them around you like I want to. We have a code...Johnny and I...an unbroken pact not to take from the other something the other wants or had first. I have to honor that code."

I was astonished...and hurt...and angry. "First of all, Johnny doesn't own me. I am my own person. And, second of all, even if I did break up with Johnny tomorrow, who says I would come running straight back here to you? And third of all, a code of honor? Really? Is it freaking 1750 and someone forgot to tell me?"

Charlie moved to stand by the window. He put his hands in his pockets and turned to look at me. His face was unreadable. "I'm sorry, Emma. I shouldn't have kissed you. I couldn't help myself. I wanted to know what it was like, but it was wrong and I'm truly sorry. Can we just forget it happened?"

I stood up and went to the door. My heart hurt and it was hard to breathe. I was confused and angry and a million other things. But forget his kiss? I could never do that and I wasn't afraid to tell him so, no matter how pathetic I sounded.

"Maybe you can forget, Charlie, but I can't. And your song? It's a lie. Every word of it." I choked back a sob as I opened the door and ran down the stairs as fast as I could. I heard Charlie coming after me. I ran for the front door and just as I reached for the knob, Charlie grabbed my arm, stopping me up short.

"Wait…Emma…please." He was breathing fast and his grip on me was firm and strong. "You're right. I can't forget the kiss. But my song? It's not a lie…it's a fantasy…a dream…in my head…in my heart. But please don't call it a lie."

I looked down at his hand on my arm. I started to pull my arm away but I had another idea. And I knew it was risky and potentially painful. My body was too alive and thrumming with heat to leave without taking the risk. I wanted to show Charlie…just one time…his fantasy.

I closed the distance between us, catching him off guard. I reached up and wrapped my hands around his neck and pulled him down to me and kissed him…hard…crushing my mouth to his…making sure he felt every fiber of my lips. I molded myself into him to make sure he felt every part of my body. He put his arms around me and held me as I pushed my tongue into his mouth. He welcomed it in, as I'd hoped he would. I kissed him until I thought my heart would burst and then I stopped, pushed his arms away from me. He stumbled backward a step but caught his balance. He was winded and somewhat shaken up by my assault on his senses. I opened the door.

"I just wanted to make sure you really don't forget my kiss, Charlie, because I will never forget yours." I stepped outside and said over my shoulder, "I live two blocks away. I don't need a ride."

"Emma…wait! I'll take you home." But I ignored him. I walked as fast as I could, considering I was wearing heels. I heard Charlie walking behind me but keeping his distance.

"I'm following you home, Emma. I want to make sure you get home safe."

I didn't answer him, nor did I look back, but I gave a wave of my hand over my head and continued on. I walked the two blocks to my house and headed up the drive. I let myself inside and when I looked out the tiny window in the center of the door, Charlie was still there at the end of the driveway, looking up at my house. I turned off the porch light and ran to my room. I could hear the TV in my dad and Nanette's bedroom…canned laughter from a sitcom. I dropped my purse on the loveseat, slipped off my shoes and curled up on my bed. I felt hollow inside and cold outside. I didn't fight the tears as they fell onto my pillow and when Johnny called me again a few minutes later, I didn't ignore his call this time.

Chapter Nineteen

Johnny

I couldn't wait to get back home to Emma. I'd talked to her on the phone earlier and she'd told me about the job at Charlie's music store. I was glad she wouldn't be working at the mall. I hated the mall and if she'd gotten a job there, I'd have had to spend more time there than was humanly possible—or Johnny Beaumont possible anyway. Teaching guitar lessons was a much better option. I'd texted Charlie and thanked him for helping her get the job. I felt a lot better knowing she'd be working where Charlie was. Lately I'd had the feeling that our relationship was changing somehow…and not in a good way. But I knew what we needed. We needed another trip to Lake Crescent. Emma had loved it there. And with the Fourth of July holiday coming up next weekend, I was fairly certain that's where we'd be. I'd been celebrating Independence Day at the Channing's cabin most of my life. Of course, there would be more people there this time but I'd find a way to carve out some alone time with Emma. Maybe I could talk her into going on an overnight camp-out by the lake.

Over dinner we told Grandpa Beaumont stories. I was proud of my grandma for holding up so well. She was going to spend some time with my Aunt Kathy and her family at their home on the other side of Kalispell and later in the summer or maybe in the fall she would come out to Westbrook to our house. I was glad. I didn't want her to be alone. After dinner I went out to the front porch and dialed Charlie but got his voicemail. I dialed Emma's number and hers went to voicemail, too. "Hey, babe. Call when you get this. I miss you but I'll see you tomorrow. I'm coming straight over as soon as we hit Westbrook. I love you." I hung up the phone and stared out at Grandpa's garden for a while. I wished like crazy I could smoke some of his new wave basil right now. Even a beer would be nice but my parents would never go for that. Grandpa Beaumont wouldn't have minded though.

Fuck it…I'm stealing a beer, I said to myself as I made my way out to the garage where Grandma had a spare fridge. My brother Scott was there, helping himself to a Bud Light. He didn't even have to ask if I wanted one. He tossed me one and I found us a couple of cooling sleeves on Grandpa's work bench. Good. Now Mom would think we were having sodas if she came out on the porch. Scott and I went out to the front porch and settled into the wicker chairs, toasted Grandpa and watched the sun set. When it was totally dark, Scott went inside. I took out my phone to call Emma again. I needed to hear her voice before I went to sleep tonight. And this time tomorrow she'd be in my arms.

Chapter Twenty

Charlie

"See that girl, Charlie? I want her." Johnny grinned like the devil as he pointed at Madeline Smith, the hottest girl in eighth grade. She was beautiful, blonde, blue-eyed and big boobs—she had all the B's covered. I'd secretly admired her for weeks but I'd kept it to myself. And now Johnny had claimed her by speaking up first and so I was shit out of luck.

"Hey, Chuck…I'm trying out for quarterback for freshman football. No one can touch me for quarterback…except maybe you…but you don't want to be quarterback so I'm going for it." I'd been thinking of trying out for quarterback on the freshman football team most of the summer but I hadn't mentioned it to Johnny because he had never once even hinted that he cared about football. And now he'd called it first.

"As long as you're not interested, Chuckster, I'm going for it—I'm gonna run for sophomore class representative." Johnny in politics? So what if it was high school government. I couldn't run against my best friend even though I'd hinted at a possible run at the end of freshman year. Why hadn't I definitively spoken up then—claimed it for my own? Was I sabotaging myself with Johnny purposely?

Emma was impossible to shake. I could still smell her on my shirt. I could still feel her in my arms…a perfect fit. But the taste in my mouth was the hardest thing to erase. She'd tasted incredible and her lips were freakishly soft. She was so real and so vivid and so present in my mind that sometime before dawn I gave up trying to sleep to do something I hadn't done in a really long time. I slipped into a pair of running shorts, a t-shirt and my tennis shoes and I went for a run. I started slowly, jogging down the block, testing my leg…checking to see how it would hold up. As long as I paced myself it didn't hurt. I ran the two blocks to Emma's and glanced at her house as I passed. It was dark and quiet just like the rest of the neighborhood, except for the newspaper deliveryman, throwing the daily news out his passenger-side window into driveways.

I ran toward town sticking to the sidewalks until they ran out and I had to move to the dirt roadside along the two-mile-long rural area that led into Westbrook proper. There was little traffic this time of morning and I welcomed the solitude. My brain raced faster than my legs could ever hope to though, and there was no way I could outrun it. I'd fucked things up with Emma and now Johnny would be home tonight and I'd have to act normal. I'd have to act like I hadn't kissed his girl…act like I hadn't held her in my arms. And the worst part was…I'd have to pretend that I hadn't noticed she'd wanted me as much as I'd wanted her. Next weekend was the Fourth of July and Johnny would be expecting to come up to Lake Crescent like he always had since we were kids. He'd want to bring Emma. Of course, after last night, she might not want to be anywhere near me. But I wouldn't be able to avoid her and Johnny forever so I'd just have to suck it up and find a way to deal.

My leg began to ache so I slowed and walked around in circles on the side of the road catching my breath. I stood a minute and watched the sun come up over the east side of Westbrook painting the sky first pink and then a brilliant orange. Finally I turned back and headed home at a slow pace to give my leg a break. I'd probably made at least a mile and a half before giving in to my aching leg so that felt like progress—three miles of progress. If only I'd made progress exorcising Emma from my mind. But when I got back home and stood under the hot shower spray, she was still with me…still making me crazy…still making me want something I couldn't have.

"Sweetie, are you and Will planning to go up to the lake for the Fourth?" asked my mom.

"I guess so. I haven't talked to Will about it. You and Dad going?" I asked as I sat down at the kitchen table with a bowl of cereal and a glass of grape juice.

"We can't go this year. Your dad was asked to go to Costa Rica on a humanitarian mission. He's actually replacing an ophthalmologist who was supposed to go but had to drop out due to a family emergency so your dad's going in his place. And I wasn't planning to go anyway because Cheryl asked me to help her cater a wedding. It'll just be you and Will and any friends of yours you want to invite…but Charlie, just because there won't be any adults there doesn't mean you can drink or smoke or do whatever it is you teens like to do these days that would make a parent crazy or that can get you arrested. You know this, right?"

I put my spoon down and stared at my mom in wonder. "Seriously? No beer or meth or orgies? Really, Mom? Cuz…what's the point in going then? We may as well just stay here and read the dictionary and hang out at the mall."

She grinned at me and walked over, wrapping her arms around my neck.

"Ha…ha…Charlie. You and your sarcasm. I've missed it. But you know what I mean. I'm required by law to say my parental spiel and I'll say it to Will, too. But I trust you boys…you know I do." She kissed the top of my head and left me to my cereal.

I smiled to myself as I tipped the bowl and drank the milk. If there was one good thing that had come out of the accident, it was the close-ness that had developed between me and my mom. She'd quit her job and stayed with me in Seattle every day. My dad had been there a lot at the beginning but he had a clinic to run and so Mom had been there through all the surgeries and physical therapy. We could have easily gotten on each other's nerves but I couldn't remember a single argument between us. I'm sure I couldn't have been the easiest guy to live with, especially those first few weeks. My mom was a saint.

Will came in then and sat down across from me. "I just passed Mom in the hall and she gave me her 'talk' about drugs and alcohol. She and Dad aren't coming to the lake for the Fourth. Did she talk to you?"

"Yeah. Just now. You taking Amanda?" I kept a poker face when I asked. The thought of spending time in close confines with Will's cur-rent flavor was an unpleasant one.

"I'm sure I will. Did Mom say anything to you about fireworks?" Will grabbed my empty bowl and filled it with cereal and milk, and using my spoon, began to eat. I raised an eyebrow at this but let it slide.

"No, but she will. There's no way she or Dad will let us do our own. But Crescent Springs will have good ones over the north side of the lake so it'll be cool."

"Probably so. Johnny going?"

"I would imagine. I'll ask him." I nodded toward my cereal bowl. "How's your breakfast there, Will?"

He finished his cereal and pushed the bowl back toward me. "Good, thanks. I'm off to work. The grocery store awaits." He gave me a salute and disappeared out the back door.

I grabbed my keys and my guitar. I had three back-to-back lessons this morning, one of whom was the Munson kid. My plan for him today was to help him master how to hold a guitar properly. He still thought it was some kind of weapon or digging device. And my other plan included asking the boss for some studio time. He had a small recording studio in the back of the store and I wanted to record a couple of songs so I could prepare for the Jenkins audition which I intended to put in a request for before heading to the cabin for the holiday weekend.

I parked the Durango in the mostly empty parking lot and went inside. Luke was setting up the cash register as I passed him on the way to the lesson booths. He had his cell phone shoved between his chin and shoulder so I waved as I passed him, not stopping to talk. I'd ask him about using the studio later. I smelled coffee brewing in the small employee break room so I stopped in for a cup. I wondered if I would see Emma. Just thinking about her was causing the idea of coffee not to sit well in my gut. As I sipped from my cup I heard the Munson kid's voice in the hall and I rolled my eyes. I wanted to file this kid in the lost cause bin but with my luck he'd turn out to be a Grammy-winning artist someday so I forced myself to smile and met him in the booth to suffer through the lesson.

Three students and three hours later I came out of my booth needing more coffee and food to get me through the two lessons I had to give this afternoon. I had some time to kill so I decided a trip to Wendy's was in order. Just as I walked out of the store, a silver Honda Civic pulled into the parking spot next to my Durango. Emma turned off the engine and stepped out of her car, stopping in front of me. She was wearing sunglasses, hiding her green eyes and I noticed her hair was pulled back in a long, sleek pony tail. She wore jeans and a pink blouse and already I could smell her perfume…the scent of wildflowers and oranges swirled all around her.

"Hey, Emma," I said, testing the waters. I shoved my hands in my pockets just to give them someplace to be.

She glanced down, then toward the store and finally at me. "Charlie."

"How many lessons do you have today?" May as well talk shop until I knew where I stood with her.

"Just three today…but I have five tomorrow. Why do so many people want to learn guitar?"

I laughed. "Maybe so their moms will put videos of them playing on You Tube so they can get famous."

"Maybe," she said. She pushed her sunglasses up on her head then, revealing her beautiful emerald eyes. I swallowed hard, resisting the urge to step closer to her.

"You OK?" I asked, my voice quiet.

"Of course. Why wouldn't I be?" I noticed her cheeks pinking up as she spoke. So she wasn't totally immune to me then...or to the situation we were in anyway.

"No reason. So Johnny'll be home tonight, right?"

"Yep." She shifted her purse over her shoulder and looked at the store. "Well, I better get in there. Don't want to be late on my first day."

"Yeah, right. Good luck." She started to walk away but I couldn't let her go like this. "Emma...?"

She stopped, turned and stared up at me, a questioning look on her face.

"Are things OK between us?" Inside my pockets, I clenched my hands into fists to keep from grabbing her and pulling her into my arms.

"You tell me." Her voice was soft...quiet...her expression neutral, not giving anything away.

"I want them to be."

"Then we're fine. I've gotta go. See ya, Charlie." And she turned and went inside the store. I stood there a second looking after her, then shook my head in frustration and got inside my car. I headed to Wendy's for a burger that I wasn't looking as forward to now as I had been before seeing Emma. Things were clearly not OK between us but I would follow her cue. If she wanted to act like nothing had happened then that's the way I'd play it, too.

When I returned to the store, my first student was already there. I spent the next two hours listening to two boys with Justin Bieber hair play guitar badly. At least the second kid had shown some promise and actually listened when I explained the difference between major and minor chords. I gave him some sheet music and told him to practice it for next time and walked with him out into the hall. Emma was just coming out of another practice booth with a kid who couldn't keep his eyes off of her. I wondered how much about playing the guitar he'd been able to grasp when it was clear his head was in an Emma cloud. Not that I could blame the kid. Emma started to walk past me but I touched her arm, hoping she would stop.

"Hey, Em...could we talk a sec?" I wasn't exactly sure what I was going to say to her...I just didn't want her to leave yet. I didn't like the tension between us and I wouldn't feel better until I tried to resolve it.

"Let's walk out to the parking lot," she said, heading out into the store. She stopped for a moment to speak to Luke. He asked how the lessons had gone and told her he'd see her tomorrow. I waved good-bye realizing I still hadn't asked about using his recording studio but I promised myself I would do it tomorrow. I followed Emma out to our cars. She unlocked her door and turned to me. "You want to sit in my car?"

I nodded and got into her front passenger seat...or tried to. I had to move the seat all the way back first so I could fit inside. Her car seemed tiny after my Durango. She settled into her seat and turned toward me.

"What did you want to talk about?" I couldn't tell from her tone of voice what kind of mood she was in or if I was about to make a huge mistake. I just knew I didn't want her to go yet.

"Can we talk about last night? About the kiss? Both of them?"

"What about them?"

"You're not going to make this easy, are you?" I asked, forcing a grin.

"Make what easy?" she asked, blinking at me, her face completely expressionless.

Dammit. I felt frustration building as I fought to control my emotions. "About how I kissed you and I shouldn't have and then how you kissed me and maybe you shouldn't have…? And how we should handle that moving forward?" I realized I sounded ridiculous even as the lame words rolled off my tongue. "I just want to be sure we're OK—me and you—and that we're friends and that you and Johnny are…"

"Charlie…really…you made your point loud and clear last night with your ancient code of honor thing. I get it. Girls have codes, too. As for the kiss, well, I'm not sorry for either one of them. But it doesn't have to change things and it doesn't have to affect anything to do with Johnny." She stopped speaking and glanced out her window then turned back to me. "Last night I was just a little…shall we say…emotionally charged…probably because of your song. But I'm OK now—back to normal. So, we'll just get on with it. Oh, and by the way…Johnny texted me earlier about the Fourth of July. He said you guys are going to Lake Crescent and he wants me to come, too. But I'll understand if you think that would be too awkward. I can tell him I have to do something with my dad and Nanette."

"No, you don't have to do that. Johnny won't come without you and I know how much he loves the lake." I couldn't even imagine being at Lake Crescent without Emma there and I wanted to my punch my own face for feeling that way.

"I don't want to cause problems," she said, looking away again. She sighed and leaned back against her seat. Without thinking I reached over and took her hand in mine. She looked down at it and then at me but she didn't push me away.

"It would cause more problems if you didn't come…for Johnny, I mean. So, yeah, I want you there. It'll be fun." Her skin was soft. I needed to let go of her hand but I couldn't. I wished she would push me away and make it easy but that didn't happen either.

"You're holding my hand, Charlie. Is this like the kiss you shouldn't have given me? Are you doing something you shouldn't be?" She looked down at our hands and I started to pull mine away but she grabbed it with her free hand and held it tightly. "Am I doing something I'm not supposed to do by holding your hand now?" She turned her gaze on me and our eyes locked.

The air in the car suddenly seemed to dissipate making it hard to suck oxygen into my lungs. There was no mistaking the electrical charge passing between us in the small confines of her car. I had to get out before I made the same mistake I'd made last night—before I kissed her again. Because that was exactly what I wanted to do. I pulled my hand from hers and opened the door.

"I'll see you later, Em. Tell Johnny hi for me." I got out and shut the door and went straight to my Durango. I started the engine and drove out of the lot. At the traffic light on Main Street I glanced back and saw that Emma was still sitting in her car. She was slumped over her steering wheel and I felt my heart constrict in the strangest way. A horn sounded behind me, annoyed at my distraction and not reacting to the green light fast enough. I cursed, hit the dash with my palm and pressed my foot down on the accelerator. I drove home and went up to my room. I had an urge to damage something but out of respect for my mother I decided not to. I could hear her in the hallway reorganizing the linen closet and I didn't want to have to explain why I'd felt it necessary to put a hole in the wall or tear the door off its hinges.

I finally calmed down and went over to my desk and booted up my laptop. When it was up and running I went on to the Jenkins School of Music and Theatrical Arts website and filled out the online registration form requesting an audition. I also checked on the status of my application for admission which showed as pending. I was a bit ahead of myself considering I still had another year of high school facing me, but I didn't want to risk missing a chance of getting in. I was well aware of how competitive the school was. When I was finished I put my computer away and went downstairs for something to drink. The house was quiet. Mom must still be upstairs organizing things—her favorite hobby along with baking. I caught sight of a pie on the stove and decided I'd have a piece. It was blackberry and still warm from the oven. I ate a huge piece with a glass of milk. It was good and made me feel better. And then my phone buzzed with a text message. I pulled my phone out of my pocket and checked it. It was from Johnny: hey, chuck…heading to airport now—home in a few hours. we are on for lake crescent. cannot fucking wait. see you tomorrow.

I didn't respond. I finished my milk and decided to distract myself with more pie. I was having a very strong urge to text Emma and I knew what a mistake that would be. I was going to have to find some willpower where she was concerned or there would be major hell to pay. And I so didn't need that.

Chapter Twenty-One

Emma

I had a new mission in mind: to accept that Charlie was my friend and nothing more, and that would have to be that. If I was so easy to resist then I would show him that he was, too. Not that I fancied myself such a great catch…but…I knew I wasn't imagining the way Charlie had kissed me—that had been no ordinary kiss. He had felt something for me, I was certain. But if he could ignore his feelings, then so could I. And so I put him out of my mind. Even when his face and his voice kept trying to force themselves back into my head, I just kept shutting the metaphorical door on them. Even though every time I closed my eyes I could still feel his lips against mine, I mentally wiped away the sensation. I distracted myself by going online and filling out the form on the Jenkins website requesting an audition. I also submitted my application for admission. And then I showered and headed over to the music store to teach my lessons.

I saw Charlie's Durango in the parking lot but I didn't see him. I had several lessons in a row and when I was finished, he was gone. And the sting of disappointment I felt at not seeing him annoyed me even as it made me ache.

"Now that is what I call a welcome home kiss," Johnny whispered against my cheek. We were in his car in my driveway. He'd come straight from the airport, after stopping at his house to get his car. "Hmm…you taste like spearmint. I'm thinking you must've missed me just a little bit, huh?" I started to smile but he kissed me again, capturing my lips with his.

"Of course I did," I said softly, when I was able to come up for air. I snuggled against him and closed my eyes, breathing him in. This was Johnny…not Charlie…and I needed to remember that at all times. I looked over his shoulder into the darkness as he held me, letting myself relax. I'd met Johnny in his car because, as I'd told him on the phone, my dad and stepmother were having a 'discussion' about baby names and it was getting weird and I didn't want to subject him to it. And while that was somewhat true, I really just wanted to be alone tonight.

We'd only been in his car for a couple of minutes but it was long enough for Johnny to be able to tell that I wasn't quite myself, in spite of my attempts to act normal. I held him tightly for a moment and then he pushed me back a little, frowning.

"As much as I love this warm welcome and you making me feel like the king of the world in a Leonardo DiCaprio in Titanic kind of way, I'm worried...," he said, rubbing his thumbs over my wrists gently. "Is something up, Em? You OK?"

I tilted my face up to his. He brushed strands of hair off my cheek and ran a finger along the line of my jaw.

"I'm fine...really. I started teaching guitar lessons at the store and it was kinda fun. I have all boy students...they're all like twelve or thirteen. I have a bunch more tomorrow."

"Lucky boys. You wanna teach me guitar?" he said, kissing the tip of my nose. "Or better yet...I'll be a guitar and you can play me...hmmm...yeah...I like that idea."

I chuckled and leaned back against the seat. "You're goofy. Now onto another subject... Fourth of July and Crescent Lake. When are we leaving? And who all's going?"

Johnny sighed. "As far as I'm concerned too damned many people are going, which reminds me...I kinda want one more person to go just to balance things out. So far it's my brother and his girlfriend, Mila, and Will and his girl, Amanda, and you and me and Charlie...which makes Chuck the odd man out. So I was thinking...what if we invited Kerry or Claire to sort of round things out? You think one of them would be a good match for Charlie?"

I picked up a length of my hair and began to twirl it around my fingers. "Oh, boy. Charlie said he doesn't want any fix-ups. And anyway I think Claire has a boyfriend."

"Yeah, but it would be awkward to have four guys and three girls. And just for the record, babe...," He leaned over, pulling me across the console into his arms again, "I'm not sharing my girl with anybody." He tilted my face up to his and kissed me...a long intense kiss that I assumed was meant to drive his point home. He slid his hand around my back and slipped it under my shirt, pressing it against the small of my back. He began to rub his hand up and down the knots of my spine, under my bra. I tensed up for a moment but then immediately relaxed and let him massage my shoulder blades. He slid his other hand beneath the front of my shirt, pressing his fingers into my stomach. I leaned closer to him and he caught my hand as I reached under my shirt to slow him down.

"Your skin is so soft, Em…you feel so good," he murmured against my lips and when I didn't stop him, he let go of my hand and slid his fingers under the front of my bra, caressing my breast. I'd let him do this to me before but it had been awhile. I didn't want to send mixed signals to him, but ever since he'd been applying more pressure to have sex I'd been hesitant to get us into situations where it would be hard to resist. He cupped my breast in his hand and started to lean down, when I caught his cheek in my hand and brought his face back up to my eye level. I shifted away from him just out of kissing reach.

"I don't know about fixing Charlie up. It doesn't seem like a good idea," I said. Johnny leaned back, opening his eyes wider. He removed his hand from underneath my shirt.

"Uh…OK…but it could be awkward…don't you think? Everybody all paired up…except Charlie? Your concern for him is really sweet but he needs a little push so he can start living again. I really want you to ask Kerry Westfall."

"I guess I could ask her but she probably already has plans," I said, trying to mask the annoyance threatening to creep into my voice.

"What? You don't want to ask her? Don't you want Charlie to have a little female company?"

I shifted in my seat and adjusted my shirt. "It's not that. It's just… oh, never mind. I'll text her tonight and see what she says. But, hey, Johnny…I've gotta go. I don't want to leave Popcorn alone for too long. She meows a lot when she's lonely." I reached for the door handle and started to open it.

"Wait…hold up, Em," Johnny said, grabbing my hand. "What's up all of a sudden? You seemed awfully happy to see me a minute ago and now you have to go take care of a needy cat that will have to do without you all weekend? What's with the sudden change of mood? Is it that time of the month or something?"

I should have called him out on his rude comment but I decided to overlook it. I brought my hand up to his cheek and he turned his lips into my palm, kissing it.

"I'm sorry," I said. "I don't know what my problem is. I think it's the whole pregnant stepmother thing. But I will ask Kerry about the lake. I do need to go though. I have an early lesson tomorrow." I pulled him closer and kissed him. "I'm glad you're home."

Johnny pulled me into his arms, the center console crushing my rib cage, and kissed me good night. "I love you, Em. I'll see you tomorrow."

Kerry was thrilled with the invitation—a little too thrilled. "My parents and sisters are going to my grandparents for the weekend and I didn't want to go so this is perfect," she said. "But are you sure Charlie is OK with this? Does he think this is a set up? What if he doesn't like me? What if he won't even speak to me? What if he..."

I tossed a pillow at her, cutting off her list of 'what ifs.' We were in my room with Popcorn crawling all over both of us, purring loudly and wanting constant attention.

"Charlie won't mind your being there, and as long as we don't act like it's a set up then he won't think it is. And I'm sure he likes you. It's not like he doesn't know you. Haven't you been going to school with him for years?"

She nodded and stared off into space in a dreamy trance. Popcorn stretched, curled up on her lap and settled in for a nap. I watched her absentmindedly scratching Popcorn's ears. "OK, when do we leave? And what should I bring?"

I blinked back a wave of negative emotion. I'd really hoped she wouldn't be able to go or even want to go. But I knew Johnny would ask if I'd invited her and I didn't want to get caught in a lie. "A bathing suit, hiking shoes, toiletries...you know...the usual. We're leaving Saturday at noon. We'll be back Monday evening."

Kerry rubbed Popcorn's head and sighed. "I'm nervous...but excited. And, Emma, thanks for asking me. But...does Charlie actually know you're inviting me? I mean, it's his cabin, right? Maybe we should ask him first."

"I'll let him know. You'll be my guest so he won't mind." I studied Kerry for a minute. She was tall with big blue eyes and long blonde hair. And her boobs were every boy's fantasy. I felt a twinge of jealousy flicker through me. I had a feeling Charlie might be happier to have Kerry there than he would ever admit and that thought bothered me. I shrugged off the negativity that was altering my mood.

Kerry's phone rang, startling Popcorn who jumped off of her lap and into my arms. She took the call and a moment later said, "That was my sister. She needs a ride home from the mall. You wanna come along?" She got up and moved over to the door.

"No, thanks. I've got a guitar lesson this afternoon. But we'll talk before Saturday. Johnny and I will pick you up." We walked to the front door and I waved her off. I went into the kitchen and found Nanette decorating cupcakes in elaborate designs.

"Wow. Those are nice. What's the occasion?" I asked, resisting the urge to stick my fingers into the bowl of frosting.

"No occasion at the moment. I just felt like baking. These are vanilla with orange frosting. But your dad and I are going to a picnic Sunday afternoon for the Fourth with some of his work people so if these are good I'll make more Sunday morning. What are your holiday plans?" She made a fancy swirl on top of a cupcake and handed it to me.

"Oh, I forgot to tell you...I'm going with Johnny up to Lake Crescent for the Fourth—up to Charlie's family's cabin. The same place we went before. We're leaving around noon Saturday." I peeled back the cupcake wrapper and took a bite. It was heavenly.

Nanette looked up at me. "Did you ask your dad if you could go?"

I narrowed my eyes at her over the top of the cupcake, wondering what her deal was with my social schedule. "No, but I'll tell him when he gets home tonight."

Nanette sat down at the table with a cupcake and looked up at me. "OK. Oh, I forgot to tell you, your mom called while you were at work."

"She called the house phone?" That was strange considering I had a cell phone and she could reach me on it anytime.

"She said she called you a couple of times but you never called back she was worried." Nanette polished off her cupcake and peeled the wrapper off of another one.

"I didn't notice any missed calls but I'll check my phone. Thanks for letting me know." I finished my cupcake and fixed myself a glass of iced tea. As I headed to my room I stopped in the doorway and said over my shoulder, "Before we leave Saturday I'll make sure the litter box is clean and Popcorn has enough food and water...but she might get lonely and cry...a lot. Will that be a problem for you? I'll keep her shut inside my room."

I watched in fascination as Nanette started in on her third cupcake. "She'll be fine. I'll check on her. How'd you like the cupcakes?" she asked. "They're Martha Stewart's."

"They're awesome. Maybe I should make some to take to the cabin this weekend." I let the Martha reference roll over me.

Nanette's eyes brightened. "How about I make a couple of dozen for you? Some chocolate and some more like these?" She held up a cupcake and I feared she was going to eat that one, too.

"Thanks, that'd be great but only if you want," I said, inching down the hall away from her gorge-fest. I'd heard of eating for two but I hadn't realized it started so soon in pregnancy. At the rate Nanette was going she'd be the size of British Columbia before her second trimester.

My phone beeped with a text message as I climbed the stairs to my room. I pulled it from my pocket expecting it to be Johnny. I was shocked to see Charlie's name on the screen. I opened the text and read: i got a response from jenkins about my audition...nothing definite just that they'd let me know by end of august if i get one. have you sent in your request yet?

My hands began to shake. I read his text again as my heart hammered against my ribcage. I typed a response: i sent in the request but haven't heard back yet…will let you know when/if i do.

He responded quickly with: you'll hear from them. i've got a good feeling for both of us.

In my room I could hear Popcorn meowing for some company. I snuggled her into my arms and lay back on my bed wondering if I should continue texting Charlie. I knew I shouldn't but I didn't want to break the connection yet. I texted back: i hope so. i still haven't mentioned it to johnny. have you? His response: no…no need to bring it up until we know about the auditions. we should just stay quiet until we have something definite to announce, ok? I typed back: agreed. oh, before i forget, kerry westfall is coming with us to the cabin. i hope it's ok. probably should've asked you first. I waited…and waited…but got no response. The lack of contact left me feeling out of sorts and listless. I might have made him mad mentioning Kerry but I couldn't just spring her on him at the cabin. I was edgy now…I could feel energy coursing through my veins and I had a sudden urge to climb Mt. Rainier. Thankfully it was a little too far away or I just might have done it.

I glanced at my phone and decided I would call my mother. I checked my phone for messages first but if she'd really called my cell phone then something had to have malfunctioned. I had no missed calls or voicemails from her. Just as I started dialing her number another text came through. My heart rate sped up as I glanced at it. It was Johnny: i want you. Whoa. I couldn't help smiling to myself at his directness. I didn't know why I responded the way I did but my ego might have had something to do with it: what do you want with me? I could just imagine his laugh at that response. He answered quickly: i'd rather show you than tell you but here's a hint: my hands and mouth all over you. and that's not all. Oh, wow. That's what I got for asking. Johnny never was one to dance around directness. I thought for a minute before answering. Finally I typed: it's the 'all' part that scares me. He answered back: nothing to be afraid of, em, i promise it'll be perfect. are you on the pill? I felt a knot forming in my stomach. I didn't want to text anymore but I decided I'd rather answer this question in a text message than face to face so I typed back: yes. He responded: good girl. i've gotta work tomorrow but I'll see you after. say hi to popcorn. i still haven't met her yet. i love you. I typed back: night, johnny. you're still incorrigible. And finally from him: yeah, but you love me. I sighed and dialed my mother. She finally answered and we talked a while. All was well in Portland. It sounded like she was possibly keeping something from me…almost like she wanted me to ask probing questions but I didn't take her bait. After a while we hung up and I got ready for bed. Tomorrow would be a busy day. I had several lessons to teach and Popcorn finally had a vet appointment. And then I had to pack for the weekend. I felt anxious about the weekend…excited to see Charlie and nervous about Johnny and his expectations. But I was getting ahead of myself. Everything would be fine—no sense borrowing trouble.

Chapter Twenty-Two

Johnny

"Looks like we're the last ones here," I said as I parked my car behind my brother's Explorer. Charlie's Durango was already parked in front of his brother's Jeep Wrangler. I noticed all the windows of the cabin were open along with the front door. Just as I turned off the engine, Will's bimbo Amanda and my brother's extremely fine babe Mila walked out onto the porch. Amanda was a very attractive girl but she was also a first class bitch, a state of being which cancelled out her hotness. But Mila was a fucking wet dream—all boobs, doe eyes and long, brown hair. I glanced over at Emma and Kerry and saw them both trying not to stare at the two girls, who were wearing extremely tiny bikinis. And even though Emma was by far the hottest girl in the universe and the only one I wanted, certain parts of my body were suddenly begging to differ. I noticed that Emma's gaze had now shifted to me, her eyes narrowed. I gave her a guilty grin and hopped out of the car.

"Hey, Johnny," Amanda purred the words like a horny kitten and I had to fight not to roll my eyes.

"Amanda…how's it going?" I grabbed bags out of the back of the Escape and rounded the front of the car, stopping in front of her. She was blocking my path. "Mind if I get by you? This shit's heavy." She grinned and stepped to the side. When I got to the door I stopped to make sure Emma and Kerry were coming. I should've introduced them but decided I'd let them take care of that themselves. And sure enough, I heard Emma take the lead and make the introductions.

I took the bags of food to the kitchen and went back for my overnight bag. The girls had moved into the living room and were talking about bathing suits or something to do with clothes. I saw Charlie, Scott and Will out on the back deck already drinking beers without me. I dropped my bag on the floor and joined them. "You guys couldn't wait for me? Where's my beer?"

Scott pointed to a cooler at the end of the table. "Help yourself, dude. Where's your other half?"

"Chatting with Amanda and Mila. Emma brought a friend…Kerry Westfall," I said as I grabbed a Corona from the cooler. I glanced over

154 | Kellie Bellamy Tayer

at Charlie to see his reaction at the mention of Kerry. He played it cool, drinking his beer and remaining quiet.

Scott sat up straighter in his chair, frowning. "Kerry Westfall... hmmm. Why does that name sound familiar?" He gave me an evil grin. "Didn't you do her...I mean...date her once or twice a few years ago?"

I frowned. I couldn't believe my fucking brother remembered. And now that he'd brought it up, he could let it slip in front of Emma. Charlie knew I'd had a fling with Kerry but he wouldn't say anything. He was the epitome of discretion. And I was certain Kerry hadn't mentioned anything to Emma because, if she had, I surely would've known by now. I needed to do some preemptive damage control ASAP.

"Seriously, Scott. That's ancient history and Emma doesn't need to know so please... keep your mouth shut about it. Kerry won't say anything." When I'd asked Emma to invite her, it hadn't occurred to me that anyone would remember our very short history. I barely remembered it myself. I guess I'd have to take Kerry aside and make sure she kept it on the down-low.

"Who cares if she knows? You've done most of Westbrook...surely Emma knows that, right?" Scott finished his Budweiser and tossed the empty can into a recycle bin that someone had thought to put in the corner of the deck.

I walked over to Scott and loomed over him. "Shut your fucking mouth, Scott. You're a motherfu..." I cut myself off at the sound of Emma's voice coming from behind me.

"Hey, what's going on out here?" she asked. She was standing on the tracks of the sliding door staring at all of us. "You guys aren't arguing already, are you?"

I went straight over to her and draped an arm around her shoulders. "Arguing? Who's arguing?" I pulled her out onto the deck and the other three girls followed. Mila went straight to my brother and sat down on his lap. When he put his hand around her bare waist and draped it over her thigh I had to find something else to look at. Amanda did the same to Will but he didn't seem to be paying her much attention. He was staring off in the direction of the lake, his eyes glazed over. I wondered if he was already drunk. Emma pulled away from me and she and Kerry went to sit beside Charlie who was still strangely quiet. The dude hadn't even said hello to me.

"Hey, Charlie," said Emma. "You know Kerry, right?"

Kerry's face turned red as Charlie leaned forward in his seat and finally spoke. "Of course. How's it going, Kerry?" His voice was flat and his face impassive, giving nothing away. I had a feeling he was annoyed about something and I suspected I'd hear about it eventually. I was just about to crack a joke when Amanda stood up from Will's lap and walked over to the railing of the deck and draped herself over it. And with very little clothing on, it was quite a sight. As much as I hated the bitch, I couldn't help but admire her assets. Emma caught me staring and spoke in a loud voice.

"We need music and food. Johnny...did you bring in the cupcakes?"

And just like that, whatever weirdness was in the air seemed to dissipate. I went out to the car to get the tray of cupcakes Emma's stepmother had baked and Charlie went inside and put on some music. The sound of the Black Keys filtered outside from an iPod set up in the kitchen. Charlie turned up the volume and more beer bottles were opened along with wine coolers for the girls although I noticed Mila had a bottle of Corona in each hand. I had a feeling beer wouldn't be the only thing she'd be double-fisting before the day was over—damn but Scott was a lucky bastard. I gave my head a shake and turned my attention to Emma. I intended to get her alone as soon as possible...which made me wonder about the sleeping arrangements. I hoped my shithead brother hadn't taken my room but he probably had.

"Anybody wanna go for a swim?" asked Will. "Come on, Amanda. Let's break in that little bathing suit of yours." He shoved the last of a cupcake in his mouth and pulled his t-shirt over his head then stepped onto the path leading down to the water. "Anybody gonna join me?"

"I'm not about to get this bathing suit wet," said Amanda. "And who even knows what's crawling around in that lake."

"Isn't that what bathing suits are for? Swimming?" I asked. God, what a fucking prima donna.

"I'll join you," said Emma. "Kerry, how about you? Wanna change and go for a swim?" Emma got up and headed back inside. Kerry followed. I heard Emma ask Charlie which room they'd be sleeping in.

"You and Kerry can have the one you used before. I'll slum it and let Johnny bunk with me," said Charlie, giving me the eye through the screen door.

When the girls disappeared down the hall I joined Charlie in the kitchen. He was making himself a sandwich and I decided I'd have one, too. "What's up, Chuck? You're awfully quiet today."

Charlie set down the knife he was using to spread mustard on a piece of bread. "What's up? Uh, let me think...how about I told you no fix-ups and yet you bring Kerry? Speaking of which...why haven't you told Emma about your little fling with her? Come to think of it, why hasn't Kerry said something? This is so gonna come back to haunt you, dude."

"It's cool. I'll talk to Kerry and make sure she's not holding onto any residual issues regarding our little fling which happened something like three hundred years ago and lasted...oh...maybe all of five minutes." Jesus Christ, what was with people?

Charlie finished making his sandwich and put it and a handful of potato chips on a plate. As he passed me on his way back out to the deck he stopped and turned to me.

"Hey…Johnny…do you still keep track?"

I cocked my head to the side. "Keep track of what?"

"Your conquests." He didn't wait for an answer which was lucky because the answer I wanted to give him was a punch in the mouth. I watched as he went back out on the deck, settling himself in a lounger with his food and a Coke and proceeded to talk to Scott and Mila.

Now I was slipping into a funk. There were entirely too many people here and I had a feeling this weekend was going to end up sucking big time. But then Emma walked into the kitchen and I felt a million times better just looking at her. She was wearing a two-piece bathing suit with palm trees on it, visible through a long, white and very sheer cover-up. Kerry wore a blue one-piece and seeing her—and her boobs—in it reminded me of why we'd had that fling so long ago. She caught me staring and moved past Emma out to the deck.

"You coming?" Emma asked me.

"I'll walk down to the water with you. I'm not quite ready for the lake yet." I left my sandwich on the counter and followed Emma down to the water. Will was standing waist-deep in the lake while Amanda stood on the shore, hands on her hips, scowling.

"Come on, Amanda. It's nice out here. I won't let any sea creatures get you. Emma's coming in…she's not afraid." Will pushed his sunglasses up on his head and beckoned to Amanda. She responded by flipping him the bird.

"I'm going back inside. There is no way in hell I'm getting into that cesspool."

"Jesus fucking Christ, Amanda. It's a lake…a very clean lake. Don't be such a baby," I said, resisting the urge to shove her in. She flipped me the bird, too, made a face and stalked up to the cabin. I glanced over at Emma and Kerry and shrugged. "What a bitch."

"Alrighty then," said Emma, grinning. "I'm going in." She stripped off her cover-up, slipped out of her flip-flops and waded in. Holy shit but she looked hot in that swim suit. I stared at her breasts pushing up against the V of the top, noticing there were coconut designs right where her nipples were. Holy fuck.

"Hold up, babe," I said. I stepped closer and pulled her to me. I whispered in her ear so Kerry wouldn't hear, "You look amazing. Do you have any idea what's going through my head right now?" I ran my hand down her bare back, stopping at the top of her bathing suit bottom. I pressed her into me and wished the world would disappear except for the two of us.

"I can guess," she smiled. "Behave…I'm going in the water." She lowered her voice. "Kerry doesn't want to go in. She just wants to sunbathe. Why don't you go keep her company for a few minutes—make her feel welcome."

I nodded as she pulled out of my embrace. I noticed that Kerry had dropped a towel on the ground and had plopped down on it. I took the opportunity to handle my potential crisis. I walked over and squatted down beside her.

"Hey, Ker…can we talk a minute?"

She looked up at me, her eyes hidden behind large sunglasses. "You don't have to worry, Johnny. Emma doesn't know and I wasn't planning to tell her. It was a long time ago so no worries."

"OK, thanks. But just to be sure…you're OK, right? This isn't weird for you or anything?"

"Please. If this was weird it would mean I still had feelings for you. Like I said…it was a long time ago. We've all moved on, right?"

I stood up. "Right…thanks. I'm gonna head back up. I left my sandwich somewhere."

Well, that was a load off. Kerry was a nice chick. A nice, hot chick. Oh for fuck's sake, Beaumont, what the hell is wrong with you? Ha. I knew exactly what was wrong with me. I wanted Emma. Bad.

I retrieved my sandwich and returned to the water's edge to watch Emma in the lake…which did absolutely nothing for the current state of my psyche. I realized that if I didn't do something soon I might lose my mind so I decided to drink some more beer. Beer always helped me get myself together. I'd brought another bottle of Corona and I drank it down and felt myself relax. I watched as Emma joined up with Will and they started swimming out to the diving dock. It was pretty far out there and I felt my gut tense up. I wasn't entirely comfortable with her being out that far out even with Will, who may be a little on the drunk side. I sighed in relief when I saw them reach the dock and climb up onto it. They sat side by side, their heads close together, talking. I wondered what in the hell they were talking about. As far as I knew, Will didn't even know Emma. OK, so now I was feeling jealous. Especially when she threw her head back and laughed loudly enough for me to hear her all the way up here on the shore. A shadow fell across me and I looked up to see Amanda standing over me.

"Aren't they just having a sweet time?" she said sourly. "How cute."

"What the fuck is your problem, Amanda?" I asked, wishing she would leave.

"At the moment, your little girlfriend is my problem."

"Emma is no threat to you. You could be out there with Will, you know."

"Oh, I know she's no threat. She looks like she's twelve. I have Barbie dolls bigger than her."

"Go home and play with them then." I looked up at her. "What the fuck does a smart guy like Will see in you anyway?" I glanced at her boobs and her long legs. "Never mind. You don't have to answer."

"Now who's jealous?" she said, casting a scathing look down on me and stalking back up to the cabin. I shook my head in disgust and heard Kerry laugh behind me. I turned to stare at her.

"What's so fucking funny?"

"Meow," she said, giggling.

I looked back out at Emma and Will. They both dove into the water at the same time and began to swim in circles around the dock. It looked like they were racing. Eventually they swam to shore and I met Emma with her towel. I wrapped her in it and held her against me. She was shivering.

"The water is cold but so refreshing," she said, her teeth chattering. "You should have come in with us. It was fun."

"I will next time," I said. We walked back up to the cabin. Charlie was standing in the kitchen eating a cupcake. Emma dried herself off on the deck before coming inside.

"You wouldn't want to make a couple of sandwiches for me and Kerry, would you, while I go clean up?" Emma asked me.

"Coming right up," I said.

I made a couple of turkey sandwiches and left them on the counter. I was keenly aware of Charlie watching my every move. "Where'd everybody go?" I asked him.

"Scott and Mila are in their bedroom and I'm pretty sure Amanda is off somewhere sharpening her fangs or maybe she's in the garage changing the oil in her broom."

"Seriously, dude. You're brother is a great guy—really smart and nice and all, but his taste in women is totally fucked. Can he not see beyond the big tits and hot ass that there is a first class fucking bitch living inside that pretty facade?"

Charlie laughed. "Maybe we should stage an intervention before it's too late and try to save him from a fate worse than death."

"No shit…Amanda makes death look like a fucking vacation in the Caribbean." I could feel Charlie's earlier dark mood lightening. Maybe the weekend wouldn't be so bad after all.

Emma and Kerry returned and after a joint meeting to discuss the evening's menu, Will suggested a hike. Of course, Amanda was having no part of that and immediately disappeared again. Mila and Scott had eventually emerged from their bedroom looking disheveled but were both game for a hike. Emma walked past Charlie and bumped him with an elbow.

"You coming, Charlie?" she asked.

"I think I'll pass. I'll stay here and keep Amanda company." He turned away so no one but me could see him roll his eyes and cross himself. I had to bite my tongue to keep from losing it. I walked over to the cupboard where spices were kept and pulled out a bottle of garlic powder. I set it down on the counter and grinned at Charlie.

"Just in case," I said under my breath. "Maybe there's a wooden stake in the garage. Dude, I'm just trying to help." He shook his head and smiled.

We all put on shoes and headed down the path. And for the next three hours we walked along the lake path and through the woods. Emma, Kerry and Mila seemed to be bonding. Mila and Scott hadn't been together long but she seemed like a cool enough chick—a lot better than fucking Amanda, that was for sure. I started feeling sorry for Will for being stuck with Amanda. I couldn't help but notice how much happier and more relaxed he seemed when she was out of sight. I also noticed that he kept making excuses to talk to Emma and I was beginning to get annoyed. We returned to the cabin to find Amanda in a funk on the deck and Charlie in hiding. We all ignored her and, after cleaning up, we regrouped in the kitchen. Charlie finally turned up and took over the lighting of the grill. I walked over to him and pulled the neck of his t-shirt away and examined his neck.

"Good. She didn't get her fangs in you...lucky bastard." He pushed my hand away and struck a match, lighting the crumpled newspaper inside the grill.

Mila made a salad while Emma peeled potatoes and Kerry fried them. Amanda sat on her perch at the end of the island counter and did something with her nails. We barbecued burgers and hot dogs and sat out on the back deck eating until the sun went down, casting an orange sunset over the water which got Emma excited, as did the tiny sliver of moon that appeared over the north side of Lake Crescent.

"Look, Charlie, it's a waxing crescent," she said. Charlie looked up at the moon then glanced at Emma. Some look passed between them like they knew something no one else did and I felt paranoia creeping up on me.

"Anybody wanna jam?" asked Will. "Charlie and I brought our guitars."

Emma jumped up. "I did, too. I'll get it."

We all assembled on the deck and played music until after midnight. Even Amanda sat and listened and didn't cause too much trouble.

But I could tell she was seething with jealousy at Emma's immense talent. Eventually we had to quit when Mila almost face-planted into Scott's lap. Everyone was sleepy and went their separate ways. Kerry said good night and went to bed and I took Emma by the hand.

"Come with me for a sec out to the front porch so I can tell you good night properly," I said. She set her guitar inside the living room and followed me out onto the porch. I took her in my arms and held her tightly. I tilted her face up and kissed her…finally. She tasted sweet like honey.

"We haven't been alone and I've been waiting to kiss you all day. You know we could sleep under the stars down by the lake…just me and you." I ran my hands through her hair and pressed her body against mine so she could feel how much I wanted her. "What do you say?"

She sighed into my chest. "Johnny…no…I'm sleeping in my bed. You're sleeping with Charlie, remember?"

"Charlie doesn't do it for me…but you…oh…you do it for me big time," I whispered, kissing her neck.

"I'm tired," she said against my chest. "I'll see you in the morning, OK?"

I wanted to argue but I held back my protest. "Tomorrow then, alright? Me and you…alone."

She answered me with a kiss and went inside. I brushed my teeth and went to Charlie's room and crawled into the twin bed under the window. He wasn't there so I waited up to talk to him. My eyes grew heavy waiting and eventually I fell asleep.

The next morning when I woke up I noticed that Charlie was still not in his bed. Either that or he'd come and gone while I was sleeping. It wasn't even messed up as if he hadn't slept in it. The house was quiet as I went to the bathroom to take care of business. When I finished I stopped outside Emma's door. It was ajar and I pushed it just enough to peer inside. It was empty. I shuffled out to the kitchen where Scott and Mila were having toast and juice.

"What's up, guys?" I asked as I walked over to the sliding doors to look out on the deck and the lake beyond.

"Amanda and Will went into town. Apparently her royal highness was having a mental breakdown about sunscreen or mosquitoes or something to do with protecting her skin and she wasn't letting up until he took her to the general store. Damn, but I'd like to be a fly on the wall when she realizes there's no Sak's Fifth Avenue in Crescent Springs," said Scott.

I nodded. "No shit. Any chance he'll leave her ass there and come back alone?" I asked in all seriousness.

Mila giggled. "You guys are funny. Amanda's not all bad."

Scott and I rolled our eyes and ignored her. "Where's everybody else?" I asked.

"Kerry's in the shower and Emma and Charlie went for a walk. They've been gone a while," said Scott.

I poured myself a glass of orange juice and went out on the back deck. So Charlie and Emma had gone for a walk...together. I convinced myself that was a good thing. Maybe she could get a feel on how Charlie was doing and see if there was any chance he'd make a move on Kerry tonight. Once we got the fire going and everybody settled in for the fireworks over the lake, maybe he'd realize that he missed having a girl in his life. Especially if we all got drunk. Yes, that sounded like a plan. Just as I finished the last of my juice Charlie and Emma emerged from the trail that bordered the lake. They were walking close together, looking awfully serious. I put my glass down and went out to meet them.

"There's my girl," I said, swooping in and grabbing Emma around the waist. "Where'd you guys go?"

"Just part way around the lake," said Emma. "But the bugs are kinda bad. I think I swallowed a mouthful of gnats or something."

"Thanks for the heads-up. I was gonna kiss you good morning, but maybe I'll wait till you brush your teeth or eat something." She grinned at me and I kissed her anyway. "Where were you all night, Charles? Your bed looked unslept-in this morning."

"I was there...briefly...you just didn't see me. But you make a lot of noise in your sleep so I moved out to the couch. No offense, but I see separate bedrooms in your future when you finally get married some day."

"Ha, ha. Emma won't mind. I'll get her some earplugs." I looked at Emma, gauging her reaction to my comment. She gave me a look I couldn't decipher. I knew my inference probably rattled her but she was not going to show it. A weird look passed between her and Charlie though and it was enough to get under my skin. I swear there were some weird vibes floating around this place.

Back at the house the girls made breakfast--pancakes and sausage. Afterward, Will got the boat out and we took turns tooling around the lake. At first, Amanda refused to go out on the lake, but Will promised her a weekend in Seattle if she'd go with him so she took him up on it. We all shook our heads in disgust that it took bribery to get her to do something fun—not that she found it fun. We could hear her complaining all the way up on the shore. Mila and Scott went out for a while and then, in a shocking move, Charlie and Kerry went out for a ride together.

I nearly fell over I was so excited at the thought of them getting together. For some reason, it was becoming very important to me that my best friend have a little romantic action in his life. I wanted Charlie to feel what I was feeling. Emma and I finally took a spin around the lake and when we returned we ate lunch. I noticed that Kerry and Charlie were talking and again, I felt hopeful that maybe something was brewing there.

All day long I was thinking about the fireworks and being alone with Emma. She'd seemed distant today but I was looking way too forward to tonight to let anything get me down. After we'd cooked out steaks and chicken on the grill, Will and Scott went to the fire pit down by the lake and started the fire. Charlie and I dragged coolers filled with beer and other libations we'd all sneaked from our parents' liquor cabinets and set up a makeshift bar near the fire. Emma brought out the fixings for s'mores and spread it all out on a towel and began to assemble them. And when Will and Amanda had a disagreement about something stupid and left us alone, Scott cleared his throat and got our attention.

"OK, I have an idea. Let's play a drinking game once it gets dark and we're watching the fireworks. It's called the Amanda Drinking Game. Every time she bitches about something, we drink a shot. We won't tell Will...no sense making him mad, although I have a feeling he'd probably prefer to just get drunk in advance so as not to have to listen to her mouth. But we'll play until she either goes back to the house or one of us keels over."

"You've got to be kidding me," said Charlie. "As intriguing as that sounds, it's also unhealthy. You know we'll all be plastered within ten minutes. I'd like to keep my liver in working order, if you don't mind."

"Then just do beer shots. But I'm doing vodka shots. How about you, Johnny?" Scott asked.

"OK, I'm in, but I don't necessarily want to get drunk tonight."

"Count me in," said Mila.

"I'll do whiskey shots," said Kerry.

Emma glanced at her and frowned. "You drink whiskey?" she asked.

"Sometimes," said Kerry. "You gonna play, Emma?"

I answered for her. "No, I'm rationing Emma's alcohol intake." I looked over at her and her frown deepened.

"I can play if I want." She was sitting on a log and now she crossed her arms over her chest and glared at me. I heard a child-like, petulant tone in her voice.

"You don't even like alcohol," I reminded her.

"Maybe I'm planning to change that." I raised my eyebrow at her and shook my head. I noticed Charlie suddenly looking morose and wondered what was up with him.

Will and Amanda joined us then and we all settled around the fire on blankets. Will brought his iPod and turned on some classic rock, while Scott surreptitiously passed around shot glasses. It had gotten dark and fireflies were flashing in the trees. A crescent moon hung over the lake. We made s'mores and cracked open beers. I leaned back and pulled Emma off the log she'd been sitting on, settling her into my lap and putting my arms around her. "You were too far away," I whispered in her ear.

Kerry and Mila were seated on adjoining blankets talking while Charlie poked a stick in the fire and Scott sat rigidly on a blanket holding an open bottle of vodka in one hand and a shot glass in the other with a Corona wedged between his thighs. I glanced over Emma's head and saw him frown and cock his head in Amanda's direction. She was being quiet and apparently not living up to Scott's expectations in the bitchiness department. Our game was gonna go bust if Amanda didn't get mad about something. I decided to kick-start the game.

"Hey, Amanda…care for a s'more? I'd be happy to make you one," I asked as sweetly as possible. Scott grinned and nodded at me. Charlie rolled his eyes. Even the girls looked excited.

"No thanks. I don't do s'more's. Chocolate gives me acne."

"I'll drink to that," Scott practically screeched. He poured a shot of Stoli and downed it. He wiped his mouth on the back of his hand and grinned from ear to ear. Kerry downed a whiskey shot she'd already poured from a nearby bottle.

"Hit me up, Scott," said Emma, passing him her shot glass. When Scott filled it and passed it back, I intercepted it and drank it before she had a chance to snatch it back.

"Johnny! That was mine!" She shoved me and jumped up. She took a beer from the cooler and popped the top like a pro and began to chug it. When she came up for air, her face contorted as if she'd sucked a lemon.

"Hey, now. Slow it down, girl. You're not used to drinking." I held my arm out to her and she sat down beside me again. She took another slug and shuddered.

Amanda burst out laughing. "Oh, this is going to be a fun night. I can tell. Little doll's gonna get sloppy drunk tonight!"

"Drink up," said Scott. He tossed back his vodka shot and followed it with a pull on his Corona.

"Watch it, Amanda." I could deal with her bitchiness for the sake of the game but not if it came at Emma's expense. I noticed Charlie wasn't drinking and Kerry and Mila were more interested in making s'mores at the moment. Will looked like a zombie staring off into space again. There was definitely something up with him.

Suddenly a cracking sound followed by a burst of light over the lake turned our attention away from Amanda…for about two seconds until she complained about how loud the fireworks were. Everyone drank their shots except Charlie and me. Emma tipped her head back and finished the beer.

"Whew! I did it. But beer tastes gross," she said.

I took the empty bottle out of her hand and pulled her back against my chest. "How about you relax and watch the fireworks. I'll make you a s'more."

"I don't want a s'more. I'd rather try some of Scott's vodka," she said. I stared at Emma in surprise. It was like she'd been taken over by aliens. This was so not like her.

I tightened my arms around her and tilted her chin so I could look into her eyes. "What's up, Em? You don't drink. Why tonight? Just have a Coke or something." I leaned down and kissed her lips. She was beginning to smell like a distillery. She tasted like one, too.

She surprised me by turning completely around in my arms and kissing me hard on the mouth. It was exactly what I'd wanted from her all day…just not in front of a crowd. But I kissed her back, tasting her tongue and lips and feeling myself getting carried away. Fuck it…if alcohol made her feel this way I guessed I could let her drink a little more. When she pulled away and gave me a sweet smile I didn't stop her when she had Scott pour too much vodka into a red plastic cup.

"This little show just keeps getting better and better," said Amanda. She'd been sitting on Will's lap but he suddenly brought his legs up and dumped her onto the ground. "Hey! Why'd you do that? My shorts are all dirty now! Dammit!" She jumped up and began to dust off her ass while Kerry, Mila, Scott and Emma all downed their drinks. I watched in horror as Emma drank way too much vodka way too fast. She tossed the empty cup and swayed into my arms.

"And that's it for drinking for you, Emma. Now we're gonna relax and watch the fireworks." I held her in a vise grip and she went slack against me and looked up at the sky.

"Look, Shonny…itsh sho pretty," she said, her words slurring.

"Look, the doll is drunk," said Amanda. "Someone's getting lucky tonight."

"That's it." Will jumped up and grabbed Amanda by the arm. "You and I are going for a walk." He dragged her back toward the cabin. We heard her cursing and protesting with every step.

"Thank god," said Kerry. "She is definitely weird." She reached over and tapped my arm. "Is Emma OK?"

"She's fine but she can't have anymore to drink. I'm cutting her off." I kissed the top of Emma's head and she sighed. We watched the fireworks in silence for a few minutes. I saw Charlie get up and start gathering the empty bottles. After shoving them all into a garbage bag he disappeared in the direction of the cabin. He'd been quiet throughout the drinking game and Amanda debacle.

"Hey, Kerry? Why don't you check on Charlie. He's acting strange. Maybe you could feel him out...see what's wrong," I said.

"I don't know what you think I can do but, OK," she said. She got up and grabbed her blanket and left.

Emma squirmed in my arms. "Hey, Shohnny...you wanna go for a shwim?" She started to get up but didn't get far before falling back into my lap.

"Absolutely not. You've had too much to drink and you drank it way too fast. You're not gonna feel so good in the morning, babe." No way in hell was I letting her near the water tonight.

Scott and Mila were in the middle of a heavy make-out session that looked like it needed to be moved to a more private location. "Why don't you two get a room already?" I suggested.

Scott stood and pulled Mila up with him. "That, dear brother...is a very good idea. Good luck with...," he shook his head and pointed to Emma. "She's gonna regret this tomorrow." He gave me a salute and they walked off, leaving me and Emma alone.

I stood and helped Emma to her feet. She was unsteady but able to stand without falling over. She reached down and grabbed the blanket and began to walk toward the water, swaying back and forth, dragging the blanket along behind her. "Come on, Shohnny. Letsh go for a shwim."

I followed her down to the shore and grabbed the blanket from her, spreading it out. I turned back just in time to see her strip her t-shirt over her head and step out of her shorts. She stood in front of me in her bra and tiny little underwear and it took everything I had not to lose my shit. She wobbled on bare feet toward the water's edge and I ran after her just as she fell over onto the sand.

"Em...what are you doing?" I grabbed her t-shirt and shorts and tossed them up onto the blanket. I helped her up and moved her over to the blanket, laying her down on it. I stretched out next to her. "Emma... babe. This is why I don't like you drinking. You're a lightweight...you know that."

"Shorry. I just wanted to cut loosh tonight. I told you I'm not ash perfect ash you think I am," she slurred. Her eyes were half-closed and she was shivering, goose bumps covering her body. I glanced down at her stomach, ran my hands up and down her arm, feeling the tiny bumps of cold flesh. She put her arms around my neck and pulled me down and

I kissed her until I thought I would explode from wanting her so much.

"Come on, Shonny. Ishn't thish what you wanted?" She ran her tongue around my lips and I groaned in sweet agony. I slid my hand under her bra and kissed the swell of her breast. Her nipples were hard and I wanted them in my mouth so badly I could already taste them. I wanted to devour all of her. I ran my hand down her stomach to the top of her underwear slipping my hand inside. I caught myself before I went too far even as she squirmed against me. But, oh, my god, it would be so easy...

She pulled me down on top of her showing surprising strength for someone so small and drunk. She ran her hand down my chest and moved toward my crotch and as soon as I felt the pressure of her hand there I knew I was at a crossroads—the proverbial fork in the road. It would be so easy to take her right now, right here. But would she even remember it in the morning?

"Come on, Shonny, What are you waiting for?" she whispered against my neck, her fingers fumbling at the button of my cargo shorts.

"Oh, god, Em," I moaned against her mouth. "I want you so badly... but..." I leaned back and looked into her eyes. They were glazed over. I wasn't convinced she even knew who I was at the moment.

"I'm cold," she murmured, her teeth beginning to chatter. I bent down over her, covering her with my body for warmth. She ran her hands under my shirt and I seriously knew I had to stop this now because I was on the verge of ignoring the conscience I'd only just developed since I'd met Emma. I kissed her again, not wanting to stop but knowing I was about to cross a line if I didn't get myself under control.

"We need to get you back to the house, babe. Come on, let me help you get dressed." I sat up and began to put her t-shirt and shorts back on her.

"I thought thish was what you wanted," she said, her face puckering up. Two fat tears rolled down her cheeks and now I felt like a fucking asshole. I adjusted her clothing and hugged her against me...tried to smooth away the gooseflesh.

"It is, babe, but I want your first time to be perfect and this...this is not perfect. You're drunk and cold and not completely coherent. I love you too much to let it happen this way." I wiped away her tears and stood, pulling her up with me. I shook the sand out of the blanket, then wrapped her in it and lifted her into my arms. I carried her practically weightless body up to the cabin and took her to her room. I noticed Kerry wasn't in the room. "Do you need to go to the bathroom before you sleep?"

"Hmm, hmm," she nodded. I helped her to the bathroom and waited in the hall for her to finish. Back in her room, I tucked her in, pulling the blanket up to her chin. I set a box of tissue and a small trash can next to her bed, just in case. She was already breathing heavily as I backed out of the room, bumping into Kerry in the hallway.

"Hey…is Emma OK?" she asked.

"She's asleep but she's gonna feel like shit tomorrow. If she pukes during the night, come get me, OK?"

"I will. Night."

I went down the hall to the kitchen and grabbed a beer from the fridge. I sat at the counter and nursed it, letting my emotions and my body cool down. I was still on fire for Emma and figured it would take more than a cold Corona to put the fire out but I would deal with it. My body literally ached from wanting her.

"How is she?" Charlie sat down next to me with a glass of water.

"Passed out in her bed." I shook my head back and forth. "I don't know what got into her tonight."

"Maybe it was the Amanda Effect. God knows it helps to be drunk when in her company."

I chuckled and took another pull on my Corona. "For a while there I felt more like Emma's fucking father than her boyfriend. I can't believe she got drunk. She even took off her clothes and tried to go into the lake."

Charlie set his water glass down rather hard on the counter and pushed it aside. I glanced over at him and saw that he'd closed his eyes. He was working his jaw back and forth as if trying to work out tension from it. Finally he turned to me.

"You…didn't…take advantage of... the circumstances…did you?"

"Fuck no. I'm not that big of an asshole. Sure, I was tempted…it would've been easy…but no, I would never do that to her. I told you I love her. She's the one, and I would never do anything to fuck that up—not intentionally anyway." I finished my beer and stood up. "I'll sleep on the couch tonight. I want to be able to hear Emma if she gets sick in the night. You can sleep in silence in the bedroom. Night, Chuck."

He didn't answer as I moved into the living room. I lay down on the sofa with a throw pillow and an afghan and tried to make my body relax and my mind settle down. It wasn't the easiest thing to do. When I closed my eyes I saw Emma's half-naked body. Damn it…this wasn't how I'd expected to spend this night.

Chapter Twenty-Three

Charlie

We'd gone for a walk that morning at the cabin and talked about music. The lake was quiet and still and Emma had been enthralled by it. We never mentioned the kiss or addressed our attraction to each other. We'd talked about career possibilities and Johnny. I'd wanted to touch her…to hold her hand…to run my fingers through her hair…a million forbidden thoughts had run through my head, but we both had acted as if nothing was amiss. And when we returned to the cabin, Johnny was there waiting for her. I'd watched him hold her and kiss her and it hurt… like a constant stabbing sensation in my chest. I'd felt my depression rippling like a flag caught in a sudden gust of wind. Drinking had helped for a while until the effects of the alcohol had worn off and then I felt worse. I didn't like this roller coaster feeling and it occurred to me that maybe I should listen to my doctor and see someone after all—just to talk…maybe just once.

"Ready when you are, Charlie. Give me the sign," said Luke. His voice bounced off the wall of the silent studio. I worked out the kinks in my shoulders and settled onto the stool, my guitar in the ready position. I adjusted my headphones, strummed a few chords and took a breath, then nodded once to Luke. He nodded back, counting down from three on his fingers and I began. I'd practiced all night and now adrenaline and the music swept me along as I played "She's Mine." I paid no attention to Luke in the control room as I sang each verse. When I finished, I sat still and waited for Luke's guidance.

"I don't want to change anything yet, Charlie. That sounded perfect. Play your other song now." Luke counted me down again and I played my other song, "Never Again." I'd written it when I was up in Seattle recovering. Luke had me play it three times before we were both satisfied with the result.

"Give me a few minutes and then let's see what we think," said Luke as he listened to my music in his headset. I sat on the leather couch and tried to relax…tried to let the tension in my limbs melt away. The stiffness I'd been experiencing in my leg eased and I flexed my toes inside my shoes. I felt good about what I'd done in the studio and I was anxious to hear what Luke would do with my songs. He beckoned me over to the boards.

"Check this out," he said as he pushed some buttons on the panel. I listened with my eyes closed as my voice and my guitar filled the small studio with sound. And I was pleased. Luke had added a drumbeat and a bass rhythm and I loved the sound of it. When both songs ended he clapped me on the shoulder. "Well done. This is special, Charlie. You've got something here. Keep writing…and don't stop."

We talked a few minutes more and then I headed out to my car. I felt buoyant but also fearful. I'd been thinking about my chances of getting the Jenkins audition and Emma and wondering what the future held. A few months ago I'd've bet money that I had no future at all, but now…anything seemed possible—maybe not with Emma, but with my music at least.

Still wanna listen to my song? Six little words with so much power. Just seeing her name on my phone was enough to disturb my equilibrium. I was sitting in my room, staring at a sheet of blank paper, contemplating lyrics to a new song that was trying to write itself in my head when she texted me. I typed back: of course…can't wait. A few seconds later, she responded: johnny's at work and i'm home alone. you wanna come over? I closed my eyes for a second before I answered. If I said yes my roller coaster could come off the tracks and crash. I wondered how many people died on roller coasters every year. I texted back: give me 10 minutes? And she answered: see you then.

"You're really stupid, Channing." I spoke to my reflection. "Really Class A stupid." I changed my shirt, put on some cologne and walked downstairs. My mother was making more pies and the smell of baking apples made me feel better.

"I'm gonna run an errand," I said as I passed through the kitchen. She smiled and waved me out the door. I walked slowly to Emma's house, taking the longer route through the back of the neighborhood. We'd been home a week now and I hadn't seen Emma since the holiday weekend. We hadn't even bumped into each other at the music store. Even Johnny had been keeping a low profile. He'd mentioned some huge landscaping project he had to help his father with at the mayor's house and I guessed that had been taking up most of his time lately. I turned up Emma's street and just the sight of her house was enough to make me feel off balance. I wanted to walk slower but figured I'd end up looking like a lost zombie. I wanted nothing more than to see her, but I feared it might not end well...ha...I knew it wouldn't. But I couldn't pass up a chance to see her—alone—no matter how painful it might prove to be. I stepped up onto her front porch and she opened the door, welcoming me in.

"Hey, Charlie. Thanks for coming," she said. "I wasn't convinced you would."

I shrugged. "I told you I'd return the favor. I want to hear your song. Oh, and I got an email back from Jenkins about auditions. Did you know we have to send in a tape or a video of our music? Apparently they need to evaluate us before they commit to giving us an in-person audition. I'd actually already cut a couple of tracks on a CD at the store with Luke's help before I knew that. He could help you, too, if you want. He has that recording studio in the back. You've probably seen it."

I followed her up the stairs—apparently we were going to her room. I could hear Popcorn meowing down the hall. "Yeah, I got the same email. That's why I texted you. I want to see if you think my song is good enough to record cuz if it's not, I'll have to sing a cover and I'd really hate to do that."

I looked around Emma's room...noticed the purple walls and frilly white curtains. She had a lot of books and I noticed that the guitar lying across her bed was not the same one she'd had at the cabin. "Nice Gibson," I said. "That had to cost a fortune." I walked over and ran my hand along its shiny surface. Popcorn jumped up on the bed and nuzzled her pink, cold nose against my wrist. I picked her up and held her up to my face. "She's put on weight."

Emma smiled and sat down in the chair by her desk. "Yeah...she eats a lot. I think she remembers you. You hear her purring?"

I sat down on the end of Emma's bed and put Popcorn beside me. I glanced at Emma...she seemed different...sort of sad. "You OK?" I asked.

"Sure...hand me the guitar?" She held her hands out and I placed the Gibson in her arms. I noticed her hands were shaking. When she placed it across her lap she almost disappeared behind it. She strummed the strings and looked up at me. "It's called 'Crescent Moon.' Ready to listen?"

"Can't wait." And I really couldn't. I listened as she played the opening notes, noticing everything about her...the way her hair was pulled all the way over to the side out of the way of her right arm...the way she tilted her head down to the left...the sure and confident way she played as if she were master of her instrument...which I was pretty sure she was. She looked beautiful as she played and her voice was smooth and pure as she sang. She had perfect pitch. I wanted to push her expensive guitar off her lap and pull her onto mine and kiss her until she begged me to stop. I listened to her lyrics:

In the night sky
all the way high,
there's room just for two
on my crescent moon

The view from up here
is so crystal clear
and the earth goes away
but you and I stay

There's no right or wrong.
There's only this song
to tell you,
to tell you,
to tell you,
I want you

The water below,
The ebb and the flow,
The pull of the moon,
Let's make it soon.

No time to wait.
Let's open the gate.
There's nothing to lose.
You don't have to choose.

There's no right or wrong.
There's only this song
to tell you,
to tell you,
to tell you,
I need you.

It's waxing, it's waning.
It never stops raining
but we're high and dry
in our private sky.

There's always a risk
in that first kiss
so baby let's fly
and never ask why

There's no right or wrong.
There's only this song
to tell you,
to tell you,
to tell you,
I love you

When she finished we were both quiet. She looked up at me and I saw tears in her eyes. Just as she'd heard the words of my song and understood the message, I heard and understood the meaning of her song. At first I didn't move as I stared at her, a war waging in my head...a war I had no chance of winning. So I surrendered, and in my moment of weakness, I made a terrible, beautiful mistake. I got up from the bed and walked over to Emma...removed the guitar from her hands and leaned it gently against the bookshelf beside her desk. Neither of us spoke as I reached down to her, took her hands and pulled her up into my arms, enveloping her in my embrace. She tilted her face up to mine and I leaned down and kissed her. She was so warm and responsive, her mouth so delicious. I thought of John Mayer's song, "Your Body is a Wonderland" and the line about candy lips and a bubblegum tongue and it made so much sense—that's exactly what Emma tasted like. She wrapped her arms around me and molded herself into me and any control I might have had began to slip away.

Somehow we ended up on her bed, nestled into the pillows. She lay on her back and I leaned over her, kissing her, tasting her lips, her tongue, her neck. Every part of my body was alive and awake and hers was, too. She moaned against my mouth and the words she whispered against my lips nearly caused me to spontaneously combust.

"I want you, Charlie," she said softly. I looked into her emerald eyes, the pupils huge and dark with desire and I groaned against her, consumed with a burning need. Her hands began to roam...down my arm and up again. She touched my neck and ran her hand down the front of my shirt. When her fingers grazed the skin above my belt line I had to fight not to go crazy. My war was back on and though I didn't outwardly show it, I was in a full-on internal battle for my self-control. She took my hand and pressed it against her chest and I threw down my invisible white flag as I felt her breasts through the thin material of her t-shirt. I slipped my hand under her shirt, under her bra and I knew I was done for. She was so soft and so damned perfect. I wanted to taste every inch of her. She moaned and moved against my hand, her lips pressing into my neck. I was out of my mind at this point, not caring about childhood codes of honor or betraying best friends. All I cared about in this moment was Emma, touching her, tasting her, taking from her what she had been unable or unwilling to give Johnny or anyone else up to now…taking the gift she was offering me…the gift of her body…the gift of her.

I pressed my lips against her ear. "Are you sure, Em?" My hand rested against the waistband of her shorts, my fingertips just under the button.

She turned her face so her mouth caught the corner of mine. I felt her tongue tease the edge of my lips and I groaned in sweet agony—the girl was killing me. "I've never been more sure of anything," she whispered.

"I want you, too…you have no idea how much…or maybe you do," I chuckled as she pushed the palm of her hand against the evidence of my desire. She reached up for my belt buckle and started to unbuckle it as I tugged at the button of her shorts. I kind of felt bad for her because I knew my self-control was non-existent and her first time would be over faster than I wanted it to be. And I couldn't let myself think about getting another chance to show her that it could be…would be better…the next time. I sighed as I felt her soft skin under my hand…soft as velvet.

"Anybody home? Emma? You here?"

Emma jumped up so fast that Popcorn, who'd been sitting on the floor beside the bed, went vertical as if she'd been shot out of a cannon.

"Ohmygod…Johnny!" Emma gasped. She rolled off the bed and we both stood and quickly adjusted our clothing. She smoothed the blankets, restacked her pillows and ran a hand through her hair. "Sit on the couch and act normal."

"You want me to hide in the closet?" I whispered. I'd walked here so it wasn't like my car was going to give me away.

She shook her head and pointed to the loveseat. I sat down and she handed me her guitar. I placed it across my lap and ran a hand through my own hair, hoping it wasn't sticking up all over. She walked over to her bedroom door and stepped out into the hall. "Hey, Johnny. I'm up here. Charlie's here, too."

Johnny entered her room, a puzzled look on his face. "Chuck? What're you doing here?" He glanced down at the guitar and smiled. "Don't tell me…let me guess. You guys are gonna make a video of yourselves playing and singing and put it on YouTube, aren't you? Trying to get famous? Maybe get a record deal and make some college dough?" He pulled Emma into his arms and kissed her on the mouth. I felt the pain of it like a fist to the gut.

Emma forced a laugh. "Oh, man...you caught us. But, no...actually I called Charlie to see if he could help me tune my guitar. I was having trouble getting the notes to sound right. I probably need new strings or something."

I strummed a chord, purposely making it sound bad. "Yeah...I think maybe it's time for a re-string. I'll show you the ones I buy for my guitar next time I see you at the store." I was amazed at how normal I sounded. "I probably should go. I've got a lesson soon." I stood up and put the guitar down on the bed. I suddenly noticed Johnny's dirty clothes...and his smell.

"You reek, man," I said, moving toward the door.

Johnny laughed. "I know. The fucking mayor's wife is driving me insane. We've been there the whole fucking day planting flowers and shrubs and shit. I haven't been home to shower yet."

Johnny's language in front of Emma was annoying me. "Well, while you're washing your body, wash your mouth out with soap while you're at it. You shouldn't use that kind of language in front of Emma."

Johnny raised an eyebrow. "Oh, my god, Charles. I had no idea you'd gone into the priesthood. You don't want to date Kerry and now you find cursing offensive. Wow. Please promise me you aren't going to molest little altar boys, too."

Emma cleared her throat and picked up Popcorn who was now sniffing around Johnny's feet. "Thank you, Charlie, for helping me. I'll check on those strings when I come in tomorrow for lessons."

I glanced from her to Johnny and back again. I didn't bother responding to his snide comment as I nodded and said good-bye. I hated leaving like this, but Johnny was pissing me off. As I made my way down the stairs I heard Emma lay into him. I headed for home...taking the shorter way...and walking a lot faster than I had earlier. Once again I was acutely aware of how wrong Johnny and Emma were together. He wasn't good enough for her. I went up to my room and got ready to go to the store for my evening lesson. And I couldn't help but wonder if maybe I wasn't good enough either.

Chapter Twenty-Four

Emma

"You can be so horrible, Johnny. That was mean what you said to Charlie." I pulled away from him and moved toward the door. I wanted to get us both downstairs and out of the intimacy of my bedroom. He grabbed my arm as I was about to cross the threshold, stopping me up short.

"Hey...come on. I was only kidding but, seriously, he's been on such a fu...fricking...high horse since he came home. It's ridiculous."

"Well, he's right. You do swear a lot. And not that I'm opposed to cursing...I do it sometimes, too. But you...you say fuck like you say hello or pizza. It's disrespectful." I'd always overlooked Johnny's language before, but now that Charlie had commented on it, I realized that it had bothered me and I'd allowed myself to grow used to it.

"I had no idea it was disrespectful to use the words hello and pizza. I'll make a note of that." He went to put his arms around me but I put my hands on his chest, stopping him.

"Ha, ha...very funny. You know what I mean. And, please don't touch me. You're sweaty and you really do stink." I headed for the stairs and he followed me down to the kitchen.

Johnny was quiet. He stood beside the refrigerator staring at me. Finally he said, "I didn't realize I was hurting your feelings. You know me, Em...I say whatever I think. I don't have a filter on my tongue. No one's cared before how I express myself...well, except for my mother, but she doesn't count. But if it'll make you happy, I'll watch my mouth." He moved toward me and I turned away, opening a cupboard and getting out a glass.

"I'd appreciate that...thanks. You want something to drink?"

"I should go home...take a shower...make myself smell good. And maybe when I come back later, I'll get a warmer reception."

I felt guilt stabbing at my conscience. "Actually, I have some stuff to do tonight. I've got lessons to prepare for tomorrow and I'm supposed to see Claire later." And now I could add lying to my guilty conscience.

"I've hardly seen you since we got back from the lake, between your lessons and my work. And now you're seeing Claire? But, hey, at least Charlie got to spend some quality time with my girl today. Glad someone did. I'll see you later, Em. Tell Claire I said hi."

He was hurt. I could see it on his face and hear it in his voice. He turned and walked to the front door…slowly. I knew he wanted me to come after him and I almost did, but I forced myself to stand firm, holding onto the counter to keep from running after him. I felt badly about hurting him but I needed to be alone. Charlie was still so present in my mind that I wanted nothing more than to go to my room and cuddle Popcorn and relive what had happened between us. I heard the door slam and I slumped against the counter and let out a pent-up breath. Inside, I was swirling with emotions that I'd had to contain while Johnny was here—emotions that had me reeling. I poured myself a glass of iced tea and went back to my room. I sat down on my bed and Popcorn immediately joined me, crawling on my lap, meowing and purring with not a care in the world. How I wished I were a kitten.

I thought about Charlie. I touched my lips, and with my eyes closed, I could almost feel his kiss as if it were happening right this second. My body actually shook with a power surge just thinking about what had almost happened between us. I wrapped my arms around myself, imagining Charlie here with me…holding me…touching me. I was going crazy…aching for him. I glanced down at my phone and considered texting him. I needed to restore some kind of connection between us so I could relax. Because at the moment, I felt like a bomb with its pin removed. I was going to explode any minute if I didn't talk to Charlie. I picked up the phone and clicked on his name and typed: hey… johnny's gone. he's not happy with me right now but he'll get over it. you never did say what you thought of "crescent moon."

A few minutes passed during which time I agonized that everything I felt for him was only one-sided. I imagined that Charlie was just like Johnny and he would say or do anything for sex. I tricked myself into believing that all boys were exactly alike and they only wanted one thing from a girl. I was certain Charlie was just using me. Yep…he was Johnny with darker hair and blue eyes. And then my phone beeped and when I read his words I knew I was wrong to think those things about Charlie, who could never be like Johnny: it was beautiful just like its composer and lyricist. let's record it at the store tomorrow for your audition tape. you'll need one more song for the tape—they require two. i'm sorry i caused a problem for you with johnny—it wasn't my intent. and I want you to know that i treasure you. sorry if that sounds corny…i've been told there's a 40-year old man trapped inside my 17-year old bod,. but it's true…i do.

I fell back onto my pillows nearly crushing Popcorn who meowed loudly and skittered away. I clutched the phone to my chest and squeezed my eyes shut against the tears that threatened to fall. His words were beautiful...he was beautiful. My fingers trembled as I texted back: thank you. what a beautiful thing to say. and for the record, i also treasure you.

"Emma? You home?" Nanette tapped on my door and pushed it open. I sat up and swiped quickly at my face, hoping she wouldn't notice my emotional state.

"Yep. What's up?" I tried to make my voice sound as normal as possible.

"Could you help me in the kitchen? I just got groceries and some of the bags are heavy. The doctor said not to do any heavy-lifting. I bought bottled water and jugs of juice and milk. Could you give me a hand getting the bags in from the car?"

"Sure." I followed her downstairs and brought the groceries in while she sat at the table, eating Chips Ahoy like popcorn.

"Would you mind putting the groceries away since you're down here? I read on the Internet that pregnant women aren't supposed to lift their arms up overhead because it could cause the umbilical cord to get wrapped around the baby's neck."

I closed my eyes in a slow blink before responding. "At this stage of the pregnancy, does the baby even have a neck?" I asked, not even kidding. I began to empty the bags of canned goods and produce.

Nanette looked at me like I had three heads. "Of course. It has everything...more or less. I'm going for my first ultrasound tomorrow so I'll get to see him...or her. I'm trying to talk your father into coming with me but he says he has some interview he can't reschedule." The chipper tone of her voice rang false.

That sounded like my dad. Ignoring his children was his modus operandi. I guess it shouldn't surprise me that he was starting so soon in Junior's life. I noticed the sad look on Nanette's face and my heart went out to her. "What time's your appointment?"

"Nine o'clock."

"My first lesson isn't until eleven. I could go with you if you want," I made the offer even though going to Nanette's doctor appointment was the last thing I wanted to do. But I sensed she didn't want to go alone and I didn't like seeing her sad.

She brightened instantly. "Really? You'd come with me? That would be really sweet, Emma."

"Sure." I put the rest of the groceries away and then went back to my room. I'd left my phone on my desk and I noticed I had a missed call from Kerry. I lay back on my bed and called her.

"Hey, Ker...sorry I missed your call. What's up?" Popcorn jumped up on my stomach and began to purr loudly. I scratched her tiny ears while she kneaded my stomach like bread dough.

"Did you hear about the party at Purgatory Pass? It's Saturday night and I guess a bunch of kids are having a clam bake and kegs and music. I saw Claire at the mall a little while ago and she told me about it. She's going with Jason. Had you heard?"

"No. I don't know anything about it. Sounds fun though. You going?" I wondered if Johnny was in any way involved in this party… or his brother.

"I'm thinking I might. Actually…I wonder if Charlie would go with me? Not that I have the courage to ask. But I thought if you were gonna go, you could ask him…?"

I closed my eyes. Kerry wanted to go with Charlie. Charlie wouldn't want that…and neither did I. But since I couldn't say that, I said instead, "I'll see what the plans are this weekend but I think Charlie and his family are going to be busy. It seems like he mentioned something about going away somewhere."

"Really? Oh, well, his brother must not be going because he's one of the ones throwing this party at Purgatory. I think Scott is, too. I'm surprised Johnny hasn't mentioned it to you."

I was growing frustrated with this conversation and wanted off the phone. As luck would have it, another call was beeping in. I glanced at the dial. "Hey, I'm getting a call from Johnny right now. Maybe he's calling to tell me about it. Can I get back to you?" We said good-bye and I switched over to take Johnny's call.

"Hey, babe," Johnny's voice sounded deep…and a little slurred.

"Hi. What're you up to?" I asked, sitting up on my bed and pulling at a loose thread on my comforter.

"I miss you. And I don't like the way we left things earlier. I need to talk to you about something, OK?"

My stomach knotted. If he was going to bring up the topic of sex again, I might just throw the phone out the damned window. I swallowed a lump of irritation. "OK, what?"

Johnny was silent a few seconds and I wondered if he was still there. Finally he spoke. "Ever since the Fourth you've seemed a little… distant…and it's been bothering me. But I've had time to ponder and I think I know what's wrong."

Oh, boy. I was almost afraid to hear his theory. He couldn't possibly know what was going on in my head…or my heart.

"OK…what's wrong?"

He cleared his throat and let out a deep sigh. "That night…at the lake…when you were a little drunk…you remember what happened that night, right?"

"Barely…I remember making a fool of myself, if that's what you're referring to." I really didn't need or want to be reminded of how

I'd acted that night. At the time I'd been marginally aware of my actions but completely unable to stop myself from acting like an idiot.

"No, baby. You didn't make a fool of yourself. You were drunk but you were adorable. You took off your clothes and made me an offer I didn't want to refuse...but I did. And I just want you to know that my....pardon the use of this word...rejection...of you that night was hard for me. I wanted you more than you know, but I didn't want to take advantage of the circumstances and I'm worried that by not taking what you were offering me that you felt rejected and humiliated. And I just wanted you to know that I wasn't rejecting you...I was saying no to the situation. Am I making any sense here?"

Aw, Johnny...so sweet. I did remember what happened, and the next morning when my shame had washed over me, I'd been thankful for his resistance. I wouldn't have guessed he'd had it in him. "It's OK. I didn't feel rejected. You were a gentleman and that means the world to me. Thank you for looking out for me."

"So...we're OK then...me and you?" He sounded fearful of my answer.

"Of course. Did you have to get liquored up to tell me all that? You sound a little slurry." I chuckled so he wouldn't think I was criticizing him.

"I might have had a beer or two...or three," he said. I could hear the smile in his voice. "And just so you know, the next time we're in that situation, we're both gonna be straight up sober...which reminds me...my brother and Will and some other people are having a party at Purgatory Pass Saturday. A lot of people are going...even Charlie. Let's you and me go, too."

"A party on the beach? Who coming to this party?"

"The usual suspects...Will, Scott, a bunch of their friends and a bunch of us seniors. We're having a clambake which is code for beer and weed but you didn't hear that from me," he laughed raucously in my ear. I rolled my eyes and shook my head, glad Johnny couldn't see the expression on my face. It all sounded so juvenile. But...if Charlie was going to be there...

"Sure, why not?" I said. We talked a few minutes more and I told Johnny I had to go down for dinner. I ended the call and debated calling Kerry back but decided not to. Talking to her would lead to talking about Charlie and I didn't want to engage in evasive measures to avoid the subject of her dating him. All I wanted now was to think about Charlie...to daydream about him...to wish I had magical powers so I could conjure him up, right here in front of me. Just thinking about him made my body tingle in the most illicit places. I sighed and went down to see about dinner. It smelled like Nanette, aka Martha Stewart, was making something delicious and I was suddenly ravenous.

Chapter Twenty-Five

Johnny

The road leading into Purgatory Pass was congested with cars and motorcycles, most of which I recognized. From the look of things it was going to be one helluva party. Will and Scott had gone up earlier with a bunch of other guys to get the fire going and set up the bar. It had rained off and on all morning but by six o'clock the clouds had cleared and the temperature had warmed up a few degrees. It promised to be an exciting night. Emma sat beside me in cut-off jeans and a tight white tank top. I could see her lacy bra through the material and the sight of the outline of her breasts was distracting my driving. They were begging to be touched. The car swerved and Emma let out a yell.

"Oops...sorry, but that was your fault," I said, reaching over and taking her hand. "I can't stop staring at you."

"Do I need to drive?" she asked, giving me a look. She pulled her hair back and around over her right shoulder and turned toward me. I was glad she'd brought her pink Portland hoodie along...because when the temperature dropped after sunset and she got cold, I probably wouldn't be the only one staring at those round, perfect tits.

"I've got things under control." I found a parking spot and pulled off the road. I grabbed my jacket and a twelve-pack of Corona and Emma grabbed the chips and dip and we made our way along the side of the road toward the Pass.

We walked around the rocky entrance and entered the beach of Purgatory Pass, named for its isolated location along the Olympic Peninsula. The Pass was a favorite hang-out for teens from local schools. And we always had a plan in place in case the cops decided to get nosy. Hopefully we wouldn't have to implement the plan tonight. On one side of the beach were massive cliffs, on top of which tall western hemlocks disappeared into the fog. And on the other side of the beach the Pacific Ocean roared like a deranged lion. At least that's what it sounded like tonight. The surf looked rough and the tide was coming close to the area we planned to use for the clambake. As we stepped over the debris of rotting logs, seaweed, seashells and stones of various shapes and sizes, I could hear my brother and Will and several other guys debating whether to move the site up higher or stick it out in hope that the tide wouldn't reach our spot. Emma spotted Claire and Kerry and went over to talk to them while I joined my brother and the other guys around the fire pit. In the end we decided to leave the pit where it was and erect a makeshift barrier of logs around the side that faced the ocean.

Charlie finally arrived and dumped a couple of bags of food onto the ground beside the fire. He looked over at me and nodded but didn't approach me. We hadn't spoken since we'd seen each other in Emma's bedroom the other day, except for a short texting conversation about this party. I stood still with a cold Corona in hand and watched him for a second. He appeared to be searching the crowd for someone. When his eyes settled on Emma, Claire and Kerry and his expression changed, I felt a small burst of happiness. Kerry was here and it was obvious the sight of her was having an effect. He started toward them and I did, too, noticing the crowd around us had gotten larger. There were probably fifty or more of us spread out around the beach on logs or blankets. The pit was hot and several Westbrook High seniors had taken charge of the clams and hot dog roasting. Music blared from someone's iPod speakers and several girls appeared to be already inebriated, judging by the wobbly sway of their dancing. I noticed the fiery orange and hot pink colors of the sky as the sun set and made my way to Emma. She loved this time of evening and I knew the sunset was probably getting her excited…as would the glowing moon hanging low beneath the clouds over the ocean.

"I don't even know half of these people," Emma was saying when I walked up beside her and slipped my arm around her waist.

"That's because a lot of them are from Kenilworth. Apparently word of our little shindig got out and they decided to crash us," I said, squeezing her closer to me. I looked over at Charlie. "Hey, Chuck. How's it going?"

He raised his beer in the air and said hello. I noticed Kerry inching slowly toward him and I wondered if Charlie was paying attention. If he could pull himself out of his own weird headspace long enough, he'd see that Kerry was his for the taking.

"You hungry, babe?" I asked Emma. "I'm gonna have a hot dog. You want one?"

"I'm starved," she said. We all made our way over to the fire. Claire had wrapped herself around Jason Flanagan, one of Westbrook's star football players. Kerry was talking to Charlie and I was hoping he'd offer to get her a drink or something, but so far he'd been quiet while he nursed his beer. I thought back to a year ago when Charlie was often the life of the party—laughing, joking, rough-housing—and I hardly recognized him anymore. He wasn't the Charlie Channing I knew and I wished like fuck there was something I could do about it.

"Hey, Beaumont! What the fuck's going on with you these days?"

I recognized the voice of Doug Farnsworth, Kenilworth's first-string quarterback. We were rival teams and we Wolverines were the current division champs, something they didn't like to be reminded of. I was quite sure showing up at our clambake uninvited was their way of getting a dig in—apparently they liked to torture themselves—seeing us only served to remind them of what they didn't have and wanted badly. I really hated this guy and his posse, several of whom were here tonight.

"Not much, Farnsworth...how about you?" I asked, not really giving a rat's ass but hoping to avoid unpleasantness if at all possible. I stepped casually in front of Emma. I hated having her subjected to this asshole.

"Ready for football this fall, dude?" he asked. He tossed back his beer and then crushed the empty can, tossing it somewhere over his shoulder onto the sand. I shook my head in exasperation because I knew what was coming next. Sure enough, Emma stepped around me and moved closer to Doug.

"Hey...don't litter. We have trash bags." She glared up at him, her hands in tiny fists at her sides.

Doug raised his eyebrows and looked down on her. He cocked his head to the side and I prepared myself to strike. "Well, hello there, sexy. Do your parents know you're here?"

In less than a second I was in his face, pushing my chest into his. "She's with me, asshole...back off."

Doug stepped back an inch or two and grinned. "Whoa there, Beaumont. No need to get all territorial." He looked around me at Emma. "But, are you sure you're old enough to be out this late?"

"You, motherfuck..." I started to say, as I brought my hand back to strike. But before I could break his face, two very strong arms grabbed me and pulled me backward. I stumbled in the sand but didn't fall.

"Cool it, Johnny," said my brother. "Come on...no fighting." He turned to Doug. "Farnsworth...? Chill out already. We don't need the cops here so if you can't control yourself, I hear the Quinaults are partying tonight on their reservation. Why don't you go crash their party?"

Doug didn't respond. He just laughed and he and his posse walked over to the fire and helped themselves to our beer and food. Scott grabbed my arm and gave me a death glare. "Calm the fuck down, John. Have a beer and a hot dog and try to have some fun."

I jerked my arm out of his grip and looked around for Emma. She had retrieved Doug's empty beer can and was walking over to a trash bag that someone had laid over a rock not far from the fire. I joined her and we fixed ourselves hot dogs and I found us a log to sit on far enough away from Farnsworth and his pack that I couldn't see them without craning my neck. Charlie and Kerry came over and sat down on an adjacent log. We were further from the fire here and closer to the cliff wall than the water and already I could feel the coolness of the evening air.

"Farnsworth is such a motherfu…" I caught myself just in time. "Jerk," I finished. "I hate that guy."

"He seems like a bully," said Emma. "Not to mention a litterbug."

I couldn't help but chuckle at that. "And you're going to save the world, one litterbug at a time, aren't you?"

"Somebody has to," she said. She took a bite of her hot dog and, naturally, ketchup splattered all over her white tank top. "Ahhh…," she mumbled around the food in her mouth. She dropped the remainder of the hot dog onto the ground and jumped up.

I shook my head. Charlie had a grin on his face which he was trying to suppress.

"Wow, Emma. That was awesome," said Kerry. She pulled a napkin out of her pocket and passed it to Emma who tried to wipe away the mess to no avail.

"Dammit! This tank top is brand new. Son of a gun!" Emma screeched. "I'll be back. I'm gonna run down to the water and see if I can wash it out before the stain sets in."

"You need help?" I asked.

"No. I'll be right back." She dashed off, jumping over logs and passing the fire pit then disappearing into the darkness.

"Anybody need a refill?" Charlie asked. "I'm gonna grab another beer."

"I'm good," said Kerry. "I'm still working on this Coors Light." She held up her bottle and gave Charlie a cute smile, which he didn't seem to notice.

I shook my head. I had a Corona in the pocket of my jacket so I was good for now. Charlie walked off to find beer and I took a moment to question Kerry about her status with him.

"So, Ker…you and Charlie…?" I left the question hanging.

She pursed her lips and shook her head. "I don't think he's interested. We've talked a little but when I try to get personal he just clams up, pardon the pun."

"He's a tough nut to crack. But I think he likes you. I saw the way he was looking at you earlier. He's still not quite himself though, because of the accident. Just give him time."

Kerry shook her head. "I don't know. Are you sure he was looking at me?"

"Of course. I was watching him. Just be patient. He'll come around." I pulled my Corona out of my pocket and twisted off the top.

Someone turned up the music and a lot of people were dancing around the fire. A girl I didn't know took her top off and was prancing around in her bra and very tiny shorts. Kerry looked over and giggled.

"That does not look like a bathing suit," she said.

I watched the girl in fascination. She certainly seemed to be having a good time. I saw some of Doug's posse ogling her and hoped the poor girl wasn't with one of those assholes. I didn't see Doug and wondered briefly where he'd got off to. What jerks these Kenilworth idiots were. I realized that Emma had been gone a while. How did long did it take to wash ketchup out of a tank top anyway? I'd give her a few more minutes and if she didn't turn up, I'd go find her. Someone had brought out weed. I could smell it from here. I enjoyed my Corona—and the scent of pot—while I waited for Emma to come back.

Chapter Twenty-Six

Charlie

There was a time when I enjoyed a good clambake aka excuse to gather around a fire on the beach, smoke pot and get wasted as much as the next guy. But none of that meant anything to me anymore. It was quite amazing how nearly losing your life could change your perspective on what mattered most. I looked around at the people I'd grown up with and realized they were stagnant…unchanging. Still drinking beer…still smoking pot…still looking for quick hook-ups with whoever was willing…and I didn't want to be a part of it anymore. I tossed my empty bottle into a garbage bag and looked over to where Johnny sat talking to Kerry. I knew she was interested in me. It wasn't hard to figure out. But her efforts were wasted on me. I wished I could tell her that, but I didn't want to hurt her feelings. Because there was only one girl I wanted. One girl who was off-limits to me and with every passing day I was caring less and less about honoring that damned pact I'd made with Johnny years ago. I felt guilty just thinking it. I was a terrible friend.

I decided I would leave this stupid gathering and go home and work on my new song. But I wanted to say good-bye to Emma first. Just seeing her here tonight and being unable to touch her…kiss her…be with her… was killing me. But I couldn't just leave. I looked back over to where Johnny sat with Kerry and saw that Emma still hadn't returned. I frowned and walked around the fire pit, scanning faces to see if she'd joined another group though that seemed unlikely. I didn't see her anywhere and her absence had me rattled. It didn't take that long to clean a stain out of a shirt. I began to walk around the area where people were partying, looking for her in the crowd and when she still didn't turn up, I headed around the rocks toward the cove. It was dark now, but under the light of the moon I had a good view of the coastline. I walked a few yards and caught sight of tiny footprints in the sand leading away from the water's edge…and then much larger footprints alongside those tiny foot prints that turned into prints that appeared to have been dragged away from the water and around the bend in the direction of the cliffside. My heart rate went into triple-time as my breath caught in my throat. I began to run…as fast as my stiff leg would carry me. I screamed her name as I ran.

"Emma!" I rounded the bend and saw them in the sand. Doug Farnsworth was on top of Emma and she was fighting him with everything she had. She was naked from the waste up and trying to scream against the hand he had pressed over her mouth.

"You motherfucking son of bitch!" I screamed as I ran toward them. Doug looked up in surprise and released his hand from her mouth. She screamed, twisting away from him and began to crawl away on her hands and knees. I didn't think twice as I dove on top of him and began to pummel his body with every ounce of strength I had. I hit him in the face with my fist over and over again. I heard Emma crying and screaming at me to stop but I couldn't stop. I didn't want to stop until I'd broken every bone in his body. He'd had a chance to get about two jabs into me but I hadn't even felt them as I continued to pound him into the sand. I was no longer in control as I poured my rage into his body. I ignored his pathetic pleas to stop...his sad apologies and his cries to get off of him. He didn't stand a chance against the fury that burned inside me.

"Charlie! Please! He's down. He can't hurt me anymore. Please stop!" I heard her begging me and her voice broke through my wall of rage. I stumbled backward, away from Doug who lay in a bloody heap on the sand, and looked over at her. She had an arm across her breasts, covering herself. She was shaking and crying and reaching her free hand out to me. I ran to her and pulled her to me and we both shook as she cried into my chest.

I could hear voices in the distance getting closer to us. I let go of Emma and stripped off my t-shirt, yanking it down over her head, but not before catching sight of the ugly bite mark on her left breast. I felt the fury rise inside me again as I pulled her into my arms.

"Jesus, Em...are you OK? What did he do to you?"

She tried to speak through her sobs. "I was washing my shirt in the ocean and he just showed up and started..." Her voice broke as she continued to cry uncontrollably. I held her tight, stroked her hair and pressed my lips to the top of her head.

"Sh...sh...you're safe now. I'm so sorry. I've got you." I looked up just as Johnny, Scott, Will and several others rounded the bend and found us. Doug was starting to stir and trying to get up.

"You're dead meat, Channing. Dead fucking meat," Doug said, spitting blood into the sand. He staggered toward me but didn't get far before he fell, his feet unable to find purchase in the soft sand in the state he was in. His face was bloodied almost beyond recognition. The blood glistened in the moonlight.

"What the fuck is going on?" Johnny yelled. He looked at Doug, nearly unrecognizable now, trying again to stand, and me, bare-chested, with Emma in my arms, sobbing, wrapped in my giant t-shirt. Intense rage bloomed across his face in the moonlight. I watched as he put the pieces together of what had transpired and advanced on Doug. He let out a growl that would scare a grizzly and was on top of Doug in less than a second. And then Will and Scott were on him instantly, dragging him off of Doug who had no fight left in him. Doug's friends turned up then and within moments a battle waged.

"Johnny!" Emma screamed. "Oh, my god! Someone get help!" She began to jump in my arms, trying to break free, but I held on tight and made the decision to get her out of there away from the violence. I didn't ask her first...I just scooped her up in my arms and began to run away from the fight. "Charlie! He's gonna get hurt!"

"He'll be fine," I gasped and prayed I was right about that. I ran until we were out of sight of the fighting and I sat her down on a rock near the water. I sank down on the sand beside her. She wiped her face, streaked with tears and dirt, and slid off the rock into my lap. I held her against me as she cried. I could feel her tears dripping down onto my bare chest. I rocked her and let her cry until she finally cried herself out.

"Charlie...I poked him in the eye and I kicked him in the balls. It felt good," she whispered, her words coming out between ragged breaths. "But...I couldn't get him off me. He's awful. He took my bra off...and tore up my tank top. I don't even know what happened to them. He threw them somewhere. Why did he do this?"

I stared up the beach over her head. "Because he's a fucking asshole. We need to call the police and report this."

"A fucking asshole. That's what Johnny would say. But I don't want to call the police. I don't want to have to relive this for the record." She leaned back then, suddenly noticing I was shirtless. "Are you cold?"

"Don't worry about me. Hey, they're coming." We stood up and walked toward my brother and Scott and several members of the Westbrook High football team. Johnny looked murderous. He had a black eye and cuts on both cheeks. Blood trickled down like red tears, disappearing under his jaw into his neck. But when he saw Emma, his face softened and he came to her with his arms open. She pulled away from me and went to him. I looked away.

Scott went up to Emma. "They're gone but we should report this. Emma, we can't let that asshole get away with doing this to you."

Will stepped forward then and handed a white bundle to Emma. "I found your clothes." Johnny snatched them from Will's hand before Emma could get them and shoved them into his pocket.

"I'm going to kill that asshole." He turned to Will and Scott. "You should have let me take him out. He's gonna pay for this."

"And then you'll be the one in jail so forget about revenge. Let the law handle it," said Scott.

"I don't give a fuck about the law! Goddammit!" Johnny looked down at Emma. "What did he do to you? Did he rape you?"

"No…please let it go. He didn't rape me. He tore off my bra and ripped my shirt and…and…and…put his mouth on my…" She crossed her arms over her chest and turned away, trying not to cry.

Johnny let go of Emma and paced around in a circle, frantic. "Son of a bitch. I'm going after him. I'm gonna fucking kill him." He kicked out at the sand, raising his fisted hands above his head. "I've gotta take care of this now." He started back toward the cliffs but Will and Scott each grabbed an arm and prevented him from leaving.

"No! There are other ways to handle this. And they're long gone by now. They might have gotten in a few punches on us but those assholes dragged Doug out of there fast when they realized they were outnumbered." He tapped Johnny's shoulder, making sure he was listening. "Control yourself and think of Emma right now," Scott demanded. Johnny tried to jerk away from them but they both held on tight. He looked at Emma and again, he calmed down a fraction. He reached for her.

I spoke up then. "We need to get her home—away from here. Let's go." I stepped toward her, wanting to take her in my arms, but Johnny was there, picking her up.

"I'm so sorry, baby, that I wasn't there for you. But I promise you he'll pay for this. No one touches you and gets away with it…no one." He looked around at us over the top of Emma's head and I could see in his eyes that he wanted revenge.

We walked back toward the party which had dwindled down to less than a dozen people. I noticed that Claire and Jason and Kerry were gone. The few stragglers who remained were making a half-assed attempt to clean the place up. We headed down to the road where our cars were parked. I dug in my pocket for my key and pressed the button to unlock the door. Johnny opened his door and helped Emma inside. She called out to me as I was about to get into my car.

"Charlie, wait," she said. She got back out and ran to me, throwing herself into my arms. It was unexpected and caught me off guard. "Thank you so much for…for…saving me. If you hadn't come, it could have been worse. You were…are amazing." She pulled my head down and kissed my cheek and whispered so only I could hear, "I love you." I held her tight…just for a second…and let her go. And then Johnny was there, hugging me, too.

"I owe you for this. You saved my girl. I will never forget this, Chuck. You're the best friend anyone could ever hope to have." He patted my back and then let me go. I didn't say anything to either of them as I walked away. I got into my car and drove off. Later, back home in the quiet of my room, I stared down at my hands. My knuckles were dirty and sore but surprisingly unmarked. My arm throbbed and my leg ached like it used to right after the accident…like it had after the surgeon put it back together. I went into the bathroom and took a shower…washed away the sand, blood and filth of Doug Farnsworth from my hands. And when I finished in the bathroom, I did something I hadn't done in a long time. I got drunk…well and truly obliterated. I knew I'd regret it…that I'd be hung over and feel like shit tomorrow, but tonight I just didn't care.

Chapter Twenty-Seven

Emma

Johnny took me home and we sat in my driveway for a while. I clutched the hem of Charlie's t-shirt in my hands as I sat in the passenger seat, trying to feel him against my skin. I wanted him with me so badly that I wasn't sure I could function. I felt dirty and exhausted and sick to my stomach. And I knew deep down that Johnny wouldn't be able to let this go.

"I don't want to call the cops," I pleaded." This could wind up in the police blotter and it's my dad's beat—crime and accidents. He'd see the report come in at the station and I don't want that."

Johnny was staring out the window, working his jaw back and forth, drumming his hands on the gear shift. Finally he turned to me, his eyes glassy. His voice was low and...flat. "If that's what you want, babe...fine. But this isn't over. Farnsworth isn't getting away with this. I'm gonna fix this. I promise. He's not gonna hurt you again."

"I'm not afraid of that jerk. But you have to promise me you won't go after him. Something bad would happen and I couldn't bear it if you got in trouble with the law. He's not worth it. Promise me you'll let this go...please?"

"I can't make any promises. Well, except one...and that is I promise that no one will ever hurt you again. It kills me that I didn't come to look for you sooner. I blame myself for this happening to you, but thank God for Charlie. Fuck...oops...I mean...dammit...I didn't even ask him if he's OK."

I reached up and ran my fingertips lightly along the cuts on his cheeks. His eye was swollen and black and blue. I took his hands in mine and gave them a squeeze. "He seemed OK. He didn't even get a mark on him that I could see. I saw that jerk hit him once or twice but Charlie didn't even seem to feel it. But...hey...I'm gonna go inside. I need to take a shower and wash this sand and the feel of everything off of me."

Johnny glanced at me for a second then pulled his hands out of my grasp. He opened his door and came around to my side and opened my door. He pulled me out of the car and into his arms and held me so tight it almost hurt. "I love you, Em. I'm so sorry about this. I don't ever want to let you go. I could come in and sleep on your floor if you want."

I looked up at him and smiled. "Don't be silly. I'll be fine. I love you for offering though. I'm gonna go. I'll see you tomorrow, OK?"

He nodded and leaned down to kiss me. It was a sweet, slow kiss and it made my heart ache. He was reluctant to let me go but I finally extricated myself from his embrace and went inside.

Upstairs in my room I stripped out of my shorts and underwear and tossed them into the clothes hamper. I placed Charlie's t-shirt on the end of my bed and went into the adjoining bath to shower. Under the shower spray I glanced down at my body and saw for the first time the marks that Doug Farnsworth had left on me—bruises on both hip bones and a bite mark on my left breast. In my quest to fight him off, I had barely felt the pain he'd inflicted. I tried to wash the marks away but I knew it was impossible. I dried myself off and put my hair up in a towel and went back to my room. I sat on the end of the bed and watched as Popcorn emerged from her hiding place in my closet and jumped up to purr at my elbow. I picked up Charlie's t-shirt and buried my face in it, breathing in his essence. Then I held it up and looked at the front of it. It was navy blue and had a faded white peace sign on it. I shook my head at the irony as I slipped it over my head. I could smell him on it—his cologne…his scent…and it made me dizzy…dizzy enough to fall over onto my pillow. Popcorn immediately jumped up on my chest and sat, staring at me…meowing sweetly. Tears slid down my temples and were absorbed into the towel wrapped around my hair. And I knew I needed to comb out my tangles and make an appearance downstairs so Nanette and Dad would know I was home and in for the night.

They were in the family room watching TV, cuddled together as usual on the couch. I stuck my head in and said hello, then I went to the kitchen for some toast. When I finished eating I went to my room and noticed that I had several missed calls and text messages. The calls were from Claire and Kerry as were the texts. They'd heard about the incident on the beach and were checking to see if I was OK. I texted back assuring them I was. I expected Johnny to call or text me any time and was surprised when he didn't. I brushed my teeth and lay on my bed with Popcorn tucked into my neck and closed my eyes. It was going to be hard to sleep tonight but I would have to try. I kept seeing Doug Farnsworth sneaking up behind me, drunk, grabbing me, telling me he was going to love getting a piece of Beaumont's girl. He'd dragged me up the beach by my arms, under the cliffs, ripped off my tank top and bra. I'd tried to scream but he'd clamped his hand over my mouth and nose and for a moment I thought I would suffocate. I touched the tender spot on my breast…felt the raised skin from his bite there. Thank God for Charlie. He'd saved me. How I wished he were here now to save me from bad dreams.

A sound awakened me. Popcorn was curled up next to me and she raised her head and stretched while I pushed myself up on my elbows, blinking in the darkness trying to figure out what it was. Then I saw my phone glowing on my nightstand. Someone had sent me a text. I reached over and picked it up, noting the time: 3:45 a.m. It was from Charlie: you're probably asleep and won't see this until morning, but i just wanted to tell you i love you, too.

"Oh…Charlie…," I whispered in the darkness. Instant tears formed. I pushed myself higher up on my pillows and typed a response with trembling fingers. My heart pounded an endless thunder against my ribcage. are you ok? i'm worried about you. saying thank you for what you did tonight isn't enough. you're my hero. I pressed send and while I waited for a response I fought the damned tears.

A minute later came his text: i'm ok but drunk. i was gonna come over and throw a rock at your window but i could get arrested for drunk walking so i decided to stay put. i don't usually drink to excess but to-night seemed to warrant it. don't let that piece of sh** break your spirit. if you decide to turn him in, i'm right there with you. and i didn't want to fall asleep until i said it back. we're gonna figure this out, em. night, angel.

I grabbed a pillow and shoved my face into it to stifle my sobs. I shook so badly that I must've scared Popcorn because she meowed once loudly, jumped off the bed and ran back to the closet. I turned off my phone and slid down my pillows, hugging one against my body, pre-tending it was Charlie. I missed him with an ache that hurt beyond what was tolerable. I pulled the pillow away from my face and glanced at my window. He was only two blocks away. I could be there in three min-utes. I could be in his arms, in his bed, holding him, and maybe…just maybe…time would stop and we would never have to say good night again. I turned over and settled under my sheet and cried myself to sleep.

"Emma…wake up."

I opened my eyes to the sight of my father standing on my bed-room's threshold. He looked scary, filling the doorway, his face serious. Something was wrong. I sat up, my heart pounding. I noticed the clock on my nightstand…9:30. I'd slept later than usual.

"What...Dad...is Nanette OK?" He was scaring me...just his presence alone, in my room, a place he never set foot in, was unnerving me to no end.

He came into my room and stood by my bed. "Emma...Johnny's been arrested. He's in the Kenilworth jail. I just got the call from the office. I'm on crime-watch this weekend so I'm going there now and I thought you'd want to know."

I tore out of the bed and began to dig for jeans in my closet. "Oh, my God, Dad. What did he do?" Oh, please, oh, please, oh, please... don't let him be a murderer...don't let him be a criminal...let this be a mistake, I pleaded with unknown gods as my panic rose. I could barely see through my tears as I slipped into a pair of jeans and tennis shoes. I was still wearing Charlie's giant t-shirt and I didn't bother to change—it would give me comfort. Nausea took hold of me as I looked up at my dad.

"He beat up a Kenilworth football player. He was arrested at his house earlier this morning by the Westbrook police and then transported to Kenilworth's jail. If you're coming with me, you should drive your own car and you'll need to stay out of the way no matter what. Once I'm finished at the station I'll have to get downtown to the paper. I won't have time to bring you home. Will you be able to control your emotions and not make a scene?"

"I'll be fine," I said, running a brush through my hair. I caught sight of my reflection in the mirror over my dresser, noting the combination of puffy eyes and dark circles and I knew I looked frightful but I didn't care about that now. I needed to get to Johnny. I ran downstairs after my dad and hopped into my car. I followed right on his tail as we drove into Kenilworth. My mind raced with a million crazy thoughts of what Johnny might have done after he'd dropped me off last night. I'd assumed he'd gone straight home but I guess I should have known better. I thought about texting or calling Charlie but I knew not to use my phone while driving in the agitated state I was in. I felt a tug at my heartstrings when I drove past the area where Charlie's accident had occurred. A few minutes later I parked beside my dad's Nissan in the Kenilworth Police Department's visitor's lot. I rushed to catch up with my dad. Once inside I waited impatiently, pacing back and forth, while he talked to someone at the window. A door opened and a police officer walked out, followed by Johnny and his father.

"Johnny!" I yelled and ran toward him. I threw my arms around him and held on tight. He stiffened and pulled my arms away, but not before leaning close to kiss my cheek and whispering softly, "hush, baby...no talking."

I stepped back, astonished, trying to read him. He was telling me something with his eyes and though I was scared and confused, I held my tongue. I watched as the police officer handed him a plastic bag with his wallet and keys in it.

"Stay away from Doug Farnsworth, son," said the police officer to Johnny. The officer then turned to face Mr. Beaumont. "You posted bail pretty fast, Andy. Keep him out of trouble. And call your lawyer. Farnsworth's gonna need surgery to fix his face. It's gonna cost you."

"Thanks, Sam. I appreciate your taking care of Johnny like you did." Mr. Beaumont glanced over at Johnny and frowned.

My dad approached Mr. Beaumont then and I felt my heart fall. I hated my dad's job right then. "I'm Anthony Davis with the Westbrook Daily News...and I'm also Emma's father...I think we might have met once before." He said the words to Mr. Beaumont as he looked at Johnny with curiosity and interest. "You care to tell me what happened last night, Johnny?"

"Absolutely not!" said Mr. Beaumont. "This whole thing is a mistake. Johnny's not talking to anyone except our lawyer."

My dad looked from Johnny to me and then back to Johnny again. I saw something dark pass over his face. "Fine. I'll read the police report for my story. And until I know exactly what happened last night, I'd appreciate it if you would stay away from my daughter." He stepped toward me and pulled me away from Johnny.

I yanked away from him. "No! I'm staying with Johnny. You can't stop me, Dad."

My dad pointed at the front doors. "Go home, Emma. We'll talk later. Go home now."

Angry tears welled in my eyes. There was no way my dad was going to be a real dad now—not when Johnny needed me most. Whatever Johnny had done to end up here, he'd done because he loved me and I wasn't leaving him now. "You can't make me."

Before my dad could respond, Johnny said, "It's OK, babe. We'll get this straightened out and when we do, I'll talk to your dad—off the record. It'll be OK. Go ahead home."

I threw my arms around him and squeezed him hard, then moved past my dad, giving him a death glare on my way by. I ran to my car and immediately dialed Charlie's number but he didn't answer. I had to see him now. I had to know what had happened last night after the clambake.

I drove straight to Charlie's house just in time to see him and Will walking out their front door. I parked at the end of the drive and jumped out of the car.

"I just saw Johnny at the jail. What happened last night?" I had to fight to control the hysteria in my voice.

Charlie looked exhausted and hung over. "You saw him? How'd you find out? Johnny didn't want you to know," he said, running a hand through his dark brown hair.

"My dad told me. He's a reporter for the Westbrook paper and crime is his beat. But, please tell me. Did Johnny go back out last night and do something to that guy?" I looked from Charlie to Will.

"No. Johnny was home all night...well, until the cops came and took him away. He'd wanted to go after Farnsworth but Scott and I held him hostage. We knew he'd probably kill the asshole if we didn't keep watch over him." Will glanced at Charlie as he spoke. They both looked rung out and exhausted.

"I'm gonna go down there and fix this. Johnny didn't do this. I don't know why the cops arrested him for something I did," Charlie's voice was low and gravelly. "I was just on my way down to the station."

I couldn't imagine my gentle, sweet Charlie in jail. "Wait...Johnny was just released into his dad's custody. Let's go talk to him first."

"He's out? Maybe the charges got dropped," said Will. He walked to his Jeep Wrangler and opened the door. "I want to go with you, but I have to work at the grocery store this morning." He looked back at his brother. "Charlie...don't do anything until you talk to Johnny."

Charlie walked toward my car. "Let's go see Johnny...and then I'm going to the station."

We climbed in and I started the car. When Charlie was buckled in, I reached for his hand. He seemed so forlorn...I couldn't stand to see him like this. "We'll get this straightened out, Charlie. You were defending me and you can't get in trouble for that. Nothing bad will happen." I squeezed his hand and reversed the car out of the drive. Charlie sat slumped in the seat and remained quiet as I drove. I could see the wheels turning in his head and I wondered what was going through his mind but I didn't say anything. A few minutes later we parked in Johnny's drive and walked to the front door.

Johnny opened the door and immediately pulled me into his arms and kissed the top of my head. "Hey...come on in," he said. "Let's go out on the back deck." We followed him down the front hall, through the kitchen and through sliding doors to the deck. I glanced out at the kidney-shaped pool, its water clean, clear and shimmering in the morning light. Charlie sat down in a chaise and stretched out his legs. Johnny sat and pulled me onto his lap. I felt shy and awkward sitting on him like this but I didn't try to move away. Johnny needed me close right now and whatever he needed, I would give it.

"Why'd they arrest you? I did this...not you," said Charlie. "I'll get this straightened out...don't worry."

"No! You stay out of this, Chuck. Farnsworth ID'd me as the one who beat the shit out of him and I wanna keep it that way. You don't need to be dealing with any of that asshole's shit." He squeezed me to him and frowned. "Sorry, babe...but I can't guarantee control over my language right now."

Charlie looked up at him in surprise. "No...no...you're not going down for something I did. Farnsworth knows full well I beat him up. No way I'm letting you take the heat for it."

Johnny stamped a foot on the deck causing me to jump in his arms. He hugged me to him and glared at Charlie. "What you did was save Emma...something I should have done. I should have been there for her. This was my mistake and I am going to fix it."

I tried to loosen myself from Johnny's tight hold on me. "What's going to happen next? What were you charged with?" I asked him.

"Assault in the first degree. I'm gonna do time."

"What?" I cried...shocked not only by his words but also by the way they'd so nonchalantly rolled off his tongue. "No!" I threw my arms around him and cried into his neck. "This can't happen!" It was suddenly hard to breathe...my lungs threatened to shut down.

Charlie had been leaning forward in his chair, his elbows resting on his knees. I'd seen the tenseness in his shoulders...the way his body was coiled tight like a cobra. Suddenly he stood and headed to the sliding doors. "No, you're not. I'm going down and turn myself in."

Johnny pushed me gently off his lap and went to Charlie, blocking his exit. "Listen, Charlie...please. Just sit your ass down and listen to me."

Charlie hesitated but didn't sit back down. He and Johnny locked eyes. Johnny spoke with an intensity that frightened me. "Farnsworth ID'd me as the assailant. He told the cops I was the one who beat him up...over some old rivalry shit...that I was lording some sort of superiority over him. His posse backed him up...they all ID'd me. I could've maybe understood Farnsworth being confused considering how messed up he was, but his idiot friends were very sure of themselves. I mean...look at my face. I have a fucking black eye and cuts on both cheeks. I look fucking guilty." He took Charlie's arm and twisted him around to face their reflections in the glass of the sliding door. "Look at your face, Chuck. Not a mark on it." He grabbed Charlie's hands and looked at his knuckles. "You managed to beat the shit out of that fucking asshole and not get a mark on you...and that... my friend...is your saving grace."

Realization dawned as I understood Johnny's intent. He was protecting Charlie...to be the hero. I felt sick to my stomach. Neither of them deserved to lose their freedom over that jerk Farnsworth. There had to be something I could do. "The police know that Farnsworth attacked me, right? That Charlie was only defending me…do they know all the facts?"

Johnny took me in his arms again. "Baby…I didn't want you brought into it. I know Farnsworth…he'd only deny attacking you and you'd get dragged into this mess and I can't let that happen to you."

"Wait, wait, wait," I said, moving away from him. "This is…no…no…how is your going to jail and Farnsworth getting off free as a bird going to help anything? How is it going to help anybody? He's the one who should be in jail…not you…or Charlie." I began to shake…tears falling in torrents down my cheeks. Johnny reached for me but I backed away, closer to the deck railing.

Johnny's body tensed. His face reddened and I could see that he was working on his self-control. His voice was filled with barely contained rage as he answered. "I want nothing more than for that fucking asshole Farnsworth to pay for what he did to you, Em…but I had to make a split-second decision in front of those cops in that interrogation room. And I chose you and Charlie over making that asshole pay. I will not let you get dragged into this fucking mess and I absolutely will not let my best friend go to prison for a crime I should have committed—not that beating the shit out of Farnsworth was a crime—in my eyes he got off fucking easy…but I won't let you both suffer for this—no motherfucking way."

Charlie began to shake his head back and forth as he slid the glass door open. "Fuck you, Johnny."

I gasped…my knees shaking, threatening to buckle under me. "Charlie…?"

"I don't need anybody to fight my battles. I'll handle this my way." He stepped inside to the kitchen but Johnny was in front of him in an instant.

"No…fuck you, Charlie. Don't be a fucking idiot. No one's gonna believe you. Let me do this my way. Don't be stupid."

Charlie hissed in Johnny's face, "then you…don't be a fucking martyr!"

I feared they were going to fight…that one would strike a blow on the other and I couldn't stand back and let it happen. I dashed inside and pushed myself between them…and without giving any thought to my actions I reached under my shirt—Charlie's large, peace-sign t-shirt—and pushed my jeans down below my hips. I grabbed the hem of the shirt and lifted it up to my neck exposing my bare breasts and abdomen to them. "Maybe they'll believe this…" I cried, my body shaking.

Charlie and Johnny both looked at my body—at the greenish, bluish bruises on my hipbones and the angry purple bite mark on my breast. I felt my insides shaking with nerves that seemed to have come loose from their moorings, flailing wildly inside of me.

"Jesus, Emma!" Johnny yelled. He shoved himself between me and Charlie, blocking Charlie's view. He touched the bruises on my hips and pressed a finger gently onto the mark on my breast, then grabbed the shirt from my hand and pulled it down over me, covering my evidence. "Oh, Jesus fucking Christ."

Charlie began to move backward out of the kitchen, down the hall toward the front door, staring at me and Johnny as he moved. His face was twisted in fury, his eyes hard as two dark stones. He brought his hands up in fists and for a second I was afraid he was going to punch the wall. "I messed up...son of a bitch...I messed up."

"What...messed up what?" Johnny asked, his voice sounded husky with emotion. "What do you mean, Chuck?" He began to slowly inch toward Charlie.

"I stopped too soon. I should have killed him." He turned his gaze on me, his eyes brimming with tears. "I'm so sorry, Em. I've gotta go." He turned to leave but Johnny rushed to the door, preventing his departure.

"Don't do anything stupid, Chuck. Stay here...come on...please," Johnny pleaded, his voice surprisingly quiet and controlled.

I spoke up then. "You can't leave without me. I drove, remember?" I came toward him, taking his arm, but he pushed my hand off of him.

"I can walk. It's only a couple of miles. Please move out of my way, Johnny."

"No. You're not going anywhere. Stay here until you're calm," said Johnny.

In a quiet yet menacing voice, Charlie responded, "Move the fuck out of my way...please." Again I saw the tightness in his shoulders... felt the quiet strength exuding from his pores.

Johnny stepped aside and let Charlie leave. We watched as he walked down the driveway, past my car and out into the street. Johnny turned to me and caught me as my weak knees finally gave up supporting me, and held me tight against him.

Chapter Twenty-Eight

Johnny

"Sh...sh...come here," I whispered against Emma's cheek. "Come with me." I took her hand and led her upstairs to my room. I knew my mother was at Mass, probably asking God to forgive her son for his many sins, and my dad was in his study more than likely trying to reach his lawyer who was somewhere on vacation at the moment. I felt badly that my room was trashed but neatness had never been one of my strong suits. I grabbed a bunch of clothes off the floor and shoved them into my closet and put empty beer bottles into my trash can. I smoothed the blankets on my bed and sank down on it, taking Emma with me.

"What's gonna happen to you... and Charlie?" she said, sighing into my shoulder.

"I'm not even gonna freak about it anymore. My dad's lawyer will fix this." I sat up suddenly, thinking of something that made me want to puke my guts out. "Emma...fuck...baby...I hate to ask you this... but..."

"What? Ask me...what?" She pushed herself up into a sitting position and stared back at me with those emerald eyes that turned me to mush every time I looked into them.

"Maybe I should take a photo of you...of your...you know... marks...in case the truth comes out on its own...or if Charlie really does go down to the station and makes a fucking fool of himself."

"Yes! Do it." She jumped up and ripped the giant t-shirt over her head and pushed her jeans down below her hips. "Where's your camera? Does it date the photo automatically? My phone does."

I gulped. Oh...my...god... I fought the rage that threatened to undo me at the sight of Farnsworth's attack on Emma's body. I pulled my phone out of my pocket just as she tossed me hers. "Stand up against the wall." She did as I asked and I took photos of her hips and breast. Then I took her phone and took the photos again. I didn't know what the hell I was doing or if this even made sense but at least we'd have some photographic evidence if we ever needed it.

Suddenly Emma chuckled. "Did you just trick me into sexting?"

I dropped our phones on the bed and stepped closer, pulling her into my arms. I ran my hands up and down her bare back and groaned, feeling the dull ache in my body intensify with every pass of my hand over her soft skin. It was so fucking wrong to want her so badly right now but fuck all I did. She rubbed my back softly on top of my shirt and I wanted so desperately to feel her fingers on my bare skin. I wanted her more in that moment than I ever had but I knew it was wrong and I had to stop...stop my selfish desires and think of her and...Charlie. I groaned and stepped out of her arms and helped her back into Charlie's t-shirt.

"We need to know what Charlie's doing...but I can't leave my house. I'm under some sort of house arrest bullshit until I go before the judge next week."

"I want to go to the police and tell them what really happened. I'm not afraid. And I don't believe they'd put Charlie in jail. Charlie and I can go together." I heard the pleading tone in her voice and I felt myself waver. But it didn't seem like the right thing to do.

"I don't think you should do it. I can't have Charlie getting arrested. It's too risky. I don't want to take the chance of it all going wrong. It would kill me for Charlie to spend even one day in fucking jail, Em. And they'd have to look at you...at your...body. I can't stand any of this shit."

Emma seemed suddenly excited. "No...no...I can feel that this is right. No matter what, the truth is always the right path. I'll make them see that Charlie was only defending me. It's what I want. I have to go get Charlie and we can fix this...shit...as you call it."

I paced around in my room, breathing hard. "Oh, my fucking god. Something tells me this is a mistake that's gonna backfire badly but I can't stop you. But promise me, you'll come straight back here."

Without warning she threw herself into my arms and kissed me. "I will...and don't worry. It'll be OK. I promise."

I closed my eyes and shook my head in resignation. We walked downstairs and she kissed me one more time, then bounded down the porch steps to her car and waved as she drove off. I felt sick to my stomach. I went to the kitchen and fixed myself a cup of coffee and sat down at the table to wait...for my father to reach his lawyer...for my mother to get home from church and tell me that God was my fucking co-pilot and for Emma to execute her mission. This was so fucking messed up.

Chapter Twenty-Nine

Charlie

I didn't go home when I left Johnny's house. He lived less than a mile from the police station so I walked straight there. It felt good to move—to make my legs carry me. My bum leg actually felt stronger today. My arm ached, but otherwise I felt powerful. There was something to be said for righting a wrong. My only worry was that Farnsworth wouldn't get what was coming to him, but I had to let that go for now and concentrate on saving Johnny from a sure prison sentence. I walked through the doors of Westbrook's police station, only then remembering I should have walked home for my car and gone to Kenilworth's station. Purgatory Pass was in Kenilworth's jurisdiction. Dammit. I looked around the reception area and since no one seemed to be paying me any attention I went into the restroom to heed the call of nature before I walked home to get my car. I glanced at my phone and noticed I had a text from Emma. I hadn't even heard my phone beep. I opened it and read: just left johnny's. coming to get you. i'm going to the police station too. see ya shortly.

I closed my eyes for a moment against the annoyance I felt in my gut. "Dammit, Emma," I said under my breath. I dialed her number as I took care of business and then walked out of the bathroom and through the front doors of the station. I walked out into the parking lot and stopped when she picked up.

"Where are you?" she asked.

"I walked to the police station…Westbrook's station. I know I need to go to Kenilworth."

"Stay there. I'll pick you up and we'll go together."

"Emma, wait, I don't think you…," but she'd already hung up. "Son of a bitch!" I yelled into the air.

I waited down by the road and within a few minutes Emma pulled her Honda Civic over to the side of the road and unlocked the door. I climbed in beside her and started into the speech I'd been preparing while I waited for her.

"They're gonna make you take off your clothes, Em. And take photos and shit. You're gonna have to relive the whole thing all over again. Are you prepared to do that?"

Emma straightened up taller in her seat. "He didn't rape me, Charlie. He only tried to. I'll show them the bruises. Johnny took pictures of them on my phone. Maybe they can use the photos and I won't have to show them the real thing. I don't even care about that. All that matters is that Johnny...and you...don't go to jail because of that piece of shit Farnsworth."

I almost laughed at her language choice. Curse words sounded so foreign and...sexy...coming from her mouth. Damn. She drove fast but mostly within the speed limit and we were there in no time. We went inside the station and I asked at the window if I could speak to Johnny's arresting officer. We were told to wait in the lobby. Emma sat close to me and about five minutes later an Officer Samuel Marks called us into an empty room.

"What can I do for you two?" he asked.

"You were the officer who arrested Johnny Beaumont for beating up Doug Farnsworth, right?" Emma started. But I wasn't about to let her do the talking. I reached over and put my hand on her arm, letting her know I wanted to handle this my way. She frowned at me as the officer nodded his answer.

"You arrested the wrong person. I'm the one who beat up Doug Farnsworth. Johnny wasn't even there when it happened."

The officer cocked his head to the side and regarded me intently. "And your name is?"

"Charlie...Charles...Channing."

"And what is your connection to Johnny Beaumont?"

"I'm his bes...his friend."

The officer continued to stare at me. His gaze raked over my face and down to my hands which I self-consciously moved under the table to rest on my lap.

He turned then to Emma. "Didn't I see you here this morning?"

"Yes. I'm Johnny's girlfriend, Emma Davis."

Officer Marks leaned back in his seat and appeared to be suppressing a smile. "So tell me, Charlie, what happened?"

I glanced at Emma, wondering if I should tell the whole truth. I so very much didn't want to drag her into this. I swallowed hard and opted for complete honesty. "I came upon Doug Farnsworth attacking Emma and I intervened. I beat him up to...to...protect her."

Officer Marks seemed to consider my words. He looked back and forth from me to Emma. He asked her, "Is this true, Emma?"

She nodded vigorously. "Yes. I'd gotten ketchup on my shirt and I'd gone down to the water to rinse it out and he found me there and he...." She squared her shoulders and continued. "He grabbed me and pulled me away toward the cliffs and began to assault me."

Again the officer shifted his gaze back and forth between us. He took his sweet time responding. "Pardon me if I have trouble believing this, but…" he looked at my face and I knew what he was going to say. "You don't have a mark on you. Your bes…uh…friend…Johnny Beaumont, on the other hand, has cut cheeks and a fierce-looking shiner. Now…I saw the condition of Doug Farnsworth's face so, pardon me for finding it hard to believe you had anything to do with it."

"It's the truth. I was very angry at what he was doing…had done… was planning to do to her…and I reacted out of fear for her safety."

"Let me see your hands, please."

I closed my eyes for just a second. He would never believe me now. I had no explanation for the lack of marks on my hands other than the way I'd hit Farnsworth…mostly uppercuts. It wasn't my fault that asshole had such a breakable face. I brought my hands out from under the table and held them out for him to see.

"And not a mark on your hands either. Johnny, though, had quite some discoloration on his knuckles." He looked at Emma then. "Let me guess…you probably don't have a mark on your body either, do you?"

Emma jumped up from her seat and for a horrifying second I thought she was going to pull the shirt up over her head again. I moved to stop her but she reached into her pocket and pulled her cell phone out and clicked a few keys until she'd found the photo she'd mentioned to me earlier in the car. She slid it over to the officer and he looked down at it.

"Are these marks still visible on your body?" he asked, his gaze raking over her chest. I felt the rage trying to take hold again and I fought it down.

"Yes. That photo was taken less than an hour ago," she responded.

The officer studied the photo far too long before standing up. "I'm going to have a female officer photograph you. You can make a statement about the marks on your body…and write down who made them on you. You need to be honest, Emma."

She sucked in a breath. "I am being honest. Doug Farnsworth did this."

"Are you sure about that? Are you sure it wasn't someone else who put those marks on your body? Did you and Johnny have a lover's quarrel? Did Doug Farnsworth maybe come along and see what was happening and intervene on your behalf and end up with his face bashed in? It's OK to tell the truth, Emma. No one can hurt you here."

I stood up abruptly, so fast that the chair I'd been sitting in shot out behind me. "She is telling the truth. I should know. I was there. Johnny would never in a million years lay a hand on her."

Emma began to cry. She stood up, too, and I saw an intense fierceness wash over her face. "You've got it all wrong! I told you what happened. How dare you accuse my...Johnny of doing this!"

I moved around to stand beside her. I wanted more than anything to put my fist in the smug face of Officer Marks. It took every ounce of restraint I had not to.

The officer pushed back from the table and stood. We were eye to eye now. "Calm down there, son. I just need to make sure I have all the facts. You two have a seat while I go find a female officer." He left us alone and Emma collapsed in my arms.

"Oh, my god! Charlie. This is going all wrong. This is what Johnny was afraid of—that they wouldn't believe you. What have we done?" She sobbed in my arms as I held her, staring off into space, my mind racing with scattered thoughts. Since when did telling the truth sound so false and criminal? I looked down at the top of Emma's head, thankful I was holding her now because if I let go of her, I knew I would unleash the adrenaline that was currently coursing through me and destroy this room. It would be so fucking easy to turn the place into a pile of rubble.

The door opened and a female cop entered the room. She handed me a piece of paper and a pen and instructed me to write down my statement. She then led Emma from the room. I resisted the urge to vent my anger on what little furnishings were in the room and sat back down to write out my statement. A few minutes later Emma returned and was given a sheet of paper to write her own account of events. The female officer stayed in the room and when Emma and I were finished she took the statements and left. Office Marks returned and beckoned us out into the hallway. He walked us to the front door and stopped.

"I understand that you both care for your friend. But lying to protect him won't help anyone. You two need to go home and think things through. If you need to come back and...amend...your statements, I'll understand. Sometimes you remember details later...that you didn't think of at the time. And just so you both know...I know Johnny Beaumont's family. I know Johnny has a reputation for being a bad-ass. He's managed to never get arrested for his antics until now. It was bound to catch up with him sooner or later. You'd both do well to steer clear of him. Go on home and rethink your priorities...and your friends." He started to turn away but stopped himself. "And Emma, telling the truth about what happened to you could potentially save another girl from the same fate. Think about that." He walked away and I had to pull Emma out the door to keep her from attacking the officer.

"Oh, my god. I've ruined everything. They don't believe me! Charlie...I can't ever face him again. What have I done?" She was uncontrollable. I supported her as we made it to her car. I took the keys from her shaking hands and settled her into the front seat. I got in and adjusted the seat so I could fit behind the wheel. Damn these tiny-ass cars. I drove back to Westbrook, barely noticing the passing vehicles and scenery.

"It's going to be OK…I promise." I said the words but not really sure I believed them. "I'd like to know why Farnsworth lied…why he said Johnny beat him up when he knows it was me." I'd always known about the rivalry between the two starting quarterbacks. It had never been Kenilworth versus Westbrook at the football games. It had always been Farnsworth versus Beaumont. And senior year was Farnsworth's last chance to annihilate Johnny on the field. I guessed he doubted his quarterback skills…enough to take Johnny down now so he could make his sought-after victory easier to grasp. But I wouldn't let it…no way.

Emma reached over and placed her hand on my knee and turned her teary gaze on me. "He can't go to prison…he won't…will he?"

"No…never gonna happen," I said, shaking my head. "There were too many witnesses. The whole Westbrook football team will vouch for Johnny. Don't worry." I drove into Westbrook and headed toward Emma's house. I would walk the rest of the way home. As I pulled into her drive she started to protest, wanting to take me home.

"It's only two blocks." I put the car in park and got out, coming around to the passenger side. Emma walked straight into my arms, locking hers behind me and holding on tight.

"What're you going to do now?" I could feel her lips moving against my chest as she asked. I rubbed my hands up and down her back and wished I didn't have to let her go.

"I'm gonna make some calls and get this straightened out. But I'm not going to tell Johnny what just went down at the station. He doesn't need the added stress. And now…," I pulled her hands from me and held her at arms' length, "I want you to go inside, try to relax and not stress. You have a busy week ahead of you…lessons and recording your audition CD for Jenkins. We need to get them to the committee for evaluation. Luke will help you…OK?"

She looked up at me with tear-filled eyes and all I wanted was to wipe the tears away and hold her. "I can't even think about that now. Suddenly it doesn't seem important." She dashed away the tears and let out a soul-cleansing sigh.

I frowned at her. "It is important. Now go inside, have some iced tea, play with Popcorn, and leave everything to me." I leaned down and put my lips close to ear. "I love you." I heard her sharp intake of breath as she turned her head a fraction, putting her lips in close proximity to mine. "I'll be in touch." I brushed her cheek with my lips and turned away, heading down the driveway and home. I didn't look back.

Chapter Thirty

Emma

"Don't worry...this isn't for the public's reading pleasure. I filed a three-sentence bit for the blotter and left it at that. Now I want to know what happened. Were you there when Johnny beat up that Farnsworth kid?"

My dad was actually acting like an involved parent for once and I wasn't thrilled with his timing. I'd managed to get this far in life without too much parental involvement and I preferred to keep it that way--to protect the independence I cherished. "Johnny didn't do it."

My father stood in the doorway of my room like a sentry, looking more serious than I'd seen him in a long time. "Then who did?"

I sighed and walked over to my closet, reaching in and scooping Popcorn from her warm place in the far corner. I cuddled her close to me...listened to her soft meows. "I'll tell you what happened but you might freak...or not...I don't know."

"I'm listening." He stayed put in the doorway and listened as I told him about Farnsworth's assault and Charlie's coming to my rescue... how Johnny had come upon us after the worst was over but then got into a fight with Farnsworth's friends. He didn't say anything as I spoke but I watched as his body language began to make an awful lot of noise—clenching fists, angry eyes, increased breaths.

"Of course I'm freaked. Why wouldn't I be?" He came toward me then, giving me a total head-to-toe scan. "Did he hurt you?"

"I'm fine. Charlie pulled him off me in time." There was no way in hell I was going to show my father what Farnsworth had done. "Farnsworth said Johnny did it...but he didn't. He wasn't even there."

My father paced the room a few minutes asking more questions and promising not to go to the station or call anyone and make this worse than it already was. Eventually he left me alone in my room but not before staking a parental claim. "I'd still like you to keep some distance from Johnny until this blows over. I'd feel better if you two cooled things off a bit."

I started to balk but realized he might be right, although for entirely different reasons. I knew I'd protested this morning to him about being ordered to stay away from Johnny, but now I wasn't going to fight his edict. I agreed to his request but when he left, I called Johnny immediately. I needed to let him know why he might not see me for a while.

"Hey, baby…what happened at the station? And why aren't you here with me?"

I should have taken time to prepare an answer before calling him, but it was too late now. "We wrote statements and I showed them the photos you took of me. They said they'd check into things and get back to us." Not exactly the truth but not a total lie either. I ignored his other question for the moment.

"Well, I have news." Johnny sounded apprehensive, now that I took a moment to really listen to his voice. "The football team is going down together to write out statements on my behalf. Even Claire and Kerry are going and a few other Westbrook girls who were there and sitting around the pit. Of course, their statements are going to nullify my confession, but I'll deal with that when the time comes. If it ends up being a case of 'Charlie said versus Johnny said,' Farnsworth will finger me and Charlie will be safe. I'm not letting him go down for this."

I let out a pent-up sigh. I didn't know what to say. I loved Johnny for wanting to protect Charlie, especially in light of our disastrous attempt to tell the truth, but what good was it if he went to jail? "Are you doing OK?"

"I'm fine, but I'm missing you badly right now. Why don't you come over for dinner? My mom's home and holed up in her room. She's upset about something…she was upset before this whole Farnsworth shit happened…oops…sorry, baby. She's been spending a lot of time in her room. Now that I think about it, she's been acting strangely since Grandpa B's funeral…maybe even before then. And my dad's hardly ever here anymore but thankfully he showed up to bail me out of jail. He was quite ready to believe the worst about me. Any other time that would have pissed me off, but I don't care right now. All I know for sure is, I need you in my arms and then I'll feel so much better…so…come for dinner?"

I closed my eyes and felt my heart sink as guilt and shame washed over me. Shame for knowing he needed me and not being there for him and guilt for feeling thankful to my father for not allowing me to go to him. I was the worst kind of girlfriend and I knew Johnny deserved better. I swallowed hard and responded, "I can't. I'm so sorry…but… my dad is sticking to his directive that I stay away from you for a while."

Johnny didn't answer. The silence from his end thickened until I felt it coming through the phone, grabbing me in a chokehold. "Johnny…?" I whispered his name.

"I'm here. It's OK. I understand…I think. No worries. I'm gonna go check on my mom. I'll talk to you tomorrow. I love you." He hung up before I could say good-bye. I threw the phone down on my bed, dangerously close to Popcorn's sleeping form. She dived off the bed and headed back to her refuge in the closet. I collapsed on my pillows and tried to sort my scattered thoughts. I wanted to call Charlie...but then again, when didn't I want to be in contact with Charlie Channing? I grabbed my Gibson from its case and sat down on the edge of my loveseat and began to practice the songs I needed to record this week for the Jenkins audition. The distraction of my songs helped and soon I was lost in the music.

The week was going by in a blur. I was busy with lessons and worried about Johnny's date with the judge which was coming up on Friday. I was also nervous about recording my songs with Luke. He'd happily agreed to stay for a couple of hours after the store closed Thursday night to help me. I'd seen Charlie a few times in passing at the store but we hadn't spoken much or even texted. I was pretty certain he was avoiding me, but I was afraid to know for sure so I kept to myself and suffered in silence. Even Johnny was quiet—not calling or texting much, except around bedtime to tell me good night. He alluded to problems at home but didn't elaborate so I assumed it had to do with the Farnsworth mess.

And now it was Thursday and I was in the booth, sitting on a tall stool, trying to hold my guitar securely on my lap, giant headphones affixed to my head. I'd thought Charlie would come and listen—I'd asked him to—but he hadn't said yes or no. I was fairly certain he was just upset about Johnny and probably worried about how Johnny's date with the judge would affect him. I told myself not to take his ignoring of me personally. I tried to change the direction of my thoughts as Luke made adjustments on the sound board. He dimmed the lights to set the mood and told me to nod when I was ready to begin. I strummed a few chords, getting the feel of the guitar and the opening notes of "Crescent Moon."

When I felt ready, I gave him the sign and he counted me down... three...two...one...and I began to play. It took several takes before we were satisfied and I was relieved when Luke finally gave me a thumbs up. I waited a few minutes for him to give me the sign to sing my other song. It would be the first time anyone had heard it besides Popcorn. I'd written it just this week. It had come to me during the night...waking me up from troubled sleep and begging me to write it down. And just as Luke began to count me down again, I saw Charlie slip into the booth and sit down on the couch behind him. My heart literally leapt inside my chest, like a horse hurtling out of a gate at the sound of a gunshot starting a race. I stumbled a moment and missed my cue but Luke only smiled and counted me down again. I sucked in a silent breath and began to play "Did You Ever…?"

Did you ever wonder why
One heart lives, another dies
With no regrets, no good- byes,
Just a shifting of the tides?

Did you ever… did you ever…
No, I never promised you forever.
I only promised you hello
And one more kiss before I go.

Did you ever wonder who
Would break the one and only rule
Not to take what one claimed first
To never quench unending thirst?

Did you ever… did you ever…
No, I never promised you forever.
I only promised you hello
And one more kiss before I go.

Did you ever wonder when
Or even if there'd be an end
To love that started out so right
But faded out with morning light?

Did you ever… did you ever…
No, I never promised you forever.
I only promised you hello
And one more kiss before I go.

Did you ever wonder how
To get from then and back to now?
It can be done I know it's true
And next time love will stay with you.

Did you ever… did you ever…
No, I never promised you forever.
I only promised you hello
And one more kiss before I go.

Did you ever... did you ever...
No, I never promised you forever.
I only promised you hello
And one more kiss before I go.

I glanced up in time to see Charlie jump from the loveseat and dash out the door. My heartbeats ricocheted inside my chest as I slipped from the stool and ran out of the booth. I laid my guitar down on the seat and brushed past Luke who looked up at me, his eyebrows raised in surprise, his mouth in an O shape. I heard him call my name as I ran after Charlie down the hall.

"Charlie! Wait! Please!" He turned the corner and I saw him go into the employee break room. The room was dark but a security light in the ceiling cast a reddish glow about the room. He was standing at the sink, his back to me, his hands propped on the edge of the stainless steel. His head was down and his body rigid. I wanted to move closer to him, desperate to touch him, but afraid of his reaction. "Charlie...? What's wrong?"

Slowly he turned to me and spoke...quietly...his words barely more than a whisper. "What are we doing, Em?"

I moved closer to him, brought my hand up to touch his arm, but he stepped aside just out of my reach. I felt his rejection like a fist to my stomach and the pain of it brought instant tears. "I thought you said we'd figure this out...that together we'd figure out how to tell Johnny that..."

He closed his eyes, shaking his head back and forth. "I don't see how...how to do this...without destroying him. Look what he's doing... now...for me. Taking the blame for something I did...and what am I doing to thank him? Only falling for his girl is all. Only setting him up for heartbreak. Jesus...Em...he wants to spend the rest of his life with you...did you know that?"

I suddenly became aware of the low hum of the central air conditioning and the nip it brought to the air. Goosebumps popped up on my skin and I shivered, as much from the temperature as from the words Charlie had just uttered. "He told you that?"

Charlie let out a slow breath and ran his hands through his thick brown hair. He looked up, finally, and caught my gaze in his dark blue one. "Yes...you're 'the one,' he says. Jesus...you're his reason for living."

I gasped, bringing my hands to my face, shaking my head from side to side. Oh, Johnny...oh, no...sweet Johnny...who I already knew loved me that much. He'd told me so on more than one occasion...but... now...hearing Charlie say it, only made it hurt more. Because I knew

218 | Kellie Bellamy Tayer

there would be no happy ending for Johnny...not with me...even as much as I loved him.

"Everything OK in here?" Luke appeared in the doorway. "I'm finished with your songs, Emma, if you want to hear them. They sound amazing. I'm thinking one of these days I'd like to hear you and Charlie together. I think your voices would blend well."

Charlie cleared his throat and glanced up at Luke. "Yeah, she sounded amazing. I've gotta go. I'll see you guys tomorrow." He disappeared like a ghost into the dark hall.

"Did I interrupt something?" Luke asked, no doubt taking in my splotchy face and dejected expression. "You OK?"

"I'm great. Let's go listen to the music, shall we?" He nodded and I followed him to the studio. We listened to my songs...how he'd added some percussion to the chorus of one song and a bass line to the other. They sounded amazing and very real. I was happy with the results but I had a hard time feeling it. Because all I felt at the moment was sadness at the knowledge that we were all going to get hurt.

Chapter Thirty-One

Johnny

"What the fuck are you doing here, Channing?" My father and I had just arrived at the court house and Charlie was sitting on a bench just inside the door. He was wearing dress pants and a button-down shirt. Add a tie and suit coat and he could be a fucking lawyer.

"I'm here to turn myself in—again," he said. He stood and came toward us, his face a stone mask.

"Like hell. Go on home." I saw my dad's lawyer walking our way. "Go...now," I hissed. I glared at Charlie hoping he would get lost before he did something we'd both regret.

"Johnny, Andy," said the lawyer, shaking both of our hands. He turned his attention to Charlie. "Are you one of the witnesses?"

Charlie opened his mouth to answer, but I cut him off. "No...he was just leaving."

"Johnny!"

Fuck...Emma.... I turned toward the door just as she cleared security. She ran to me and I pulled her in close. "What the hell are you doing here, baby? You shouldn't be here." I looked down at her clothes. She wore a navy blue dress and fancy shoes—damn it all if she didn't look like a lawyer, too...a fucking hot lawyer. She and Charlie were clearly here to impress someone.

She looked up and gave me a nervous smile. "Why not? I'm the reason all this crap is happening. Shouldn't I be allowed to speak in front of the judge, too?"

I shook my head in exasperation. I was just about to try to convince her to go home when I heard a lot of commotion at the front of the building. I jerked my head in the direction of the front doors just as they opened and most of the Westbrook High football team walked in. "Jesus Christ," I muttered under my breath.

And it was all downhill from there. We were called before the judge, an old gray-haired, familiar-looking dude who seemed like he should have retired twenty years ago. I was asked to enter a plea and, ignoring my lawyer's advice to plead not guilty, I pled the Fifth Amendment instead. My plea was immediately interrupted by Charlie who jumped to his feet and shouted his own plea—of guilty—followed by the football team's collective outburst that I was innocent. The courtroom erupted into chaos and I slumped in my seat, my head in my hands, fully expecting the whole lot of us to be carted off to jail cells.

The judge slammed his gavel down and called counsel to approach the bench while police officers told us all to shut up and calm down. I had the feeling the courthouse hadn't seen this much excitement since its inception.

My father was livid. I could see he was confused by the outburst and was barely containing his annoyance. We waited several minutes for them to discuss whatever the hell they were discussing and finally the judge spoke.

"It seems to me that we have a bit of a conflict here. I want to see if I have the facts straight." He pointed to me. "You just executed your Fifth Amendment rights…is that correct, son?"

"Yes, sir," I said, sitting up straighter in my chair. He pointed toward Charlie.

"And who are you?"

"Charles Channing."

The judge shuffled some papers and picked one up and read it. He looked at Charlie over the top of his glasses. "Are you the same Charles Channing who submitted a statement claiming to be Mr. Farnsworth's assailant?"

"Yes, sir."

He turned to the other lawyer. "Where is your client?"

"Mr. Farnsworth is currently at his home recovering from the savage beating inflicted upon him by John Beaumont."

"I object!" shouted my lawyer.

The judge glared at him. "Do you see any jurors in here, Houston? What? No? Then save your objections." He picked up another handful of papers and waved them around at the audience. "And am I to assume that all of these statements were submitted by the lot of you hulking beasts, claiming John Beaumont's innocence?" A chorus of 'yes, sirs' rang out in the courtroom. The judge scratched his head in apparent confusion. He studied the statements for a few minutes, paging through the sheets of paper. He pulled another sheet of paper from the pile and studied it, along with some photographs. I felt my heart sink. I couldn't see the photos from where I sat but I had a feeling I knew what was in them. I watched as the judge scanned the courtroom, his eyes settling on the area where Emma was sitting.

"Does anyone else have anything to add before I try to straighten this mess out?"

Without missing a beat, Emma exclaimed, "I do!" I turned to stare at her, along with everybody else. Even standing up she was nearly the same height as the rest of the seated crowd. I closed my eyes and hoped for the best.

"And you are?" asked the judge, who clearly seemed to be enjoying the theatrics playing out in his courtroom.

"Emma Davis."

The judge picked up the photos but thankfully didn't turn them around toward the crowd. "You're the same Emma Davis who submitted a statement on Mr. Beaumont's behalf as well these photos of an assault on your person allegedly inflicted by Mr. Farnsworth?"

"Yes."

"Were you a witness to the beating of Douglas Farnsworth?"

She looked at me and then at Charlie and hesitated. Oh, Jesus, she was going to ruin everything. I couldn't let her tell the truth. I jumped up and turned to her. "No, Emma! Don't answer that!" My lawyer grabbed my arm and yanked me back down to my seat.

"Control your client, Mr. Houston," said the judge, an amused grin on his face. He asked her again. "Miss Davis…do you know who attacked Douglas Farnsworth?"

I held my head in my hands and waited.

"It was self-defense. He was attacking me and I had to defend myself."

Oh, my good god. Did my tiny little Emma who barely weighed a hundred pounds soaking wet expect the judge to believe she'd beaten Farnsworth? I peeked up at the judge. He looked like he was about to laugh. Like this was funny. Yeah…it was fucking hilarious.

The judge cleared his throat. "According to your statement, Charles Channing interrupted an assault on you by Doug Farnsworth and beat him in your defense. Is this correct?"

"Yes."

"Are you saying you also assaulted Mr. Farnsworth?"

"I'm saying I defended myself from being raped by Doug Farnsworth. I have the marks to prove it."

I felt sick. This was not going the way I'd expected. It should have been cut and dry. Fuck.

"I see." The judge looked at the photos for far too long and I suddenly had the feeling the entire world had gone to shit. Finally, he shoved everything aside and leaned over the wooden surface of his bench and looked directly at me. "Here's what I'm getting out of this mess. The only person who definitively identifies you as the assailant is the victim, Doug Farnsworth, who is not currently present in the courtroom. Every other witness in the room—and there are far too many of them to ignore—claims you, in fact, did not attack Doug Farnsworth.

You have conveniently decided to plead the Fifth, which I find interesting considering it doesn't jive with the statement you gave to the police, but that's neither here nor there for the purposes of this hearing since it's the plea you enter today that matters. Mr. Channing here, who, according to the officer's statement, has no visible marks on him that one would naturally incur in a nasty fist fight, claims to have been protecting Ms. Davis who has just announced that she, in fact, assisted Mr. Channing in the beating of Mr. Farnsworth. So you can see why I find all of this a bit…bizarre."

I wasn't sure if I was supposed to answer so I looked at my lawyer for guidance. He shook his head and stared at the judge. The opposing counsel fidgeted in his seat. He seemed about to speak when the judge continued.

"I'm turning this soap opera back to the Kenilworth police for further review. When the department can put the facts of the case together into a more cohesive picture we can proceed. I'm going to remand John Beaumont into his father's custody until such time as everyone can get their shitake mushrooms together. Speaking of which, it's lunch time and I'm starving." He directed his final comment to Farnsworth's lawyer. "You have a week to get your case together or the charges will be thrown out. And the next time you're in my courtroom, bring the complainant. I'd like to meet Mr. Farnsworth." The judge stood and smiled around the room. I had the feeling he wanted us to applaud. I took a closer look at his nameplate on the front of the bench: Judge Ralph Bollinger. I hadn't paid any attention to his name before but I suddenly realized who he was. I'd just this week planted twelve rosebushes in his yard and trimmed his overgrown hedges. I'm sure my father was aware of this but no one else seemed to be. I didn't know if this was a conflict of interest or not but I sure as fuck wasn't going to mention it to anyone. And I couldn't complain about today's outcome either. I'd gotten a reprieve—a temporary one—and I was grateful. I must have done a damned good job with those hedges.

Chapter Thirty-Two

Charlie

I sat in line at the Wendy's drive-up waiting to place my order. The line was long enough that I had time to dwell on the last hour which I'd spent at the therapist's office. I'd finally told my mother I'd see someone and she'd made me an appointment. I'd dreaded the whole idea of it, but it hadn't been as bad as I'd expected. The therapist had seemed normal. For some reason I'd assumed that all people who listened to other people's problems for a living were a little bit crazy in their own right. But Dr. Lowry had been easy to talk to and understanding of my tortured soul, such as it was. I decided therapy was at least better than going to the dentist and figured I'd keep going for a while. I placed my order and drove home where I knew my mother would be waiting to find out how it went.

I'd sent my audition tape into Jenkins and now that it was officially August, I checked my email constantly waiting for word. Emma had sent hers in, too, and I figured she was just as anxious as I was for a response. I hadn't seen her much the last few days and I wondered if she missed me as much as I missed her. I wasn't sure which was harder—being near her and not able to be with her the way I wanted to, or staying away from her altogether. Either way I was miserable. What I needed was Lake Crescent. It was time to go back to my refuge. School would be starting in less than a month and I hadn't been to the lake nearly enough. My brother and his friends were planning a 'back to college' party at the cabin this weekend, but I had no interest in partying with him and Scott and their degenerate friends. But the weekend after...yes, I'd go then and get in some lake time.

My phone beeped with an incoming text from Johnny. He'd been keeping a low profile lately, working long hours for his dad. I knew he was anxious about the Farnsworth mess—I was, too—and I hoped this text would be good news: hey...what're you doing? can you come over for a beer later? i've got good news on the assworth front.

I smiled as I responded: sure, see you around 7?

Johnny texted back that seven would be great. I wondered what the news was—at least it was good news. I suddenly had a strong urge to communicate with Emma…strong enough that I couldn't ignore it. I texted her: how are you? johnny says he has good news about farnsworth. has he talked to you?

A minute later she responded: hi. yes. i don't know what the news is but i'm going over to his house later. i'm not supposed to be seeing him for a while so my dad thinks i'm going to a movie. i miss you.

I read the last three words and closed my eyes. Oh, god…Emma, I miss you, too…more than you know. I wanted to type those words but I didn't. I couldn't help but grimace at the irony that we were both missing something we'd never had. I was too conflicted about Johnny and our damned childhood pact to allow myself to dwell on the possibility of making Emma mine. I texted: ok il'll see you there. I pushed send and felt badly that by not returning her sentiment, I could be hurting her feelings. I shoved my phone in my pocket and went outside to wash my car. I filled my head with the sounds of Muse's latest CD while I scrubbed and waxed…anything to keep Emma out of my head. Of course, it didn't work.

"So, now Farnsworth is saying he can't remember who beat him up," said Johnny. "He claims it was too dark on the beach and that he'd had a little too much to drink and everything's a blur."

I was stunned. This didn't sound like Farnsworth. "How is this possible? He knows full well it was me. What's his deal?" I didn't believe this problem was going to go away so easily. I watched as a slow grin began to form on Emma's lips.

"So will they drop the charges? Will this be over?" she asked. We were sitting on Johnny's back deck. Someone in the neighborhood was grilling out and the smell was making me hungry.

"I'm not sure what's going to happen, but I think I know what happened," said Johnny sounding cryptic. I raised an eyebrow at him and waited for him to elaborate.

He finished his beer and stretched his legs out in front of him. "Will and Scott are friends with some of the Kenilworth players who graduated last year and I know for a fact that the two of them were hanging out with those dudes last weekend. I think they somehow got them to strong-arm Farnsworth into changing his story and going to the cops with a new version of events. Scott told me today that Farnsworth is saying he can't remember who beat him up and he's running scared. I would be too, if our brothers and their bad-ass friends were threatening me with god knows what. I think he's trying to save face, which is ironic considering the condition of his face at the moment." Johnny laughed raucously at his own joke. He reached over for Emma's hand, bringing it up to his mouth to kiss her palm. I glanced away to look at the pool. This sounded too good to be true and Johnny's mouth on Emma's hand was too hard to take.

"Just because that idiot changes his story doesn't mean the charges will be dropped, you know," I said.

"I know," said Johnny. "That Officer Marks is an asshole. I think he has it in for me. But he's only one guy and I doubt the decision to make the charges stick or not rests with him anyway. I'm hoping my idiot lawyer will call tomorrow with some news."

Emma pulled her hand from Johnny's grasp and began to fiddle with her Coke can, twirling it round and round in her hands. I hoped to god it was empty. She looked puzzled. "Do you think this Farnsworth guy will forget about all this and let it fade away?"

Johnny laughed again. "Oh, hell no, babe. If the legal system doesn't take care of it, I have no doubt Farnsworth and his followers— the ones Will and Scott didn't get to—will take care of things on their own around the time school starts and football season gets underway. The thing is...I don't know who they're gonna come after—me or Charlie. Who knows? They may want revenge on both of us. We'll have to watch our backs."

The sound of loud voices drifted out onto the patio from inside the house. Johnny glanced through the sliding doors, a worried look coming over his face. "Dammit! My parents are fighting again. They've been at each other's throats a lot lately. Sorry you guys...it might get loud." He stood up and walked closer to the sliding doors, his head cocked to listen.

"What's going on with them?" Emma asked. I noticed her hair seemed to be glowing with a halo of light cast from the setting sun. It was starting to get dark and she looked downright angelic sitting there across from me. I felt my gut twist at the thought of running my hands through those black strands of silk. I swallowed and looked over at Johnny. He looked agitated.

"I'm not sure. My mom's been crying a lot lately and my dad has been acting like a first-class prick. I've asked them both what's going on and neither one will say, so I'm guessing it's financial, but who the hell knows. But business certainly is booming. We have more clients than we can handle these days." He moved away from the door and sat back down on the chaise. "Hey, Chuck...you do realize that school's gonna start in a few weeks and before that I'm going to be starting football practice and you're gonna have marching band…so…I was thinking… how about another trip up to Lake Crescent before all the madness starts, assuming I'm not in prison?"

"I'm not marching this year. I don't feel like it. It'll be a nice change to actually get to sit in the stands and watch the games." I'd missed last year because of the accident and I'd realized my passion for marching band had faded along with a lot of other things in my life…except for the things I couldn't have. "But…yeah…I was thinking of going up to the lake soon. Will and Scott are planning some hedonistic weekend of college debauchery this weekend but the weekend after would be good. And then you'll have football practice right after that…so…it's a good way to end the summer."

"You think you're dad'll let you go, Em?" Johnny asked her. "I mean…if I'm not about to become inmate number 1234567, maybe he'll relax his rule…which, I might add, you're blatantly breaking by being here tonight." He walked over to stand behind Emma's chair. He put his arms around her neck and began to kiss the side of her face. I looked down at my hands and mentally chastised myself for inviting him to the lake. I hadn't exactly planned to do that…but I knew I wasn't fooling myself. I wanted Emma there even if it meant Johnny would be there, too.

"I'm coming to the lake no matter what. If my dad gives me trouble about it, I'll just have to wear him down. But I forgot to tell you that I'm going down to Portland to see my mom Friday. I'll be back Monday in time for my afternoon lessons. I haven't seen her in a while and she wants me to come down at least once before school starts."

"Well, damn. I guess it's a lucky break for me I have to help my dad with a huge landscaping project Saturday and Sunday…it'll keep my mind off of missing you," Johnny said, coming around in front of Emma's chair and pulling her to her feet so he could wrap his arms around her. I could see in her body language that she wanted to resist his embrace and that made me feel marginally better. But I couldn't stand watching him with his hands all over her and I knew I needed to get out of there.

"I'm gonna head home. I'll see you guys later." I left them on the deck and walked to my car, opting to walk around the side of the house instead of passing through the house's interior. I didn't want to run into Johnny's parents. Every so often I could hear a loud voice coming from one of the back bedrooms. Whatever was happening between Mr. and Mrs. Beaumont, it didn't bode well for a happy ending.

When I got home Will was sitting at the kitchen table eating ice-cream. I got some for myself and joined him. "I was just over at Johnny's. He told me Farnsworth's recanting. You know anything about that?"

Will grinned at me through a mouthful of strawberry ice-cream. "I plead the Fifth."

I laughed. "That seems to be the popular plea these days. But seriously...what's up with his change of story?"

"Let's just say, that not all of Kenilworth's football team—past and present—are fans of Farnsworth. Apparently they've been wanting someone to bash that fucker's face in for some time now and you, little brother, are a hero in their eyes. They know it was you and not Johnny. Farnsworth's posse are a bunch of dope-heads but they didn't see you beat Doug because their asses were all sitting around the fire pit with the rest of us while you were saving Emma from that asshole. Now, I have a prediction about this, bro: the charges will be dropped against Johnny and the cops won't come after you because there are no witnesses and...," he hesitated before continuing, "Farnsworth will come after you for revenge. He may be a fucking asshole but he's only human and humans are naturally inclined to want to get even...so watch your back...and Johnny's, too."

I nodded and finished my ice-cream. I hated to think that Will was probably right about Farnsworth. Johnny had said the same thing earlier, so I'd have to assume that Doug would come after me at some point. I put my dirty bowl in the dishwasher and went up to my room. I was tired and looking forward to turning in early. I wondered if Emma was still with Johnny. My thoughts always turned to her at night when I wanted to sleep. I picked up the new Daniel Silva novel and tried to concentrate on the plot. Eventually I got caught up in it and I was able to tuck Emma away in the corner of my mind for a couple of hours. But I knew she'd still be there, taunting me, in the morning.

Chapter Thirty-Three

Emma

It seemed strange to be back in my old room in Portland. Mom had made some changes to the house since I'd been living in Westbrook and I was surprised at how different the place looked. She'd gotten rid of a lot of stuff—there was a chair missing from the living room and the baker's rack was gone from the dining room. I noticed that the closets were neat and tidy and…sparse. She'd painted my room white and it looked awful. But the biggest change I encountered was in my mother's bedroom. While she was out picking up dinner from my favorite Italian place, I'd stuck my head in her room to see if she'd made any changes in there, too. I opened the closet where my father's clothes used to hang, expecting to see my mom's clothes there, or at the very least nothing at all. But what I saw nearly made my heart stop. The rack was filled with men's clothes—suit jackets, dress shirts, jeans, t-shirts and rows of men's shoes on the floor beneath the clothes. I stared in shock at the sight of it all, trying to comprehend what I was seeing. I turned around then and studied the room. I opened a couple of drawers and found men's underwear, socks and t-shirts. In the adjoining bathroom, I opened the medicine cabinet and saw men's cologne and a toothbrush and shaving supplies. I blinked my eyes for a moment, taking it all in. I supposed I shouldn't be so surprised that Mom had a man in her life. After all, it was her cheating that killed the marriage in the first place. I wondered who the man was…if it was the same one who she'd been seeing when she was married to Dad or if it was someone new. I heard a car in the driveway so I quickly closed the medicine cabinet and the closet door. I ran downstairs just as she was coming in the back door, her arms filled with way more food than two people could eat.

"Wow, you got enough to feed an army." I took the bags from her hands and set them on the counter. When she didn't respond I glanced over at her. She had a strange expression on her face. I stared and waited for her to say something.

"Um…we're having guests for dinner tonight," she said.

"Guests?"

"Yes. I want you to meet someone…a man I've been seeing. His name is Robert."

I opened my eyes wide in mock surprise. "Robert?"

"Yes. We've been dating a…while now…and it's kind of serious so…I wanted you to meet him." As she spoke she took a stack of plates from the cupboard and began to set the table. I counted the plates—six of them.

"Just how many Roberts are coming?" I asked.

Mom laughed nervously. "Well, he has three kids and they're coming, too."

I felt nauseous. Dinner with my mother's boyfriend and his three kids? No wonder she was in such a big hurry to get me moved up to Westbrook…she'd needed room in the house—my house—for her new family. I wondered if my brother knew about this. Eric was stationed at an Air Force base in California. It suddenly occurred to me that I hadn't had any communication with him except for a few Facebook exchanges and emails.

"Three kids? How old are they?"

"Six, eleven and fourteen…and they're all girls." She looked at me as she answered, gauging my demeanor. She was expecting a reaction out of me and I decided to give her one.

"Do they live here, too? Did you throw me out to make room for them?" I could feel my blood pressure rising as my heart began to pound harder.

"Emma! How can you say that? I did not throw you out…and no, they don't live here. They live with their mother. And can I assume you've been snooping around and found some of Robert's things around the house?"

I didn't answer. I went to the refrigerator and took out a pitcher of tea. I poured myself a glass and took a long drink…and immediately spat the mouthful out into the sink as soon as I got a taste of the sugar—it was sickeningly sweet. "God, mother. This is awful. Since when do you drink sweet tea?" I grabbed a paper towel and wiped my mouth.

"Robert and the girls prefer sweet tea so I've started making it that way."

I couldn't believe it. So she was catering to them and their wishes now? I looked at her and shook my head in disgust. "Well, I am your daughter and I do not drink sweet tea. And you should have told me about Bob and his darling daughters before I got here instead of waiting to tell me now."

She continued setting the table, laying out the silverware and glasses. She didn't say anything and the silence was louder than a bomb's blast. I heard a car in the driveway and glanced out the kitchen window. A man and three red-haired girls were just getting out of a dark blue minivan. "Bob and the girls are here. Are they spending the night? Maybe I should call Liane and see about spending the night with her. I wouldn't want to be in the way."

"Emma...stop." She frowned and went to the door to let them in. I wanted to grab my bags and leave now. I could stay at Liane's or better yet I could go back to Westbrook. I could see Johnny—or Charlie—and I could get away from this ridiculous love-fest that I wanted no part of. But I swallowed my annoyance and put on the perfect daughter act.

Dinner was excruciating, Bob was weird, and his daughters, Brandy, Sherry and Crystal, who were apparently named after the contents of Bob's liquor cabinet, were the most bizarre creatures I'd ever met. I quietly endured the evening for my mother's sake, but I came to the determination that it would take a court order to get me to come back to Portland.

The weekend dragged. I had to endure Bob and his daughters for most of it. They were quite awful and I thought Monday morning would never come. I'd wanted to leave Sunday afternoon but my mother had insisted I stay for Bob's birthday dinner. But come Monday, I was up and on the road by eight o'clock, driving myself back to Westbrook—to my real home. Portland wasn't the same and neither was my mother. I actually looked forward to going back to Nanette and her baby drama. Anything was better than my mother's life, which didn't have room for me in it anymore.

Chapter Thirty-Four

Johnny

"You're a lucky son of a gun, John," said my dad. We were loading equipment at Beaumont's Greenhouse and Landscaping in preparation for a big job on the Quinault reservation. It was going to be a long day and I was dreading it, but with Emma in Portland, I knew I'd be glad for the distraction. And by the end of the day, I'd be too exhausted to dwell on the fact that I missed her like crazy.

"I'm aware of that." I climbed up into the cab of the truck and fastened my seatbelt. I looked over at my dad, noticing that he looked older and tired. "What's going on Dad? What's happening between you and Mom? I know it's something serious so don't think you can just blow me off."

Dad gripped the steering wheel hard enough to turn his knuckles white. He cast a sidelong glance my way. "Your mother and I are having some problems but we're working them out. I don't want to talk about it and I don't want you to worry. And for god's sake, don't ask your mother any questions. She's a little fragile these days. Please just drop the subject. If I want you to know anything just be patient. I'll tell you when I'm ready, but for now...no questions."

I started to protest at the wimpy answer but thought better of it. I'd just have to hope for the best where my parents were concerned. At least things were looking up on the Farnsworth front. The lawyer had called yesterday to tell us that the charges were being dropped against me. With Doug's change of story and no eyewitnesses except Charlie and Emma, whose accounts apparently didn't match the supposed evidence collected by the cops, there was no case. Of course, I knew it wouldn't end there. I had no doubt that Farnsworth and I...and Charlie... would have a run-in again in the future.

Chapter Thirty-Five

Charlie

Johnny's car was in the shop getting new tires so we'd decided we'd all ride up to Lake Crescent together. I had just finished my last guitar lesson of the day and had stopped by my house to pick up a few things. I packed up the car, said good-bye to my mom, who handed me a freshly baked apple pie to take with us, and headed over to get Emma. She was waiting for me on the porch.

"Hey, Charlie, we'd better get a move on before my stepmother comes out and asks me to move something. She's been rearranging the furniture once a week since she got pregnant. Oh, wait…let me rephrase…I've been rearranging the furniture for her once a week because she can't move or lift anything heavy. She's making me crazy."

I laughed more at the sight of her all fired up than at her stepmother's addiction to home decorating. "I take it your dad didn't have a problem with your going off to a cabin in the woods alone with two guys again?"

She rolled her eyes. "Now that the charges against Johnny have been dropped, my dad is back to burying his head in the sand where I and my activities are concerned. I feel sorry for my future little brother or sister."

I gave her a sympathetic grin as I tossed her bags into the back of the Durango. We drove over to Johnny's and I parked on the street in front of the house--three of the Beaumont's cars were parked in the driveway. It seemed strange to see most of their vehicles there at the same time. Just as we got out of my car to walk up to the house, Johnny burst out of the front door and ran down to meet us half-way.

"Hey, guys…slight change of plans." He was breathing hard and his face was red. He was definitely upset about something. "We're having some family drama right now and I can't leave. My mom is a wreck, my dad isn't talking, and Scott and I are trying to figure out what the hell's going on. Something has been brewing for weeks under that roof and I think it's going to come to a head before this day is over."

Emma hopped out of the car and put her arms around Johnny and hugged him. "I'm so sorry. Do you need me to stay here with you?" I felt my heart sink at her question.

"No…I want you guys to go on ahead. It could get ugly around here and I don't want you sitting at home worrying when you could be enjoying the lake. I'll stay here for my mom and in the morning, assuming no one killed anybody, I'll get my car from the shop and drive up to the lake. "

"Are you sure?" I asked. "We could wait till tomorrow if you want." It wasn't what I wanted but I had to make the offer. The thought of being alone with Emma at the cabin tonight was turning my brain inside out.

"Positive. You guys go ahead and I'll drive up tomorrow. I'll let you know what's happening here as soon as I know myself." Johnny lifted Emma off the ground and kissed her. I tried not to let it bother me. After all, he was unwittingly giving me a gift…a gift I didn't deserve, but I couldn't think about that right now. We said good-bye and watched as Johnny ran back inside his house. Once inside the car, Emma turned to me, her eyes troubled.

"What do you think's going on with his parents?" she asked me.

"I have no idea. They always seemed to have the perfect marriage but I guess no one really can know for sure what goes on behind closed doors. I guess we'll just have to wait and see." I left the neighborhood and pulled out onto the main road. Emma played with the radio until she found a song she liked. As we drove along, we talked about everything under the sun. She told me about her mother's boyfriend and his daughters and talked about her stepmother's weird habits. I asked about Popcorn and her eyes lit up. It was evident that finding that little kitten had made her extremely happy. While she talked, I watched her--more than I should have, considering I was driving a vehicle, but she was so damned beautiful, sitting there next to me in white shorts and a tight red tank top, flip flops on her feet and her hair pulled back in a low pony tail. I noticed her toe nails were painted red and I had a vision of massaging each one of her toes individually. I blinked and shook my head against my wayward thoughts.

It was late afternoon when we arrived at the lake house. We'd stopped at the little store in Crescent Springs to pick up a couple of steaks, some salad fixings and a loaf of French bread. Once at the cabin, we unloaded the car and Emma went to work fixing the salad and slicing the bread.

"I'm starving," she said. "I can't wait to eat."

I went out on the deck and started the grill. I stared at the briquettes…tried to count them…anything to keep my thoughts off of Emma. I glanced up through the sliding door and caught her staring at me. She looked away quickly and went back to slicing bread. Once the grill was hot I went inside and moved past her to turn on the radio. We were standing close now and I was keenly aware of her...her perfume, her hair, her body. My own body tensed, my mouth watered and my heart started a jackhammer sensation against my ribs. Oh, my god...I could already feel her in my arms and I wasn't even touching her.

"Salad's ready," she said softly. I gave her a sideways glance and swallowed. I needed a distraction or else I was going to kiss her. I grabbed the steaks and went back out to put them on the grill. A minute later Emma came outside with two cold Cokes and handed me one. She leaned over the railing and stared out at the lake as Bruno Mars began to sing about being locked out of heaven. I knew the feeling. Her back was to me and it took everything I had not to walk over to her and pull the band from her hair and run my fingers through it. I stared at her body, the curve of her backside, the swell of her breasts pressing up against the railing and a million volts of electricity fired inside me. If she turned around now, she'd see the effect she was having on me—I wouldn't be able to hide it. I could literally taste her sweetness on my tongue. I fought to suppress a groan and turned my attention to the steaks. I turned them over and avoided looking at her.

"There's supposed to be a half-moon tonight. I checked moon phases on my phone earlier. It'll be pretty over the lake. Maybe we should go for a walk around the lake after dinner," she said. She took a sip of her Coke and went back inside the kitchen, returning with plates and silverware. I plated the steaks and we carried out the salad, bread and fresh drinks to the patio table. Once I was seated and eating, I felt better about controlling myself where she was concerned. I just had to get through this one night and Johnny would be here tomorrow and this temptation would be over. I could do this.

"Sure...a walk would be good. It's warmer than usual which is nice. August may be hot everywhere else in the nation, but usually it's cooler here, at least at night." Oh, my god, I'm talking about the weather, I thought, as I chewed my steak. We finished eating and carried the dishes inside. Emma stacked the dishwasher, without breaking any dishes, while I cleaned the grill and tidied the kitchen. She went to the bathroom and I went back out onto the deck. It was twilight now and the sky was slowly turning to indigo. The water shimmered and the night sounds began to play...chirping crickets and birds rustling in the leaves. I could even hear the gentle lapping of the water on the shore.

"This place never gets old, does it?" Emma spoke softly beside me.

I looked over at her. "No, it doesn't." She was standing close to me—too close—and I felt the first strike against my self control. I swallowed and looked back at the lake. It was darker now and the half-moon was peeking over the tree line, making its way slowly over the water. The mountains in the distance looked like silent watchmen. "I wonder what's happening with Johnny's folks."

"I just checked my phone. He sent a text and said they were all about to have a family meeting or something and he would be in touch later." She leaned forward, staring off into the twilight. "Look at all the fireflies."

I watched their golden lights blinking on and off in the gathering darkness. A soft breeze blew through the trees and I caught a whiff of her perfume...cherries and vanilla and some exotic flower. It made me dizzy. I closed my eyes for a second.

"You didn't bring your guitar?" she asked. Was it my imagination or had she somehow moved even closer to me?

"No. You didn't brings yours either," I said, glancing down at her.

She turned to face me and smiled. Her eyes seemed to sparkle in the moonlight. I felt another blow to my resolve as I let my gaze linger on her lips. And when she licked those full, beautiful lips I was done for. I groaned audibly and stepped away from her. This couldn't happen.

"Are you feeling it, too, Charlie?" She stepped toward me.

"Oh, I'm feeling something...yeah...and I shouldn't be..."

"Give me your hand. I want to show you something." She held her hand out to me and I knew if I touched her, there'd be no turning back. I put my hand in hers and she grasped my fingers, pressing two of them to her wrist. "Do you feel that?"

I closed my eyes and felt the rapid beat of her pulse. She moved closer and placed her hand against my chest, pushing against it. My own heartbeat gave me away and if she were to glance down, she'd know that wasn't the only part of my body pulsating. I placed my hand over hers and held it there. "Emma..." I shook my head slowly back and forth, hoping she would be the strong one because I knew I didn't have it in me...not anymore.

"Kiss me, Charlie. I need you to kiss me."

And I did. I pulled her into my arms and I kissed her lips...so soft... so pliant...so ready and willing to be consumed. I slipped my tongue inside her mouth as I ran my hand down her back and over her tiny, perfect ass. She groaned and pressed her body into mine. Her tongue was magical, tangling with mine in perfect rhythm. There was no question now that we were on borrowed time. I pulled back a fraction to look into her eyes. Her pupils were large, masking the green color of her eyes. "Emma...I want you...so badly."

"Then take me. I'm all yours," she whispered against my lips. I didn't even hesitate. I took her hand and led her inside the cabin and down the hall to my bedroom. It wasn't completely dark in the room—I was able to see her and for that I was thankful. I didn't want to miss a thing. I took her in my arms again and kissed the corners of her mouth.

I reached back and pulled the band from her hair and watched as the long, black, strands loosened and fell around her shoulders. She was so damned beautiful. It was hard to breathe just looking at her.

"Give me a second? I need to get something from Will's room," I said, noticing that my ability to speak normally was hindered by my unsteady breaths.

"OK."

It only took me a second to find what I needed. Will was always prepared for moments like these. I grabbed a few condoms and went back to my room, dropping them onto the nightstand. She looked from them to me and for a moment I thought I saw a look of fear on her face. I didn't know if it was a Farnsworth flashback or something else, but I sensed I needed to tread carefully. I hugged her close. "It's OK, Em... we don't have to..."

"I want to...but...you should know that...I've...I've never...I mean...I'm a...a...virgin...so I'm a little... you know...nervous," she said, her words tumbling out on a long puff of air.

"Ah...I see...it's OK." I put two fingers under her chin and tilted her face up to mine. I already knew this about her and it made me so incredibly happy knowing I would be her first and I hoped to god her last. "I'll talk you through it...or kiss you through it as the case may be." I grinned and leaned down and kissed her. "Your lips are filled with some kind of drug...I'm under the influence."

She emitted a soft giggle and kissed me back, her tongue tracing a path around the interior of my mouth. I groaned and slipped my hand under the front of her tank top. "Your skin is so soft." I slid my fingers under the bottom of her bra, taking my time, giving her a chance to change her mind. But she moaned and pushed up against me and I lifted her bra up, over her breast and I cupped her in my hand. Oh, my god...she felt like powder, her skin was that soft. I brought my hand out from under her tank top and pulled it over her head. I reached behind her, under her hair and unclasped her bra. Before I pulled it away from her, I closed my eyes for just a second to prepare myself for the sight of them, even though I'd seen them before, briefly. I opened my eyes and put my hands on her, cupping her breasts, running the pads of my thumbs over her dark nipples. I saw a faint mark on her left breast but I didn't comment on it. I didn't want anything to spoil this moment. "My god, Emma...you are so...something else," I whispered. I pulled her toward the bed and she lay down on it. I stripped my t-shirt off and lay down next to her. I trailed my fingertips between her breasts, down her stomach and stopped at the waistband of her shorts, and with each inch of my fingertips' journey, her body quivered and trembled under my touch as goose bumps formed on her skin. I leaned down and took her breast in my mouth and sucked. She arched her back and moaned as I leaned across to take the other breast in my mouth. Holy hell…this was…in a contradiction of terms-- excruciatingly amazing. She tasted like heaven. She moaned and grasped my hair in her hands, pulling my head up closer to hers.

"Oh…it feels so…so…," her soft voice trailed off. I looked up into her eyes, waiting for her to finish her statement, "so amazing…so good." She pulled me down on top of her and kissed me with a fierceness that killed the last of my self control. Her hands were suddenly everywhere… rubbing up and down my back, across my chest, in my hair and on my face. I sucked on her lower lip, pulling it into my mouth and I let my hand go again…down her stomach, past her bellybutton… and under the top band of her shorts. She trembled under my palm as I slid my hand down further inside her shorts, my fingers sliding into her warmth. She gasped, her hips coming up off the bed, her body pressing into my hand as I stroked her.

"Oh…oh…oh…," she moaned, her eyes closed. Suddenly she shook and gasped and I felt her release as I leaned down and kissed her lips. She continued to rock her hips against my hand, trembling and shaking.

I whispered against her mouth, "That was a beautiful sight to see. And it's only the beginning." I removed my hand from her shorts and pushed them down to where she could kick them off. I looked down at her naked body, taking her in. "You are so beautiful, Em. I love you."

"I love you, too." She reached for the button of my jeans, never taking her eyes off of mine. She fumbled with the button, her hands shaking, and I helped her. I unzipped my jeans and slipped them off along with my boxers. I pressed my body against hers, reveling in the feel of skin on skin. She glanced down at me, her eyes widening, and again, I thought I saw that look of fear. I needed her to know she was safe with me.

"Touch me, Em," I said against her mouth. I ran my tongue over her lips, causing her to moan again. She ran her hand down the length of my body and this time I was the one quivering. She took me in her hand and gave me a gentle squeeze. "Oh, god…this is the sweetest torture," I moaned. I knew I didn't have much time before my will to hang on gave out. I reached behind me for a condom and tore open the wrapper with my teeth. I rolled the condom on and positioned myself above her.

"I don't want to hurt you, angel, so we'll take it slow…well, as slow as is humanly possible." I kissed her beautiful mouth…her chin… her neck and the space between her breasts. Propping myself up one elbow, I ran my hand down the length of her body and she involuntarily arched upward off the bed. I slipped a finger inside of her to make sure she was ready. She was more than ready.

"Oh…Charlie…I think it might…happen again…everything feels so…alive…down there."

I couldn't help but chuckle at that. "That's a good thing." I spread her legs apart and positioned myself between them. "Look at me, Emma. Keep your eyes on mine. Don't look away." I slowly pushed into her, resisting the urge to go full throttle which is what my body was naturally inclined to do. Her eyes opened wide…wider…her mouth forming an O, her body slightly stiffening. I could tell she was holding her breath and I worried I was hurting her so I stopped a moment. "Breathe, angel…just breathe." When she didn't say anything, I pushed on, past the point of resistance until she began to relax. She brought her legs up, making it easier for me to enter her and with one final push we were finally joined. "You OK?"

She nodded and grabbed my head to pull me down to her mouth. We kissed and began to move in rhythm together and I knew I wouldn't last long. I pulled my mouth from hers and groaned low in my throat. I rocked, probably a little harder than I should have, and let myself go. I heard her sweet whimpers…soft cries…and I stilled…trying to calm myself. I'd made a few sounds of my own and I hoped I hadn't frightened her. As my body came down off its high, I leaned down close to her ear…closed my eyes. "You feel so good, angel. And the sounds you make…the sweetest, sexiest sounds…you're like your own symphony." I kissed her temples and tasted salt. Her hands were in my hair, holding me to her but I leaned back to peek at her face and saw tears. "What is it, Em? Did I hurt you?"

She shook her head back and forth and pulled me down for a kiss. I felt something in this kiss…an urgency…a message…she was telling me something with this kiss and I was listening.

Finally she spoke. "No…you didn't hurt me...quite the opposite. I never knew it would be like this…so…otherworldly. Beautiful things always make me cry—you know that—a turquoise lake, a crescent moon, a fluffy, white kitten…you…and the things you do…the way you make me feel."

I chuckled. "Otherworldly, huh? Yes, it is that. And thank you… for giving me this gift…the gift of your body. I will never stop wanting this now…wanting you…you know that, right? " I slowly pulled out of her and rolled to lie next to her. I discarded the condom into the trash can beside the bed. Emma snuggled into my shoulder and I held her, my hand rubbing up and down her back, feeling the soft skin…loving the feel of it.

"I hate to tell you this, Charles Channing, but…," she stopped...

turned her face up to mine. I saw a glint in her eye.

"But?"

"But, I think you may have just created a monster," she giggled.

"Oh, yeah? Well, let's see if that's true." I glanced down at myself. "It's a little shell-shocked at the moment, but in the right hands, I think we can work something out...the three of us."

"Ooh...let's see...shall we?" She pushed me back on the pillows and moved on top of me.

"Oh, god," I moaned as she leaned down to kiss me, her tongue finding mine, her breasts molding into my chest. "I was gonna suggest we have some apple pie and go for a walk in the moonlight, but I think that's gonna have to wait." It didn't take long before the movement of her lower body against me, the feel of her hands on my chest and her tongue and lips blending with mine had me ready again. And this time, I had more control. I rolled her over onto her back, slid the condom on and eased into her. We moved together, her eyes locked on mine, and when I finished before she did, I slid out of her and with my hand, I watched as she exploded against me, emitting soft cries of pleasure and moans of ecstasy. I knew in that second that if I lived to be a hundred, there would never be another moment in my life that would match this one...that could ever come close to equaling the taste, touch, smell, sight and sound of Emma Davis's body uniting with mine.

Chapter Thirty-Six

Emma

It was still dark when I awoke to go to the bathroom. I slipped out of Charlie's arms and stole quietly from his bed. I relieved myself and had a drink of water. My body still hummed from Charlie's lovemaking and I smiled to myself as I washed my hands. I felt different now…I felt loved in a way I never had before and I knew that I would never be the same girl I was yesterday. I didn't want to be that Emma anymore. I was Charlie's now. I thought back to that moment…the moment I first felt Charlie inside of me. It had hurt at first, but the pain had turned to pleasure so fast it was like I'd only imagined it. He was so gentle with me and so perfect—everything about him was so incredibly perfect. It seemed as if the last eight hours had happened in a dream…the most beautiful dream. I sighed as I looked in the mirror at my swollen lips, mussed hair and flushed cheeks.

This is what love looks like, I thought, as I turned off the light. I tiptoed back to the bedroom, slipping into the warmth of Charlie's arms. He tightened them around me and I turned to him…pressing my lips into the space just beneath his ear and kissing him there. My body was on fire for him…thrumming with a heat I couldn't contain. I ran my hand down his naked chest…let my hand drift slowly and gently into that magic place beneath his bellybutton. He shivered, groaning low in the back of his throat and turned his face to me, planting his lips on mine. I was starting to scare myself with the depth of my feelings, and as I slipped my tongue inside his mouth, I felt a sense of urgency so intense that a surge of longing coursed through my limbs. I burned for him.

"Charlie…"I whispered against his lips. "Is it wrong to want you so much? Is it normal?"

He leaned back and in the dim light of the pre-dawn sky from the window I saw the corners of his mouth turn up in a smile. "Oh, god, no, Em…it isn't wrong and, as for normal, we'll make our own normal." He kissed me, his tongue making a slow turn inside my mouth. I whimpered from the taste and feel of him. I shook with a surge of passion so strong I felt like I'd been electrocuted. His hands began to move over me…down my arm, over my breasts, across my hip. I pulled him to me and felt his erection against my abdomen.

"Oh, god…Charlie…please…" I was gasping now. His tongue trailed down my throat and he sucked my breasts and I convulsed. I was going to die…right here…right now…if he didn't give me what I so desperately needed. "I want you inside me." I didn't even care how brazen those words sounded. I wasn't myself…I was the new Emma now and the new Emma wanted Charlie Channing's body in the worst way. "Please."

"I have created a monster, haven't I?" he whispered as he reached for a condom on the nightstand. "Lucky for me I'm not afraid of monsters." He slipped it on and shifted his body on top of mine. As he slid inside of me I wrapped my legs around his waist and tried to swallow him whole—I would have if I could. "You feel so good, Em…so warm… so…so…ah…ah…"

I moved beneath him…raking my nails down his back, hoping I wasn't hurting him but unable to control the sensations flowing through me and the power they were giving me. He moved rhythmically inside of me and I felt my body tighten and tense. He gasped…his breathing became labored.

"Jesus…Em…you're so…un…real," he groaned out the words. He thrust once more hard into me and his body spasmed, jerked, and finally he stilled on top of me. I held him close, not wanting our connection to be severed. A fine sheen of sweat had broken out over his body and I felt the dampness of it on me. He panted into my neck and I continued to hold onto him…not letting him go…squeezing him tightly into me with my legs and my arms. "Em…you're…kinda strong…all of a sudden…," he gasped.

I relaxed my hold on him and he slowly slid out of me and pulled me into his arms. I grabbed his hand and pushed it down and within seconds he gave me the release my body ached for. I cried out, unable to control the emotion and the intense feeling of the moment. I kissed him long and slow, knowing I could kiss him forever and never want to stop. "I love you," I said, meaning it with every heartbeat…every breath.

"I love you," he said. He held me and over the next minutes, I felt my body relax. My breathing returned to normal…exhaustion overtook me. Finally, satisfied and content, I slept.

"What time is it?" Charlie asked, looking for his phone on the nightstand. "We slept late."

Bright light was streaming in through the sheer lace curtains—it did feel rather late. I found my phone on the floor where it had fallen last night. It was on vibrate so I hadn't heard it alert me to any calls or texts.

"Oh, geez...it's almost ten o'clock," I said, scrolling through the texts. There were several from Johnny. I read them, jumping from the bed in a panic, my heart pounding. "Oh, my god! Johnny's on his way here. He texted at 8:45 saying he was just leaving. He could be here any time."

Charlie stood up and pulled me into his arms. "You go take a shower and I'll..." he glanced around the room, "clean up in here, just in case he comes in here. Don't panic...everything's going to be OK." He kissed me then and as much as I wanted to stay in his arms, my fear of Johnny catching us outweighed my desire for Charlie's lips. I nodded, gathered my clothes and dashed off to the bathroom at the other end of the cabin. I rushed through my shower and once I was dressed and had my hair combed out, I felt more in control of our circumstances. We should have taken some time last night to discuss how to handle Johnny and the way we would break it to him that we wanted to be together, but we'd been too caught up in each other to think of much else.

I glanced out the living room window on my way to the kitchen, fearing Johnny's car would already be parked out front, but only the Durango was there. In the kitchen, Charlie was frying bacon and making coffee. His hair was damp from a shower and my eyes drank in his body. I went to him, desperate to put my arms around him but fearful of Johnny's imminent arrival.

"Hey, beautiful," said Charlie. "I'm making us some bacon and eggs. Johnny just called me. He stopped in Crescent Springs to get something and he'll be here in a few minutes." He set the spatula down on the spoon rest and turned to face me. He could clearly see by the look on my face that I was freaked out about what was going to happen with Johnny today. He shook his head at me, giving me a reassuring smile. "Try not to worry, angel. We're gonna work this out. I know I've gone back and forth on the whole Johnny thing and our childhood pact and our friendship, but Emma, I can't stand back and watch you with him. And even if you break up with him to become a free agent, I'm not gonna let you go. You're mine now and we'll make him understand, OK?"

I felt tears threatening to fall and I tried to blink them away. I was just about to answer him when I heard a car door slam out front. "Oh, shit...he's here. Charlie...I don't think I can do this...now...I don't know how to do this without hurting him." I dashed my tears away and composed myself.

Charlie didn't respond. He turned back to the stove and flipped the bacon just as Johnny walked into the room. Johnny stopped beside the kitchen table and dropped his car keys onto a placemat. He stood looking at us, not speaking. Charlie turned from the stove and he and I both stared at him, his expression one of utter sadness and exhaustion. I felt my heart crack at the sight of his sad face. He tilted his head to the side and opened his arms to me. I felt Charlie's eyes on me as I walked across the kitchen and into the circle of Johnny's arms. He kissed me... hard on my mouth...hard enough to hurt, but I didn't flinch or protest. He held me tight against him, rocking us from side to side. I had never seen him like this and I didn't know what was happening—both in his family and inside of him. Johnny didn't show his vulnerability like most people, so his current state was hard to take. I let him hold me for a moment before stepping back to look into his eyes, my hands in his. He stared at me as if he could see into my soul and for one horrifying moment I thought he already knew—that he could plainly see I had fallen in love with his best friend.

"Last night...my family...," he started, glancing away toward the sliding doors leading to the deck, "my family kind of went to fucking shit." He released my hand and slumped into a chair at the table. He pushed out the one next to him and asked me sit beside him. Charlie turned off the stove and joined us, taking the seat across from mine. "I don't even know where to start."

"What happened? Is your family OK?" I felt breathless and shaky, not knowing what was happening.

His face reddened and I saw his eyes water...he was fighting hard not to cry...not to show weakness. Finally he answered, and as he spoke, I watched his body tense, the muscles in his arms flexing. "My mother has cancer—ovarian cancer."

I gasped then clamped a hand over my mouth...felt tears form instantaneously. Johnny reached for my hand and gave it a squeeze. I glanced at Charlie who sat, immobile, watching Johnny. I could see in his eyes that he was fighting tears, too.

"But wait...cuz there's more....there's more fucking shit...and I hate this...I hate this for my mother...as much as I hate the fucking cancer in her body I hate this..." He let go of my hand and pushed back from the table, standing, his hands gripping the edge of the oak. He was shaking, his body coiled like a snake, ready to strike. I watched as a myriad of emotions washed over his face and, for the first time ever, I was afraid of Johnny Beaumont. I held my breath as I waited for what he would say—or do—next.

Charlie stood up and moved to stand between me and Johnny. "What's going on, Johnny? What more is there?" His voice was quiet...calm.

"My goddamned father is having an affair...with his best friend's fucking wife." He suddenly lashed out at the chair, kicking it against the wall. He picked it up and raised it, ready to hurl it across the kitchen but Charlie grabbed it from his hands, set it down, and took hold of Johnny's arm. Johnny continued through clenched teeth. "I mean... who does that, Chuck? Who the fuck cheats with his best friend's wife? While his own wife has fucking cancer? Who does that?" He laughed...a harsh, almost menacing laugh. "Of course, he started the affair before he knew about the cancer...not that the timing matters...but can you fucking imagine what my mother is going through? She finds out her asshole husband is having an affair with his best friend's wife and the next day the doctor tells her she has goddamned cancer. Can you believe this shit?" He shook off Charlie's arm and began to pace...around the island...over to the stove where he picked up a piece of bacon from the skillet and dropped it back down again. He stopped at the fridge... opened it...closed it...and then turned his gaze on me. I sat at the table, frozen, speechless, my heart thumping so hard in my chest I thought for sure it would burst right through my chest wall. He walked over to me and knelt beside my chair. His eyes were red and so...hurt. I couldn't stand it. I pulled him against me and held him, his shoulders shaking in silent sobs.

"I am so, so, sorry," I whispered against the top of his head. I ran a hand through his thick blond hair, noticing it had gotten long and lighter from so much time in the sun. I looked up at Charlie who stood by the sliding door watching us. His hands were in his pockets and the expression on his face spoke volumes.

"Thank God I have you, Em, and Charlie." He cocked his head sideways to look at Charlie for a moment then turned his face back into my lap. I stroked his hair, rubbed his back, waited for him to pull himself together. He straightened and reached up to cup my face in his hands. He pulled me toward him for a kiss and I responded to him because I knew he needed it. Charlie moved then...came to Johnny and put his hand on his shoulder. Johnny released me and stood. He embraced Charlie briefly and let him go, then sat down beside me again at the table.

"My father is an asshole. He doesn't deserve my mother...my mother who wouldn't hurt a fucking soul and has never done anything to deserve to be treated this way. I hate him."

"Jesus, Johnny. I don't even know what to say. I'm sorry...this is all so...," Charlie waved his hand, at a loss for words. He walked back over to the stove and put the bacon on a paper towel to drain. "I'll finish making us some breakfast."

"I'll get coffee," I said. I ran my hand along Johnny's arm as I got up to get three cups from the cupboard. I avoided Charlie as I poured coffee and set out cream and sugar. I purposely kept my mind focused on Johnny so I wouldn't think about my and Charlie's dilemma.

Charlie made scrambled eggs and toast while I sat with Johnny. He brought the food over to the table and we passed the platters around in silence. As Johnny ate, I noticed the tension ebbing from his shoulders and neck. I asked him if he'd gotten any sleep last night.

"No...maybe an hour or two. We listened to my fucking father apologize over and over...the weakest damned apologies, too. He's only sorry he got caught. He actually said...and I shit you not...he actually said..., 'this never would have happened if I'd known you were going to get cancer.' Now...can someone tell me what the fuck that even means? Jesus Christ. My mother and her piss poor cancer planning. If she'd only gotten fucking cancer six months earlier, my dad would have been faithful? Really? That's all it would have taken to honor his marriage vows? Better timing? Can you believe that shit?" He slammed his fist down hard on the table, causing his coffee to splash over the side.

I was stunned. I glanced at Charlie who sat straight and stiff in his chair, his face an impassive, unreadable mask. Johnny got up and poured himself more coffee while I wiped the coffee mess with my napkin. He held up the pot and we both shook our heads. I couldn't eat or drink anything else. My stomach was nervous, the eggs not sitting well. When Johnny came back to the table I asked, "How is your mother? Who's with her? Is your father still...living...in the house?"

Johnny leaned back in his seat and let out a long sigh. "Yes, the asshole is still in the house—in the guest room. He says the affair is over but I have my doubts. And my mother, who traditionally doesn't do well in emergencies, is surprisingly phenomenal...I mean...so brave." His eyes welled with tears and he tried to smile. "Her doctor said the cancer was detected early and her prognosis is good. She has to have a hysterectomy...next week...and then she'll have a short course of chemo. They're not sure if radiation will be necessary...it'll depend on what they find when they remove all of her...you know...female parts." He fought to choke back a sob. "And Scott's with her today but I'm gonna have to go back tonight." He looked at me. "You'll come back with me, right, Em? I know you were looking forward to being here for the whole weekend but I feel like I've hardly seen you lately. I miss you like crazy. I seriously just want to go somewhere for a few hours and be alone with you."

Charlie suddenly moved from his trance-like position at the end of the table. He pushed the chair back, the legs screeching loudly on the floor. "We'll all go back. It wouldn't be the same here without you... two...anyway...and Johnny...," he stood and moved to stand behind Johnny, placing his hand on the back of Johnny's neck, "I know it sounds trite, but…if you need anything…or your mom…just say the word."

Johnny smiled over his shoulder at him. "Thanks." He turned to me and tilted his head, "Emma…you look beautiful. I mean you always look beautiful…but today you look exquisite…like you're glowing or something. Being here is good for you, isn't it?"

My eyes widened in surprise. I swallowed a lump in my throat and felt my face redden. My stomach clenched and it suddenly seemed nearly impossible to take a breath. Every organ in my body suddenly seemed to want to stop working altogether. I opened my mouth to say something…to thank him…deflect his compliment…anything…but speech failed me.

Johnny started to laugh. He glanced over at Charlie who was standing at the sink. "Look at this, Chuck. She's speechless. My little gorgeous princess here is at a loss for words." He got up from the table and pulled me to my feet, crushing me into his chest. His fingers filtered through my hair as he pressed his lips to the top of my head. "What did you two do last night anyway? Did you bring your guitars?"

"Nope—no guitars. We cooked out…steaks on the grill…and watched a movie…that's about it," said Charlie. He began to clean up the breakfast dishes, keeping his back to Johnny. I extricated myself from Johnny's embrace and found my voice…finally.

"Thank you for the sweet compliment." I needed to get out of this room. It felt like the walls were closing in. "I've got to use the ladies' room…be right back." I started to walk away but before I got two steps, Johnny caught my arm and pulled me back, kissing me…a long, passionate kiss that threatened to undo me, but not in the way he intended. He finished the kiss and held me close.

"I don't mean to get all sentimental on you guys—emphasis on the 'mental' part—but I am so frickin' lucky to have you two in my life. A beautiful girl who's all mine and a best friend whose loyalty I never have to question. I'll never have to worry about getting stabbed in the back by my best friend…I mean…shit…how many guys can let their girl and their best friend spend a night alone together in a cabin and not have to worry for one minute that he'll be cheated on. My dad's best friend should have been so lucky." He cupped my face in his hands and caressed my cheeks. "I just needed to say that. Now go to the bathroom, babe, before you pee your pants."

I forced a smile and disappeared down the hall to the bathroom. I'd never once looked at Charlie while Johnny was speaking. I was too afraid of what I'd see on his face…in his eyes. I leaned against the door…my body shaking. Even my teeth began to chatter. This was all such a horrible mess…the worse kind of nightmare. I sank down onto the edge of the bathtub and buried my face in the towel that hung on the rack beside me. I had a terrible feeling that I knew how Charlie would want to handle this. I knew, deep in my aching heart what was right. Charlie would never betray Johnny—not after he'd poured his heart out to us...certainly not after everything he'd suffered in the last twenty-four hours. And I couldn't betray him either. If ever Johnny needed me...it was now. I had to be the person he thought I was—the faithful, loving, supportive girlfriend that I'd always tried to be...had intended to be...until I'd made the tragic mistake of falling for his best friend. I stifled my sobs in the towel, hopeful that they couldn't hear me. I cried for Johnny's mother and for Mr. Beaumont's best friend and for Charlie and for me. But mostly...I cried for Johnny.

Chapter Thirty-Seven

Johnny

"Emma and I are going for a walk around the lake. We'll be back in a bit," I said to Charlie. He was sitting on the deck staring out at the water. I suddenly noticed that he didn't look right...like maybe he had a headache or was in some kind of pain. "You OK, Chuck? Your leg hurting?" He was rubbing his hand up and down his thigh like he was trying to force an ache out of it. He pulled his gaze away from the water and looked up at me. It was obvious something was bothering him.

"What? Oh...yeah...my leg's bugging me today. It acts up every once in a while. It's nothing I can't live with." He stood and moved past me into the kitchen. Emma came around the corner then. She looked from me to Charlie and back to me again. I became aware of that weirdness that I sometimes sensed in the air here at the cabin when Emma and Charlie were in the same room. I shrugged off the weird feeling and beckoned Emma to come to me.

"Ready for a walk?"

She glanced again at Charlie whose back was to her and nodded, then followed me down to the lake. I looked up at the sky...it was a perfect day to be at Lake Crescent—huge white cumulus clouds, the water sparkling in the bright sunshine, the air heavy with the scent of pine and earth. "Damn...I wish we were staying till tomorrow. But you understand why I need to get back to my mom, right?" I grabbed her hand as we walked side by side along the lake path.

"Of course. Your mom needs you. And the cabin isn't going anywhere. We'll come back again another time." I heard sadness in her voice and I felt badly that I'd brought her—and Charlie—down with my family drama.

"Can you believe I start football practice Monday? This summer has flown by," I said, giving her hand a squeeze.

"It has, hasn't it?" she agreed, her voice low.

I glanced over at her. She looked as sad as she sounded. I stopped walking and pulled her to me, tipping up her chin with my fingertips so I could look into her eyes. "What's wrong, Em? Is it my family shit bringing you down? I'm sorry about that."

She put her arms around me and placed her head against my chest. "No...I mean...of course, my heart is breaking for you and what your mother is going through. I was just thinking that she's lucky to have you in her corner. You're a good son and I love the way you love her."

I coughed...cleared my throat...struggled to speak without sounding like a blubbering idiot. "Oh, Jesus...the pedestal you have me on has a very weak foundation, babe. I haven't been the greatest son over the years. It's a fucking shame it takes something like what's she going through now to make me realize how much better I could have been... could be now...for her."

She tightened her arms around me. "Don't dwell on the past. The only thing that matters is now...and the fact that your mom needs you and you're there for her." She leaned back to look at me. "True story, Johnny Beaumont...you're a good guy. Don't ever let anyone—yourself included—tell you differently."

I smiled...a huge, wide smile...and lifted her up so I could reach her lips. I kissed her, tasting her sweetness, my tongue needing to feel every corner of her beautiful mouth. I let her slide down my body to the ground and the feel of her pressing against me started a fire in my crotch that quickly threatened to consume me. I groaned at the sweet pain of the ache spreading through me. I rubbed my hands over her back, down to her backside and cupped her ass in my palms. She stiffened in my arms but I didn't let it bother me...I'd caught her off guard. I continued to touch her, to feel the softness of her skin, to rub her back, until she relaxed against me. I leaned down so my mouth was next to her ear. "You know, Em...you and Charlie have been the only bright spots in an otherwise very shitty summer. Just being with you makes me feel a million times better. I love you, babe."

She hugged me, pressing her face into my chest. We stood together...quiet and unmoving...until I noticed that she was ever so slightly quivering...shaking...in my arms. I leaned back to see her face. She was crying silently, tears rolling down her cheeks. Just ahead, close to the shore I saw a flat rock, wide enough for us to sit on. I led her to it and we sat side by side, my arm around her back. "Why the tears, babe... what's wrong?"

She leaned forward, resting her upper body on her knees, her face turned away from me. I slid my hand under her shirt, rubbing her bare back, kneading it with my fingertips. She felt so tense. Finally she spoke.

"I don't know...I just feel emotional today...just...you know... thinking about things...life in general...worried for you."

"Ah...it's OK. I feel good about my mom's situation...well, her health anyway. She'll beat it...I mean...fuck...she's a Beaumont...in a manner of speaking...so she'll be OK. As for the other...problem...

Scott and I'll make sure she comes out OK on that end, too. I'm gonna make my idiot father step up and be a man. He's gonna do right by my mother or else he'll be dealing with me…and it won't end well for him. Nobody fucks with someone I love and lives to tell." I bumped against her and she turned to me. I grinned and she seemed to relax. In the back of my mind I thought of Doug Fucking Farnsworth who had fucked with someone I loved and lived to tell. It burned me to think about it. Emma stood up and walked over to the water's edge. She picked up a handful of flat stones and skimmed them out across the water. I watched her for a few seconds and then got up, needing to feel her in my arms again.

I wrapped my arms around her and buried my nose in her hair, breathing her in. She was still trembling and though I didn't really know what was causing her tremors, I did know what was causing my own internal quaking. I wanted her…badly…so much so that to wait much longer could be my undoing. "Let's go back to the cabin…to my room. I want to be alone with you," I said quietly into her hair.

"We're alone here," she said, shifting in my arms.

"You know what I mean. I want to make love to you. I need you." I stepped back to look at her but she turned her face away, avoiding my eyes. I cocked my head to the side and raised an eyebrow, trying to read her. "Em…?"

She let out a long, shuddering breath and looked off somewhere behind me. "I…I… can't…because…I'm…I'm…" she stopped. I noticed her face was red and she looked like she was about to cry again.

"You're what?"

"I'm…I'm…on my period." Her voice quavered as she said the words.

I laughed, a feeling of relief washing over me. "Ah, I see." I took her hand and we began to walk again along the path. "For the record, I don't even care about that, but…I want your first time to be perfect and being on the rag would definitely interfere with your pleasure…so… we'll wait till you're finished. I've waited this long…," I squeezed her hand. "I can wait a few more days."

We walked along in silence for a while along the water's edge. I stole occasional glances at Emma's profile as we walked. She seemed to be lost in thought but I didn't press her to talk. I was disappointed at the timing of her body which made me think of my idiot father in an ironic way. But I would endure. I'd undoubtedly have to take matters into my own hands later until she gave me the all clear. It wouldn't be the first time I'd had to take care of myself waiting for Emma.

Chapter Thirty-Eight

Charlie

A battle raged inside my head and my heart was caught in the crossfire. There was no way around it—I would have to choose one over the other—Johnny, whom I'd known nearly all my life, my best friend and keeper of all my childhood secrets, my partner in crime and my closest confidant...the one person who'd always had my back, in spite of his behavior in the months after the accident...or...Emma, whom I'd known for all of three months, but who was now indelibly imprinted on my soul...Emma...the one person above all others who made me feel whole again. In a perfect world I could have them both and Johnny would understand and even give us his blessing. But in the real world, it was a case of either, or...my past...or...my future...both of them stuck in the abyss that was my present. I had only one second to make my choice...they were both going under...fading away...and I knew I couldn't save them both...

Jesus Christ! I sat up in bed, my heart pounding, my t-shirt soaked in sweat. I hadn't had a nightmare in months and this one had been a doozy. I leaned forward, resting my head and shoulders on my knees while I waited for my heartbeat to regulate and my breathing to slow. I tried to remember the bad dream but already, in the minute I'd been awake, the details had faded. All I could remember was having to make a choice...between what was... and what could be. I'd had only seconds to save Johnny...or Emma...from sinking into the dark depths of Lake Crescent.

"Goddammit!" I muttered as I got up from the bed and went to take a shower. I didn't need the nightmares. I didn't need the drama. What I needed was Emma...even though Emma would cost me Johnny. Hell, it would cost more than Johnny—it would cost a peaceful existence. Because if Emma and I were together, we would have to live with Johnny and his demons and that thought alone was enough to give me pause. I felt the weight of depression taking hold again. I didn't want to feel this way anymore. I glanced at the clock on my nightstand and saw that I was going to be late for my lessons if I didn't get my depressed ass moving. My phone rang just as I was pulling out of the garage. It was Emma.

"Hey," I said, feeling my heart race.

"Hi. Are you on your way to the store?" She sounded breathless.

"Yeah. I'm running late. I've got the Munson kid this morning. Fun times."

"I have at lesson at nine o'clock. Meet me after?"

"I have three lessons in a row. Why don't we go to Wendy's for lunch at noon?"

"I'll see you there…and Charlie…I love you."

She hung up before I could say it back.

"I'm going with Johnny tomorrow to the hospital. He wants me with him while his mother's in surgery." Emma toyed with a French fry, making swirly patterns with ketchup on a napkin.

"Of course. I'd come, too, but I have a doctor appointment in the morning." I stared at my burger, wishing I had an appetite for it.

"What kind of doctor appointment? For your leg?"

I hesitated, hating to lie to her but knowing it was for the best. She didn't need to know I was a fucked up mess inside and that I needed a therapist to help me get my shit together.

"Yeah…just routine."

She pushed her food aside and reached across the table, her palms facing up. I glanced around the restaurant before placing my hands in hers.

"Tell me what to do, Charlie. I don't want to hurt him, especially now when he's down so low, but I want to be with you—only you."

I sighed…closed my eyes against the bright sunlight shining across our table. "I've thought of nothing else since we got home from Lake Crescent. I don't have any answers. Let's just lay low until after his mother's surgery. Once she's on the mend, we'll sit down with him and tell him. I don't want to hurt him either but I can't be without you." I had a sudden flashback to the many times over the years Johnny had taken something I'd wanted because he'd spoken up and claimed it first, but I didn't care this time. I didn't care that Emma had been his first. This time I would speak up for myself and take what I wanted…what was mine…and let the chips fall where they may.

"I need to get back. I have one more lesson and then I'm free. Johnny had football practice this morning and he has to work for his dad this afternoon. Then he'll be with his mom this evening. I probably won't see him until tomorrow at the hospital." As she spoke she began to rub her foot against my leg—slowly up and down—under the table.

I cocked my head to the side and stared at her. She looked sexy as hell, looking at me with those big green eyes filled with desire…for me. I felt a jolt of electricity hit me hard below the waist. I fought to stifle a groan. "My mom won't be home this afternoon…if you want to come over…?"

She smiled. "Oh, I want to come, alright."

I grinned…shaking my head in wonder. "I bet you do. OK then, little monster…come over after your lesson. Maybe you should leave your car at home and walk to my house…just in case."

We left Wendy's and went our separate ways. I'd wanted to kiss her good-bye but it didn't seem like a good idea to kiss her in public. Westbrook wasn't the smallest town in the world but still, it was rare not to see someone you knew when you were out and about. I drove home and parked my car in the garage. I decided to clean my room while I waited for Emma to come. I stripped my bed and put on clean sheets and ran the vacuum. I went into Will's room for some condoms. My brother had a never-ending supply hidden in a bag in the back of his closet. I put a few in my nightstand drawer and then went out to wait for Emma on the porch. Just as I sat down my phone alerted me to a new email. I opened it and saw that it was from the Jenkins school. I sucked in a breath, my heart slamming against my chest as I read: Congratulations, Charles Channing. You have been selected for a resident audition at The Jenkins School of Music and Theatrical Arts in New York City. Your audition number is 22 and your scheduled appointment time is 11:00 a.m. on December 19. Please see the attached document for important information about the auditioning procedures and recommended preparation to make your audition a successful one. Good luck.

Wow. I'd gotten the audition. I was a step closer to my dream of being a professional musician…an educated professional musician. Excitement bubbled up inside me. If I'd heard from Jenkins then Emma probably had, too. I couldn't wait for her to get here. I paced around on the porch waiting, going crazier with every step—both from excitement about Jenkins and the thought that in a few minutes I would have the most beautiful girl in the world in my bed. I glanced down the street just as Emma rounded the corner. She saw me and broke out in a run and when she got close enough for me to see the huge grin on her face, I knew she'd heard from Jenkins, too.

She bounded up the porch steps and came to a halt in front of me. I kept a poker face while she caught her breath. "I heard from Jenkins…I got an audition…December 19. Did you hear from them yet?"

A slow grin spread across my face. "Yep. Same date, too. Congrats, angel." I opened the door and as soon as we were inside, I shut the door and pressed her up against it. "My god, Emma Davis...I thought you'd never get here." I began to kiss her...all over...her lips, cheeks, temples, anywhere my lips found skin. She wrapped her arms around me and pushed her pelvis into me and I was nearly done for. "Let's go to my room."

We ran up the stairs and I had no more than shut the door and locked it than Emma was tearing at her clothes, pulling her t-shirt over her head, stepping out of her jeans, pushing at her bra straps, breathing hard as if she'd just run a marathon.

I grabbed her hands and steadied her. I looked into her heavy-lidded eyes...kissed her softly on the mouth. "Easy little monster...let's not rush this."

"I'm sorry," she panted into my chest. "I just...can't help myself. I want you...so much...that it actually...hurts." She started to jump... little bounces...up and down in front of me. The movement was doing things to her breasts that nearly knocked the air out my lungs. I raised my eyebrows in surprise, cocked my head to the side and grinned.

"Well, then, let's get rid of your pain, shall we?" I took off my shirt, stepped out of my jeans and boxers, then helped her out of her little, white lacy panties. When we were naked, I stared at her, my eyes taking in every inch of her. I admired her like the work of art she was. Her body quivered with desire and I bent down and took her nipples into my mouth, each in turn. Her legs turned to liquid and she crumbled into my arms. "Whoa there, Em...you OK?"

"Oh, my god, Charlie...will it always be like this? Will I always feel faint and earthquakey?"

"I sure as hell hope so," I said, taking her hand and leading her to my bed. I settled her into the pillows and began to explore her body. I wanted to feel every inch of her. She brought her hand down and began to stroke me, causing my entire body to spasm. "Oh, man...Em...if you touch me like that, I'm gonna explode way sooner than either of us wants me, too."

"I'm sorry...I just want it all...I mean I want all of you...ooh...I just want..." she panted, tugging at me to come closer to her. I leaned over her, taking her mouth, plundering it with my lips and tongue, feasting on her. I snaked a trail down her neck and across her breasts, touching them, tasting them, sucking them, as her body quivered and quaked. Her nipples were dark rosebuds...silky soft and so damned delicious.

"Angel...look at me," I whispered. "I'm going to taste you and I already know how good it will be." I ran my hand along the curve of her hip and slid it across her upper thigh. I slid two fingers into her and she squirmed against me. I closed my eyes...reveling in the velvet heat. I withdrew my fingers and she whimpered, lifting her head to look at me. I slid down and positioned myself between her legs. I parted them and slid my tongue across her sweet spot and she bucked against me. I had to hold her hips in place until she could get herself under control. She tasted every bit as delectable as I knew she would. I stroked her with my tongue...listened to the symphony of sounds escaping from her throat. She gripped the blankets in her fists, her head thrashing back and forth on the pillows as I continued to lick her and within moments, I felt the explosion of her body against my mouth. I kept up my rhythm until her movements slowed. And I knew I couldn't wait a second longer. I needed to be buried inside of her. I crawled up the bed, grabbed a condom from the nightstand and ripped it open. When I had it on, I leaned over her and whispered in her ear, "Angel...do you have enough strength to be on top this time?"

Her face lit up. "God, yes," she said. I lay back against the pillows and she climbed on top of me, straddling my hips. I groaned in anticipation as she lifted her body above me and with my hand as a guide, I helped her lower herself onto me. "Ooh...ooh...Charlie...will it...fit? Ah...ah...," her face contorted and I stopped her.

"You don't have to do it this way, angel, if it hurts too much." But...oh, god...how I wanted it to be this way.

"I can do it." Her voice was shaky as she lowered herself the rest of the way onto me. "Oh, my god...I feel so...full," she whispered. She brought one hand up and touched the spot on her chest under which her heart lay. "It's like I can you feel you all the way up here."

"Take it slow, baby. I know this is new for you. But you should know how amazing you are...and how incredible you feel...so beautiful...so sexy." I reached up to move her hair out of the way of her breasts so I could see them move as she began a rhythmic ride over me. I ran my thumbs over her nipples, pinching them softly between my fingers, making her gasp. I had only seconds to take in her beautiful breasts and full pink lips, currently in the shape of an O, her eyes heavy-lidded with desire, before my tenuous grip on my self-control slipped away and I couldn't hold back any longer. I reached down and grabbed her hips, pulling her down hard as I lifted my pelvis to meet hers, cementing our bodies and I let it all go. "Ah...Jesus...Emma...oh...my god..." I shook...my body one volcanic mass of smoke and ash...erupting inside of her.

When my spasms subsided she slid off of me and came to rest in the crook of my arm. I wrapped her tightly in my embrace, unable to get her close enough. She held me and began to kiss me...the sweetest, softest kisses. I was molten lava in her arms. We lay still and quiet for several minutes. I listened to her breathe…every breath so soft and fragile. I felt so overwhelmed with love for her in this moment that I actually feared for my manhood. It wouldn't take much for me to become a crying mess in her arms.

"I could do this…literally…all day, every day," she whispered against my neck. "I mean it, Charlie."

I grinned down at her. "Well, damn, girl…I guess that makes me the luckiest man on earth." I kissed her lips, preparing myself to do it all over again, when her cell phone rang.

She sat up, her face flushed…from lovemaking and probably the sudden interruption. "It's Johnny. I have to answer." She got up and pulled her phone from her purse and said hello.

I listened while she talked to him. She didn't say much…he was doing most of the talking. Finally she hung up, dropping the phone back into her purse.

"He's getting off early from work and wants to have dinner with me. He's just getting into the shower now so he'll be at my house soon."

"I guess I knew this couldn't last forever." I sighed, wishing like crazy it could.

"I'd better go. I'm going to have to shower before he comes for me. Although…," she walked across the room and stopped in front of me, her eyes locking on mine, "I don't want to wash you off of me. I love the way I smell and feel after having you inside me."

I groaned and looked up at the ceiling. "You're killing me, Em." I swept her into my arms and kissed her feverishly. She returned my kisses with the same fervor and I thought, for just a moment, that I might actually lose my mind. I pulled away from her. "We've gotta stop. I can barely control myself as it is…and…you've gotta get home before he comes."

We got dressed and went downstairs. As she turned to go, she said, "We're going to have to tell him about Jenkins. He needs to know there's a possibility that we could be going to school in New York next year."

I sucked in a breath…held it…then let it out slowly. "OK. But don't say anything tonight. I want us to tell him about Jenkins together."

"OK. I'll call you tonight. I love you so much, Charlie. I don't think you even know how much."

I leaned down to kiss her, pulling her lower lip into my mouth for one more taste. "Angel…if there was a way to measure love, I bet I would win."

She snuggled up against me and kissed the Nike logo on my t-shirt. "There isn't…it's immeasurable. So that makes us even. I'll call you later."

I watched her walk away. She turned back to wave numerous

times. I gripped the railing of the porch to hold myself in place...to keep from running after her and taking her back to my bed. When she finally disappeared around the corner I went to my room, took out my guitar and began to play.

Chapter Thirty-Nine

Emma

"How was Johnny tonight?" Charlie asked me. I was tucked into my bed, Popcorn crawling all over me, purring and pawing at my blanket. We were on the phone but in my imagination he was lying here next to me.

"Exhausted. He isn't sleeping and now with football, plus working long hours for his dad, I'm really worried about him. And Mrs. Beaumont has to be at the hospital at six in the morning. He probably won't get any sleep tonight either. I told him I'd get there by 7:30. I'll stay till I have to get to my ten o'clock lesson at the store."

Charlie sighed. "He'll be OK. But, Em...we need to tell him about Jenkins and about us. I don't want to have to hide my feelings for you. I want to be able to hold your hand in the halls at school and kiss you senseless in public places."

I didn't answer right away. I wanted the same things but...Johnny was too fragile right now and I couldn't bear the thought of hurting him...not now. "We'll play it by ear. Let's see how things go tomorrow, OK?"

We said good night and I tucked Popcorn into the crook of my arm, and tried to still my thoughts so I could sleep. I watched the clock for a long time before sleep finally pulled me under.

My heart ached for Johnny and his family. I could barely breathe as he sat beside me on the couch in his living room. His father and Scott were at the hospital and he would be heading over their soon. This day had not gone as anyone had expected.

"The fucking doctor was so sure the surgery would solve everything. That she'd be OK, have a few chemo treatments...maybe some radiation...and that would be that. They're all fucking idiots."

I didn't know what to do...how to comfort him. "So what are they saying now?" I asked softly, worried I'd ask the wrong thing.

"Well, it's in her lymph nodes. So this means heavy duty chemo

264 | Kellie Bellamy Tayer

and definitely radiation. She's gonna get a whole lot sicker before she even has a shot at getting better." He suddenly stood up and began to pace around the living room. "You know what, Em? I blame my asshole father for this. This is all his fault. He's a selfish fucking bastard." He picked up a framed photo of his parents from the fireplace mantel and raised it above his head.

I jumped from the couch and ran to him, unable to control the tears streaming down my cheeks. "Please, don't throw it," I cried, reaching for the frame. He placed it in my hand. I put it back on the mantel. "You know this isn't your father's fault."

He pulled me into his arms and held me so tight my ribs ached. He cried into my shoulder, his body shaking. "This is so not fair," he cried, his voice muffled in the sleeve of my blouse.

"I know." I whispered, my heart aching more with each passing second. "We have to think positive thoughts…put good vibes in the atmosphere. She's gonna be fine…I can feel it. You have to be strong for her even though it's so hard."

He leaned back and looked down at me, his brown eyes so troubled and lost. "You're right." He kissed me--a feather-light kiss—so different from the usual Johnny kiss. I put my arms around him and held him.

"Come with me, Em," he whispered against my cheek. He brushed his thumb along my jaw, caressing it softly. He clasped my hand in his and started toward the stairs. My stomach instantly tightened…my heart began to race inside my chest. We climbed the stairs and went inside his room. I swallowed a lump of apprehension. I didn't know how to handle this situation without hurting him. He shut the door and pulled me with him onto his bed, pushing me back against the pillows. "I love you so much and baby, I've never needed you more than I do now. I need to feel you…every inch of you…I'm going crazy and you're the only one who has the power to calm me and make feel like life is worth fucking living…pardon my French."

I opened my mouth to say something…intending to redirect his thoughts some other way, but he swooped down and captured my open mouth with his, kissing me with an urgency that I knew was borne of fear and an unknown future. His tongue sought mine, sweeping inside my mouth from side to side. He slid his hands under my blouse, under my bra and cupped my breast and my body instantly betrayed me, my back arching upward. He was moving so fast…my brain couldn't keep up with the frantic state of emotions coursing through him. His lips moved down to my neck and he brought his hand out from under my bra and began to unbutton my blouse. I had to stop this…but I was so afraid of his reaction that for a moment I was paralyzed with fear.

"I want you so bad…baby…so, so bad," he said against my lips. He reached under me and with one slick move, had my bra unfastened. He pulled it away exposing my breasts. He took one in his mouth and began to suck and goose bumps broke out all over me. Why couldn't I move? I didn't want this. I wanted Charlie…Charlie…oh, my god, Charlie. I had to swallow my fear of hurting Johnny…rejecting him… and act now, before this went so far that to suddenly stop could start a war neither of us had a chance of winning. I wanted more for Johnny than this. He slid his hand into my pants, moving down, and I finally faced my fear enough to stop him. I would fix this another way.

"Johnny…hang on," I grabbed his wrist, stopping his hand from moving any further.

He groaned. He looked up at me, his eyes heavy-lidded with desire, his breathing erratic. "No, baby…please, not this time…not when the only thing I need to feel better is the one thing that only you can give me. I want to make love to you. I need to be inside you." He began to shake his head slowly back and forth. He leaned over me, pressing his mouth against my breast, sucking it, moaning, pulling his hand from my grip and caressing my other breast. I was dying inside.

I took his hands and pushed them away so I could lean over him. I began to kiss him and I knew he loved this…loved my taking charge. I had to do this one thing for him but I had to do it my way so my con-science would wound me without killing me. "My period's not quite fin-ished but I can still help you…give you what you need." I ran my hand down his chest, stopping at the waistband of his pants. I could plainly see the outline of his erection pressing against his zipper.

He sighed but didn't speak. He unzipped his pants and pushed them down. When his body was exposed to me, I shuddered…with fear but not repulsion. This was Johnny. And I did love him. In some weird dark corner of my mind I felt I owed him this much. I reached down and took him in my hand and began to stroke him. I kept my mind blank and my eyes averted from Johnny's. His hips began to move and I could tell he was nearing his release.

"Emma," he gasped, "Take me in your mouth." I tensed, not ex-pecting this. He brought his left hand up to the back of my head and gave it a gentle push. "I want to be in your mouth."

I was frozen in place, unable to move…too fearful to move. He pushed a little harder on the back of my head. And in that moment I felt I had no choice, but I promised myself this would never happen again. I leaned down and gave Johnny what he wanted. It only took a few sec-onds before he exploded and I fought my gag reflex with everything I had. When his body seemed to relax, he took my arm and pulled me up the length of him. I felt like a rag doll in his hand. He kissed me, brush-

266 | Kellie Bellamy Tayer

ing my hair away from my face. When he spoke, his voice was so soft and quiet, I could barely hear him.

"Thank you, baby. I needed that so bad. You have no idea."

I lay my head down on his chest and fought my tears. I couldn't let him see me cry because, in Johnny's eyes, I had no reason to cry. He pulled up his pants and I fastened my bra and buttoned my blouse. I needed to get out of here. I needed to be alone to think about what I'd done and to try to figure out who I was becoming…someone I didn't like very much right now.

We went downstairs and walked out to our cars. Johnny hugged me good-bye and planted a tender kiss on my lips. He told me he'd give me an update on his mother's situation as soon as he knew anything. We drove out of his neighborhood and when we got to the main highway, he turned toward Westbrook's city center and I turned the opposite way toward home. I passed the entrance to my neighborhood and headed toward Pacific Beach, just south of the Indian reservation. I parked my car and headed to the rocks where I sat, staring at the ocean. The surf was rough…and dangerous. Seagulls flew overhead, swooping and turning circles around fallen logs and rock formations. I brought my knees up to my chest and leaned over them and began to cry. I stayed there until I was completely cried out. It was getting dark and I needed to get home but I didn't want to face anyone…not my stepmother or my father, not anyone. I thought of Charlie then. How could I face him now? But he didn't know what I'd done. He couldn't ever know. Suddenly a hysterical giggle escaped my mouth. I was cheating on my boyfriend with his best friend—on whom I'd just cheated with my boyfriend. What a fucked up mess I was in. I didn't deserve either of them.

Chapter Forty

Johnny

I needed to see Charlie. It had been a while since I'd hung out alone with my best friend and I really just wanted us to talk. With Charlie I could be myself…say whatever the hell I wanted without embarrassment or fear of being judged. We'd had a few bumps in the road this summer, but we seemed to be nearly back to normal with our friendship and that fact gave me a great sense of relief. Of course, I could talk to Emma about anything and she would listen without judging or criticizing, but sometimes a guy needed his best friend.

I parked in his drive and shoved the six pack of Budweiser into a brown paper bag I'd sneaked from our garage fridge and grabbed the pizza I'd bought at Alfredi's Pizzeria on the way over. Charlie was expecting me—he was waiting for me on his back deck. I walked through the quiet house and as I passed through the kitchen I saw several pies sitting on the kitchen island. They looked awesome and I hoped we'd get to eat one after the pizza.

"Hey, Chuck," I said, setting our dinner on the patio table. "Please tell me one of those pies in there is for our dessert."

Charlie chuckled. "Unfortunately no, but we have some leftover blueberry cobbler in the fridge. I can hook you up with some after we eat if you still have room."

"Sounds good," I said, grinning. "Where's your family? I haven't seen Will much lately. He still with the vile Amanda?"

Charlie rolled his eyes. "Yeah…sort of…but he's in the process of breaking up with her. She's like a bad rash though. He just about gets rid of her but then she keeps coming back. And my parents are out to dinner. It's their anniversary today."

I shoved a piece of pizza in my mouth to avoid commenting on his parents' anniversary. I hoped to god my parents would get another one to celebrate when theirs came around in the spring. Not that my asshole father deserved another year with my mother but that was beside the point.

"How's your mom?"

I swallowed my food and took a long swig of my beer. I glanced out at the Channing backyard...noticed some weeds that needed pulled and some bushes that could use some trimming.

"She's doing OK. I was just with her. Her spirits seem good but she could be faking...trying to be brave for me and Scott. My dad's kissing her ass right and left trying to make up for being a shithead. Oh, Chuck...you'd've been proud of me and Scott the other day."

Charlie took a bite of pizza and raised a questioning eyebrow at me.

"Let's just say...Scott and I had a little fireside chat with Daddy Dearest about Mom. We told him be better stay away from his BFF's fucking floozy and devote his every breath to Mom or we were gonna kick his ass to Vancouver—Canada, not Washington. And the best part? He didn't even balk. He sucked it up and promised he would. It was like we were the fucking parental units and he was the dickhead kid who got caught with his pants down...literally. I fuckin' loved making him face the music."

"Wow. Good for you...for taking care of your mom like that." Charlie sipped his beer and stared off into the flower garden which I noticed needed some serious work, too.

"How are things with you? When you gonna get back in the dating world?" I really wanted Charlie to find someone. Maybe he would when school started back and he was swimming in a sea of females every day.

He gave me a strange look. "I'm just fine. And I don't really give dating too much thought. It hasn't been a priority. How's football?"

"Great. Exhausting...but really good to be back on the field. It's gonna be different without Will and Scott. They're the best tight end and wide receiver in the history of Westbrook High, but hopefully last year's second stringers will fulfill their potential this year. Can you fucking believe we start school in less than two weeks?"

"Yeah. It's gonna be strange to be back after missing all of last year. I'll feel like the new kid on the block."

"Ah, you'll be cool. Everybody'll be pumped to see you again. You should've let me throw you a welcome home party this summer."

Charlie shook his head. "That was the last thing I needed. I'd rather slide back into things under the radar. Who knows, maybe the student body won't have noticed I was gone the entire year."

"Emma was new last year but she fit in so fast, it was like she'd gone to Westbrook all her life. She can make friends with anybody and everybody loves her."

Charlie shifted in his seat and turned away from me. "I bet."

"Speaking of Emma..." I said, letting my voice trail off, waiting to see if he would prompt me to finish my statement. Sometimes I had the feeling he wasn't all that keen on her and it bothered me.

He didn't say anything, but he did look my way, his eyebrows raised over his beer can.

"We hit a rough patch this summer...me and Em...but I think things are getting better. It's just been a weird summer in general—with so much drama—and work and shit...for her and me...but things are calming down finally. We had a really nice...shall we say...encounter... in my bedroom yesterday...finally. It was just what I needed." I finished my beer and reached for another.

Out of the corner of my eye I saw Charlie's posture change. He stiffened in his chair...grabbed his thigh and began to rub it hard. I glanced over at him and his face was contorted as if in pain.

"You got a charley horse?" I asked, wondering if there was something I should be doing for him.

He shook his head back and forth and stood. He looked so tense I thought he must really be hurting. "Just an ache. I'll be right back." His voice sounded thick and unnatural. He disappeared inside the house.

Damn...poor dude, I thought. I helped myself to more pizza and studied the rhododendrons. They needed attention, too. I could work miracles with those babies. I finished my beer and pizza and lay my head back on the chaise, letting my body relax. All the football and landscaping had me feeling sore and tight. I noticed it was starting to get dark as I closed my eyes to rest them for a second. I wondered what Emma was doing right now, thinking I'd go see her after I left Charlie's since she was so close and I missed her like crazy. Several minutes passed and I was getting very comfortable in the chair, close to falling asleep. I suddenly realized it was totally dark and Charlie still had not returned. I got up and gathered our empty cans and the pizza box and took everything inside to the trashcan. I looked longingly at the pies then glanced around the living and dining rooms. It was dark and quiet everywhere. Charlie's absence was beginning to freak me out so I went upstairs to look for him. I stopped outside his closed bedroom door and knocked softly a couple of times.

"Chuck? You in there? You OK?"

The door suddenly opened. Charlie was standing in the doorway. His face was red and he looked...angry. His hands were clenched into fists and his breathing sounded labored. He must be hurting more than I realized. He was seriously freaking me out.

"Dude...what's going on? Is it your leg?" I asked. I actually took a couple of steps back to look him up and down.

"It's everything...my whole goddamned body hurts today, Johnny. I think I need to go to bed. Sorry to cut this short." He shut the door in my face and left me standing in the hall wondering what in the hell had just happened. I went downstairs and ran into Will in the front hall.

"Hey, man. What's up?" he said, giving me a friendly punch on the shoulder.

"Not much. Hey, Will…I was just having pizza and beer with Chuck and he suddenly disappeared on me. I found him in room. He doesn't look good…says his whole body hurts. Is this normal for him? Should we be doing something? I'm really worried about him."

Will frowned. "Huh. He usually seems OK. But, I'll go check on him. Thanks for letting me know."

We said good-bye and I drove straight over to Emma's house. I pulled up in the drive, noticing the house was dark. I took out my cell phone and dialed her number but it went to voicemail. I sent her a text and waited a couple of minutes but got no response. She had mentioned earlier something about hanging with Claire and Kerry today so maybe they were at the mall. I reversed the car and headed for home, thinking about Emma, worrying about Charlie and hoping everybody in my life was going to be OK.

Chapter Forty-One

Charlie

My hand ached like a son of a bitch. I stared at the bloodstains on the carpet thinking I should spray them with Resolve before they set. I sat on the end of my bed…pulled a few splinters from my knuckles and stared at the wounds I'd inflicted upon myself in my violent rage. It occurred to me that this was how my hand should've looked after I'd beaten the hell out of Doug Farnsworth. My mother would kill me when she saw the mess I'd made of the door to my closet. But right now, I didn't give a flying fuck about the closet door, the blood-stained carpet, my messed up hand or my life. I just didn't care about anything.

My phone dinged with an incoming text message. I moved like a robot over to my dresser and picked it up. It was from Emma: just got home from the mall. saw a movie with claire and kerry. i miss you. I stared at the words on the screen like they were in Portuguese. I could read the words but I didn't have a fucking clue what they meant…not the last three words anyway.

I dropped the phone on my bed and thought about what Johnny had said earlier. My gut twisted and I felt nauseous. He'd fucked Emma. That was the part my brain couldn't comprehend. I'd been so sure of her…so sure she was mine and I wouldn't have to share her much longer with Johnny. I certainly hadn't expected to share her that way. Hell, I wouldn't share her that way. If she could flip-flop so easily, then he could fucking have her. Rage began to build inside me again and I knew I was going to break something else. I looked around the room wildly… saw my guitar…remembered the latest song I'd written for Emma on that fucking thing. I walked over to it…picked it up…ran my fingers over the fret board. I played the song from memory in the quiet of my room. I called it "Happenstance."

> It's so strange how two hearts meet.
> A random moment on a street,
> A passing glance, a twist of fate,
> A chance encounter, running late.

And just like that you found me,
Or maybe I found you.
Maybe it was happenstance,
A wish I made came true.

It's so strange how souls are bound
By threads and chains and common ground,
By hands and eyes and lips and skin,
By holding out and giving in.

And just like that you found me,
Or maybe I found you.
Maybe it was happenstance,
A wish I made came true

It's so strange how stars align
Making sure you see the sign,
Fire, water, earth and air,
A map unfolds, the truth is there.

And just like that you found me,
Or maybe I found you.
Maybe it was happenstance,
A wish I made came true.

And just like that you found me,
Or maybe I found you.
Maybe it was happenstance,
A wish I made came true.

And just like that you found me,
Or maybe I found you.
As long as we're forever,
It doesn't matter who.

I stood up from the bed and grabbed the guitar by the neck and smashed it to fucking hell against the already wrecked closet door. I swung it repeatedly until it finally broke into pieces all around me. I was making so much damned noise that I didn't hear Will walk into the room. I didn't know he was behind me until he grabbed what was left of the guitar out of my hand and brought me down onto my bed in a head lock and held me there until the rage inside me dissipated. I went limp...quiet...spent. And to his credit, my brother kept his silence, except to tell me where I could find him when I was ready to talk.

I woke up at three a.m., amazed I'd been able to sleep at all, but knowing I wouldn't be able to anymore. I needed to see Emma. I needed to tell her it was over. Somehow I needed to get past this. I found my phone and sent her a text. I typed fast so I wouldn't change my mind: you awake? i need to see you. Within seconds she responded: i'm awake. want to meet at the corner at the school bus stop? I typed back: on my way. I had to get this over with. I needed to do it now. The sooner I ended whatever this was with Emma, the sooner I could try to get my life—and my mind—back...not that I was under any illusion that being the old Charlie Channing again was even a remote possibility. I felt sick and betrayed and angry, but I promised myself I wouldn't lose it in front of Emma. I would be quick, matter-of-fact, unbending...no matter what kind of scene she made.

She was already there when I got to the bus stop. Her hair was mussed from sleep and her face looked pinkish in the light from the street lamp. She smiled when she saw me and went to put her arms around me but I grabbed them in my hands and stopped her in her tracks. Her smile faded...I heard her suck in a breath.

"Charlie? What's wrong?"

"It's over. Us...me and you. No more."

She began to cry. Her lips quivered and I watched as the tears rolled down her cheeks. She looked so vulnerable and beautiful that I felt my resolve weaken. So she'd made a mistake with Johnny. Maybe I could forgive her. Maybe it hadn't meant anything. Maybe...maybe... but, no...in my head I kept seeing Johnny on top of her, kissing her, touching her...I was losing my mind just thinking about it. I had been right with my initial inclination to honor my and Johnny's childhood code of honor. I should've obeyed our pact. But I hadn't, and now I would pay the price for that betrayal. And if Emma had truly loved me, she would never have let Johnny screw her. I couldn't get past it.

"But...why? I love you. I want to be with you. We can work things out. We can do it right so Johnny isn't crushed. You said you loved me. You said we'd..."

"Stop, Emma. It's over. I knew Johnny long before you and he deserves my allegiance. What you and I have...had...was a mistake. It never should have happened. So it ends now...we can't see each other anymore. Johnny's been through hell this summer and he deserves happiness. He's my best friend and I can't...I won't hurt him. And if you were any kind of a girlfriend, you wouldn't hurt him either."

"Oh, my god...no...please...you can't mean this," she sobbed. She threw her arms around my waist and again, I took her arms and pushed her away.

"I do mean it. Go home, Emma. It's over. I'm just sorry I let it go this far."

"No! I won't let it be over! I love you. Please, tell me what happened to make you do this. Is it Johnny? Did he find out? Is it something I did? Please tell me what's wrong so I can fix it. I love you." Her sobbing grew louder. She paced around me like a trapped animal looking for a way out...or perhaps in this case...a way in. Her breathing was erratic...her eyes crazed and teary in the lamplight.

"You don't get to decide, Emma. I do. And I say it's over. I made a mistake and I'm fixing it now. Good-bye." I backed away from her. She took a few steps toward me, reached for me. I shook my head and walked away. I didn't look back but I heard every sob. She'd wake the neighbors if she didn't get her shit together. When I rounded the corner out of her line of sight I stopped and hid behind a tree to watch her. I needed to make sure she went straight back home and got there safely. She stood there for the longest time crying, her arms wrapped around her body. I felt every one of her sobs like a blow to my chest. For a minute I thought she was going to come after me. But she didn't. She finally walked home. I watched her body shake and convulse with every step. I went back home and grabbed a couple of beers from the fridge and drank them in my room. As soon as I finished the second one, a wave of nausea hit and I barely made it to my bathroom in time before I vomited into the toilet. I went back to bed and lay there, thinking about the blood on the carpet and the smashed closet door. Then I remembered my guitar—my favorite guitar. I'd destroyed it beyond repair. The cold fingers of depression took hold of me and I sank into it, wishing for sleep and a way out of the darkness.

Chapter Forty-Two

Emma

"You're starting to scare me. If you don't tell me what's wrong I'm going to call your father...or your mother." Nanette stood in the doorway of my room staring down at me. I was in bed and wanted to stay there all day. I was exhausted...nauseous...drained of energy. I just wanted Nanette to leave me alone and go away.

"I'm fine. I ate something that upset my stomach and I threw up a couple of times during the night...and now I have a migraine. I just need sleep." I turned my back to her, hoping she'd take the hint and go.

"I never knew vomiting and a headache could make someone cry like that...like their heart's been broken. And your eyes are swollen. Are you allergic to something, too?"

I wanted to tell her I was allergic to her, but I held my tongue. Why couldn't she just disappear? "I've got a summer cold. I'll be fine after I sleep. So, if you don't mind..."

She sat down on the edge of my bed and put her hand on my hip. I fought the instinct to shift away from her. "Emma...I know you're not sick. Not physically anyway. Did you and Johnny have a fight?"

I buried my face in the pillow and answered her...my voice muffled. "No...I told you I'm sick. I don't mean to be rude but...please leave me alone."

She stood up. I heard her walk to the door. "I'm going to call your father. He needs to know you're sick."

I rolled over and sat up, pushing my hair out of my face. "No! Do not call my father or anyone. I'll be fine. Yes...we had a...a...fight... but we'll work it out. I really do have a headache though. I just want to sleep."

"Do you want to talk about it?" Her voice was soft and...maternal. I guess she was getting in practice for Junior.

"No...but...thank you. I'll be fine." My phone buzzed just then. I reached for it on the nightstand, praying it would be Charlie. I glanced down at it—Johnny.

"Johnny?" she asked. I nodded.

"OK. I'll leave you alone. Talk to Johnny...he's a sweet guy.

Whatever happened, find a way to work it out. There are few things in life worth fighting for…but love is probably the fight most worth the beating. If you want to talk, I'll be here." She gave me a sweet smile and went downstairs.

I sighed and read Johnny's text: hey, baby. just left practice. heading to hospital to see my mom, then coming to see you. I don't have to work for my dad this afternoon. I want to take you on a picnic. fried chicken or turkey sandwiches? both? brownies? cupcakes? both? lol.

My eyes burned…my head throbbed. Tears fell onto my pillow. Charlie…Charlie…why…why did you do this? Nothing made sense. I'd cried all night…made myself insane trying to figure out what had gone wrong. It was obvious something had happened with Johnny. They must have talked, but…about what? I reread the text. I didn't want to face Johnny. I couldn't put on a happy face and act like I didn't have a care in the world. For a second I considered calling my mother and asking her if I could move back home. I could graduate with my friends—my real friends whom I'd known all my life. But my mother wouldn't want me there. I would get in the way of Bob and his liquor cabinet full of daughters. I felt like a displaced citizen. I could just keep playing the sick card until school started and then figure out how to get through the days until graduation. Oh god…graduation…Jenkins… Charlie could end up there…I could, too…no, I couldn't go to college there now. Maybe I should join the military like my brother Eric. I could join the Marines and make my father proud—a daughter with bombs and guns and camouflage. Oh, yeah…he'd love that. My phone buzzed again, scaring me…making me jump. I looked down at it: ok, since you're not specifying, I'll get it all. call me or text. I miss you…where you at?

I typed back: Home…sick in bed…not sure a picnic is a good idea today. I hit send and settled back against my pillows. Popcorn bounded up and sat in her usual place on my chest staring down at me. I took some deep, calming breaths in an attempt to relax. Charlie's voice resounded in my head…telling me it was over…it was a mistake…he was sorry it had happened. How was this possible? I needed to talk to him. My heart began to beat fast…faster…I would go over there and find out why he'd changed his mind about us. I'd force him to talk to me and I wouldn't leave until this was fixed. I sat up on the edge of my bed, feeling stronger. Yes…I could work this out. Charlie didn't get to trash my life…break my heart…tear me up inside…without telling me why. I jumped up and went to shower and brush my teeth. Once I was clean and had some make-up on, I felt better. My eyes were still puffy but I couldn't help that. I dressed in pink shorts and a white tank top, slipped on a pair of sandals. I left my hair down…spritzed on some perfume. I looked good, in spite of the eye situation. I went downstairs…Nanette was in the kitchen watching the Food Network and making whatever Rachael Ray was cooking, right along with her. I slipped quietly out the front door without her noticing…and came face to face with Johnny.

"Hey…babe…you feeling better? Where're you off to?" Johnny took my hand and pulled me to him.

I closed my eyes, frustration setting in. "I needed fresh air." I looked up at him. His hair was wet and he smelled like Armani. "I thought you were going to see your mom." I was aware that my voice sounded flat and emotionless.

"I was but you said you were sick. I wanted to make sure you were OK…see if I could get you anything." He pulled me over to the wicker loveseat…sat down and pulled me down with him. He put his arm around me and settled me into his chest. "What's wrong?"

I sighed. "Migraine."

He bent his head down for a closer look at my face. "Your eyes are puffy. Have you been…crying?" He shifted in his seat to face me.

I felt tears forming. Dammit. I didn't want to cry in front of Johnny. "Maybe a little. I didn't sleep because of the stupid pain in my…head."

He leaned over and pressed his lips against my forehead. "Aw…I'm sorry, babe. That sucks. How's your head now? Did you take anything for it?"

"Yeah. It's better, but migraines always leave me feeling drained."

"Why don't you come with me to see my mom? And then we can stop at Kentucky Fried Chicken and get some food and go to the beach. The ocean air will help your head…not to mention fried chicken…" He chuckled and nuzzled his nose into my neck.

My stomach chose that moment to growl loudly. I pressed my hands against it and felt myself smile involuntarily. "Hmm. I am kind of hungry."

"OK, then. Let's go see Mom. She'll be so happy to see you. She's feeling better and she's been asking about you. They're letting her go home Saturday."

I nodded. I didn't want to go anywhere but I needed to keep busy… to keep moving. And I didn't want to blow off Johnny's mother. I'd have to wait till later to see Charlie…and I would see him. He owed me an explanation and I wouldn't rest until I got one.

"I bet your mom's stoked to be getting out of the joint," said Will to Johnny. "Scott was just saying she's getting sprung this weekend."

We'd run into him and Scott in the hospital lobby. They were arriving just as Johnny and I were leaving.

"Yeah. She's feeling better...anxious to get home. Hey, where's Chuck? I called him earlier and sent a couple of texts but he never responded."

Will's face darkened. He glanced at Johnny first, then at me and back to Johnny again. "He's...uh...gone...for awhile."

My heart began to pound...my skin tingled with goose bumps. I felt light-headed. Johnny frowned at Will.

"What do you mean...he's gone? Gone where?"

"He and my mom went up to the cabin. They're gonna stay up there till school starts, I guess. He's been a little down lately and she felt like he needed to get away. You know next week is the anniversary of the accident and Sarah's..." His voice trailed off.

Johnny tensed. He took a couple of steps backward. "Of course I know the fucking date."

"Calm down, John," said Scott. "Don't get upset."

"Don't tell me to calm down. I'm calm. But Charlie should've said something to me...talked to me about this. Why'd he run off without coming to me?"

I glanced around the lobby. I needed to get out of here. The walls were closing in and I felt sick to my stomach. I didn't like the way Will was looking at me...as if he knew the truth.

"Charlie's not in the greatest shape...emotionally. He needs time away...alone. Just leave him alone for the next week...let him get his head together." Will turned to Scott. "Let's go see your mom and then I've got to get to the grocery store. I'm working the afternoon shift today."

Johnny grabbed Will's arm. "Will you give him a message for me? Tell him to call me...text me...something? So I can know he's OK?"

Will nodded, glanced at me one more time, his eyes giving nothing away, and he and Scott went to the elevators. Johnny took my hand and steered me to the revolving doors. I felt like I was in a vacuum... hearing nothing, seeing nothing, feeling nothing, except a dull ache in my chest and a swirling sensation in my stomach. We walked in silence out to Johnny's Escape. Once we were buckled in, he turned to me. "You see Charlie sometimes...did you ever notice anything wrong with him? Like depression or sadness?"

I swallowed, unsure how to answer. I glanced around at the parking lot, trying to buy some time. "Um...no...I don't think so..."

"I was with him last night. We were talking...just a normal conversation...and suddenly he grabbed his leg like it was killing him and he abruptly got up and went to his room. I waited a few minutes and when he didn't come back, I went looking for him. He was in his room and wouldn't come out...told me his whole body ached...so I left. It was strange and his face looked...I don't know...angry...I guess...or pained. I'd assumed it was physical pain, the way he was rubbing his leg, but maybe it was another, different kind of pain...emotional pain... maybe I should've paid more attention...forced my way into his room and stayed with him." He started the car and headed out of the lot.

I was afraid to ask, but I had to know... "What were you and Charlie talking about, just before his leg started to hurt?" I held my breath as I waited for Johnny to answer.

Johnny thought a minute. "I think I'd been commenting on what a shitty summer it had been and I mentioned that you and I had had a rough spell but that we were OK now...that we'd had a nice afternoon alone together and I felt better about our relationship. I think that's what we were talking about anyway."

I sucked in a breath. "You told him we had a nice afternoon? What does that mean? Do you talk to Charlie about us...I mean about... our...you know...?" I stopped, unable to say the words. I felt sick at the thought of Johnny talking about private things with anyone, but especially with Charlie.

He reached over and put his hand on my thigh, giving it a gentle squeeze. "Our sex life? No...I mean...not in detail. He is my best friend though. Don't tell me you don't sit around with Claire and Kerry and talk about sex with your boyfriends. All girls do that."

"No, all girls don't do that. I don't kiss and tell and you shouldn't either. Dammit, Johnny! It's no one's business what we do behind closed doors!" I was seething with anger. I needed to get out of this damned car and go home. I pushed his hand off my leg and turned toward my door, away from him.

Johnny clucked his tongue. "Or don't do behind closed doors, as the case may be."

I looked over at him. He was looking straight ahead at the red light. "Take me home."

"Em...come on. Whether I said anything to Charlie or not about our sex life, it's not like that caused his leg to suddenly hurt so much that he had to run to his room and then go to the lake with his mother for the last week of summer vacation...Jesus Christ!"

"Take me home...now." If he didn't turn the car around and take me home, I would get out at the next light and walk.

The light turned green and Johnny slammed his foot down on the accelerator. I jerked in my seat as he shot through the intersection. He turned into the parking lot of a strip mall and parked. "I'm not about to take you home until you tell me what the hell is the matter with you.

What the fuck's going on, Em?"

I was beyond agitated. I spoke through clenched teeth. "Johnny... please...I just want to go home. I don't feel well and I just...," my voice trailed off.

"You just what? Talk to me, Em...you just what?"

I turned to him, my eyes watery...I just wanted Charlie. "I just don't feel well. Please...?"

Johnny unbuckled his seatbelt and leaned across the middle console. He got as close as he could to me. He held out his hand, palm up in my lap. I looked down at it and, almost against my will, I placed my hand in his.

"I'm sorry. I'll take you home, but I need to know something first..." I swallowed a lump of fear...turned to him. His eyes looked sad and mine were tear-filled. I waited for him to speak.

"Baby...this whole summer has been one fucked up piece of bad news after another. My grandpa dying, the Farnsworth debacle, getting arrested, my mom getting cancer, my dad cheating with his best friend's wife and now Charlie running off to Lake Crescent to deal with whatever demons are inside of him...and I have been keenly aware that next week is the one-year anniversary of the accident and Sarah's death. Just because I haven't mentioned it doesn't mean I don't remember, because, believe me, I remember alright. I've dealt with a load of shit all summer. But you, Emma, have been my rock through it all. You can't crumble on me. I love you so fucking much. I will always be here for you. You mean more to me than anyone on earth. Please don't pull away from me now. I can't lose you. Please be the one thing...the one person I can count on...the one person who won't leave me. Tell me your mine... please."

My shoulders shook. My stomach heaved. Charlie was gone. He didn't want me. He'd thrown me away without explanation. But Johnny was here...right in front of me...always with me...taking care of me... loving me...baring his heart and soul to me. And I knew in my heart that I did love him. Not the same way I loved Charlie, but it was love...a love I couldn't ignore. I had to find a way back to Johnny...steadfast... solid...dependable...loving...beautiful Johnny. He wouldn't leave me. He'd never hurt me—he'd cut off his own damned arm before he'd ever hurt me.

I squeezed his hand...looked into his beautiful, troubled, brown eyes...felt my brain split in two and said, "I'm yours."

Epilogue Part One

Johnny

It had been a hell of a summer. I wasn't a fan of school but it was senior year so I was psyched to be heading back to the halls of Westbrook High…and back to the football field playing quarterback for my team for one last season. I'd be the big man on campus…everybody wanting a piece of Johnny Beaumont and I was cool with that. I liked being the center of attention, conceited as that might sound. But more than anything, I was just plain happy to have my girl with me…under my arm… in my sights. Emma Davis was the most important person in my life— the best thing that had ever happened to me. I loved her in a way that scared me sometimes. She was like a vital organ…impossible to live without. Which reminded me, we needed to talk about college soon… about going to the University of Washington together. And Charlie, too. I wanted the three of us to go there together. We were a team, the three of us…albeit a slightly fractured team. I wished we'd spent more time at Lake Crescent this summer—that place had magical healing powers. I was glad Charlie had gone there with his mom—he'd needed it. He'd be OK. I could feel it…just like my mom…she'd be OK, too. I drained the last of my Budweiser and tossed the can into the recycle bin beside the grill. I could hear my mom singing along to the radio in the kitchen... trying to be brave. She was going to start chemo tomorrow and I was going to be there with her. I wanted to go to every chemo session with her. I planned to be the man my fucking father wasn't, even if he was trying to make things right. I stood up from the deck chair…pulled my phone from my pocket. I wanted to send a good night text to Emma: just wanted to say good night and tell you I love you. see ya tomorrow. I hit send and headed inside, a smile on my face, thinking that, yeah, it's gonna be a good year.

Epilogue Part Two

Charlie

I took my new guitar out of its case and laid it across my lap. It wasn't as perfect as the one I'd destroyed…it had no history…no memories attached. I regretted ruining my old guitar, but at the time, it'd seemed like the perfect outlet for my frustration. I thought of Lake Crescent and being there with Mom. Grace Channing was an amazing mother. I was lucky to have her. Thinking of my mom made me think of Mrs. Beaumont. I hoped she was going to be OK. Johnny certainly seemed confident about her prognosis. I tightened the strings, tuning, adjusting, working out the kinks so I could get the perfect sound. I played chords for a while, getting the feel of my new instrument. I began to play a new song I'd written at Lake Crescent…it was mostly just a tune at the moment, very few lyrics…just snatches of phrases really:

dancing around the island…black hair…green eyes…pink lips… golden skin…colors and whispers…

dancing waters…crescent moons…fireflies…soft skin…gentle touch…glances and kisses…

dancing flowers in the breeze…goose bumps… Popcorn clouds… making love…the afterglow…

Yeah, it was gonna take some work to make this song take shape, this song I'd named, "Emma's Dance." I wondered if it was too late to tell her I loved her. That I never meant to throw her away. That I was hurt and felt betrayed. That I wouldn't share her. That she made me feel whole even when she was the one breaking me apart. That I could forgive her anything. That maybe there was nothing to forgive. That maybe I'd misunderstood. That she was mine.

I played for hours, until my fingers bled.

Epilogue Part Three

Emma

Senior year. I could hardly believe it. One more school year and then I would be free to go anywhere I wanted...well...not completely free. I'd come to realize that a person wasn't truly free when their heart belonged to someone else. Or in my case, to two people. I loved them both...Johnny and Charlie...the two best men in my life. Not even my own dad made rank...not that I didn't love him, too, but Dad would never change. I hoped Nanette didn't expect Dad to change diapers and administer two a.m. feedings, because that was never gonna happen.

Popcorn sat on my bed purring, watching me pack my new book-bag with school supplies. I'd forgotten to cut off the price tag and its movement was making her crazy, batting at it with her tiny white paw, nipping at it with her teeth. I watched her awhile and then my mind began to drift. I sank down on my loveseat...took a sip of iced tea. The ice had melted and the tea was watery now, but it still tasted refreshing. I lay my head back on the seat...closed my eyes...and thought of them:

Johnny—so handsome and athletic...with his beautiful brown eyes and silky blond hair, that he'd let grow out over the summer. He'd gotten a tattoo on his chest—a huge tattoo—of a tree trunk covered in vines. It was beautiful and had cost a fortune. He'd had it done by an Indian on the reservation. He had a heart of gold, Johnny did...and a no-holds-barred outlook on life. He was something else. I loved him.

Charlie—so gorgeous and tall...dark hair that curled around the ends and those endless navy blue eyes that turned black when lit with desire. I'd noticed the small scar on his jaw, but I'd never mentioned it. I'd never mentioned any of his scars from the accident. They were as important as the parts of his skin that were flawless. I thought of the way he looked in the moonlight at Lake Crescent...ethereal. He had a gentle spirit but there was a fire inside him that burned continuously. I sensed it when he was near. His hands...so big and confident when he wrote songs...when he played his guitar...when he touched my body and set it on fire...on fire for him. I loved him more.

To be continued in:
Crescent Moon

About the Author

Kellie Bellamy Tayer is a former journalist turned flight attendant. She is the author of several novels that can be found on Amazon and in book stores:

Talisman trilogy:
The Gypsy Thief
The Dark Prince
The Shadow King

Her memoir,
This is Not a Fairy Tale: How I Found Love Online and Almost Lost My Mind

She lives in Cleveland, Ohio, though her heart resides in the Pacific Northwest.

www.ingramcontent.com/pod-product-compliance
Lightning Source LLC
Chambersburg PA
CBHW070637260626
47161CB00007B/2740